A LAND APART

VOLUME 2

REBELLION

By

VIC SELBY

The characters and situations in this book are entirely imaginary and bear no relation to any real person or actual happenings

Published by Mirotosa

ISBN 978-0-9576150-3-8

Also by Vic Selby in this series
A Land Apart – *Betrayal*

Acknowledgments
Heartfelt thanks go to my daughter Rosemarie for her
cover artwork and helpfully constructive criticism
and to Megan for her invaluable help with proof
reading

To my good friends and old comrades
for their support

TABLE OF CONTENTS

FOREWORD

The year is 1314. In Northumberland the Radulf family are awaiting news of a battle between the armies of their king, Edward II of England and Robert de Bruce, king of Scotland. Young Walt Radulf, his two sons and pregnant wife Katherine anxiously await news. Walt's father, Sir Walter de Radulf the elder and most of their manor's troop of mounted cavalry had mustered with King Edward's forces to fight the Scots under King Robert de Bruce.

Sir Walter has gone to extreme lengths to maintain his hold on his land and his wealth. This included clandestine meetings with his old friend, Robert de Bruce, who was in his youth associated with Walter's sister for three years until her death. Despite agreements made with Bruce for the protection of his land from Scottish raids, open warfare between armies meant that Sir Walter, as the king's knight vassal, and his mounted troop, subsidised by the state, had no option but to obey the call to muster under their sovereign's flag and do battle with the enemy.

England's rulers in this period showed more concern with their French possessions and their frequent squabbles with the northern earls, than the fate of the borderlands. As a result northern areas such as Cumberland and Northumberland became lawless, with local earls and barons making the law in their area as they saw fit. These laws were often applied and interpreted to fit the purpose of landowners such as Sir Walter Radulf and his friends.

The story follows the Radulf family as Sir Walter's son, Walt, embarks upon treasonable actions, leading him into dangerous situations which could mean the destruction of his family and his own violent death. He desperately needs friends to help him to redeem himself and keep his head. Unfortunately he has made a lifelong enemy of the leader of his local priory in Tynemouth, and Prior Gregory is determined to see him hung for treason. Walt and his supporters can only strive to find ways to keep his head on his shoulders, his family safe, and hope to retain his widespread land holdings.

GLOSSARY

Burn. Scottish and border counties name for a stream.

Chausses. Medieval armour of mail for the legs.

Constable. The keeper of a military castle or, on a lower level, the law enforcer in a town or manor assisting a bailiff.

Cotehardie. A close-fitting outer garment with long sleeves, hip-length for men and full-length for women, often laced or buttoned down the front or back.

Demesne. Part of an estate occupied, controlled by, and worked for the exclusive use of, the owner.

Destrier. A heavy war-horse or charger.

English (language). A mixture of Scandinavian, Saxon and Norman, with strong regional dialects. Nowadays referred to as Middle English. The written word had no formal spelling and could vary according to the view of the writer, i.e. Bite could be written as bight, biht, bihte, or any other variations, perceived by the writer to mimic the sound of the word.

Eyre. A court hearing made by an itinerant judge (justice in Eyre) in medieval England.

Garron. A small sturdy pony bred and used chiefly in Scotland and the borders. With road hooves they were ideal for the soft moorland when travelling away from regular roads and bridleways. Also used as pack animals, for light cavalry and mounted infantry by both Scots and English in the border regions.

Groat. A Middle English silver coin equal to four silver pennies.

Hauberk. A long defensive shirt, usually of mail, extending to the knees.

Heriot. A fee due to the overlord of a manor by the inheritor.

Horsebread. Pea and bean supplementing, or being added to grain in times of poor harvest, or as a cheaper option than whole grain bread.

Kirtle. A woman's gown.

London Tower. Early name for the Beauchamp Tower, which was later named after Thomas Beauchamp, Earl of Warwick, imprisoned there in 1397.

Maid. A term generally used to describe a young virgin in medieval times, although sometimes referring to an older unmarried female servant.

Mazer. A large drinking vessel of hard wood or pewter.

Pele House/Tower. A small fortified tower, for residence and for defence during an attack.

Quintain. A target mounted on a horizontal pole, usually pivoted on a vertical pole with a counterweight at the opposite end to the target. Used for practice from horseback or on foot with a variety of weapons.

Reeve. Overseer of workers. Normally an elected serf with some ability in penmanship and knowledge of letters and numbers. Often responsible to a bailiff.

Reiver. A plunderer. (Scottish and English borders). Lawless clans of the border valleys whose lifestyle was to rob livestock from their neighbours.

Serf. Servant, slave.

Snood. A pouch-like hat or elaborate net for holding a woman's hair in place, especially Scotland and the north of England.

Solar. Private room or bedchamber.

Trencher. Originally a thick slice of bread, used as a primitive form of plate for eating and for slicing meat. By the 14th century it became a square or circular wooden or metal plate.

Uisge Beatha. (Water of life). The Gaelic name for an early form of strong fermented and distilled grain mash which evolved into today's Whisky.

Villein. A class of tenant holding land on his master's demesne and providing labour or rent in recompense.

Yeoman. A tenant farmer holding the leasehold, land. Or a rank ascribed to a castle guard or military escorts. Also known occasionally as a freeman.

MAP

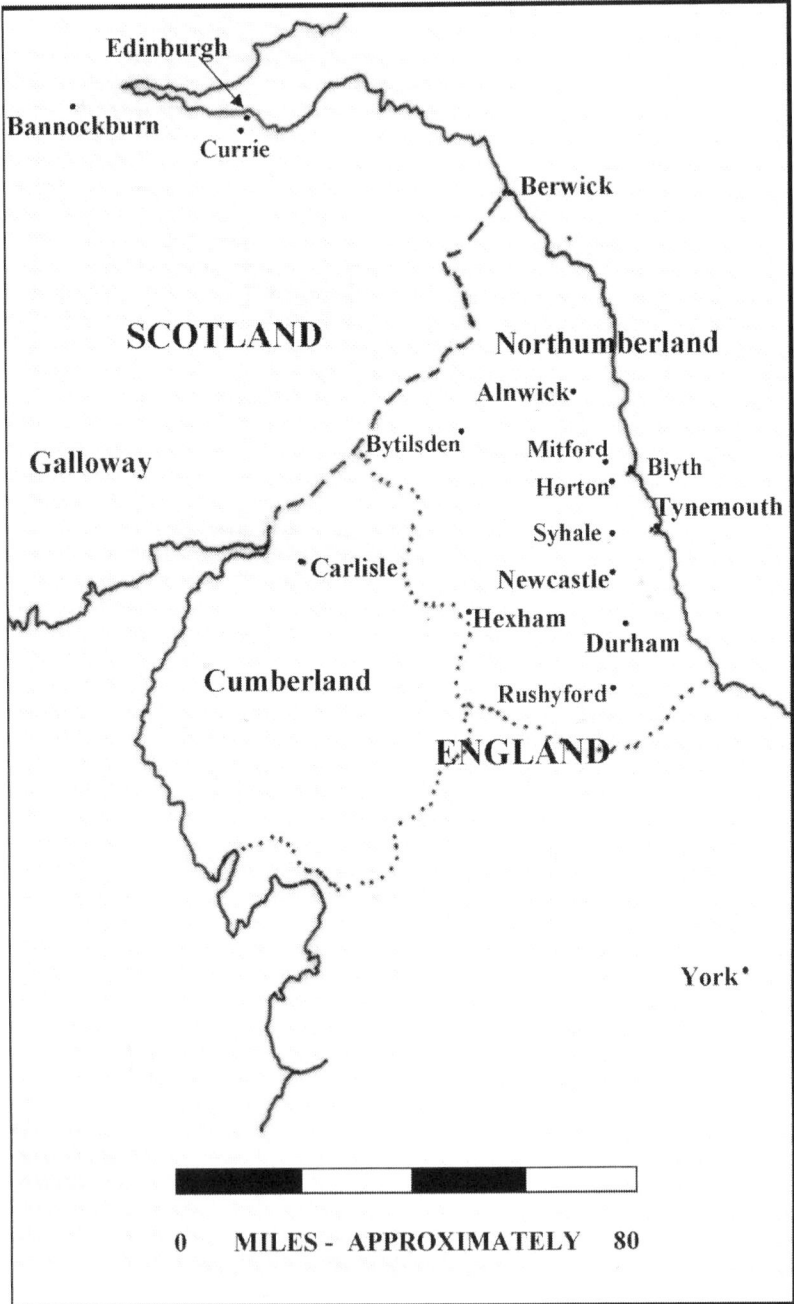

Edinburgh

Bannockburn

Currie

Berwick

SCOTLAND

Northumberland

Alnwick

Galloway

Bytilsden

Mitford

Blyth

Horton

Tynemouth

Syhale

Carlisle

Newcastle

Hexham

Durham

Cumberland

Rushyford

ENGLAND

York

0   MILES - APPROXIMATELY   80

iv

CHAPTER 1

After the battle

July the first 1314. The sunrise over the hills and dales of Northumberland was casting edges of red to the black clouds of the early summer morning at Syhale Manor. It was an ominous looking sky, but the inhabitants of the manor had more to worry about than the old saying of, 'red in the morning, shepherds' warning.' They had known wars with the Scots as long as folk could remember, and now, somewhere north of the border another battle had raged and they had heard only conflicting rumour as to its outcome, none of which was reassuring.

Walter de Radulf, known to his family as Walt to avoid confusion with his father of the same name, his pregnant wife Katherine, and their two boys Walter and Alexander arose early. Walt had overruled Katherine on the name of their firstborn, insisting that it had been a family tradition for generations to name the firstborn Walter. The child was now generally referred to as young Walter, or young master Walter.

The entire household, including the servants, were anxious to hear definitive news of the battle. There was a sombre air around the house as the family went about their tasks of morning ablutions which generally involved no more than a splash of water to the face from the trough in the yard to freshen and assist wakefulness. There were jugs and bowls in the bedchambers for family members, but in the summer months they would generally use the trough along with the others. The servants were busy with preparations for breakfast.

Walt's fifty-eight year old father, Sir Walter de Radulf, had been summoned, and departed over three weeks ago to muster at the border with the king's army. He had taken his squire Thomas Gesthill, his sergeant at arms Nicholas Heddon and a troop of mounted infantry, leaving behind just three troopers for his family's security. Walt had suggested he go in his father's place, but had been told forcefully that it was a knight's summons and not for a stripling, who should look after his wife and his family.

1

Who is to know what is happening? Walt thought. The English army, led by King Edward the second, was to do battle with the army
of King Robert de Bruce, the self proclaimed king of Scotland. Edward's aim was presumably the final punishment of the disobedient Scot and the relief of his castle at Stirling, besieged by Bruce's army, more than one hundred miles north of the Radulf manor at Syhale. The only comforting thought was, that it was said that Edward's army was expected to outnumber the enemy by two to one. Unfortunately the English king was not renowned for his leadership, normally preferring to avoid battle and run for shelter.

Gathering in their family room for breakfast, the Radulfs were attended by their housekeeper Jeanne Jensen, nursemaid Tilly, and Katherine's personal servant Annie Foster. Walt sensed the tension was also present in the servants; many had been with the family since before he was born. Jeanne had been taken in as an orphan of war when a young child and was now betrothed to Aidric Johansson, one of Sir Walter's senior mounted troopers.

Walt, the eldest of Sir Walter's two sons, at twenty four was two years senior to his brother William, who had a share in his uncle Harald's corn merchants business in York where he and his wife Freda currently resided.

With breakfast over, Tilly had taken the children into the feasting hall to play, as Katherine made her concerns known. 'Walt, do you not think we should have heard news by this time? I have a fear that something dreadful has happened. What can we make of the rumours of defeat?'

'It is more likely to be bad for the Scottish army. The odds against them are strong, and we should have little cause for worry' Walt replied, doing his utmost to hide his own concerns.

Katherine, who was a shrewd observer of people, was still worried, and odds were not part of it. 'Your father has been in a funny mood for a while, and he spent much time with the soldiers on the quintain before we knew there was to be a battle, and he has been leaving more of the estate work and decisions to you. Have you ever known him to be so keen to be in a fight?' she asked.

'No,' he replied, 'but surely he does not want to die?' He could have bitten off his tongue, after realising what a stupid remark he had made, and seeing the effect on his wife.

Unable to control her emotions any longer and dwelling on Walt's reply, Katherine felt tears come to her eyes as she expressed her next worry aloud.

'Walt, has it occurred to you that he lost his will for life after your mother died. I fear he intends to give his life in battle and join her, where he would be happy again.'

Walt was shocked; he had noticed the difference in his father, but never suspected that he was so deeply troubled. 'I hope to God you are mistaken Katherine,' he said quietly.

***

On the outskirts of the village of Cramlington, around four miles north of Syhale, four Welsh archers were making their way south, after fleeing the battle at Bannockburn two weeks previously. Their party was ten strong when they first fled the scene of slaughter, hiding in woods and making slow progress from one hide to the next until they were sure they had left Scotland. They had not dared to beg for food, knowing that to be spotted on the run north of the border would definitely mean capture, and if not death, the removal of two of their fingers once it was known they were enemy archers.

The leader of the group, Cethin ap Gwyn, had reluctantly let five of the men head to the west soon after they had arrived in England. He had encountered difficulties maintaining his authority over one, David Thomas, who continually questioned his decisions. David wished to head southwest on the shortest route to Wales, whereas Cethin believed that returning to Wales was the surest way of being sent back to Ireland, from whence they had been taken to fight in the king's Scottish war. The remaining four stayed with Cethin, including Petrus Crofter, the English archer who had assisted them until they had arrived at his home near Mitford.

Planning to lose themselves in the north and try to join some small militia, where they may never be found and sent to Ireland again, Cethin had asked the English archer if he had heard of a place called Syal, apparently the home of some friendly mounted troopers he had conversed with, prior to the battle.

'You mean Syhale,' Petrus had told him. 'Keep on to Cramlington and ask directions again, you will only have about another four miles to walk.'

And here we are in Cramlington, Cethin thought.

***

Approximately one hundred and fifty miles north in a Scottish field near St. Ninians, about half way between the battle site at Bannockburn and Stirling, Sergeant Heddon and Aidric Johansson, the only Radulf men among other mounted infantry troopers, were tied and shackled along with hundreds of other prisoners, after the complete rout of the numerically superior English army. They had heard that there were more prisoners in other camps. Many knights held separately from the common soldiers were also prisoners, and were considered by the Scots as good bargaining fare to exchange for Scottish knights captured in previous encounters and imprisoned in England. The sergeant did not hold out much hope for them as common soldiers. *Who would want to pay ransom for us?* he thought. He discussed their situation with Aidric, who said he had an idea he would like to test. He broke his word to Sir Walter and related to the sergeant what had transpired in Galloway many years ago.

'I saw Sir Walter and Sir Robert, first appear to fight, and then go into the cottage of an old crone. They were alone for a long time together after the old woman came out and ran around the hill sticking stakes into the ground. This provided us all with some amusement but we had no idea as to the purpose, other than to be rid of her. When the two knights reappeared they seemed friendly and not like enemies at all.'

'Do you mean that Sir Walter was a traitor?' the Sergeant asked incredulously.

'No Sergeant, but think about it, I think he did some sort of deal. Why have Scottish regulars never attacked Syhale during the raids? We only ever had to defend against reivers and outlaws. I should see if I can get an audience with King Robert, maybe it would be to our advantage. We have to explore any opportunity. What is the worst that can happen? Nothing or I get a kicking for insolence. I tell you the man knows our master, believe me.'

The sergeant persisted with his defence of Sir Walter. 'We have seen him pay ransoms.'

'Yes,' replied Aidric, 'but have you ever seen any stock driven off or a ransom openly demanded. It was usually a private meeting in the house with only Sir Walter and the Scottish commander.'

Sergeant Heddon capitulated, and without enthusiasm said, 'you may as well try then, do you think he will remember you?'

'No Sergeant, it was the squire who accompanied him and brought back his horse while they talked, but if I can gain an audience, I know enough to convince him I am genuine and I am sure he will recognise the colours as we wore full colours for the meeting.'

'Colours; in Galloway?' the sergeant replied, shocked, 'they must be friends then.'

Aidric laughed, 'not until we reached the deserted vale of Urr, for recognition by Bruce's men.'

The next morning their captors brought them some watery porridge. There was a bowl and a spoon for every four prisoners. Aidric, claiming he had important information, asked the guard if he may speak to his officer. He received a kick for his trouble and told to speak only when spoken to. Nevertheless, about an hour later he was hauled to his feet and taken, shuffling in his leg chains, out of the prisoner area to a tent. Inside was a Scottish knight in armour, seated at a small table with a bowl of porridge and a jug of ale in front of him. Aidric stood silently in front of the table while the knight looked him up and down. He was not going to speak first and get another kick from the guard standing behind him.

'Well man, speak up, I cannot wait all day,' the knight said.

Aidric explained who he was and who he worked for. He also said he believed others of his troop were prisoners, and that he believed that Sir Walter de Radulf was known to His Majesty King Robert de Bruce, he begged the knight to speak to the king on behalf of Sir Walter who was also involved in the battle somewhere. The knight merely indicated that he understood, he made no promise as he dismissed Aidric, who was then led back to the prison compound by the guard.

'How was it?' Sergeant Heddon asked eagerly.

'I do not know, but I saw a knight who listened, and then had me sent back here, just have to keep our fingers crossed and wait to see,' Aidric replied.

The Syhale soldiers were into their eighth day of captivity before Aidric admitted that his plea must have failed. They were still in the open air, in a guarded compound and chained by the legs. After a watery porridge in the morning they had received only water until evening when there was some sort of watery soup. They could not identify the ingredients but it tasted reasonable, and there was a small piece of horsebread for each prisoner. As they finished their meal, the guard returned and beckoned Aidric forward. Knowing better than to ask a question, he waited for the guard to speak. He was told to put his hands behind him, and they were tightly tied. The guard held him by his tied hands and propelled him forward, his feet shuffling due to the short ankle chains, until they reached the same tent where he saw the knight over a week ago. This time, after he was led in, the knight dismissed the guard. Another knight came into the tent, an imposing man dressed in full armour but without helm. He was a big man, *at least six feet*, thought Aidric, with reddish brown hair and full beard. Aidric was shocked, he had only seen Bruce from a distance, but he was sure this was he. Thinking quickly he gave a deep bow and bent the knee.

'You know who I am?' the knight asked; surprised.

'Yes, Your Majesty I saw you in Galloway but you probably would not have noticed me.'

'By what remains of your colours, if I am correct, you are one of Sir Walter Radulf's men?'

'Yes, Sire.'

'Who is his squire?'

'Thomas Gesthill, Sire.'

'His sons?'

'Walter and William, Sire.'

'Good, I am satisfied. This knight will take you back to the prison compound.'

Aidric's hopes fell as the knight ordered him out of the tent, but after a sharp call to halt, the king continued. 'Once there you will identify the others of Sir Walter's men, after which you will all go home.'

Aidric made an elegant bow and asked politely if there was news of Sir Walter and his squire. The king looked sad and told him that alas, Sir Walter had perished in the battle at Bannockburn; his squire was wounded and was a prisoner, being held amongst the knights.

He would also be released with them. The king said that he would hand the squire a message for Sir Walter's son, along with the knight's helm, sword and shield as a mark of respect for his late friend.

***

Walt called to Will Foster the groom and asked for his horse to be saddled. After Katherine's depressing thoughts at the breakfast table, he felt he needed to ride in the fresh air to clear his mind and reflect on what was to be done.

He rode first to the north where the estate mill rested against the burn with its large millwheel turning slowly in the race. Outside he found the mill hand Henry West with his son John. They were unloading sacks of grain from a handcart, with the help of one of his yeoman farmers. Guessing that his mill tenant, Daisy Miller was inside, he greeted them and stepped over the threshold.

Daisy had been severely mistreated during a vicious raid on their demesne back in 1310. Her right hand had been cut off by a sword, and her shoulder put out of joint, whilst trying unsuccessfully to defend her honour against one of the outlaws, who had already murdered her husband and son before proceeding to attack and ravage Daisy. A second attacker had galloped off to rejoin the remainder of the gang attacking the manor house.

Walt and Katherine, out riding, had arrived to see the horseman galloping away from the mill and discovered the dead miller and his son, too late to rescue Daisy's honour, but Walt had killed the rapist and given aid to Daisy, before riding on to assist his family at the manor, leaving Katherine to minister to the injured woman.

Some at the manor had not fared much better, with his mother Lady Agnes, receiving wounds from which she subsequently died. Their adopted cousin, Freda, now William's wife, was severely beaten, their cook killed and her kitchen wench raped. Other members of staff were killed and wounded trying to defend the manor while his father and most of the troopers had been lured away on a false trail.

They had eventually captured the whole gang, whose leader they had previous dealings with. On that occasion his father had left him and his gang in custody in Hexham, only to later learn of their escape. To avoid such a recurrence, Walt had taken charge of proceedings and all the outlaws were unceremoniously hanged and buried. Laws in Northumberland were very much administered by the landowners and barons, as no one could remember when last a king's Eyre had toured the county to administer justice.

'Hello Daisy Miller,' he called, so as not to surprise her.

Daisy appeared from her back room and immediately offered refreshment, which he declined. He asked if she had heard any news from the north, to be told that she had posed the same question to everyone who passed by without result, except for rumours of catastrophe.

Walt decided to ride along the burn to Seaton Delaval and visit his parents in law, Sir Hugh and Lady Isobel and their son, his brother in law Richard. Daisy gave him a cheery wave with her right arm upon which was strapped a leather mitten, to give her some aid to compensate for the loss of her hand.

Riding along the burn he had a feeling of nostalgia as he passed by a small grassy clearing, and remembered the illicit love making with his adopted cousin Freda, whilst he was betrothed to the carefully chaperoned, and at that time very chaste, Katherine.

Arriving at the Delaval pele, he was met by Sir Hugh's squire, Elfric, who assured him that there was no further news to be had here. After a brief visit and an exchange of small talk with his in-laws, he departed and took the southern track home to arrive at the church on the southern edge of Syhale village. Here he spent a few quiet minutes at prayer with his priest, Father Livio Tollo. After thanking the good father for praying with him, he set off home with a clear idea of what was to be done.

He would ride north and seek news of the outcome of the battle. He believed there must have been a battle. If the king had turned tail again they would have seen returning troopers by now.

Home again he put his idea to Katherine, who was having none of it. 'Is it not enough that we may have lost your father, that you should travel up to that ungodly land, and leave me with two small boys and a baby in my womb, and then to worry about the two of you. Please show a little patience, they have a long distance to travel if they were as far as Sterling.'

Walt, seeing her genuine concern and anguish, compromised: 'I will wait one week. If we have no news by then, I travel north and there will be no more argument on the matter.'

With that Katherine had to be satisfied and she reluctantly nodded her agreement.

They did not have to wait that long. Walt had just settled down to a pot of ale, when there was urgent banging on the back door.

'Keep your hair on,' shouted Jeanne as she hurried across to see what the urgency was.

Young John West virtually fell into the room. 'Strangers at the mill, Sir,' he gabbled, out of breath from running. 'Widow Daisy said I should run and fetch you, Sir. Four men, Sir, and they talk funny, foreigners I think.'

Anticipating some urgency, Jeanne had already called across the yard for Will the groom to make the master's horse ready, and Walt was already buckling on his sword belt. 'John, go and tell Trooper Guddal that I want him or one of his men mounted, to follow me to the mill as soon as he can.' Walt hurried out to the stables, where Will had just finished tightening his saddle cinch, and passed the rein to Walt as he leapt into the saddle, and galloped away north to the mill.

He did not know what to expect on arrival, but was astounded to see a trestle table outside in the sunshine. Seated at the table were four strangers, Daisy and Henry West, tucking in to a feast of bread and cheese accompanied by pots of ale.

Walt felt enormous relief that all was well. Dismounting, he tied his horse to the rail and wandered over to join them. 'Well Daisy Miller-,' he cut himself short, after noticing the sombre faces, and Daisy rushing into the mill. He took a seat at the table, and waited for her to return with a pot, and pour him some ale from the jug on the table. Walt tilted his pot in greeting to those around the table and patiently took a sip of ale, waiting for someone to explain.

Daisy placed her pot on the table. 'These men are archers from Wales, Sir. They have escaped the battleground. The fight is lost, Sir. They know little of the plight of others, only that our army was routed by Bruce's men.' The tears began, and she excused herself, running back into the mill.

'Well, is someone going to tell me more, who is your spokesman?' Walt asked, casting his gaze around the strangers.

'Me, Sir, I am Cethin ap Gwyn, and we four are Welsh archers, from the king's army in Ireland. We were brought over by the king especially for this battle.'

'Well, are you not going to relate your tale to me?'

'Yes, Sir, I certainly shall,' Cethin replied, with a slight tilt of his head towards Henry West.

'Good. Then I had better get you back to the manor where you can partake of hot stew and more ale while you tell your story. Henry West, I think you should see if Daisy is recovered and tell her that I shall have her brought to the manor to sit with the mistress.'

In a cloud of dust, a galloping Galeron arrived, to ask what emergency there was.

'It was over before your arrival Galeron, did you go via Delaval?'

'No, Sir, I was a-.'

'Never mind your excuses,' interrupted Walt. 'Get Daisy Miller up on your horse and take her to Mistress Katherine. You can also tell cook to get some potage or other hot meal ready for four hungry refugees.'

Walt, leading his horse, walked to the manor house at a leisurely pace with the four archers. They walked in silence, as if there was a tacit agreement to wait until they were seated indoors and fed, before beginning their account of the battle.

The door to the family room was closed and Walt insisted that Katherine, the children and servants remain out of the hall until the men had finished their food, and related their experiences. 'I will call you when we are ready for you Katherine. You may bring in any servants who are interested in the news, as most had friends among the troopers.'

With some hot stew inside their bellies, and another pot of ale in front of each man, they began the sorry tale of disaster and rout, beginning on the twenty third of June, with a failed attempt to take the fight to the Scots by the joint commanders, and the total chaos of the second day of battle. This time the two commanders, the earls of Gloucester and Hereford had argued. Gloucester, apparently having been accused of cowardice by the king had given the cavalry a premature order to charge, before the archers were in position. The result was total chaos and the rout of the English army.

'What happened to the heavy cavalry?' Walt asked.

'Some escaped, some killed and some captured,' was all they could tell him. Being infantrymen they had little knowledge of the knights or their squires.

'What then of the mounted infantry?' Walt asked them.

'Mostly dead or captured when they attempted to protect the unprepared archers from Bruce's cavalry,' was the response.

They did tell him that they had heard news that King Edward had escaped.

The king escaping was not unexpected for Walt, who was surprised that he had been there at all, but he wondered how such a superior army could be so easily overcome.

'How did this all happen?' he asked the men.

Cethin ap Gwyn replied. 'Sir, it was a like butcher's street, a bloody shambles. The Scots chose the battleground, our commanders argued and did not command, and when they did, they had our archers shoot our retreating cavalry. Such was the shambles that the Scottish knights and mounted infantry routed our archers and those of our mounted infantry who had not fled. Then it was all over except for being killed, captured, or seeking to hide and escape.' Cethin went on to describe graphically the scenes of slaughter until the frenzy of killing died down and the collecting of loot and prisoners, before the camp followers became numerous. 'These were more like vultures who would strip their prey and kill him if he showed signs of life' he added.

'You are not from these parts, where are you going now?' Walt asked the man.

'We don't know, Sir. We were brought from the king's army in Ireland and do not have the means to get very far without working, and to be truthful, Sir, we have little desire to return to Ireland.'

'How is it that you came upon Syhale?'

Cethin told him of his conversations with the mounted troopers on the route to Scotland and the assistance they got from Petrus Crofter from the Mitford area, who directed them.

'Do any of you ride?' asked Walt.

Cethin and two others raised their hands.

'Would you be willing to learn?' Walt asked the fourth.

He rapidly grasped the significance of the question and his hand shot quickly into the air.

'Would you like to work here?'

11

'What as?' Cethin asked.

'Mounted militia of course, with occasional farm work when required.' Walt replied.

Without exception they all nodded eagerly.

Their experiences were no consolation for Walt in his anxiety for his father, and he knew he was taking a chance on the men. 'Come with me, I shall take you over to the barracks and Galeron Guddal, who you saw at the mill, can find you beds, if he has found his way back yet.

They all laughed at his small jest regarding his trooper's punctuality.

When Walt returned from the barracks he found a small reception party eagerly awaiting news. Katherine, Jeanne and Daisy were sitting on the bench together outside the front of the house. He told them what he had learned, omitting the graphic descriptions given by the archers. Unfortunately, what he had not learned was what they were most anxious about; the fate of his father, and the other Syhale soldiers. They only knew that that the king's army had been routed by that of King Robert de Bruce.

'God help Northumberland now,' said Katherine.

Jeanne burst into tears and Daisy held onto her, also crying. Walt looked at Daisy's obvious grief, and then to Katherine, and held his hands out in a questioning gesture.

'Nicholas Heddon,' she mouthed quietly.

'Bugger me,' he said quietly to himself as he walked into the house, 'I would never have guessed; Daisy and Nicholas Heddon, I thought they were just friends.'

The next morning as Walt and Katherine were breaking their fast; Tilly had the children in the corner under the staircase feeding them at a small table. Jeanne as usual was busy organising the day's household tasks. Annie Foster came in with bowls of porridge from the kitchen. The fire in the family room had not been lit; it was too warm now for unnecessary fires. Annie had dished out porridge for all and was distributing mugs of rosehip beverage or warmed ale, when there was a knock at the back door. Jeanne rushed over in anticipation, only to be disappointed. Galeron Guddal, temporally acting as sergeant at arms stepped across the threshold and saluted Walt, saying. 'Sir, there are four soldiers lined up outside for your inspection.'

'Very well Galeron, parade them again in half an hour when I will speak with them.'

'Yes, Sir,' replied a puzzled Galeron, 'am I expected to teach those men English?'

'Ask them to speak more slowly so as not to tax your ears and you will understand their dialect. Forget Welsh, it is a secret language only for the Welsh. You must insist they speak English in barracks amongst the others, and be sure they all understand you.'

Half an hour later the men paraded again for inspection.

'Tell me again, which of you can ride?' Walt asked, for Galeron's benefit.

Three of them, including Cethin ap Gwyn, raised their hands to claim this ability. Seemingly pleased with the response, Walt handed the men over to Galeron.

'They are yours now Sergeant. Teach them Northumberland English, and we shall see what is to be done with them later.'

Galeron made no comment, but looked at Walt, waiting for him to say he was joking.

Walt was already walking away as Galeron nodded to the men to follow him to the barracks. They were halfway there before Walt shouted over his shoulder. 'I jest Galeron, but we will have no more of this ap business. Just names, tell them, and teach that one to ride.'

***

To the North of Bannockburn, the identification of the remainder of the Syhale soldiers was completed by the knight who had been present at the meeting of Aidric and King Robert. He found Troopers Botolfe Best and Sam Farmer, of the Syhale troop, who were now reunited with the sergeant and Aidric. The knight, having seen that they all wore the distinctive black and gold surcoats, said he had a messenger tour the other holding areas to check for any more of their colleagues. The messenger had returned with Squire Thomas, who had almost perished in the charge alongside his master. The knight promised the squire would be reunited with them on the morrow after a night's rest.

This news promoted excited chatter amongst the troopers which was interrupted impatiently by the knight.

'I have yet to arrange an escort for you. It will have to be a knight of authority, and a small section of mounted infantry to ensure that you have safe passage to the border. You will be loaned horses for the journey as far as Berwick which is still in English hands. From there you will have to make your own arrangements.'

Before they could ask any questions, he turned to Sergeant Heddon.

'Prepare to leave immediately after you have broken your fast tomorrow.' With that he marched off towards his tent.

The following morning after their bowl of watery porridge, true to his word, the knight came to get them. They were led through the camp site to the blacksmith who cut off their leg chains. From there they were taken to the ostler who had horses waiting and saddled.

It was here that they had their first sight of Thomas Gesthill. He looked overjoyed to see them and hopped towards them on one leg and a crutch. His left leg was broken and had been set and bound with wooden splints, and there were dirty bandages, black with dried blood wrapped around a head wound. He threw his arms around Nicholas Heddon and expressed his joy at his survival, hurriedly followed by the amendment, 'I am happy for all of you, but where is the rest of the troop?' he asked, shocked to see only three troopers to greet him. Nicholas Heddon explained how they had fought a rearguard action to help foot soldiers and archers escape the rout, and then found themselves surrounded by a much superior force, before which the few remaining from various troops had little option but to surrender or die.

With everything ready for their departure, all they needed now was their escort. A few minutes later they saw them trotting into the camp. There was a knight, in colours that seemed strangely familiar to Squire Thomas, followed by five mounted infantry troopers. As the knight reined in his horse he removed his helm and hung it by a leather strap from his pommel, he turned the horse to face his charges.

'My God, if it isn't Thomas Gesthill,' he said, dismounting and walking to shake Thomas's hand.

The squire's brain was racing, he was sure he knew this man, who obviously knew him. *Maybe it is my head wound affecting my memory,* he thought. He had been having dizzy spells when he felt he would faint. Just as he held out his hand to return the cordial

14

greeting, the name came to him. 'Sir William de Middleton. It must be many years since I last saw you, when you visited my master. We see something of your brother Sir Gilbert from time to time, but I had no idea that you were in Scotland.'

'You may know that I was a Knight Templar before the order was dissolved. The Pope issued an order for the arrest and trial of all our order in November 1307. Many in France were arrested, and after having their wealth taken and cruelly tortured, they were put to death. I was in England at the time, but unsure of the king's reaction to the Papal Bull, I thought it prudent to flee to Scotland. I had to attend a Papal court here but was protected by King Robert, and pardoned. I am deeply sorry about Sir Walter's untimely end. Now let us get mounted and be on our way, before the king changes his mind.'

Troopers Aidric Johansson and Botolfe Best assisted the squire on to his horse and secured his crutch for later use.

'Have you got the promised letter from King Robert?' Aidric asked.

Thomas nodded an affirmative, and the party set forth on their journey home. They estimated that the journey would take around four to five days. The Scottish escorts had a pack horse with essential food and every man had a full water bottle and a groundsheet rolled up behind their saddle. They would be sleeping under the stars in a makeshift shelter of groundsheets and their cloaks.

The troopers were more at ease when they realised that Squire Thomas and their escorting knight Sir William were old acquaintances. With the exception of Aidric, the other troopers had been unsure that there may not be treachery ahead. It was young Sam who put his thoughts into words as he rode up alongside Aidric and whispered, 'why should the king of Scotland release poor soldiers like us when he could keep us prisoner and make us work until a ransom was paid?'

'Hold your tongue and keep your thoughts to yourself,' Aidric replied sharply. 'Squire and Sergeant Heddon know well what they are doing and we must make no question of a generous gesture, lest we antagonise our escort.'

***

15

Katherine was returning from a visit to her mother at Delaval tower with Trooper Galeron Guddal accompanying her as escort. They were riding at walking pace across grazing land between the two manors. Galeron was finding the proximity to the mistress he adored uncomfortable. He was afraid to speak for fear of showing his nervousness, and he knew that any question of impropriety could lead to a beating and dismissal, at best.

Nevertheless he could not resist the urge to steal glances, at this angel he was lucky enough to escort. With her shiny jet black hair, dark smouldering eyes and beautifully proportioned body, *although she was filling out a little, with child again.* Galeron almost choked at the thought of his master making love to this magnificent woman.

Katherine sensed that her escort was paying undue attention and decided to lighten his mood with some conversation.

'How are you getting along with the new men, Trooper Guddal?'

Taken by surprise at being addressed, he felt himself colour up with embarrassment at having been caught out surveying his master's wife. Rapidly pulling himself together he replied with a casualness he did not feel, 'very good Mistress, they seem keen to learn our ways, and say that anything is better that returning to Ireland.'

'Yes I suppose it is Guddal, but perhaps we had better not talk about Ireland. Strictly speaking my husband is harbouring deserters if they make no effort to return to their command' Katherine reminded him.

'Their strange dialect is difficult to understand, and they say the same of us, but I am sure all will be well when we can train and ride together. The master said he would get some horses for them this week, so I don't think he has any idea of them leaving Mistress,' he replied.

It was around midday when they dismounted after reaching the yard at Syhale. Galeron headed for the soldier's quarters while Katherine handed her horse to Will Foster.

Entering the back door she found Walt in the family room with the children and Tilly. Jeanne called into the kitchen to tell Annie that the mistress was returned, and to bring in soup and bread. Today they had thick ham and pea soup, Walt's favourite. He stood up from the corner where he had been playing with his boys. 'How is your mother?' he asked.

'Much the same, she is a little steadier on her feet but her speech is not improved and when she drinks she still dribbles from the left of her mouth. Mistress Flood says that folks so stricken are in the hands of God. All she can do is offer a prayer and give God the only help she knows, in the form of her potions. She has the help of a personal servant called Cecily, who seems most kind and competent.'

They all took their places at the table and Annie served the thick tasty soup. Walt soon finished his and asked for more. 'You can tell cook to make the same every day,' he told Annie.

'No you will not' Katherine responded firmly.

'So speaks my confident wife, who when first with child carrying baby Walter would not even ride a short distance without my permission in case she harmed the baby. Here she is now five months gone carrying our third, and galloping around like a young girl. Make sure you don't give birth on horseback my dear.'

Katherine threw a piece of bread at him. 'I am still young,' she laughed, 'I am only twenty four. You can't keep me at home just because you keep me with child.'

He leaned close to her and whispered, 'do you not like being with child?'

She kissed him lightly and whispered back, 'you know I do, but I like the getting with child part more.'

'Well then,' he replied, 'one begets the other.'

'Enough nonsense,' she said. 'Get yourself back to work Husband. Those new men need some horses.'

He agreed and said he would take a man with him to Tynemouth in the morning to buy horses and tack. Katherine reflected for moment before responding to his suggestion of buying horses. 'By all means buy horses for the men, Husband, but do you think it is wise to do it in Tynemouth, when the nosey prior knows everything that transpires in that town? Go to Tynemouth if you must to seek news, but not to buy horses'.

Walt knew that Katherine had prepared herself, Jeanne and Daisy for the worst, and after she again expressed her concerns that they had heard nothing of his father or the troopers, and in view of the slaughter witnessed by the archers, Walt was of a mind to agree with her fears.

'If we do not hear anything in another week, I think we should prepare ourselves for the worst news. I will see what is happening in Tynemouth, maybe someone has news. If not I shall ride north to seek others who have returned from battle, somebody must know the fate of Edward's heavy cavalry.'

Walt was fully prepared for the probability that he was now the master of Syhale.

***

Fortunately the weather was good for the returning prisoners on their way to Berwick. The Syhale men were fraternising genially with their Scots captors. Both sides having accepted that the battle was their duty, as was their current situation. Squire Thomas had suggested at the outset that they adopt a friendly attitude to their captors, as he saw no need to make the journey unpleasant and all had readily agreed. For the first two nights as they sat around a camp fire, Sir William had regaled them with stories of the crusade, and quite honestly admitted to the excesses of the Knights Templar, whose main reason he said, for going on the crusade, had more to do with booty than saving Christendom. He claimed that he had not brought much back, and what he had, he had given to an order of monks here in Scotland as part of the king's agreement to have him pardoned.

Thomas told him about the outlaws who attacked Syhale manor and the terrible consequences for some. When asked what became of the robbers, he did not mention executions, just that they were all killed in the final battle to rid the manor of their presence. Sir William gave him a strange look but did not press for more details on their fate. He expressed his sorrow for the untimely death of Lady Agnes, who he said he had known and much respected.

It was just after midday on the second day of their travels that they approached the fortified town of Berwick. Sir William told the rest of the party to stay hidden in the trees while he rode forward to the northern gate with a flag of truce, to negotiate with the Governor.

'It is best you do not declare yourselves until we know what sort of reception you may get' he had advised. 'There may be awkward questions about why you are being released.'

He left them watching his progress as he rode from the cover of the wood. When he was within hailing distance of Berwick walls he waived his white flag of truce and called to speak with the governor. Having been told to wait, he sat patiently for around half an hour, always prepared to gallop away at any sign of danger. He was convinced that nobody in the stronghold would be foolish enough to give chase under the present circumstances. They would have no idea of the size of force he may have hidden in the woods.

Eventually a figure appeared on the battlement and identified himself as Baron Lord Berkeley, Governor of Berwick.

Sir William shouted that he had a force of arms with him and some prisoners for ransom. He thought it inadvisable to shout that they were to be freely released for all to hear. The governor naturally wanted some details of the prisoners, whereas Sir William requested that the two of them meet under a flag of truce to discuss it. The governor agreed and disappeared from the battlement to reappear through the gates around fifteen minutes later on horseback. Behind him were four mounted infantry who waited outside the gate, while the governor continued alone, reining in some ten feet in front of him. Sir William introduced himself to the surprise of the governor.

'Middleton eh?' he said. 'Thought you were dead after the hunt for Knights Templar ordered by the Pope.'

'No, Sir, as you see, I escaped to Scotland and am very much alive.'

'Well,' responded the Governor, 'you can come back now, all that is forgotten.'

Sir William smiled, 'I think I will just stay where I am for a while longer.'

'Your decision,' the governor countered. 'Now what is this talk of ransoms, and who do you expect to pay ransom for those men?' he asked.

At that point Sir William explained that no ransom was required, they were being part of an exchange agreed with an English knight.

'What knight?' the governor asked.

'That I do not know,' Sir William lied.

'Well then, you can hand the prisoners over to me. The king arrived from Dunbar last night and I am sure he would be interested in interrogating any prisoners who have been released without ransom.'

Sir William had not expected this.

'Very good, Sir,' he lied, 'they are camped about half a day's ride from here with my main force, I will return with them tomorrow.'

'Good day until tomorrow,' the governor replied, 'I am sure the king will look forward to questioning them.'

Sir William waved a salute as he turned and rode away in a leisurely manner.

'I am sure he would,' he said to himself quietly.

Back in the woods, he told the men to mount up quickly and follow him. They rode rapidly westward, well on the Scottish side of the border and away from Berwick.

Sir William explained to Squire Thomas and the others what had transpired as soon as they stopped to rest the horses and allow them to drink from a small burn.

'If they had interrogated you and realised that Sir Walter was friendly with the Scottish king, you may have all been hung as traitors or deserters, or any other charge they felt like bringing. As it is, they do not know who you are or any details of your release.'

'So what do we do now?' Squire Thomas asked.

Sir William thought for a moment and came to a decision.

'I will escort you to the border in the vicinity of Norham and you can make your own way from there.'

'Are you going to put us on foot?' Sergeant Heddon asked.

'Take the horses, I will tell King Robert what happened. Keep the horses and their tack safe, we will soon be along to collect them. Who will stop us now your king's army is in flight?'

True to his word, having reached a point on the border just north of Norham, Sir William bade them a safe journey and requested he be remembered to his brother Sir Gilbert should any of them meet him. He then rallied his escort, gave a final wave and he and his men galloped off to the north.

***

Sergeant Heddon took control of their tactics from then on. He suggested that they kept a low profile and used minor tracks and cross the river Tweed near Ladykirk. Once in England, they should follow small tracks south westwards, using whatever cover was available until they got to the east of the moorland where there was little habitation. They could then ride southwards down the east side of the wild moorland until they came to Allenton. 'Once there,' he said, 'Sir Walter has family nearby at Clennell, who will help us with feed for ourselves and our horses.'

Squire Thomas agreed that this sounded like a sound plan, and their journey to Clennell proved uneventful except for their first night when there was a ferocious rain storm. No matter how they huddled under their groundsheets, the rain was so heavy that rivulets of water were passing beneath them. The ground sheets were too small to make a decent shelter and they had received little warning of the cloudburst, as it was dusk and the darkening of the sky was not so apparent to them. They huddled together to try to use two groundsheets to cover the wet ground, and three to shelter under. It was not a very satisfactory arrangement and they got little sleep.

The next morning saw a miserable and tired group set off towards Clennell. Their route took them well clear of villages until they came near to the village of Allenton where Squire Thomas considered that they were safe. As none of them knew the way, he would enquire at the small church. Inside he found the priest putting new altar candles in their holders.

'God be with you,' said the priest as he looked round from his task. 'How can I help?'

'We are a party of soldiers from Sir Walter de Radulf's estate. We have escaped the Scots following defeat in battle and are seeking to visit Clennell.'

'You are nearby; if you came from the north you have passed the track to Clennell. Retrace your steps, cross the river Coquette by the ford you have just passed over and you will see a small stream leading into the river. Follow the track alongside that stream and you will come to their pele. Might I ask what your business with Simon Clennell is?'

'We are on our way to our master's at Syhale, and Sir Simon Clennell is his friend and manages land for him at Bytilsden' Thomas replied.

As they were talking, the priest wandered outside the church. Thomas thought he wanted to get a look at the others to assess if there was any danger from them. The moment they were outside and the priest saw Sergeant Heddon and the other three, also in their black and gold tabards he relaxed. 'You are indeed Sir Walter de Radulf's men,' he said.

'Yes Father,' replied Thomas, 'I was his squire, and I am sorry to say that Sir Walter perished at Bannockburn. We are making our way back, bearing the sad news to his family.'

'We have heard the tragic news of Edward's defeat and most around here are wary and waiting for the inevitable punitive raids to follow. Please come into the church and join me in a short prayer for Sir Walter's' immortal soul before proceeding' the priest said sadly.

They were tired and hungry and dearly wanted to get to Clennell, but they followed him into the church and said a prayer.

'Be sure to call and make your presence known early at Clennell pele as perchance Sir Simon may have positioned archers on the roof,' the priest warned them as they rode away.

As they were retracing their steps across the ford Aidric spoke up, 'I can't speak for everyone else but I feel much better for having been able to say that short prayer.'

The others murmured agreement and then fell silent, busy with their own thoughts until they came in sight of the pele tower at Clennell. As soon as they saw the tower, Squire Thomas halted them for a moment and called loudly towards the tower, announcing their presence. Having received an answering shout to advance and be recognised, he turned to his companions and advised, 'I don't know how much Sir Walter's' friends know about his dealings. I think it best if we confine our talk to our master's' death and just say that we escaped captivity. I think it best to say nothing of the knight and the escort.'

They all agreed they should not be seen to have accepted help from the enemy and the squire's approach made sense.

Sir Simon Clennell was waiting to greet them with a small party of men at arms. One of his lookouts had forewarned him that a party of soldiers were approaching and he was taking no chances, despite the call from Thomas.

As soon as the visitors got close, he recognised Squire Thomas and the colours the soldiers were wearing, and stood his men down. Calling his groom, he told him to take the horses as the men dismounted. Squire Thomas, after being helped from his horse and supported by his crutch, shook his hand and explained their position as earlier agreed.

They were all ushered inside with Aidric and Botolfe helping Thomas up the steep narrow outside steps to the first floor entrance of the pele tower, where Alice had the servants rushing around to prepare food and drink for them. She immediately got Thomas settled in a chair and began unwinding the dirty bandage to inspect his head wound. Sir Simon wanted to know all their news. They told him about the demise of Sir Walter and he was very distressed to hear that report. Alice was crying and dripping tears all over the clean dressings she was applying to Thomas's head wound. She had loved both Walter and Agnes, and could not bear the thought of having now lost her dear brother in-law. *Losing Agnes to those terrible outlaws had been bad enough, poor Walt, first his mother now his father,* she thought.

Aidric seeing her distress, quietly took the bandage from her hand and continued with Thomas's dressing. Simon moved to comfort his wife, while they told him of the shambolic order of battle, the subsequent rout and the king's escape. Asked how they had escaped, Thomas spoke up and said that the guards had been lax at night and they had managed to free themselves from their bonds. Sir Simon looked a little sceptical that it could be so easy, but made no comment. He guessed that they had some help with their escape and knew that his friend had some dealings with Bruce, but he respected the squire's common sense in not revealing such matters.

Soon they were all seated around the table, eating and drinking heartily. Young Sam Farmer had never before seen the inside of a knight's home and looked around him with his mouth agape in awe.

'Is the food not sufficient, that you have to catch flies as well?' Aidric said to the young trooper.

Much merriment was then had by all at the expense of young trooper Sam Farmer. It was the first time they had a laugh since before the battle.

Having eaten heartily, Sergeant Heddon and the soldiers were taken and handed over to Sir Simon's men for overnight accommodation with instructions to see that they were given a good breakfast in the morning.

Squire Thomas was found a bed in the tower and would join the family when they broke their fast. He thanked his hosts for their care prior to retiring, and expressed his wish to leave immediately after breakfast. It was nearly two weeks since the battle and he could not wait to get back to Syhale. He knew it was unlikely the family had news of Sir Walter, and he believed he should be the one to tell them and not some passing stranger.

***

Walt had made up his mind. He had found no new information in Tynemouth. Everyone seemed to know that the battle was lost but no more. Exasperated he pronounced, 'if we hear no more in the next couple of days I shall ride north and seek news.'

'You cannot go without an escort and you are not to leave us here with these strange soldiers' Katherine insisted.

'Very well, I shall go and purchase more horses tomorrow. I shall take with me the five new men with cart and driver. They can each ride or lead a horse on the return according to their ability. The cart will be useful on the return for any other tack I acquire in Blyth. When all five of the new men can ride, and if there is still no news, I shall definitely ride north.'

Katherine smiled, satisfied that he had heeded her warning and was heading for Blyth.

Daisy, who had been with them since the archers arrived, fearing that she had outstayed her welcome, returned to the mill with the promise that she would be notified as soon as there was any further news.

Needing some solitude to think through his situation, Walt made an excuse and headed over towards the barrack block, where he knew the new men were busy settling in. Around the back of the block was a heavy timber bench which looked out over the trail leading towards the north and the mill. To the left of this was the quintain that his father had built on the training ground, to give himself and his soldiers a good practice area for battle. It was quiet here at the moment and he let his thoughts wander.

He wondered if his younger brother William and his wife Freda had received any news of the disaster at Bannockburn. He doubted they had, but declined to send a messenger until he had some definite news of his father. *Ah Freda,* he thought, his pretty adopted cousin. *How does she like married life with my brother? She is content if her letters are to be believed.* Walt did not think she would lie about such things and was happy for her.

Freda's father had been killed whilst trying to protect his stock from border reivers. Her widowed mother had gone on to marry Agnes Radulf's brother, Ralf Clennell, with whom she subsequently gave birth to two boys, Roland and Ronald.

They enjoyed a happy life until a fateful raid by the Scottish rebel William Wallace in 1297. Both her parents and Ronald were killed. Freda and Roland were not found and assumed prisoners of the Scots, she had been around seven at the time with the two boys still small, with Roland around five or six.

Purely by chance, after a clandestine meeting between Walt's father and the young pretender to the Scottish throne, Sir Robert de Bruce in 1305, they had discovered her working as a slave at an inn where they stopped on their return from Galloway, and then only as a result of an unfortunate incident with one of their men, which led to his father asking her name and parentage. The result of this encounter was a serious falling out with the innkeeper; ending with his father removing her from her drudgery by force, and taking their fifteen year old step niece home to her aunt Agnes.

Walt, also fifteen at that time was promised in marriage to Katherine who lived with her parents Sir Hugh and Isobel Delaval and younger brother Richard in a pele tower on the adjoining estate. Unfortunately, Katherine's mother kept her daughter on a tight rein and there was no chance of any sexual encounters. This was not the case with Freda, and the pair soon began an intense covert relationship, which continued until Walt and Katherine were married. Walt was still very fond of Freda, but there were no more thoughts of lovemaking. Freda, although a pretty girl with long brown hair and twinkling mischievous eyes, could not hold a candle to Katherine's beauty, with her jet black hair, smouldering dark eyes and lithe figure, compared to Freda's more full proportions. Besides, he thought, Freda was happy with William now.

After an interval to allow her to adjust to Walt's marriage, William, Freda's junior by two years, declared that he had loved her since the first time they met. He eventually proposed and was accepted. At his father's suggestion, he went to York to take a junior partnership in his Uncle Harald Radulf's business as a corn merchant. Once there, he made a good impression on his uncle and a year later returned to marry Freda and take her away to York.

Looking around him, Walt recalled the building of the quintain two years ago. His father had said then that Bruce was gradually whittling away at the English strongholds and Edward would be forced to take a stand or relinquish any control in Scotland. It was almost as if he wished a battle to come. He certainly wasted no time in getting himself and his men away when the call to arms came. He would not hear of Walt taking his place, despite his protestations over his father's advanced age of fifty eight.

Walt began to dwell on the family history his father had told to him and tried to decide what his next move should be in the worst scenario.

As far as he could remember, his father said that the family held land at Little Haughton as far back as the latter part of the eleventh century, with his grandfather eventually settling at Syhale early in the thirteenth century on his return from a crusade to the holy land with Edward Longshanks.

Prince Edward was on his way home in 1272 when he received news of his father's death. One of his first acts, even before returning home, was to grant large areas of land to his friend Sir Walter, who died shortly after his return of a fever. Walt's father, also Sir Walter, having inherited the land, would have liked to move the family seat to his western holdings at Bytilsden, but as yet he had been unable to gain permission to build a pele tower. To build a fortified dwelling required the king's, or in the case of Northumberland, the local baron's permission. The new king, Edward II, ignored his written requests and the Baron Gilbert of Harbottle, the power in the area, repeatedly refused him. At the moment, his mother's brother Simon and his wife Alice on the adjacent estate of Clennell managed the yeoman tenanted farms for him and collected the rents through a bailiff.

Walt had the same urge to move the family seat as his father, for more reasons than the serenity of the place, when free of Scots invaders. Moving was not an option without a pele tower similar to that at Clennell. A previous manor house similar to theirs at Syhale had been easily burnt down by marauding Scottish irregulars, and now, even though it had to some extent been rebuilt to house the bailiff, after the defeat at Bannockburn, its proximity to the border would make it even more dangerous.

The family's association with Sir Robert de Bruce began when the Scot took a fancy to Walt's aunt Annabella, resulting in a child and a three year romance, until her death in 1295. Walt's mother, Agnes, was always sceptical about Annabella's death, believing that Annabella was again carrying a child, even though she was twice Bruce's age of 18 years when they met. Following Annabella's death, Sir Robert was quick to marry Isabella of Mar when her father signed over his lands in exchange for his daughter marrying an heir to the Scottish throne. 'The liaison with Annabella had the effect of forming a useful friendship, of sorts,' his mother had said, whilst making it clear that she neither liked nor trusted the man.

They had now found themselves in the difficult position of both colluding with and fighting against King Robert de Bruce, and Walt had no illusions as to the outcome.

He did not expect any favours towards his father if captured and was prepared to pay ransom. Open warfare did not figure in his father's agreement to provide intelligence to Bruce on English military movements.

After his mother's death in the priory hospital, subsequent to the outlaws' violent raid on their home, there had been a serious falling out with Prior Gregory, during which Walt had caused him to be ridiculed in front of the monks and nuns. His father had reprimanded him over his thoughtless act, but agreed what was done could not now be undone.

Walt believed that they could control the situation with the prior, and his father worried too much. 'If we can not build at Bytilsden we should improve the manor at Syhale' he had said.

Sir Walter had said, 'if I can not build at Bytilsden, I shall not waste a penny on this place. I shall look to buy more land in the Bytilsden area. One day I shall build our pele, or you or your son will build it. If you do nothing else when I am gone Son, keep my dream alive. Promise me that.'

Walt had promised his father in front of Katherine that he would strive to complete his wishes for the family. Despite his earlier reluctance to spend more money at Syhale, a month later in March 1311, Sir Walter had succumbed to persuasion and ordered a new kitchen and servants' quarters to be built, to the gable of the manor house. It was a grand affair making use of the chimney from the hall, with baking oven and a large fireplace for cooking; it was around twenty foot square with servants' sleeping area above. Most importantly, Sir Walter had constructed a new secret vault inside the alcove used for their outdoor clothes. Access was via the opening of a panel with concealed catch, and into a small double locked iron vault, containing the family strongbox. Walt believed it was probably the security of the money, previously stored in the priory vault, which had influenced his father's decision to build, especially as relations with Prior Gregory were at an all time low.

Walt and William had their early education at Tynemouth Priory, another source of argument over money between his father and the prior. William had been removed early, as had Walt, but whereas Walt had gone on to train for knighthood at Horton Castle, near Blyth, William remained on the estate until going to join his uncle in York one year before his marriage to Freda.

Walt brought his mind back to the present and came to a decision. Heading into the barracks he first came across the new man, Cethin Gwyn. 'Get Guddal to get a cart and driver and be ready immediately after your breakfast. All four of you can ride in the cart to Blyth.' Walt's recollection of Katherine's warning about the nosey prior had determined him to keep away from Tynemouth when purchasing so many horses. He continued, 'I intend to buy horses and tack for you and your men.'

====

CHAPTER 2

A king's letter

Outside they could hear Galeron mustering his new recruits. Those that could not ride were being taught, and lacking in the skills of a mounted infantryman, Galeron intended to give them plenty of training in control of the horse using spurs, knees and verbal commands, to allow for both hands to be used for fighting from horseback. He would practise them against himself and the two men at arms of his own troop. He would also take them to the quintain which Sir Walter had built, to experience further aspects of battle.

Sitting inside finishing off his breakfast, Walt was satisfied that Galeron had the training under control. After his meeting with David Brewer, the estate reeve, and their bailiff Turstan Gathergood, to discuss the day's activities, he would take a ride to the mill and see that all was well there. Afterward he would join the soldiers and see how they were shaping up to their new ways of fighting. He had every confidence in Galeron Guddal's ability to instruct them, his skills were on a par with those of Aidric Johansson and Sergeant Heddon; two of the men missing with his father along with Sir Walter's squire Thomas Gesthill and the rest of the troop.

Jolted out of his thoughts by little Walter, who having finished his breakfast had run to his father for some attention, Walt picked him up and gave him a hug.

'How is my little warrior today?' he asked. Without waiting for a reply he looked at Katherine. 'We should be thinking of getting him a pony soon.'

Katherine laughed, 'he's not yet four years old, do you not think we should wait until he is five?'

Little Walter, who never missed much, immediately began repeating, 'pony da, pony da.'

Tilly came to relieve the beleaguered parent, arriving with toddler Alex in one hand and intending to collect Walter from his father, after which she thought to take the pair into the feasting hall, out of the way.

Katherine, rising from her seat at the table intercepted her, taking Alex and saying, 'alright Tilly, leave them both with me for a while, and you can help tidy their breakfast things. Afterwards you may take them for a short walk, but keep within sight of the manor.'

Tilly thought it would definitely not be a long walk as Alex was only capable of a few steps and was extremely heavy to carry for any distance.

Later when the children had left for their walk with Tilly, Katherine rode to Delaval to visit her mother who was still recovering from a sudden unexplained collapse. She could speak fairly well now but her face was still a bit lopsided and drinking was difficult. She was fairly mobile with the aid of her stick but still suffering from the painful joints as she had long been. The village healer had said she was stricken. When questioned what this meant she had replied, 'Just stricken, it happens suddenly and they hardly ever fully recover.' She added, 'I know of no cure except time and patience.'

The two families were long standing close friends and it had seemed the natural thing to do when they arranged the marriage of Walt and Katherine when they were only thirteen, for a church union when they were of a suitable age. They had married in March 1310 when they were both twenty and their first child, Walter, was born in December of that year. It had been Sir Walter's intention to make his son wait until he was older, but at the insistence of his wife Agnes, who had long discovered her son's secret trysts with his step cousin Freda, he capitulated and agreed that the sooner they were married the better.

Katherine returned from her visit to her parents and the supper meal was again a silent affair. Katherine began to sob silently. Walt realised that she was worried, not only about her mother, but also his father, who she tended to think of more like her own second father than as a father in law. *I must do something positive,* he thought as he stood up and walked around the table. Taking her hands he pulled her gently out of her chair and onto her feet, put his arms around her and kissed her lovingly.

'I will not wait for news any longer; tomorrow I shall ride out and seek to find what has happened to Father. I will ride to the north until I find someone who knows.'

Katherine was even more upset at the prospect of Walt riding towards Scotland, and her ending up without a husband as well as a father in law.

'Please Walt no, let us give it another couple of days, and then if you have to go you must take some men with you.'

Walt considered her distress and agreed two more days and then he would definitely set out. They finished their supper in silence. Tilly had brought the children to them to say good night, and Katherine had gone with her to put them to bed and tell them a little story while they went to sleep.

They heard the sound of horsemen outside. Jeanne rushed to the door, returning disappointed.

'It's only Galeron and the Welsh troopers retuning to barracks after their day's hard riding and weapon training' she announced glumly.

Annie the housemaid began to clear away the supper things whilst Jeanne asked for instructions for tomorrow. Walt told her to sit down and wait a while as Katherine would be down shortly. Knowing of Jeanne's worries about Aidric; he took the opportunity to tell her of his decision to ride north in two day's time to seek news if they had heard nothing by then. Jeanne expressed the same misgivings as Katherine about him riding north and the dangers he may encounter, but did not try to dissuade him. Her need for news of her beloved was paramount in her thoughts. They sat at the table waiting for Katherine to come down, master and servant, both with the mutual bond of a missing loved one.

Hearing the sound of horsemen again, Jeanne jumped to her feet, suddenly excited, as she was every time she heard horses approaching, since the arrival of the fleeing soldiers.

'Probably Galeron and his troop again' Walt said.

Jeanne was not so sure; it seemed to her that the sounds were coming up from the village direction. She ran through the feasting hall, through the small porch opened the front door a little, peering into the evening gloom.

Walt, still sitting in the family room was startled to hear her loud shriek followed by a scream of, 'Aidric!'

He jumped up, in his excitement knocking over the chair, ran to the stair and shouted up, 'Katherine, come quick.'

Not waiting for her reply he ran through the hall to the front yard to see a small group of horsemen, with Trooper Aidric Johansson already dismounted, hugging and kissing Jeanne. As his eyes got accustomed to the darkness he recognised Squire Thomas, Sergeant Heddon, Trooper Botolfe Best, and another soldier whose name he could not recall. The other servants having heard Jeanne's shriek, soon joined the welcoming party.

Walt turned to Annie. 'Get cook to get hot food ready as soon as she can and break out a barrel of ale.'

Sergeant Heddon and the two soldiers had dismounted and the Sergeant told Botolfe to fetch the groom and a stable hand to take the horses. The other trooper, who Walt heard him call Farmer, was helping the sergeant to get Gesthill off his horse. Botolfe returned from the stables with Will Foster and a stable hand. Will excitedly gripped forearms all round, welcoming them all back, whilst taking the horses to unsaddle and feed.

Walt was overjoyed to see them safe, but refrained from questioning them until he had them inside and sat down with some refreshment. He was concerned about Thomas's injured leg and hastened to relieve the sergeant and his trooper, to help him into the house. Once Thomas was down from his horse, the sergeant handed him his crutch. Waiving away Walt's offer of assistance, Thomas made surprisingly quick progress into the house with Walt staying close and concerned. As they passed into the hall he whispered to Walt, 'I have a letter for you, best I give it to you in private later when the others have gone to the barracks.'

Walt nodded and gave Thomas's arm a slight squeeze to indicate his understanding. In the hall Annie had already lit candles and placed them along the table. From the hall they heard Katherine saying to someone in the family room 'where is Walt? What is all the shouting about?'

Coming through into the hall she gave a shout of surprise, followed by an enthusiastic greeting, 'welcome to you all Thomas, Sergeant Heddon, Trooper Johansson and, Trooper Best.' Looking at the younger trooper she began, 'what is your na--?'

'Trooper Sam Farmer, My Lady,' the soldier offered, before realising that he had already lost her attention.

Katherine had suddenly realised that Sir Walter was absent. There was instant silence as everyone anticipated what was to come. She continued in a hushed tone, 'where is father?'

Squire Thomas hobbled to a chair with his crutch and said, 'I think we should all sit down.'

Katherine, embarrassed that she had not realised the squire was injured, ran to his aid and helped him into the chair.

'I am so sorry Thomas I was not thinking straight, you are wounded.'

'I am alright Mistress Katherine, just a shallow head wound and a broken leg, both of which will mend. Please everyone take a seat and I will impart my news.'

They all settled in their seats to one end of the long feasting table, with Katherine sitting next to Walt, and Jeanne next to Aidric. Annie appeared with tankards of ale for all, whilst Ursula, the kitchen maid, brought bowls and spoons. She said cook was making a pot of ham and pea soup as it was quick to make and very filling, with fresh baked bread. The new arrivals all smiled with anticipation, they were hungry and looking forward to it.

As soon as Ursula and Annie left for the kitchen, Squire Thomas returned to his response to Katherine's question.

'I am sorry to say that Sir Walter lost his life valiantly in an ill-timed charge on the Scottish shiltrons at the outset of the battle,' he paused for this news to be absorbed before continuing, 'he was at the vanguard of a cavalry charge into the Scottish shiltrons, and I was alongside him. Sadly his horse was brought down and he was set upon with a flail, I saw no more, as I was also brought down, and my leg broken as the horse fell on me. I don't know if I received my head wound during the fall, or if I was clubbed, but when I regained consciousness I was tied over a horse, and a prisoner. I was later told that Sir Walter had perished during the attack.' He made no mention of the letter the Scottish king had entrusted to him.

Walt looked shocked and saddened, Katherine and Jeanne were unashamedly weeping when Annie and Ursula came in with a big platter of fresh bread and large kettle to ladle out soup for the hungry men and anyone else who wished to partake. They served it out silently with Annie bending close to Sergeant Heddon and whispering, 'why are they crying?'

He replied also in a whisper: 'the Master was killed in battle.'

As they left the room Annie could be seen tearfully passing the sad news to Ursula.

Without further ado the hungry men began to eat their soup and bread, with the exception of Aidric, loath to untangle himself from a weeping Jeanne, but soon overcome by hunger as they had not stopped since leaving Clennell, and had only taken a few oat biscuits from Alice Clennell after stating their intention to ride straight through without halt.

Walt asked Sergeant Heddon about the main battle where they had all been captured. The Sergeant explained about the lack of leadership of the English army, and the way the Scots had used clever tactics to lure them to the battlefield of their choice, and how the premature cavalry charge had failed because the Welsh archers had not been brought forward to decimate the shiltrons first. When he had finished, Walt said he would be surprised if anyone would ever want to follow this king into battle again, and he could now well understand why Sir Henry had declined. He had been let down by being deserted to hold Perth, escaped with his life only to be briefly imprisoned for a while at the whim of one of the king's favourites, after being accused of supporting insurrection. Also he would most likely have known about the changes of command the king had brought about, which further explained his refusal to fight.

'Certainly a shock defeat,' Walt murmured. 'What do you say Thomas?'

'I think many knew the outcome when it was obvious that there was no organisation for the formation of our battle lines. Morale was low to start with and then to be led by a reticent king and two squabbling earls was a lesson in how to snatch defeat from what should have been a victory.'

'You could not have put it better Thomas, sounds like a fine review of a hopeless situation.'

The soldiers eventually took their leave, with Aidric saying a lingering goodnight to Jeanne before she came inside, suppressing her happiness at his safe return due to the sad news they had brought regarding the master. Unable to cope with her dilemma of mixed emotions caused by the loss of Sir Walter and the return of her loved one, Jeanne's immediate solution to her problem was to ask permission to retire. Walt nodded his permission, asking 'please get one of the servants to organise a palliasse and blankets for Squire Thomas before you retire, he will be staying the night in the hall.'

'Certainly, Sir and thank you' she replied as she hurried out of the room.

Walt turned to Katherine, kissed her and asked if she would mind if he had some time with Thomas alone, to speak of military matters. Knowing it would likely be about his father and not wanting to intrude, she readily agreed.

'I shall be next door if you want me,' she said closing the door behind her as she went into the family room.

Thomas chatted idly to Walt for a few minutes, waiting for the palliasse to be brought in and the servants away, so they could have their privacy. He told Walt that the Scots wanted their horses and saddles returned and to expect an early visit to collect them. Annie and Ursula came in and put the palliasse and blankets down at the far end of the hall as directed by Walt. He thanked them and told them to seek the mistress's approval to be dismissed for the night.

Once the servants had left, he checked the door to the family room was firmly closed and ensured the front door was locked and the shutters barred, before taking his place at the end of the table next to Thomas, reaching over for the ale jug and topping up both their tankards.

'Now Thomas,' he said, 'tell me all.'

Thomas reached inside his coathardie and pulled out the letter given him by the Scottish king. It was sealed with King Robert's seal and addressed, *Walter Radulf the younger*.

Thomas, who had discreetly moved away to the next chair to give his new master some privacy, watched silently and sipped his ale, while Walt slowly broke the seal and carefully opened the parchment as if something might jump out and bite him. He unfolded it and held it flat on the table with his left hand, reached out with his right, and pulled a candlestick closer for better illumination. It was written in French.

Bannockburn 26 June 1314
To Walter Radulf the younger
You will know from the bearer of this letter that your father perished at the battle of Bannockburn. God rest his soul. You must know that my men have reported that he died heroically as would be expected of a knight of his standing. I must add that I was

surprised to hear of his death as I did not expect that he would have been in battle at his advanced years.

You should also know that his body has been laid to rest in hallowed ground near St. Ninians Kirk. A prayer was said by a priest of his calling.

Your man Trooper Johansson who accompanied you both on your meeting with me in Galloway had the presence of mind to seek an audience with me by mentioning your father's name. Thus it was that I was able to honour our agreement and arrange the release of all your men who were still alive and to entrust this letter with Sir Walter's squire, Thomas Gesthill.

You must know after the rout of your king's army that there is likely to be much raiding by my armies into northern England. If you wish to continue the arrangement your father had with me I will instruct my commanders to treat your lands and those of your near family with due respect. I cannot guarantee that there will not be raids by irregulars who are not part of the army, but you should be able to deal with them with your own men judging by the bravery shown by those who died or were captured here.

If you wish to continue the arrangement I had with your father please send word by messenger in the same manner that your father did, and list your land holdings and their keepers together with those of close family. I will try to avoid disruption to these wherever possible. Although they may not be visited, I cannot say your lands may not be traversed.

R de Bruce
King of Scotland

Walter carefully folded the letter and put it inside his coat. He would sound out Katherine later. She would be able to confirm his understanding of the letter. He would not enter into any agreement without her knowledge, and he knew she would not expect him to. He knew the squire was no fool and most likely Sergeant Heddon and Aidric guessed from their easy exit from Scotland that there was some friendship between the two. Well they can guess, but they only needed to know what he was willing to tell them. He decided to take Squire Thomas partially into his confidence.

'Thomas, you know that my father had a friendship with the king of Scotland?'

'Yes, Sir, but I know not why,' Thomas replied.

36

'That is easily answered. My father's sister, my aunt Annabella, was married to Robert Bruce for three years when he was a young man and before he became a pretender to the throne. She bore him a son and unfortunately died two years later. King Robert has had my father correctly buried with knightly honours. He is offering me and mine some protection from raids as long as we are not opposing him directly in battle.'

Thomas was silent and Walt was trying to think what was going through his mind, when he spoke up.

'I understand well, Sir. I knew of your father's arrangement, I was very close to him and he entrusted me with many secrets. I will also understand that you should take up the Scottish king's offer and save your lands from destruction, for that is surely what will come in the following months for much of northern England. You need have no fear of my loyalty, Sir, we must all look out for ourselves now and must stick together with those we love and trust. We could not, and can not trust our king to help us.'

Walt was astonished. 'My God Thomas that was a long speech for you, but I welcome it. Now I must go to my wife. I bid you a good night's rest.'

'Sir, before you leave I must tell you that I have your father's sword, shield and helm, given to me by King Robert. I asked Will Foster to keep them until morning, so as not to upset the mistress.'

'Thank you Thomas,' Walt replied sincerely as he helped him over to his palliasse and laid his crutch nearby, as well as placing a chair close for him to hold onto if he had to get up. As an afterthought he went into the family room and came back with a bucket.

'Just in case you need to piss,' he said, as he left Thomas to his rest and went through into the family room closing the door behind him.

Katherine, seated alone in the family room, had stopped crying but her eyes were red and looked sore where she had been rubbing them. He leaned over and kissed her on both eyes, and then softly and gently on her mouth. She responded by opening her mouth and inviting him in. Their gentle kiss soon changed into a passionate embrace. They separated after Walt said he had something important to show her. Walt noticed that her wine goblet was empty and thought she may be grateful for a refill after she had seen his news.

37

He refilled her goblet, drew out the letter from his coat which he unfolded and laid on the table without explanation. Katherine read the letter through slowly, without comment until she had finished.

'Well what does he expect you to do for his protection?' she asked, jolted back to reality.

'Advise him if I hear of any plan for a major assault, which is unlikely in the foreseeable future and maybe give him some form of assistance from time to time by gathering information.'

'You mean, be his spy' Katherine said bluntly.

'Yes, but let us view the alternative. We could have our home burnt down; our stock and grain pillaged and be robbed of our money. This could happen at any time over the next years and we have our families and our children to consider. We can expect no help from our king, who only knows how to run away. The nearest he is likely to get to Northumberland will be York if unfriendly earls chase him there.'

Katherine replied instantly, 'I understand your views, and agree that a king who shows no loyalty to his subjects cannot expect their loyalty to his crown. You do whatever is necessary to protect our way of life my dearest, and we will reconsider our loyalties when we have a ruler who respects us. So what now? Just be careful who we trust?' she asked.

Walt was relieved; he did not want to argue with Katherine, after a moment's thought he replied. 'It is a dangerous game we embark upon, which could lead to me being arrested and tried for treason. The arrangement must be kept secret, even from family, and never admitted to any who are suspicious of our immunity to raids. I will seek legal advice and try to find a way to secure this manor for you and the children in the event that I should fall out of the king's favour.'

The more Katherine thought about their situation the more she worried, but she suspected they were not the only ones who would seek arrangements with the Scots to protect their interests, mostly by paying ransoms to be left alone she assumed, and not by actively colluding with the enemy. 'You should find a benefactor, and someone to propose you for knighthood to strengthen your position,' she said.

'Good idea Katherine,' he replied.

'But first you need to prepare a document for Squire Thomas to sign, verifying his witness to the death of your father at the battle of Bannockburn. For obvious reasons, we cannot use Bruce's letter,' Katherine reminded him.

'I know, my mind is running away with thoughts on what should be done next. I will prepare a document for Thomas to sign, and then I shall remove sufficient funds from our vault to visit the priory and pay the heriot on this estate, and that which my uncle rents at Felling. Once that is settled, I shall have to journey to Bytilsden to pay the heriot there. I do not look forward to another meeting with de Umfraville, at Harbottle castle.'

Katherine laughed, you worry about him, have you forgotten that you have not been face to face with the prior since the removal of our strongbox from their vault?'

Walt sighed, 'very well, I shall go tomorrow to pay the heriot.'

'While you are there, you could perhaps have a word with Sister Amelia and Mother Rachel. I am most concerned for Squire Thomas. What if his leg has not been correctly set, and his head wound should be examined.'

'You do not expect me to take Thomas with me, surely?'

'Of course not, I expect you to return with somebody who can examine him,' she replied.

'Yes, I can do that, and maybe find out a few things that transpired after we removed our savings. I would like to have seen the prior's face when he returned from Durham. You go to bed now my dear. I shall write to Bruce, and prepare a document for Thomas to sign, after which I shall join you.'

Katherine kissed him goodnight and urged him not to be too long. As she ascended the stairs, he went to a shelf and took down ink, quill and parchment, laid a piece of parchment in front of him on the table, dipped his quill into the ink, and began to write painstakingly in Latin, using his best effort to recall what he had learnt at Tynemouth Priory.

Syhale 6 July 1314
To His Majesty Robert de Bruce King of Scotland
Sire,
I thank you for your extreme kindness in ensuring that my late father Sir Walter Radulf was afforded an appropriate Christian

burial. I must further thank you for your generous act in freeing my father's squire and our few surviving soldiers.

With regard to your kind offer of protection, I gratefully accept your terms on behalf of myself and my family. I have interests here at Syhale, at nearby Delaval, Felling and at Bytilsden. I shall instruct my agents or family at these places to display a small plaque exhibiting my colours on my properties and their own properties as a means of ready identification by your commanders. If asked for verification, all of these people would know the name of my mother and my father's wife Agnes who is sadly deceased.

I send this letter by the only route I know; that which my father used. God be with you.

I remain, Sire, Your Servant.

Walter de Radulf

Walt carefully folded the letter, wrote on the outside, **His Majesty King Robert de Bruce of Scotland.** After folding and sealing it with wax, he wrapped it in another layer of parchment and sealed that. On the outside of the package he wrote, **Allan Stewart, Yetholm, Scotland.**

Having completed the letter, he tucked it into his jacket and picked up the letter from Bruce, which he place on the embers of the family room fire, poking it gently to ensure it was destroyed.

Back at the table, he took more parchment and prepared two identical documents describing the circumstances of his father's death, ready for Thomas to sign in the morning.

These tasks completed, he first peeped into the hall. Thomas was fast asleep and snoring gently on his palliasse. Satisfied that his squire was comfortable, he made his way quietly upstairs with the candle, where he found Katherine waiting for him, and still awake.

He placed the candle on the small table by the bed, removed his clothing and turned to see his wife, six months pregnant, holding back the linen sheet for him to come in beside her. She was lying naked, as was their habit during the summer months. Her belly was well extended with the child but to him she looked as beautiful as ever. *What is it,* he thought, *that makes a woman's skin shine with beauty when they are carrying.* Her face was radiant with health, and he loved her so much he felt the pain of it in his heart. She held out her arms to him, and as he slid alongside, she kissed him and pulled him closer. 'Just be careful,' she said.

The next morning after breaking his fast, Walt went outside where Sergeant Heddon had the men on parade. With Squire Thomas being unfit to travel, he needed somebody he could trust to deliver his letter. Remembering that his father had once requested the sergeant to provide a trooper for the task, he called Sergeant Heddon to one side and quietly asked him if the trooper who had performed that task was still with them.

'Trooper Guddal' the sergeant replied instantly.

'Good. Please take him to one side and give him this letter. Tell him to wear plain clothes and head off for Yetholm to deliver it to Allan Stewart and no other. He must speak to no-one about his mission; you can tell the others he has leave of absence for personal reasons.

With the letter handed over and the trooper on his way, Sergeant Heddon retuned to his waiting troop and was about to begin a training session with them, when Walt called him aside.

'Are you sure there is not somewhere you would rather be?' he asked.

The sergeant looked uncomfortable, and muttered that he could take care of his personal business after work tonight. Walt laughed, adding to his sergeant's embarrassment.

'I am sure you can Sergeant, but somebody is still waiting anxiously, not yet knowing if you are alive. Maybe it would not hurt to take an hour off. The men can start without you.'

Sergeant Heddon thanked him with genuine feeling, and ran to saddle his horse while Walt called forward Botolfe Best.

'Get the men saddled up Trooper and give them some practice in swerving and hanging from the saddle until the sergeant comes back.'

Aidric Johansson looked confused as to why the job had not been given to him as a senior soldier and one time acting sergeant, but said nothing, knowing that his master must have some other task for him.

'Trooper Johansson,' Walt shouted. 'When you are saddled up, report to me at the house. Trooper Best please tell the sergeant, when he returns, that Aidric is escorting me today.'

Walt walked over to the stables where he told Will to saddle his horse. He also told him to care for the five horses and their tack, which the men had arrived on the previous day.

'They are not ours,' he said. 'Their owners will be calling for them one day so we must keep them in good order and have all ready to hand over.'

Will was puzzled by the arrangement but knew better than to question his master's instructions.

Back in the house, Walt found Thomas eating his breakfast and being fussed over by a concerned Jeanne. He waited patiently until his squire had finished eating, before presenting him with the document to sign, as witness to the death of Sir Walter de Radulf. Although much common practice now dropped the formal 'de' from names, Norman bureaucracy demanded full title on official documents, and Normans were mostly in charge.

Aidric appeared outside, mounted and ready, and as soon as Walt's horse was saddled, he took his saddle bags with the heriot money and the pair set off for Tynemouth.

***

Daisy Miller had not long finished her breakfast and was busy cleaning her room. Living in a mill was a never ending battle with dust. It was impossible to win but you could just keep things from disappearing completely under a white coating. She was herself showing a coating of the dust, when she heard a horse galloping down the track to halt outside. Her heart missed a beat as she dropped her cleaning cloth and ran to the door. She was the first out, followed by Henry and his son who had come out of the mill room to see who would approach at such a speed.

At first Daisy could not see who it was as he had dismounted with the horse's body blocking her view. She saw his sleeve as he threw the rein over the hitching rail and her heart began to race, it was a uniform. He walked around the back of the horse and Daisy fainted. Fortunately Henry was behind her and caught her under her arms. Nicholas Heddon ran forward and took her from him, picking her up in his arms and carrying her into her private quarters. Thinking of Daisy's honour, he left the door open as he laid her on her bed in the corner. Henry and John stayed at the door long enough to welcome him back and express their relief for themselves and Daisy on his safe return. They told him that she had fretted continuously for news. Sergeant Heddon thanked them for their help and they returned to

42

the mill room, with Henry no longer showing the pleased countenance he had shown to the sergeant's face earlier. 'Why did that bloody man have to come back at all?' he whispered to his son when he was sure they were out of earshot.

'Then why should we be happy for him Father.'

'None of your business boy, just smile and be polite like I do, we have our jobs to consider.'

Sergeant Heddon returned to the bed where Daisy lay, with a little cider in a cup and a cloth dampened with a little water from the bucket. He lifted her head gently and wiped her brow with the cool cloth. Daisy began to stir. He held the cup to her lips for her to drink. She opened her eyes and looked directly into his.

'Oh Nicholas,' she said, throwing her arms about him and sending the cup of cider flying, 'I thought I would never see you again.'

With that she kissed him like he had never been kissed before. She broke free and looked beyond to the door. 'Close the door please, Nicholas,'

'Are you sure Daisy, what will the Wests think?'

'I care not what the Wests think, but what do you think Nicholas?'

'I think I will close the door,' he said happily.

***

Walt and Aidric arrived at the priory late morning. The first person they spied was Brother Richard. Dismounting, they asked the monk if he could take their horses to the ostler for water and rest, and if the prior was available.

'Prior Gregory has gone to Newcastle' was the curt response, as the monk took their horses, Walt having first retrieved his saddlebag.

'When is he expected to return?'

'I do not know, maybe today, maybe tomorrow.'

'What about Brother Cornelius then?' Walt prompted.

'In his office.'

'Brother Richard is not very talkative today, let us hope we have a better reception from Brother Cornelius,' Walt remarked, as he strode towards the treasurer's office, with Aidric following.

At the office, Aidric made to hang back, but Walt said 'come in with me, I may need a witness to sign something.'

Brother Cornelius at least looked pleased to see them, and gave them an enthusiastic welcome. 'What can I do for you Walt, I am most sorry to hear of the demise of your father, albeit under such heroic circumstances.'

Surprised that the monk knew of his father's death so soon, Walt asked, 'how did you know of this, we only found out last night?'

'A knight returning from the battle scene and travelling southwards sought shelter here last night, and moved on this morning. He said he saw your father go down in the first charge.'

'Well Brother Cornelius, my father's death is the purpose of our visit. I have here a signed deposition by my father's squire, who was in the charge alongside him and witnessed his end. I have brought with me sufficient funds to pay the heriot for Syhale and Felling, and wish you to arrange the transfer of the deeds through the appropriate authority. Obviously there will be money for the priory for your time and expertise with these matters.'

'The prior is not here Master Walt and I am not sure my authority extends to such matters.'

'Come now, Brother Cornelius, if the prior were present, to whom would he pass this task?'

'Well, Sir, it would be me.'

'And what happens to the money and documents afterwards?'

'Priory takes its charges, and the remainder goes to Newcastle or Durham, for new deeds to be prepared.'

'So,' said Walt. 'The prior does nothing except pass it to you, so let us get on with it. There is no need for delay; Prior Gregory can be informed on his return.'

'He will not like it,' said the treasurer, as he pulled down scrolls relating to the appropriate estates from a shelf. The scrolls, relating to tithes, also gave information of acreage, from which the heriot would be calculated.

'When did the prior ever like anything?' Walt asked, with a hint of sarcasm.

Brother Cornelius looked up from his calculations, and smiled. 'I profess, I cannot recall,' he replied.

The treasurer completed his work and Walt was asked to sign a document, with Aidric as his witness. After receiving a receipt for the money, the treasurer told Walt that he would receive the new deeds direct by messenger as they would have to be signed for.

Walt thanked him and expressed his wish to have an audience with Mother Rachael.

Brother Cornelius called loudly for a messenger, and as if by magic, Brother Richard appeared almost instantly at the door.

Walt and Aidric looked at each other and smiled, they both knew the monk had been listening to the conversation, which would be repeated to the prior at the earliest opportunity. 'Brother Richard, take these two gentlemen to Mother Rachael.'

They bade farewell to the treasurer, and Brother Richard escorted them to the Mother Superior's office. With propriety, when he entered the monk stayed with them. Mother Rachel greeted Walt warmly, and expressed deep sorrow for the death of his father. He thanked her and told her that some of his men who had escaped from captivity had returned, and that Squire Thomas was badly injured. He sought her permission to speak with Sister Amelia to assess the need for a practised examination. Mother Rachel immediately asked Brother Richard to go and fetch Sister Amelia.

'Leave the door open as you leave,' she said.

The monk returned with Sister Amelia in minutes, and Walt told her of his worries for their squire's health.

'Thomas's leg is broken, and bound with a splint, which to the untrained eye seems to be alright. He has a head wound which is healing, but he still suffers occasional spells of dizziness.'

Sister Amelia suggested that she should go to Syhale and examine him.

'I will make a gift to the hospital for Sister Amelia's time,' said Walt, 'but I would prefer if we could do this without the involvement of Prior Gregory.'

'Anything you can give would be welcome,' Mother Superior replied, recalling the family's previous generous donation following the death of Lady Agnes, 'and the prior need not be involved.'

Sister Amelia said she would return with them today, if they could provide her with an escort to return tomorrow morning. This agreed, she left for the stables to have a horse saddled for the journey. They waited outside the priory until Sister Amelia appeared, mounted aside with both feet on a small ledge, and upon a sorry looking horse. A canvas bag was bound behind her saddle. Potions and overnight requirements, Walt presumed.

Aidric sighed at the sight of the accompanying nun seated precariously on her side saddle. It was going to be a slow journey home.

As they left the priory, they came upon the prior returning from his visit to Newcastle. Not wanting to involve Sister Amelia in any altercation, Walt told Aidric to carry on with the nun, whilst he stopped to intercept the prior.

'What is transpiring here?' the prior asked, waving his arm in the direction of the departing Aidric and sister Amelia.

'Mother Rachael has given her permission for the sister to examine our squire, who was wounded in battle.'

'I should have been asked before you have an audience with the mother superior,' he snapped irritably.

'I am sorry Prior, but you were not here and the matter is urgent.'

Prior Gregory could feel his temper rising, and fought to keep control and avoid his hatred of the family coming to the fore. He recalled the bishop's warning, which had a steadying influence. 'I am sorry to hear of your father's death,' the prior said at last, reluctantly and unconvincingly. 'I suppose you want a sponsor for your knighthood now?'

'I have that in progress thank you Prior.'

'I hear Sir Giscard was killed at Bannockburn,' the prior said almost gleefully, 'so who will you get now?'

'There is no need for your concern Prior I have it in hand.' Walt was damned if he was going to ask the prior for help or tell him his plans. He bade the prior good day and turned to catch up with Aidric and the nun, smiling to himself, as he imagined the prior's anger when the novice told him all about the heriot. He felt sorry for Brother Cornelius, but he had broad shoulders and had dealt with the prior's rages before.

Katherine was surprised to see the sister return with Walt. 'The squire insisted on returning to his house,' Katherine told him, 'one of the troopers ensured he arrived safely and he is now in the care of his maidservant.'

After briefly explaining the situation, he handed his saddlebag to his wife and dismissed Aidric. They tarried a short while, whilst he and the sister partook of some liquid refreshment, before taking her to Thomas Gesthill's house, where they found him relaxing with a tankard of ale and being fussed over by his maidservant.

The nun carefully examined Thomas's broken leg, feeling the length between the splints to ensure the bone was correctly in position.

'This must have been set by a trained physician,' she pronounced. 'It is correctly aligned and should present little problem, but he will need to have his splints on for at least four months, and after that he must not put strain on the leg for another two months. He will be able to ride but must take extreme care when dismounting, and walk only with the aid of a crutch under the arm to take the weight off the affected leg.'

Thomas looked horrified at the thought of being a virtual invalid for the next six months. Sister Amelia seeing the look of disbelief in his eyes, warned him, 'if you do as you are told, with prayer, and God's help, you will get better. If you disobey, praying will not help, you may be crippled for life, and you cannot blame God. Now let me have a look at your head.'

She unwound the bandage and studied his wound. It had been bleeding again so she asked the maid to bring some warm water and clean cloth for wiping, and some for bandage. She took a bowl out of her bag, and poured a small quantity of one of her potions into it. After cleaning the wound, she bathed it with her potion, and bound it with a clean bandage.

'There,' she said to the maid, 'you saw how much of the potion I used on the cloth to bathe the wound. Can you do the same twice a week until it is fully healed?'

The maid said she understood and Sister Amelia left her the bottle of potion.

'You will be alright,' she said to Thomas, 'when did you have your last dizzy spell?'

'Not since the night we came back' he replied.

'Well that could be down to tiredness as well as your wound. You tell Master Walt if you have any more, and we shall have to think again.'

Leaving Thomas in the capable hands of his servant they returned to the manor for supper. Immediately after they had breakfasted the following morning, Sister Amelia departed for her return journey to the priory, with a generous donation for the hospital and Trooper Johansson as escort.

***

Walt and Katherine rode over to Delaval to join her parents for the Sunday service at the Church of our Lady. Walt wanted to speak to Sir Hugh about his knighthood and the protection from Scottish raids. He told Hugh that he had paid a ransom fee to be left alone during raids by regular Scottish military, and that he had taken the opportunity to include Delaval, but he must be sure to display the Radulf barry of eight on his door and remember 'Agnes' if asked a question. Sir Hugh immediately wanted to know how much he should reimburse Walt for his expenditure.

'You can repay the favour some other time Hugh, and by not discussing it with anyone. You must also be aware that my ransom fee may be invalid if the raiders are irregulars or choose to ignore the agreement. In which case you must make your own arrangement and hope for the best.' He hoped that his reply would put him off from further enquiries, indefinitely.

On the subject of knighthood, Hugh agreed with Walt's suggestion of Sir Henry Percy, and wrote him a letter of support.

'A good place for your man's training as well,' he said, when told of Walt's plans to train Aidric as a squire. 'But are you sure he will stay once trained if there is no position for him.'

'He is bound to me by his terms of engagement and only I can release him' Walt replied.

On Monday morning he had intended to ride to Bytilsden but changed his mind and asked Sergeant Heddon to send a trooper to Clennell with a letter containing similar instructions regarding security that he had given Sir Hugh, and another to be sent to his brother at Felling with a similar letter. He would go later to settle the Bytilsden heriot with de Umfraville.

The messengers despatched, he set off instead with Aidric Johansson, to seek audience with Sir Henry Percy at Alnwick castle. Following the death of Sir Guiscard of Horton at Bannockburn, his wife and daughter had fled south for a more secure existence and Sir Percy would now be Walt's overlord, so he could settle the heriot and seek his knighthood at the same time.

He returned on Wednesday with a satisfied look on his face, but made no comment until they sat down to their evening meal and Katherine, unable to contain her impatience any longer, asked: 'Well then, is it all secret? Did you see Baron Percy? Is he going to sponsor your knighthood? Did you pay the heriot?'

Walt laughed and decided to tease her a little more. 'The answers to your questions my dearest, are: no, yes, yes and yes.'

'So where and when is it to be? Don't tantalise me Walt.'

'Wednesday, first of August at Alnwick Abbey,' he replied.

'That is a long way for me to travel in my condition' she said, 'it must be over thirty miles and a good days riding.'

'What about your mother's little carriage?'

'That bone shaker would certainly bring on an early birth,' she laughed, 'I think my mother only uses it because she thinks the vibrations ease her joint pains. Where will you have the feast afterwards?'

'Here with our friends and Sir Henry and his wife.'

'In that case I will remain here and make sure everything is prepared.'

'You will like them dearest; they are really quite like us and talk in a straightforward manner.'

Walt loved her for the way she had readily compromised by giving up her opportunity to see him knighted, but he now felt ashamed and guilty for teasing her like that. He walked around the table, raised her from her chair, put his arms around her and said,

'I am sorry; the lady shall go to the ball.'

Katherine stood back from him and gave him a sharp jab in the ribs. 'What are you doing to me Walt, stop teasing and tell me what is happening.'

'Sir Henry took me to see the abbot, and for a fee he will travel here and conduct the ceremony in our little church. I only have to gain the agreement of Father Livio, and he will not be a problem, he will be honoured to have such a ceremony in his humble church.'

'There must be a catch Walt.'

'The catch is that we have to accommodate the abbot and Baron Percy and his lady, plus their servants, for the night before and the night of the ceremony.'

'We have two spare rooms, one for the abbot and one for the baron and his lady. The other guests will have to sleep in the hall.

We could use some of the spare space in the barracks and maybe some of their servants that they are bound to bring with them can squeeze in with ours. Who will be your squire Walt?'

'It will have to be Thomas, I am sure he can manage with help.

'He must be the longest serving squire in the kingdom' remarked Katherine.

'Never shown any interest in knighthood,' said Walt, 'but Father trusted him with his life, and I respect that, but I must be prepared for his retirement. When such a time occurs, I would rather take young Aidric as my squire than some stranger, so Aidric can return with them on the Thursday after my ceremony to start his training, which will be short due to the skill at arms he already possesses. He has practised many knight's skills here on Father's quintain, and he is already mainly trained on chivalry and conduct.'

'So he could be a knight in another seven years if he was so inclined' Katherine said.

Walt agreed. 'His decision, but he could impoverish himself if he could not accumulate sufficient wealth to meet the expense of the position.'

After kissing his wife again, he returned to his chair and they continued their supper. With their meal completed Katherine went into a huddle with Jeanne, discussing the forthcoming banquet in a couple of weeks' time. Jeanne did not envisage much difference between this and any other feast, except for the number of guests. She imagined that the food would have to be of a similar standard. Katherine told her nothing about Aidric's forthcoming departure, albeit temporary. She thought it better that Aidric should tell her himself at a time of his choosing.

The next day around noon, Walt had just returned from visiting some of the estate tenant farms to review grain crops, which would soon be ready for harvest. He had also reminded his villeins of their obligation to provide him with labour on his demesne during the period. Just as he was entering the house, he heard a shout of warning from Sergeant Heddon. He turned and saw two things; the Sergeant had turned out the men and they were quickly taking up defensive positions. There was no time to saddle horses. Behind the barrack block, coming over the small hill from the direction of the mill and ford was a large party of mounted and armed men led by a knight. Walt quickly shouted to the Sergeant, 'Sergeant Heddon, tell your men to move out of sight and stand easy unless called. You are all to stay calm and take your orders only from me.'

Walt had identified the visitors as Scots, and thought he should know the knight leading them, but could not put a name to him. There appeared to be about fifty of them. *Pray to God there is no trouble*, he thought, *there are too many of them for us.*

They galloped past the end of the barrack building and the knight drew them to a halt in front of the house. They appeared to offer no aggression and the leader dismounted and walked over to Walt. Walt decided to break the ice and greeted him.

'I bid you good day, Sir, I know you not, but I am the master of this estate and my name is Walter de Radulf, may I know your business here, Sir?'

The knight stepped forward and held out his hand. 'I am Sir William de Middleton. I have come to collect the king's horses and their tack.'

Walt raised his own hand and the two men firmly grasped each other's forearm, as Walt replied. 'I was sure I recognised your features, Sir, are you the younger brother of Sir Gilbert?'

'The very same, I shall not visit him with this troop, but I would be obliged if you could carry a message for my brother Gilbert and the family.'

Walt nodded his agreement, taking a sealed message from his visitor and sliding into his tunic. 'Sergeant Heddon, come over here,' he called.

The sergeant marched over from the barrack block, and the knight leading the Scots broke into a broad smile.

'Good to see you Sergeant, did you all get back safely then, how about the Squire with the broken leg?'

'Everybody is well thank you, Sir' the sergeant replied.

Walt asked the sergeant to get a couple of the men to saddle the Scottish horses for their journey home. He called Aidric to him and instructed him to arrange some bread and cheese for the men.

'If there is not enough in the soldiers' kitchen, take it from ours,' he added.

'Will you come into the house with me Sir William and take refreshment?' Walt asked.

Sir William nodded his agreement and followed Walt into the house where he introduced him to Katherine, while Jeanne organised some ham and cheese with fresh baked bread.

Over their food and a tankard of ale, Walt told him that his troopers had told him they were escorted to the border by the brother of Sir Gilbert, a friend of his late father. Sir William confirmed this and again explained his reason for being with the Scots. Walt made no criticism of this. 'Who knows? I may be in the same situation myself one day. Anything can happen in these uncertain times. My men asked me to convey your best wishes to your brother when I next saw him. I have not yet had the pleasure, as I believe he is still in York with Lord Eure, but now I have your letter to deliver as soon as he returns to Mitford. Eure has not been in residence for some time now, taking your brother and his men with him to his estate in York. There is currently only a caretaker troop at Mitford castle.'

They ate and chatted some more, with Sir William commenting on his two healthy sons and the obvious evidence of another one. Katherine blushed and reminded them that it may be a girl. Talk remained mainly about family and the subject of war was tacitly avoided. Half an hour later, Sergeant Heddon knocked on the door and put his head round to say that the horses were all ready and Sir William's men had been fed and refreshed.

'Not too much refreshment I hope,' the knight called to Sergeant Heddon as he left.

Sir William thanked them for their hospitality and headed for the door, just before passing through he turned to say quietly to Walt, 'King Robert received your letter, and asked me to wish you well with your ceremony on the first of August, but we shall give such heavily defended places as Alnwick a wide berth on our return north.'

With that he strode out, mounted his horse and they all galloped away to the north leading the five recovered horses.

Walt came back inside with a bewildered look on his face.

'How the hell did he know about my knighthood next month,' he asked of no-one in particular.

'Do not make mention of the devil's house in our home,' admonished Katherine. She was superstitious about such things. 'He seems a very nice man,' she concluded.

'He has been hiding away in Scotland because he was a Templar Knight. He may seem nice now, but you would not want to be his enemy,' Walt replied.

'There have been lots of stories about Templars doing terrible things on the crusade.'

'Some may be put about by the church to discredit them' Walt said in their defence.

'Hmm,' said Katherine, not wanting to believe that the church would do anything underhand. She discounted the scheming of monks; they were in a different category.

Walt went to visit Father Livio after the Scots had left. The little priest was delighted that his tiny church was to host such an important ceremony. Walt told him he would send some of his soldiers down to fix banners along the walls and some holders in case Sir Henry wanted some of his banners displayed. The ladies he was sure would organise flowers for the altar. He told him the abbot would be here the day before and would instruct him in any part he must play in the ceremony.

Back at home he found Katherine still busy with Jeanne, planning for the arrival of the visitors on the thirty first of July. They would all need an evening meal and breakfast in the morning. Clean linen sheets were to be provided for the beds upstairs for the abbot, the baron and his wife. Guests would be the usual family and friends. Suddenly Katherine exclaimed. 'Oh my goodness!'

'What's wrong?' Walt asked.

'We have forgotten about your brother.'

'Don't worry; I will get a messenger off tomorrow. It will be short notice for him, but there are a couple of weeks yet and he and Freda are both good riders, and she has her new saddle that Father bought her at the Michaelmass fair.'

Walt left Katherine and her servants to organise the menu and extra help for the event. He said he was going to the village to discuss some important business and would take some men hunting for deer for the banquet, in the morning. He made no mention as to the nature of the business and Katherine did not ask. He was intending to see the village reeve to ensure that Father Livio had help to tidy up the churchyard and clean the church thoroughly, prior to his people arriving to hang banners and place flowers.

Messages had been sent to friends and family, food had been ordered and menus planned for the last evening of July and the banquet on the Thursday. Plenty of wine, mead, cider and ale had been obtained and arrangements made to erect tents and trestle tables with benches in the meadow at the front of the manor for the day of the banquet. This was to be a celebration that all estate tenants, yeomen, villeins and others, such as servants and serfs could attend. Outside in the meadow there would be plain food. They would have a hog roast and there would be plenty of bread and cheese and a huge cauldron of potage on the fire. The estate workers would bring their own tankards and bowls, as was custom.

Jeanne had organised extra help from the village over the two days, and Walt and some of his men had been hunting on horseback, along with hounds, short bows and boar spears to bring home meat for the banquet. They would light a small token fire in the great hall to display the deer on the spit after cooking in the kitchen; it would make the room too warm to cook it there. All the family silver would be on display. Soup would be made, salmon steamed and various other dishes of paste and bread would be served before the main meal of venison, boar and tender lamb cutlets, with a variety of vegetables. Later they would tuck into Walt's favourite pudding with apples and dried fruits from Spain, '*a potage of roysons.*'

Finally the last day of July arrived. Last minute touches were made to the accommodation. Pisspots, beneath stands with water ewers and bowls, were put into the bedchambers to be occupied by the baron and the abbot. Over in the barracks, Sergeant Heddon had their depleted troop of soldiers on parade, and was inspecting their uniforms to ensure that a good impression was made. They would be called out as an honour guard for the baron when he arrived in the afternoon. Some of them would also perform duties at the ceremony tomorrow. Walt made a mental note that one of his first acts must be to bring his troopers up to strength again before it became known to Prior Gregory, who would be delighted to pass on the information and so cause a reduction in his payments for their maintenance.

Also expected this afternoon were William and Freda. His objectionable cousin in law Mark with his lovely wife Ingrid had not been invited. Walt had seen enough of him at his brother William's wedding to Freda. He was sorry for Ingrid but knew she would understand.

Both Walt and Katherine were looking forward to the reunion. A letter every six months did little to satisfy their curiosity as to how William was progressing as a corn merchant, and how they liked their life in York.

After breakfast they kept busy checking on all the details of the arrangements not only as a necessity, but to make time appear to pass more quickly until some guests began to arrive. Walt walked over to the meadow where the soldiers were busy erecting the tents, tables and seating. Emma was supervising the erection of the roasting spit for the hog. Trestle tables on which to stand barrels of ale were being erected. The tents had no sides hung; they were only intended as shelter in case of a shower. The weather today was bright and cloudless, and they were hopeful of a similar day tomorrow.

Over at the barracks Squire Thomas, with Aidric's help, was preparing Walt's armour for the ceremony. Everything must shine like a new pin. They must burnish any suggestion of rust from even the most obscure places on the armour. The plate armour would not be worn for the ceremony, but his serfs would expect him to come out later in full regalia and show himself in his battle order, and mounted on his destrier with his lady accompanying him.

The first guests to arrive were William and Freda, just before midday. They had brought a pack horse with them, carrying their spare clothing and necessities wrapped in waterproof groundsheets. They both looked tired and said they had been travelling for five days and had stayed in Tynemouth last night, and hoped to get a little relaxation before other guests arrived. There were hugs from Katherine and Walt. Walt could not help a thumping from his heart and a stirring of his loins as he hugged Freda, and gave her a chaste kiss on the cheek. He believed that Freda must have felt it also, as she looked directly into his eyes and smiled sweetly. *Still a little minx,* he thought. He dragged his mind away from such thoughts, and stood back to survey them both. They looked well and they looked happy, so Walt was happy for them. The young couple were taken into the family room, and whilst having their midday meal, regaled Walt and Katherine with their experiences in York.

'How are you getting on with Mark?' Walt asked of William, interested to know if his cousin Ingrid's wastrel husband was behaving himself, since he had occasion to warn him of his lewd behaviour at William and Freda's wedding banquet.

'I don't know what you said to him Brother, but he appears to be afraid of me. He is still a wastrel, often late and lazy, but when he is at work he never speaks out of turn. Ingrid has learnt from her friendship with Freda that she does not have to tolerate rudeness, she is a lady of independent means and he is only there because she loves him. He now realises that he would be unwise to spoil that arrangement.'

'How is Uncle Harald?'

'Sadly, not strong enough to make the journey, but he still manages to put in a day in the office. He says the work keeps him alive.'

Freda then took over the conversation telling all about her house and their plans for improvement. It was not long, however, before she began to show some signs of tiredness from the exhausting journey over the last five days.

William made their excuses and Walt showed them to the barracks, where a large temporarily empty section of the dormitory had been partitioned off, for them to share with Freda's Uncle Simon and Aunt Alice for the next two nights. They were delighted with the arrangement, but a little less enthusiastic when told that there may also be Adam and Hugh with their wives on Wednesday night, unless they opted for somewhere else, like the family room or the feasting hall.

It was late afternoon when Sir Henry arrived with his wife Eleanor, their thirteen year old son Henry, his squire and Abbot Stephen of Alnwick Abbey. Sergeant Heddon had kept a good lookout and had his small guard of honour paraded in time for the arrival. He called them to attention, they presented their swords in ceremonial fashion, and Sergeant Heddon saluted the Baron smartly. Sir Percy looked well impressed and let his feelings be known when welcomed by Walt.

'A fine display, Squire,' he complimented, 'you have a smart body of men there, and do they fight as well as they look?'

'Without doubt, Lord,' Walt replied, 'but we are sadly depleted at the moment as most of our men were killed at Bannockburn.'

They were ushered into the main hall while their servants unloaded their personal belongings and their mounts were taken care of. The servants were shown around to the back door by Jeanne and taken to the chambers where they could arrange their master's or mistress's respective belongings. Jeanne then showed them to quarters arranged for them. The men were accommodated in the barracks with the soldiers, and Lady Eleanor's maidservant in their own maid's chambers.

As soon as Jeanne indicated that all was prepared, the guests, who were partaking of refreshment after introductions, were asked if they would wish to retire to their chambers to prepare for the evening meal, which would be taken a little earlier than usual, to allow Walt to make ready for his overnight vigil in the church before tomorrow's ceremony. All three of them expressed the wish to retire for a while before supper, and were shown to their bedchambers by Jeanne.

'Well that was easy,' Katherine said, after they had retired, 'Lady Eleanor seems quite easy to talk to. I did not expect their son, but they were happy for him to share their chamber, and Jeanne soon arranged an extra bed. I am looking forward to some conversation with her at supper.'

'I told you they were nice people, they may not talk in our Northumbrian tongue, they come from southern parts, but they are much like us in their manner' Walt replied.

'Did you notice Walt that Sir Henry does not appear to be in good health? Lady Eleanor says that after your inauguration they are to travel to Yorkshire, where her husband will seek the attendance of the skilled physician monks of Fountains Abbey.'

Jeanne announced that Sir Simon, Lady Alice, and their squire had arrived. Their mounts were being taken care of, and their bundles taken into the barracks annexe, where they were to share with Master William and his lady.

Simon and Alice entered exuberantly into the family room and embraced them. Walt thanked them for looking after his men for a night on their escape from Scotland. Simon pulled him to one side and told him that there had been a big raid in their area the previous week but theirs and Walt's land had been left alone. Walt just said they must consider themselves lucky and refrained from any further explanation. He knew that Simon was aware that he had some sort of deal with the Scots and he ascertained that Simon understood his instructions in the letter to display his colours, but did not want to explain any further or enter into a discussion about his deal with the Scottish king. Simon, respecting his position did not press for details.

They all gathered together for supper in the dining hall in the early evening. The meal was not grand but a substantial four courses with a sufficiency of wine, mead or ale according to preference. Conversation was good, and William soon found himself giving account to the baron of life as a corn merchant in York. Eleanor·was fascinated by the story of Freda's rescue from drudgery. They had also heard stories about the attack on the manor and asked if it was true that all the robbers had been killed in the final battle. Once again Walt did not wish to go into detail and made light of the robbers' demise.

'The robbers can lie in their graves and be reminded that men trained on my father's quintain are superior to vicious ill disciplined ruffians.' He smiled to himself as he thought of the irony in the fact that the robbers were laid out under that very quintain.

'Have you other guests expected?' the Baron queried.

'Yes, Lord. Sir Hugh Delaval, who is my father in law, with his wife and son, and my Uncle, Sir Adam de Radulf, with his wife and son. These two knights are my other sponsors.'

'Good, I received their letters of recommendation, and we should all have a fine time tomorrow. My lady and I briefly made the acquaintance of your two fine young boys when we came downstairs. Your nursemaid was about to take them to bed. Lady Eleanor is looking forward to making friends with them tomorrow. Our son Henry is to study at a college in Oxford when he is a little older. I am sure Eleanor will miss him greatly.'

Having finished his meal and made further small talk for a while, Walt begged to be excused to prepare for his overnight vigil at the altar. He left them all mixing well and talking freely without reservation. He had a good feeling about his banquet tomorrow.

Retiring to his solar, where the servants had placed a tub of water, he stripped naked and began to wash his hair over the tub. Kneeling before the tub with his head hanging over he did not hear the door open quietly and close again. He just felt another pair of gentle hands moving his away and taking over the task. He did not need to look; he just reached to his side and slid his hand up a slim silk clad leg.

'I want to help you with this' Katherine said.

'What about our guests?'

'They understand, and they probably will not miss me. When I left, Freda was in fine form and had them splitting their sides with laughter, with tales of some snooty ladies of York. Now that's enough for the hair, stand in the tub and let me wash you down.'

Despite Katherine's advanced pregnancy, this was more than Walt could stand, and there came a time when they needed to take a break from washing and engage in other activities to calm him down.

When he was finally thoroughly cleansed and dried, Katherine assisted him with his ceremonial attire. First he donned clean linen braes and then black hose. Katherine placed the knee length white vesture over his head to symbolise purity. He then put on a pair of black boots. He was nearly ready now. He stood while Katherine dressed him with a red robe to signify nobility. Taking Katherine in his arms, he kissed her, picked up his sword and shield.

'Go and rejoin your guests, I will see you in church tomorrow morning' he said.

They both went downstairs, Katherine through to the hall, and Walt out of the back door to where Will was waiting with his horse. Jeanne watched him going through the family room, and was soon in the kitchen urging the staff to look out into the gloom and see the majestic sight of their master in such finery.

Arriving at the church, Walt found Father Livio waiting for him. There were many candles lit in holders and a large candle at each side of the altar. Behind the altar stood a grand wooden cross with the figure of Christ carved upon it. He noticed that Sir Henry had provided some of his Percy colours to display for the ceremony to add to the colourful display of the Radulf pennants and the flowers. He faced the altar, crossed himself and approached his position in front of the alar where Father Livio was waiting. They joined each other in a short prayer, following which the priest bade him goodnight. Walt placed his sword and shield on the altar and began his vigil, which for the next ten hours would involve him either standing with head bowed, or kneeling at the altar and praying.

Katherine was up at the first signs of dawn, when she heard the cock crowing in the yard. Tilly was already awake, she would get the children dressed, knock on the doors of the abbot and the Baron

Percy's chambers, then send Annie Foster to wake the guests in the barracks. The table was already set for breakfast in the feasting hall, and Jeanne announced that all was ready as soon as the guests required it.

Katherine walked into the kitchen, to see for herself the progress there. The deer was already on the spit in front of the fire with a long iron tray to catch drips; the spit being slowly turned by a kitchen hand. Emma had someone preparing vegetables for cooking later, and there was the smell of bread already coming from the baker's ovens at the other end of the old kitchen building. Emma told her that the estate ovens had been baking for the last two hours, so there would be plenty of bread. After the current batch in the kitchen oven she would be putting in various joints of wild boar. Already the heat was oppressive in the kitchen and Emma had all the shutters thrown back and the door open. There were cauldrons swung above the fire, with puddings steaming, and soup cooking. During the day they expected salmon to be brought after the game keeper had netted them. He would keep them alive in water until later when they were required, whereupon he would give each a sharp rap on the head and hand them to Emma, who would clean them, season them, and place them on trays with butter and herbs to go into the oven at the appropriate time. It all looked a little chaotic, but Katherine knew from experience that Emma would pull it all together with precision timing at the final moment with her additional borrowed staff from Isobel's kitchen at the Delaval household, and some help from the village.

While all this was going on, Ursula was independently preparing porridge for their breakfast and rosehip beverage for those who required other than warmed ale.

Abbot Stephen came downstairs with a bag which, he explained, contained his robe and some items he required for the ceremony. He asked if he could go immediately to the church to coach the local priest on the formalities. Katherine sent for Sergeant Heddon, to arrange for the abbot's horse, and provide an escort to the church immediately. She was worried the abbot was not taking breakfast but he insisted he would obtain a morsel from the priest.

In the church, Walt having completed his ten hour vigil at the altar, looked back on his trial.

During his periods of standing with head bowed he had to keep his mind active to prevent being overcome by tiredness. He thought of the pews behind him and how if he lay down for an hour nobody would know. Then in his mind he saw Katherine scolding him for the very thought of it. 'God would know,' she was saying. After the first hour he knelt for a fifteen minute prayer session. When he again rose to his standing position he felt dizziness and a cramp beginning in his feet. He began to wriggle his toes as vigorously as he could within the confines of his boots. The cramp started to ease and his head cleared. He resolved to rise more slowly after his next prayer session. He was cold and tired and his knees felt as if they would never again straighten properly, after the long sessions of prayer kneeling on the cold stone. His legs, back and neck all ached from being held immobile in unnatural positions for long periods. He began to wonder if he would get through the ceremony without falling asleep. His first prayers were for forgiveness for his many sins; his slaughter of the outlaws in revenge for the attack on his family; his cruel joke at the expense of Prior Gregory, which had sparked the current animosity, and lastly his using of his adopted cousin Freda for his own gratification. He thanked God for Katherine's forgiveness when he realised that she had known long before their marriage of his dalliance. He prayed for better guidance for his future decisions, peace and success for his family and the opportunity to fulfil his father's dream of a fortified pele tower home, at Bytilsden.

When Father Livio finally called him in the morning to say his vigil was completed, he followed the priest stiffly to his little cottage, trying to work some feeling back into his limbs on the way. Father Livio gave him some oat biscuits and he drank a little watery altar wine. It's just as well the wine is watered, he thought, or he would certainly fall asleep.

They sat and chatted while they waited for the time to begin mass, which would be followed by the ceremony of knighthood. The time of mass would be dictated by the time everyone arrived. The only certainties of time being dawn, dusk and midday when the sun was bright enough. One of the Italian merchants who came to Tynemouth had told Walt that in Florence there was a machine for telling time on the cathedral and somebody had said they believed that something like that existed in England at Canterbury, but Walt was dubious. There were always tales about strange things that existed, but they were always somewhere else. Anyway turning a roasting spit was labour enough. Who would be able to turn a mechanism continuously to mark the time, without faltering or falling asleep?

They heard horses arriving at the church and went outside to greet his Uncle Adam with Aunt Dorothy, Cousin Matthew and their squire, Drugo Kennet. They had a pack horse with them but said they were ready for church. There was no time to go to the manor to unload their stuff. It could wait till later. No sooner had the horses been hitched and they had gone into church to pray, than Sir Hugh arrived with his son Richard, and Isobel, being driven in her little carriage by their squire. They too went directly into the church and took their seats. Father Livio explained that they may have a long wait, but they did not seem to mind as they could take the opportunity to rest before the service.

Leaving them praying and chatting, Walt and father Livio returned to the priest's cottage to find Abbot Stephen and a trooper waiting outside. On their arrival the trooper took his leave and headed back to the manor. Walt introduced Father Livio to Abbot Stephen and they entered the cottage. If the abbot was offended by the poverty of the priest's little hovel of a cottage, he made a good job of concealing it. He spoke jovially with the priest and Walt, as he went through the order of service and ceremony. He explained that he would conduct the service, and gave Father Livio instructions as to where he could be of assistance. Having taken a little ale and a few oat biscuits, the abbot suggested they go to the church, so that Walt could take up his position before any more guests arrived. Walt and the priest headed for the church, leaving the abbot to change into his vestments and robe for the service.

Inside the church Walt retook his position in front of the altar, standing facing it with head bowed. Some of the guests already in the church were asleep in the pews but the priest made no effort to wake them. Walt no longer felt tired, things were happening and his heart was starting to race with excitement, he now felt tense and alert as he did if he were about to go into combat.

After around half an hour, the main body of the guests arrived with Tilly helping Katherine with the children. Each knight had brought his squire, and Aidric Johansson was to be there to assist the crippled Thomas. Walt had invited Sergeant Heddon and six of his soldiers, specifying that the original Syhale troopers should be included plus Cethin Gwyn and two of his men. They could form a small honour guard outside the church when the ceremony was over. There would now be only one seat left for him, to sit next to Katherine while the service was conducted.

When everybody was settled inside the church, Abbot Stephen made his entry. He walked down the aisle, indicated to Walt that he should take his seat next to Katherine, made his sign in the name of the father, the son and the holy spirit, stepped to the altar and placed upon it his own golden goblet, containing holy communion wine, and a tray of communion biscuits. He turned to his small congregation, now all awake and paying close attention, and began the service.

There was a lengthy session of prayer, followed by some religious chanting in Latin led by Father Livio. Following this there was more prayer and then an extremely long sermon by Abbot Stephen about the responsibilities and duties of a knight to the Christian church. Fortunately this was followed by another short chant by Father Livio which served well to wake those who had nodded off during the sermon. The abbot then poured a small quantity of wine into his goblet, took up his biscuit and called Walt to take communion. This done, Walt remained in his position while the abbot turned and blessed his sword and shield which still lay on either side of the altar. He then called for two sponsors to attend the altar. Sir Hugh Delaval and Walt's uncle Sir Adam Radulf stepped forward. Sir Hugh took possession of the sword and shield and passed them to Sir Henry Percy, who had moved to stand in front of them. Then with the sponsors standing on either side of Walt, Adam presented his nephew. 'Lord, I present Walter de Radulf of Syhale manor, for your consideration for knighthood.' Following this the two sponsors retook their seats with the congregation.

Then began the ceremony of swearing the oath of allegiance, a long list of promises to uphold the Christian religion, be loyal to the sovereign, defend justice, never flee from battle, defend the realm, defend all ladies of honour, widows, orphans and ladies of good fame, defend the poor people against murderers and robbers, uphold the noble estate of chivalry, enquire and understand all articles contained in the book of chivalry.

Having completed his list of oaths, Walt concluded, 'All these I promise to observe, keep, and fulfil, I oblige me. So help me, my God, by my own hand. So help me God.'

Sir Henry then presented Walt with his sword and shield. Having taken them, Walt held his shield in his left hand and his sword in his right. He then knelt in front of Sir Henry with sword lowered to the floor and head bowed.

Sir Henry took his own sword and using the flat of the blade he dubbed Walt by striking him firmly on each shoulder, followed by the words.'On this first day of August 1314, I dub thee, Sir Knight. Arise, Sir Walter de Radulf of Syhale.' He then took his seat while the two sponsors rose to complete the ceremony by attaching Walt's spurs and girding his sword in place at his side, and handing him his shield.

It was over, Sir Walter Radulf walked out with his wife and children followed by Sir Henry and the rest of the congregation. Sergeant Heddon had the six soldiers already lined up outside with their swords raised in salute.

Everybody headed excitedly back to the manor, including Father Livio who was not going to miss a banquet and some free ale.

Waiting for them on their return, there was ale, fruit cordials and small morsels to allay the appetite until the banquet later. Afterwards Walt, with the assistance of Thomas and Aidric, donned his full plate armour and mounted an armoured and decorated destrier, loaned from his father in law, for a ride around the manor with his Lady and Squire Thomas, who had been helped onto his horse by Aidric. They were accompanied by their mounted guests and the honour guard from the church. Walt was aware that this was probably the only time they would see him on such a magnificent horse. He much preferred his sure footed and manoeuvrable garron. Will Foster provided wooden steps, which had also been carried to the church and back by two troopers, to assist Katherine mounting and dismounting her horse, in her enlarged situation. She was riding aside, with a step for both feet, and the same Welsh soldier was leading her horse as had performed the duty to and from the church. Walt was taking no chances with his offspring due within two months.

There were cheers and shouts from all the peasantry to see such a magnificent sight as their own new lord in his fine battle armour, and his lady in a flowing scarlet robe and black and gold cape, to help hide her pregnant belly. For entertainment there was archery for the men and the knights could practice their skills on the quintain or partake of a little one to one jousting if they preferred. Sir Walter, as people were now calling him only insisted that he did not want his celebration marred by injury, so jousting should be limited to practice swords only.

The afternoon entertainment was a great success and Katherine was content, knowing that her guests were enjoying themselves. After a brief ride around in their formal attire, she and Walt retired to change into more comfortable clothes for the remainder of the day.

The evening banquet was enjoyed honoured guests and family alike, and as normal, once the food was mainly consumed along with much ale and wine, conversation became increasingly ribald; resulting in Katherine leading the ladies into the family room; 'to chatter in a more befitting manner for our station,' she observed.

The men swapped tales and made jests for a while before Baron Percy declared he must collect his wife and retire. Walt signalled to his servant girl Ursula to fetch the baroness.

With the Percys retired, the jests degenerated to a common level, bringing a strong rebuke from Sir Hugh when his son Richard caused a stunned silence by making a lewd joke at the expense of Walt's cousin Freda.

Walt was surprised that the lad bore resentment still. It was now nine years since the two had first met and Freda had rebuffed his advances. He had gone through a long period of surly behaviour towards all the family, but Walt had thought that was long behind him, however, he could sympathise with his loss. From his own experience, he knew the attractions of Freda.

Fortunately, Hugh decided to retire and took his over indulgent son with him.

The next day after a leisurely breakfast, the guests, after lengthy goodbyes, eventually rode away to their various destinations, except William and Freda, who had come such a distance that they wished to stay for a few days longer, before setting out on the long journey back to York.

Once the family was alone and relaxed in the family room, Walt breathed a sigh of relief.

'Everyone's calling you Sir Walter now; I suppose Sir Walt does not sound formal enough for a knight.' Katherine said, with William and Freda nodding their agreement.

'Let them call me what they wish. You and my loved ones should still call me Walt or I may think you are talking to our son, who you no longer need to refer to as Little Walter. Now I must go and see that all is being cleaned up and put away, festivities are over and I shall have to consider the harvest next. I believe there is going to be a very good yield so we will be able to make use of the old kitchen area across the yard for the extra grain storage.'

The eventful year continued with a birth and a death in October. There was the birth of Walt's third son Hugh, on the sixteenth. Shortly after this was the unfortunate and untimely death in Yorkshire, of Walt's benefactor Sir Henry Percy, from some painful inner disease, which was not understood by the Fountains Abbey monks.

He was to be succeeded by his son, also Henry, who was still to attend college and would become the second Baron Percy. Walt hoped the boy would remember his father's patronage of his knighthood, and his enjoyment at Syhale playing combat games on the quintain. *I may be in need of some powerful patronage at some future time,* he thought.

Until now Syhale had not been troubled by Scottish raids but there were many tales of others who had. They could only hope that their luck would hold and the years following would be kind to them and their friends.

=====

CHAPTER 3

Hard times

January 1316. Walt and Aidric Johansson had been touring the western extremities of the estate collecting tithes and rents from those of his yeomen who could still afford to pay. As they began their homeward journey, Walt recalled his prayer as they stowed the grain in the overflow store, once the old kitchen, in the autumn of 1314. Good weather and respite from Scottish vengeance had been his prayer. *Should have prayed louder or more sincerely*, he thought. God had not heard his plea.

***

Following the disaster of Bannockburn and the good grain harvest that year, there had been unusually wet weather since, with the ground unable to be properly prepared for sowing, seed rotting in the soil and much of what did grow being destroyed before it could be harvested. The constant wet weather also rotted many root crops. Added to this were widespread outbreaks of livestock plagues due to poor grazing and a shortage of winter feedstuff, resulting in a scarcity of all staple foods, which in turn led to famine. They were lucky that they had the extra grain storage for the 1314 crop, but they had encountered much trouble hanging onto what was theirs, keeping away robbers and livestock rustlers. Despite careful rationing it was nearly all gone, and they could only hope for better weather this year.

There were no more banquets or feasts. Many meals consisted of potage, the same as the peasants ate, albeit the ingredients were a little better with more meat involved. There were no more bonuses for servants. Prices had already more than doubled and troopers were on regular guard duties at the mill, to guard against the theft of grain or flour. It had been tried on several occasions but it became a rarer occurrence after a couple of prospective thieves were hanged. It was also necessary to post a guard outside the grain store whenever they had even a small amount of grain. There was little game left on the estate, most of it had been poached, and the soldiers could not be everywhere. Even rabbits were scarce now and peasants could be seen digging for wild roots of burdock and thistle among other unpalatable things to supplement their potage.

Many of the tenants were barely able to sustain themselves, let alone pay their rents, and even if they offered extra labour in lieu of rent there was little work to do when ploughing was impossible and harvests were so small. Walt had done what he could to discharge his duty to his tenants and workers, but his own cash was now severely depleted and he would need to exploit other sources of income. He regretted the vast sum his father had spent on the new kitchen, but held his peace on the matter as he knew it would not have been built if it had not been for him and Katherine persuading him.

To crown their recent misfortunes; last year, on top of the difficulties of feeding everyone and trying to ration what grain they had in store, they had the added shock of the untimely death of Squire Thomas Gesthill; who had been back to health, with his leg well healed and performing his full duties.

It was while on a hunt with Walt last November that his horse had stumbled in the forest. Thomas was thrown from the saddle, head first into a tree trunk, and had died instantly. There was much sadness at the time and everyone from the estate turned out for his funeral. He had no relatives, so his small holding reverted to the lord of the manor, which was of course Walt, who had subsequently promoted Aidric Johansson to the rank of squire, after buying his freedom from military service, and settling him into Thomas's holding as a freeman.

Katherine had reminded him that making Aidric a freeman was a very unusual decision, and not in keeping with common practice, as it meant Aidric could leave if he wished, but she had not pressed him on the matter and his decision had stood.

Walt put these matters to the back of his mind for the moment, deciding to concentrate on trying to get home before dark.

***

For Walt and Squire Aidric, there were still many miles of hill and dale to cross before they would reach Syhale. It was a cold day but not freezing and to keep out the cold they were wearing their long heavy split riding coats, with capes rolled behind their saddles in case of rain or snow. Walt thought of the piteous amount they had collected and determined that overall it had been a wasted journey. In fact, some of the money he had collected had been redistributed amongst the most deprived of his tenants. In times of severe hardship it was his duty to protect his tenants and his serfs, to the best of his ability. *Better to have a holding with some effort of management than none at all,* he thought. The ominous dark grey clouds suddenly turned black, and it began to rain with the wind picking up sharply. The two men immediately donned their capes, and Walt studied the darkest clouds moving with the direction of the wind from the northwest 'The wind is bringing that lot quickly towards us, and I wager it will soon turn to snow. It will take us around two hours or more to get home from here, longer if we are overtaken by that weather.' Walt called to his companion.

Following his prediction, Walt set his horse to a trot, the terrain and the ground underfoot were unsuitable for a brisker pace and more likely to cause injury to the horses. There were some wide expanses of open moor to traverse between dales, and getting marooned in a snowstorm with a lame horse was not a good idea.

'Stick close to me,' he called to Aidric, 'if you cannot keep up shout. It is important we stick together when the snow comes, as it will.'

The snow did come, as they traversed the moor. The rain first turned to sleet, and then as the wind increased in ferocity, into snow, and a blizzard. They battled on for a while until it thickened, and Walt, in the lead, heard a weak shout from behind. He reined in his horse and waited for his companion to come alongside. Aidric leaned over and needed to shout to be heard above the howling wind, which was now driving the snow with such ferocity that it was forcing its way into the hoods of their capes, if they did not keep their heads turned away. 'More than around six foot apart, Sir, and I can no longer see you, I am afraid we will be separated.'

'We must continue until we get off this high ground, and can find the leeward side of the next dale.' Walt shouted. 'We are too exposed here; we shall have to find a suitable place and sit it out. At the moment I know where we are, and providing we can continue with the darkness to our rear we will come to a dale. Once those black clouds overwhelm us and the blizzard thickens we shall have no point of reference. We must hunker down before that happens or we may get lost.'

Taking the rope coiled around his pommel, Walt tied one end fast and passed the other to the Aidric. 'Tie that to your horse's halter' he said, 'I will ride at a slow walk from here.'

They rode on at walking pace until the ground began to fall away towards the next dale. Walt, unsure of his exact location, reined in, dismounted and signalled Aidric to do likewise. He shouted. 'Stay exactly behind me. We must find a safe way down into the dale keeping clear of crags and other hazards.'

Walt knew it was essential that they now found a place to shelter. They must abandon any hope of returning home tonight. Very soon the features of the landscape would be hidden by the depth of snow and great care would be needed to make any progress at all. *My God,* he thought, *how the beauty of the Northumberland hills and dales can be changed to a treacherous landscape of white death, in such a short time.* Suddenly, he stopped and Aidric almost walked into his horse.

'What is it, Sir?' he shouted.

'Something wrong ahead, the land seems to fall away too quickly. Stay here and hold my horse. Take the rope off the halter and hand it to me.'

He took the loose end and tied it around his waist. Aidric coiled up the remainder of the rope, and leaving his master a few yards, he took up the slack and looped it around the horse's pommel, from where he could pay it out slowly.

Walt drew his sword from its scabbard and walked slowly forward, with Aidric letting out rope as he disappeared from view in the blizzard, but maintaining a slight tension in case Sir Walter should fall. Walt prodded the ground in front of him where it began to fall away. His sword went through the snow and he felt it strike a hard surface of rock. He realised his assumption was correct, they were at the top of a crag the height or steepness of which he did not know. He shouted to Aidric to take up the slack and retraced his steps to the horse. He then tried to his right, swinging in a shallow arc, but he could find only rock beneath. He began to think they had wandered onto promontory atop a crag overlooking the dale. He decided to repeat the operation by returning to his horse and testing an arc to the left. If this was the same he would have to choose left or right and continue testing until he found a safe area. He could not stop now, they needed to find shelter out of the blizzard or they would not last the night.

With Aidric again taking up the slack in the rope he returned to his horse, explained their predicament and set off to his left. Once more he found rock beneath the snow and began to prescribe his arc, making probes every couple of paces. He had moved about thirty paces to his left before his sword encountered soft earth beneath. He tried a few more paces, still soft. He gave an agreed signal of two sharp tugs on the rope and felt it slacken as his squire began to move towards him with the horses. Walt took up the slack until his squire appeared.

'We are indeed atop a promontory of some crag Aidric, but there may be a safe way down here. We will continue with the rope method for safety. Let me have around ten foot and keep a slight tension on it. I will move forward and down, testing the ground in front as I go and you follow with the horses until we find a leeward area to hunker down for the night.'

Without waiting for a response from Aidric, Walt set off probing the ground in front of him at each pace. He was relieved to find that it seemed as if he had indeed found a trail that led around the side of the crag. Trying to picture the scene without the snow, he now believed he knew where he was.

After a short while they were far enough around and down to see the face of the crag and the stream running at the foot of the dale below. The face of the crag was comparatively free of snow with the bank at the base raised high from the stream. This would provide an ideal place to shelter when they got to it. In the lea of the crag the visibility was better although it was still not possible to see across the dale. The covering of snow was diminishing to make testing with the sword unnecessary. It still took them around another half hour to reach a point where Walt considered it safe to spend the night and reassess their situation in the morning.

They secured the horses after allowing them to take a drink from the stream and gave them a feed from the oatmeal they carried in a sack. Being without a tent, they put one groundsheet on the ground, and used the other to provide a rough shelter against the crag wall, weighting the bottom with large stones and jamming the top into the gaps in the crag wedged tight with smaller stones. They sat leaning against the crag still wearing their coats and capes as the ends of their makeshift shelter were open to the elements, but at least they were now sheltered from the worst ravages of the blizzard. Walt took some oatmeal biscuits from his saddlebag and shared them with his squire. 'We should eat these and try to get some sleep. It will soon be completely dark. We can try to move on at first light, assuming the blizzard has stopped by then. The journey will likely be hazardous, even in good visibility, as drifting snow totally alters the appearance of the landscape and can conceal many dangers.'

They awoke in the morning at first light. The wind had dropped, but there was still a fine dusting of snow falling. The blackness was gone from the sky to be replaced with a light grey, through which a watery sun was trying to shine. Walt looked knowingly along the dale.

'I definitely know where we are now Aidric. We should continue along this dale until we come to a trail and a ford. At that point we shall be on the easterly road to Syhale village and will have around five or six more miles to travel.'

Aidric was about to speak when Walt anticipating him said, 'I know Aidric, there are still the drifts and general deep snow to consider but once we are on the road, there are some landmarks such as trees and rocks that will likely help us to stay on the trail. There are no more crags so the main danger is falling in a deep drift. If we stay several feet apart, one can always help the other in case of accident.'

He took some more oat biscuits from his saddlebag and shared them with his squire. The remaining oats in the sack he gave to the horses, before they set off along the leeward side towards the ford, and their track homeward. Excluding accidents or another blizzard, Walt expected to be home in a couple of hours, or more.

**

Katherine awakened early after a fitful sleep. She had been awake every hour during the night, looking out at the raging blizzard outside. She had expected Walt to be home the previous evening before dark. Maybe he was caught in the storm. She heard the children creating a noise in their bedchamber which they shared with

Tilly. She swilled her face with a little cold water in a basin and hurriedly put on some clothes. Leaving her solar, she crossed to the children's room, where Tilly was trying to keep the three children under control. 'I will take these two downstairs and let you finish with Hugh in peace,' Katherine said.

She was worried that Walt had not come home last night, and there had been a terrible blizzard. She knew he had been to the west, collecting rents, or more likely deferring them. Knowing the lie of the land in between, she hoped he had been in a position to stay the night with one of the yeomen when the blizzard blew up. She was aware that he was not alone and could look after himself, but she still worried about the unexpected, and tried to take her mind away from Walt by turning her attention to the children.

Young Walter was now seven and had been riding the promised pony for the past two years. It was getting time for him to have a larger one and pass the small pony to Alex. Walter was pestering his mother to allow him to take the pony out, but Katherine said no, the snow was too deep for the small animal and its short legs.

Tilly descended the stairs with Hugh under one arm, and a bundle of dirty linen in the other hand. The dirty linen she handed to Annie to take to the laundry woman, and hearing the noise from the feasting hall she went to join Katherine who was playing with the other children. Here they could run up and down without getting in the way of the servants, who were preparing the table for breakfast. The two of them played some games with the children until Annie called to say that breakfast, in the form of their routine porridge, was on the table, and that cook apologised for the wait.

'There is nothing to be sorry for, I awakened much earlier than normal Annie. Tell cook not to worry' Katherine assured her.

Tilly took the children into the family room for their breakfast, but Katherine remained in the hall, peering out of the window and down the trail to the road, looking for Walt returning. She felt no hunger, and although she was used to Walt being away travelling on many occasions, she thought there was reason to worry, in view of the weather and his failure to appear when expected.

The children finished their breakfast and Tilly took them back into the feasting hall to run around again. Katherine was still fretting, and frequently looking out of the window; and no amount of reassurance from Tilly or the other staff could calm her worries. She

73

had not forgotten the loss of her father in law at Bannockburn, and could not even imagine how she would bear to lose Walt. The sky was still grey and looking full of snow, but the wind had dropped and there was now only a slight dusting of snow falling. She could now see some way up the trail towards the church. After what seemed an endless wait, and around mid morning, when she finally sat down to take a hot drink while watching the children play in the hall, she heard a shout for the groom outside, and instantly recognised Walt's voice.

Relieved, she left the children to Tilly and ran out the front to greet him, forgetting that she was only wearing woollen house shoes, until she realised that her feet were cold and wet.

Walt and Aidric dismounted and the groom took the horses whilst Walt retained his saddle bag with the few depleted rents he had collected. Katherine bade them both to come inside, asking them where they stayed last night.

'At the foot of a crag under a groundsheet,' Walt replied.

She got them through to the family room where they took off their heavy coats and sat down to a hot beverage and some porridge brought by cook. Katherine, now feeling relief that he was returned, took a bowl of porridge herself and sat with them while Walt told her of their eventful journey home. Refreshment and hot drinks over, Squire Aidric thanked her for her hospitality and taking his coat, departed to continue his normal daily duties on his own farm.

Once he and Katherine were alone, Walt opened his saddlebag and displayed the pitiful takings from his tenants. 'They are in dire straits Katherine, as we shall be soon, if the rains continue this summer. We have little to look forward to except the fleece market later in the year.'

That evening, after the servants had been dismissed, Walt and Katherine relaxed and he poured them both a large goblet of wine.

They sat side by side on a bench at the table, and after each taking a sip of their wine, as if of one mind, they put their goblets down on the table and came into each other's arms.

Katherine kissed her husband passionately, before whispering in his ear. 'Oh my God! Walt. You frightened me when you did not come home yesterday and the blizzard was so fierce.'

'I am sorry dearest, I realise that I put both mine and Aidric's lives at risk for a mere pittance. It will not happen again, but I must find a way to replenish our cache, or I will not be able to meet our commitments to the estate and our family. We have the fleece market in June, maybe we can make something out of that, we have not lost as many sheep as some in the area, and who knows, perhaps we shall see an end to this damnable rain in the spring.'

'How can we gain Walt? Fleeces are fewer and smaller, which has caused a rise in price, and now the prior has introduced a new wool tax. He says it is a king's tax, to pay for his army to protect him from rebellious earls and barons.'

'Who told you about this wool tax?'

'My father, he says that it will be in place before the next fleece market, and covers the whole land, at various levels, depending upon the local greed. In areas such as ours, much of the tax will never reach the king, and just go into the purses of such as the prior or the sheriff.'

Walt took a long draught of his wine as he pondered on this new challenge. 'Then I must find a way of avoiding it.'

'How can we do that? The prior knows we sell fleeces annually at the fair. To just stop would invite suspicion.'

'First I will see if there is another place not too distant where taxes are lower. We can reduce sales at Tynemouth, saying that there are fewer fleeces due to the pestilence and serious loss of stock. If I find a suitable plan, I shall use some of our remaining money to purchase more sheep. Many people are desperate to sell stock because they cannot feed them over winter, or cannot secure them from reivers; as yet we still have the advantage of being able to do both, so long as the Scots leave us alone.'

Katherine finished off her wine, stood up from the bench and took Walt's hand. 'Enough of our difficulties, let us to bed and take our pleasure, everything will be clear in the morning.'

Walt needed no second invitation. Despite six years of marriage and three children, their lust for each other's bodies never diminished.

Much later, they lay in their bed totally exhausted, with Walt on his back and Katherine draped above him, whispering into his ear. 'I would wager you have done it again Walter Radulf.'

'What do you mean, done it again?'

'Made me with child you ravenous beast.'

'You cannot know that Katherine.'

'You will see,' she said, as she rolled off him onto her back and they both fell into a deep contented sleep.

***

Over the next few weeks, Walt spent much time travelling and talking to wool traders, even paying a visit to William in York, where there were traders with wide knowledge of the king's taxes in various parts of the country. Once back in Syhale he considered his situation.

He had learned that there was a good market in Lincolnshire for wool, where ships came from the Low Countries with merchants keen to buy high quality wool for their weavers. He would still sell wool at the annual fleece market in Tynemouth to avoid suspicion by the prior who collected the wool tax from the sales, but increase his output and avoid the king's taxes on the extra. He would seek a partner in the venture to ensure they could start with a viable quantity; maybe Gilbert de Middleton would be interested. The Lincolnshire port was Boston, but the king's taxes were based on the value of the Lincolnshire wool, probably the best in the land. He decided that he and Aidric would go to Norfolk and establish contacts in the wool trade at Bishops Lynn, a port opposite to Boston, which also handled ships from the Low Countries and Germanic states. He was sure there was traffic to that port from Lincolnshire to avoid high duties. If that was the case there must be merchants who were expert at revenue avoidance. Walt knew that coastal cogs sailed from Blyth on a regular basis, carrying coal or salt to the south eastern ports. His wool could be taken to Bishops Lynn, and transferred to a foreign vessel without being landed. There would be no problem at Blyth. It was a small port, in a friendly area where nothing would be said, if even noticed, of wool being stored for shipment south. *The king's revenue would never know,* Walt thought, *and I also need to pay my soldiers, of late often without any subsidies from the king. It is through the king's own negligence, that the northern earls and barons are in control here.* There was also a lot of wool from the peasant farmers that Walt had first option on if he chose. They must make what they could when they could with the current political situation. If they could get the sheep sheared and the wool away before the Scots raided and took them.

He discussed the plan with Katherine, who declined to comment until he had a more firm proposal. She had no worries about being caught, as long as they sold some fleeces at Tynemouth. She said, 'there are too many questions Walt. Can you find a crooked trader in Bishops Lynn, and someone to take care of things at Blyth? Supposing you resolve these matters, do you think it wise to involve Gilbert de Middleton? You know your mother always said he was a hothead.'

'No need to worry Katherine, Gilbert only needs to provide fleeces and receive his share of the profits. He does not need to know how it works in Bishops Lyn or be involved other than to give me a letter of introduction to his cousin in Blyth who is a merchant.'

'And what if there are no profits?'

'There have to be profits, the Flemish and the Dutch are paying high prices for wool and without taxes we shall soon see our savings rise again.'

Katherine was still not convinced. 'You will need to take some wool samples with you for the trader to examine, so what can you do before shearing?'

'I have some unsold sacks hanging in the grain store, I have examined them and they are still in good condition.'

Katherine shrugged, 'alright, but be careful who you deal with.'

'I shall take Aidric and we should probably wait until March to make our journey. The long days travelling will give me plenty of time to consider other ways of improving our lot, by rebellious acts if it must be so. I know I am not alone in these thoughts, many more have had enough.'

Katherine took her husband's hand. 'Walt, you may not be alone in thoughts, and also in deed, but take care my dearest, you will most likely find you are alone if you get caught. Only then will you know your true friends.'

***

After securing Gilbert de Middleton's approval and a letter of introduction to his cousin Cuthbert Middleton, it was early March before Walt and Aidric set off for Norfolk with the Trooper Botolfe

Best leading a pack horse carrying some small bundles of extra clothing, and most importantly a half sack, thirteen stone sample, of wool and sufficient waxed canvas to cover it in case of rain. Walt wore a padded mail hauberk and chausses. He carried with him a white surcoat, emblazoned with the family crest. Aidric and Best were also in uniform. Walt wished to appear as a knight should, when travelling with his squire and a trooper. All were armed with sword and dagger, with Trooper Best also carrying his short bow and a quiver of arrows. Walt believed it was important, along with their show of arms, to exude an air of confidence and rank, to deter cutpurses and other opportunistic robbers.

They reasoned that the journey would take them about ten days without changing horses. They would stay overnight at hostelries and hold ample funds for their journey. Trooper Best would be responsible for the security of the wool and must hang it in a dry place clear of the floor where he would sleep each night, in the stable along with the horses. They were expecting to be returning in around one month.

It took Walt longer than he had expected to reach their destination. The weather was not as they had hoped for March. After three sunny but windy days, it began to rain. They quickly covered the wool sack with canvas to keep it dry, but their progress was slowed due to the slippery condition of the roads, which quickly turned muddy, with water filled holes that had to be carefully negotiated as they could not see how deep the holes were, and did not want any injured horses. It rained for the next four days, and they were two days later than they estimated arriving at Bishops Lynn. They found a hostelry where they settled in for a night's rest. Botolfe was in the stable with the ostler and charged with custody of the wool sack. He was instructed to give the ostler a small bonus to guard the wool if he needed to leave for his bodily functions or to eat.

'But no ale until the wool is sold,' said Walt.

The next morning, Walt dressed in plain clothes, as did his companions. They were still armed, except that Best left his sword in the care of the innkeeper. As he was dressed according to his lowly rank and a sword was not permitted for a peasant, he did not want to invite trouble for himself or his master. They had an early meal and discussed the next part of the plan, to find a wool merchant who would suit their needs. Walt suggested that Aidric stay at the hostelry and take someone in conversation, to discover where to find a wool merchant who was honest and reliable. With a bit of luck there would be some talk about the ones that were less honest as well. Walt would visit another tavern and try his luck in a similar manner. Aidric was abed when Walt returned.

'How did you get on?' he asked.

'Found one,' Walt replied. 'A merchant called Jon Monek.'

Aidric grunted. 'Sounds foreign.'

'Yes he is Flemish. What about you?' Walt said.

'Nothing, just some talk of a local man who brings fleeces from Lincolnshire at night, for a merchant they say that they do not know.'

'Did they know anything of his name?' Walt asked.

'They were not sure, maybe Jack or John' one of them said. They asked me why I wanted to know. I said I was a sheep farmer from Cumberland.'

Walt laughed; 'you do not look like a sheep farmer and what about your accent?'

Aidric was also amused by this and replied. 'They have no idea about northern accents, and I said I was a rich sheep farmer. They forgot about any more questions when I bought them all a tankard of ale.'

'Alright,' said Walt. 'We will seek out Jon Monek in the morning and see what can be arranged. Let me do the talking, he must not see any accidental divisions in our ideas which he may try to exploit.'

Walt and Aidric finished their breakfast and set about the task of locating the wool merchant. After some enquiries, they located Jon Monek in a small warehouse near the docks. He was a tall, strongly built man with fair hair and a pointed beard. His eyes were blue, small and set close. This gave his large head a strange unbalanced look. His English was good but with a strong Flemish accent.

'Good morning, what can I do for you gentlemen?' he asked, and before they could reply he continued. 'You think I smuggle wool? Now who told you that of Jon Monek, and exactly who are you two, and where are you from?'

Walt realised that tavern gossip travelled quickly in Bishops Lynn, *we were not so clever after all*, he thought, but determined to press on. 'We are sheep farmers from Northumberland, who would like to sell our fleeces to you for shipment to the Low Countries.'

Monek looked at them and said. 'Northumberland: not Cumberland then? Why can't you sell your fleeces in Newcastle?'

Walt replied. 'the taxes are too high.'

'We have port taxes here in Bishops Lynn too' said Monek.

'Yes, lower than in Newcastle or Boston, we have been told.' Walt retorted.

'Ah! So you want to cheat his majesty's revenue?' Monek said quietly, 'and you think I can help? How would you get the fleeces to me without anyone seeing a convoy of carts arriving?'

Walt decided he had to trust the man at some stage. Any problems, he would deny it.

'By boat,' he said. 'Not from Newcastle but from the small port of Blyth, where we and our friends have control. The wool sacks could be loaded there and sail to Bishops Lynn, there are regular coasters plying the route with coal and salt and calling at Bishops Lynn. They could be passed at night onto a boat to the Low Countries and need not even touch land here.'

Monek scratched his beard. 'Why cannot the boat from the Low Countries pick up the wool from Blyth? Why do you need me?'

'Because,' said Walt 'Blyth is too small and can only take coastal cogs, such as those used to transport coal or salt to the southern ports.'

'Alright, what do I get out of this and what must I do for it?' Monek asked.

'We will arrange for the wool to be transported to Blyth and be loaded at night. Once again, that is not unusual, if the boats are to catch the morning tide. The captain will contact you when he arrives in Bishops Lynn. All you have to do is arrange for the wool to be transferred to a Flemish boat.'

'Alright', said Monek. 'I give you Newcastle price for wool, less shipping cost, and you pay me half what tax should be.'

Walt laughed. 'I want to sell the wool not pay you for it. You arrange shipment from here at your cost and give me Newcastle price less twenty percent of tax value.' 'No good' said Monek, 'I say fifty percent.'

After further argument they settled on thirty percent of tax value to be deducted. Monek got cheap wool and Walt got a much better price than Newcastle would yield after the tax was paid.

'One more thing gentlemen,' Monek said. 'Before we do business, I want to see sample of wool you brought, and some evidence you are who you say you are.'

Walt looked surprised. 'How do you know we brought wool?'

Monek put his finger to his nose. 'Wool is my business,' he said.

'Let's go and look then,' Walt said.

Monek walked into the warehouse and called, 'Wally, come with me.'

A short thickset man appeared, to join them on their walk to the hostelry. Monek introduced him as William Wallingford, a man educated in wool and a business associate. On arrival at the hostelry Walt left Aidric to show them the wool, whilst he went to their room to get a standard document of introduction from his saddlebag. It was written and signed by his late father and bearing the family arms and seal. When he returned to the stable Monek professed himself satisfied with the quality of the wool. He knew he would get a good price for this wool from the Dutch. He was satisfied with their identity and now wanted money up front to finance his arrangements in Bishops Lynn.

Walt had been prepared for this, and gave him the money less the price for the sack of wool, knowing that he would see no return for another until later in the year. He did impress upon Monek that any attempt to cheat the Radulf family would be dealt with severely. Whilst waiting for Walt to fetch his letter of introduction, and while Wally was looking at the wool with Aidric, Monek had been quizzing Botolfe, and from what he had been told he had no reason to doubt Walt's threat. The deal was sealed and Walt received a receipt for his money, to be repaid with the first consignment's payment. It was agreed that a representative of the family would come to Bishops Lynn one month after each consignment to collect payment.

Botolfe went with Wally to deliver the wool to Monek's warehouse and bring back the horse. Walt, Aidric and Jon Monek went to the tavern to seal the deal with ale.

***

After an uneventful journey home, the three travellers arrived home at dusk, tired and hungry two days before the beginning of June.

Walt explained the system to Katherine, who expressed serious doubts about the advance of so much money to set up the coastal cog system.

Following a much appreciated meal, Walt determined that after just one day at home, to see to estate matters, he and Aidric would travel to Blyth to set up the warehousing. They had no time to lose; it would soon be shearing time.

With the children abed, he persuaded Katherine to dismiss the servants early and have an early night. 'Come my dear, I have not seen you for nearly a month and I need my rest.'

'You know that you will get no rest until you have made up the love I missed during your absence.'

Walt took her hand and the pair ran up the stairs like newly weds.

Jeanne, downstairs clearing up with Annie before retiring, heard Katherine giggling, the scrape of the wattle door across the floor and then squeals of excitement or delight, she knew not which. The two servants looked at each other, grinned, and carried the dirty trenchers to the kitchen, to wash and put away before retiring.

'And Lady Katherine due to give birth again in August,' Annie said.

'Such things have never been a barrier to their lovemaking,' Jeanne observed. 'Come; let us get finished, we have to be up again at dawn, to prepare for the family breaking their fast.'

'And what about you and your soldier boy, is there a barrier to your lovemaking?' Annie asked.

'Mind your tongue you cheeky wench,' Jeanne flared. 'That is none of your bloody business, and my soldier boy is Squire Aidric to you and you had better not forget it.'

Annie, feeling hurt by the strong words, and forgetting her friend's now elevated position of Housekeeper, was determined to have the last word. 'Come on Jeanne we all know he takes you to the old barn, after church on Sunday. Do not tell me it is to discuss the reverend father's sermon,' she finished with a smile.

Jeanne's response was soon to wipe the smile from Annie's face. 'My private life is not to be the subject of your frivolous gossip Annie Foster. For your insolence you may finish this work alone, I am off to bed. I expect all to be finished before you retire and that you should rise in the morning at dawn, and awaken Emma when you have all prepared for her to begin breakfast. If you fail this task or gossip about my relationship with Squire Aidric again, you will be punished. Do you understand?'

A shaken Annie mutely nodded agreement and continued alone as Jeanne ascended the kitchen stair to the servants' quarters.

***

Walt spent much of his day of administration with his bailiff and reeve. He explained that he wanted the sheep brought in for shearing as soon as possible. Another two days and it would be June so Bailiff Turstan Gathergood was to tour all the Syhale tenants, both yeomen and villein, to instruct them that all their fleeces were to be delivered to the manor before the fifteenth of June. They would be given receipts for the weight of wool delivered and receive payment after the sale. 'I am away to Blythe with Squire Aidric tomorrow and I expect everything to be well underway before I return, hopefully within the week.'

Both men knew their responsibilities, and asked no questions, knowing that Sir Walter would tell them what was in his mind when he was ready.

The next morning, Walt and Aidric set off on a leisurely ride to Blyth, where they would stay the night at an inn, and if they concluded their business in time would return the following day.

Aidric was quiet during the ride, and Walt wondered what bothered him. Finally he said. 'What ails you, Squire? I have not known you so silent, have you and Jeanne had a disagreement?'

'No, Sir. Jeanne told me that she had to discipline Annie for gossip about our relationship. I told her we have nothing to be ashamed of and such sensitivity was uncalled for over a little friendly banter. We parted with our difference unresolved.'

Walt laughed. 'Is that all? It is about time you married the girl and then you would always have a place to settle your differences.'

'Not until I have my holding in profit and saved sufficient to keep her in a proper style as should befit the wife of a squire, Sir.'

Walt had no reply for that, things were hard for all at the moment. However the interchange had broken the ice and the pair chatted freely for the remainder of the journey.

Arriving in Blyth they found an inn with stables and a room free. After handing their horses to the ostler and settling into their room, they headed for the tavern where they had some bread and ham, and a tankard of ale to wash away the dust of the journey. After their meal, the innkeeper had given them directions on they could find the merchant Cuthbert Middleton.

The warehouse turned out to be ideal, next to the wharf which Middleton owned. Middleton had a small area in the corner of the warehouse screened off, where he did his accounts. They were shown to this area and, having presented his cousin's letter of introduction, soon reached agreement on the principles of the deal. When they enquired about his payment for use of the facilities, he referred them to his cousin Gilbert, who, he said would negotiate that part, and payment would be through him. They shook hands on the arrangement and Walt gave Cuthbert a letter for his cog captain to hold and present as introduction to Jon Monek at Bishops Lynn. All Cuthbert needed to do was to see the wool loaded onto the cog, and keep clandestine record of the number and weight of sacks loaded, from Radulf and from Middleton. He should give the captain a sealed shipping list for Monek, stating the quantity of sacks and weight.. Monek could check the cargo if he wished, so there would be no cheating and everyone would be satisfied.

'What about payment for the wool?' Cuthbert asked.

'That is between us and Monek.' Walt replied.

'What about Middleton wool?'

'Between us and your cousin.'

With business concluded, both Walt and Aidric shook hands with Cuthbert and made their way back to the inn. It was still only around midday, and Aidric asked if they should head home. 'No' said Walt, 'let us relax and take a ride up the coast this afternoon. Tonight we can eat at the inn and partake of a few tankards of ale together. It is not often that we have such an opportunity.'

The afternoon was sunny but there was a cold wind blowing in from the sea. Their ride was invigorating and bracing. There was no opportunity to talk as mostly the trails along the coast meant they could not ride side by side, and the wind prevented conversation unless up close. Walt led down a narrow trail to the beach, where they could ride abreast and talk. 'We should be thankful for this wind; it will dry up the sodden ground, maybe we have seen the last of the persistent rainfall,' Walt speculated.

'Well it snowed or rained for several days every week since January, these last two days are just what is needed to dry out the ground, and dry the sheep for shearing' Aidric replied.

'We must pray that the weather holds until our wool is safely sacked and in a dry place,' Walt rejoined, before turning his mount, to head back to the inn. 'Too bloody windy,' he added.

Arriving back at the inn after their ride in the bracing wind, the pair took to their beds for a rest until their evening repast.

It was early evening when they awoke. They freshened themselves with a splash of cold water on their faces from the basin on the table and headed down to the tavern for some food. They agreed to try some of the fresh fish available, and had John Dory with local vegetables, washed down with a tankard of ale. Being early evening it was quiet in the tavern and they were sitting well away from the bar where the single men would congregate later, all wishing to be near the pretty barmaid, and hope to catch her eye as she poured their tankards of ale from the barrel.

The next day, they arrived back at Syhale to find shearing already underway. Bailiff Turstan had employed extra shearers and was determine to finish in record time. He assured Walt that the tenants were also shearing, hopefully to beat the weather. On this occasion the weather was kind to them and all the fleeces were weighed and on route to Blyth before the rain returned with a vengeance, to wash away their efforts of spring planting and turn the fields quickly back to quagmire.

'It looks as if God has not yet forgiven us our sins,' Katherine remarked as they sat around a candlelit table in the early evening, listening to the rain and wind rattling the shutters. In a normal year at this time they would be taking their evening meal with open shutters and sunlight streaming through the windows.

After their meal, when the servants had retired to the kitchen, Walt said quietly, 'if we have another year of this we shall all be in dire straits, we can expect more reivers and desperate men trying to feed their families. I shall attempt to bring our troop up to strength to combat the situation.'

'Can we afford to pay more soldiers, we have received nought from the king since Bannockburn,' Katherine said.

'We will manage,' said Walt, grimly. 'There will have to be some reductions in pay, for everyone. I know,' he continued, before Katherine could comment, 'they have barely anything now, but if reductions mean nothing then they are still being fed, which is more than can be said for many poor bastards.'

One bright point of the year was that in July, Walt and Aidric had travelled south to claim their money for the wool from Jon Monek, and Walt had been pleasantly surprised by the amount received.

On his return he professed to Katherine that the venture had been a great success and well worth the return journey for him and Aidric, despite almost daily downpours, deviations due to flooded fords and the signs of poverty, starvation and death, they had witnessed on their outward and return journeys. He did not tell Katherine that on the return journey, after making a necessary diversion due to a destroyed bridge, they were accosted by, and had to fight off robbers, who made it clear to them that it was their horses they wanted, and if they gave them up, they would be spared. There was no way that Walt would give up their mounts, or believe their promises. Of the five robbers, Walt and Aidric quickly despatched two, whilst the other three ran into a thicket where the mounted men could not follow. Once there, they began to plead for alms. 'Sir, our village is starving and just one horse will feed us for a year when salted and preserved.'

Walt was not moved; 'you had better remain in your thicket, you have a strange way of requesting alms with weapons. We shall ride on, pick up your dead friends, go back to your starving village, and let this be a lesson. If you come after us again we shall kill you.'

'Would they really eat our horses?' Aidric asked, as they continued their journey.

'Many who have served in France will have seen worn out horses being killed and used in potage to feed armies. These have not been the first would-be robbers, we have chased away, but the first determined enough to die. They have gained nothing except grief for their families with their action. We must keep our wits about us; there will as likely be more' Walt replied.

Aidric considered Walt's reply before announcing, 'I do not believe their famine can be as bad as in Northumberland, where our folk have also to contend with Scottish raiders continually taking what little is to hand.'

The one other joyous occasion that year was the birth of James Radulf on the sixteenth of August. Walt was overjoyed, he had another fine son from his wonderful wife, and he spared no emotion in congratulating her.

Tilly smiled, and took baby James from his mother when he was finished suckling. She placed him carefully in his crib, the sixth occupant of the little bed made by the estate carpenter for the master before he was born.

=====

CHAPTER 4

An act of rebellion

1317. Katherine was worried that Walt was rapidly losing patience with the thieves and rustlers. He knew very well that some of these men were from other estates to the south around Durham. They were being sent to deliberately target anyone who seemed to be riding out the bad times more successfully than they were. Walt expressed his desire to form an alliance with a powerful near neighbour to not only better protect himself, but to take the war, which was how he saw it, to the enemy; and this time it was not always the Scots but often their own kind. Katherine already suspected that he had been out recovering stolen grain and stock with his soldiers. There was always a doubt if it was actually recovered from the right people or just taken from some other estates to the south. She may worry but she would never criticise. He was her husband and lord, and he was doing what was necessary to keep his family and estate together and fed. She knew that on top of his agreement with Bruce, general ransoms had been paid by Northumberland to keep the Scots from continually despoiling the area from which there was precious little left to take. Katherine was well aware that their nest egg in the vault was seriously diminished.

Walt knew that Katherine worried about his freebooting life of rob or be robbed. He knew roughly who was doing the robbing and just needed to minimise his losses and maximise his gains, then maybe they would leave him alone, and move on to an easier target. He had built his troop of soldiers to the strength of thirty mounted troopers, including Sergeant Heddon. He would often make use of them to collect protection money from weaker estates, using some of this money to pay the troopers he used in their protection. Money from the king for troop maintenance had been seldom forthcoming prior to Bannockburn and non existent since. Most of Northumberland was on the point of open rebellion. Many of the castles were diminished, with their keepers either dead or their troops disbanded through lack of funds.

Walt heard that Horton castle was still deserted. Since Sir Guiscard's death at Bannockburn, his wife had taken their daughter and fled south to a safer environment for a widow and young lady. Also there was a problem with Mitford castle with Lord Eure not in residence, and only a few of his men still in occupation, as most had drifted off due to lack of pay.

Walt formed an alliance with Gilbert de Middleton; his father's old ally, and his current partner in evading wool tax, who also had a troop around the same strength as his. Together they had installed de Middleton in Mitford castle without opposition. The few of Eure's men, who were left, readily joined Middleton's troop with hope of improving their lot. Now, he thought, is the time to tell Katherine of these actions. He knew she had already guessed he had something he should have shared with her. 'Katherine, I have something to tell you' he proffered.

'That you are intimidating people, and demanding ransom or reward in kind?'

'How did you know that?'

'Walt we have been married long enough. I sense when you are not telling me all, and although you have very loyal men around you, I have ways of finding out.'

'Aidric?'

'No Walt not Aidric. First it was Thomas who told me that all hunting expeditions were not as seemed. I do not want to get anyone in trouble, so I will not tell of anyone else. What happened to always being honest with each other?'

'I am truly sorry Katherine, but I suppose I am ashamed of my actions.'

She walked around the table and sat next to him. Putting her arms around him, she drew him close. 'These are hard times Walt. You are feeding your family, and workers, paying a troop of soldiers, albeit a pittance, and maintaining your estates. You still have the loyalty of estate workers who you cannot pay but you see to it they do not starve. What else can you do?'

'I have formed an alliance with Gilbert de Middleton and helped him to install himself and his men at Mitford. He was pleased at last year's wool returns and wishes to continue the arrangement.'

'Be careful of him Walt, I fear he is unscrupulous and may get you into serious trouble. I would not be surprised at him committing murder or kidnapping for ransom. Don't let him take you down that road or I may lose you altogether.'

Walt promised to be careful and not to hold secrets in the future. He was also secretly worried about the outcome of his activities. As previously promised he had consulted a monk from Alnwick Abbey who was schooled in law, with regard to his transfer of his estates into his son's name. He was told that he would be wise to name his father in law as inheritor and guardian, until the boy's coming of age. He was assured that this was a satisfactory arrangement, but may not hold if his land was forfeit on the order of the king. Also, despite his will leaving his demesne to his father in law, should he be executed for treason, as the law forbade his immediate heir inheritance in these circumstances, the king could still secure the land if he thought fit. In other words, there was no defence against the wrath of the king. He thanked the monk and made a donation to the abbey, knowing that he had indeed done as much as he could to secure his family's future with the knowledge that he had one copy of the relevant documents in his vault, and another lodged with Baron Percy for safe keeping. The young baron had not forgotten his father's patronage of Walt, and the fun he had with the soldiers on the quintain at Syhale. Lastly Walt made Katherine and her father aware of the arrangement and the location of the signed deeds.

Following the blizzard in January, the remainder of the winter had been mild with little more snow. They were hopeful for a good spring, when they could get the fields ready for sowing and hope for a good harvest this year.

It had started raining in March, and through to May there was barely a dry day. The ground was sodden and the sowing was unsuccessful with much of the seed washed away or rotting.

In addition to the worries of the famine, there was a general feeling of dissatisfaction with the king's rule, or lack of it, that had reached boiling point in Northumberland. Walt called his closest associates together for a meeting. These included Gilbert de Middleton, his brother John de Middleton, his own Uncle Adam who ran his estate at Felling, Sir Hugh Delaval, John de Widdrington and Walt's trusted Squire, Aidric Johansson. He had already formed an alliance with the Middletons for their mutual defence and joined them on attacking forays, to requisition stock and money for repayment of debts, on behalf of clients who did not wish to sully their own hands with such matters. These missions could turn violent if the landholders were foolish enough to question their demands.

In line with his previous agreement, Katherine was present at the meeting. Not to the liking of some of the others but as it was being held at Sir Walter's manor they would have to accept it. Once they were all supplied with ale, Walt dismissed the servants and closed the doors. They were seated in the feasting hall so were quite private. Walt opened the meeting by thanking all for their presence and drawing attention to the subject of the lack of government. He invited de Widdrington to enlighten the gathering on the disastrous attempt by the High Sheriff to warn the king that something should be done before things were out of hand.

John de Widdrington told how his wife's brother Adam de Swinburne, High Sheriff of Northumberland, had written directly to the king to warn him of the rebellious nature in the land, and to enlighten him of the general complaints of the borderers. Unfortunately, the only effect was the sheriff being arrested for treason and borne away to the king's prison in London.

They were all incensed by this news and the rebellion was formally grounded there and then with the word to be spread to all interested parties. During the summer months nothing happened to change their minds and soon all castles in Northumberland with the exception of Alnwick, Bamburgh and Norham were in the hands of supporters of the rebellion. Baron Percy would not actively support, but agreed to take no action against the rebels. Walt took over the abandoned Horton Next the Sea castle near Blyth and installed fifteen of his men at arms there under Sergeant Heddon. A cook, a general servant, a groom and two labourers made up the household there. Walt would spend much of his time there and visit the manor whenever he could, and remain overnight when possible.

He decided to conduct his operations from Horton and thus seek to keep that side of his business away from Katherine and the manor. He left fifteen men at arms under the newly promoted Sergeant Galeron Guddal for security at the manor. The summer did not put Northumbrians in any better mood as it continued to rain frequently and most of the poor crop would again be ruined. There was still pestilence among livestock, and the inhabitants were convinced they were cursed and the king was to blame. The areas around Durham were always a little better off, because they could obtain things from the south which was not as badly affected as Northumberland, and they were not harried by Scottish incursions.

When at last news came that the king was taking some notice of their plight; many in the north had already offered allegiance to the Scots, believing they would get a better deal from King Robert de Bruce.

Walt rode to Mitford to discuss the latest news with Sir Gilbert. After a few pleasantries and a jug of ale, Sir Gilbert elaborated on the news. 'Talk is that the Earl of Lancaster is marching with an army to Newcastle at the request of the king, who is to meet him there with his own army at the end of September. There is much speculation on the king's intentions.'

Walt responded. 'I doubt he intends to go further north and take on Bruce again. The first time he was to meet Bruce when his father died, he ran. Second time he ruined his chances of success and ran. Why should we expect anything different this time? I believe it is just a show of force to warn us rebellious Northumbrians to behave.'

Sir Gilbert agreed and the only concession they made, was that it would be best to keep their activities north of Newcastle when Lancaster's army arrived.

***

One regular routine did not change in the Radulf household. Katherine announced that she was again with child, the birth to be expected next May.

Walt, as usual was delighted by the news, but Katherine pointed out that he no longer saw so much of his children as he was spending so many days away at Horton and other places.

'Well I am here today and I shall stay until tomorrow morning,' he said.

'You already have me with child so I am still safe from another.'

'Practice makes perfect Katherine my dear.'

'No need to strive for perfection Walt, just pleasure.'

Their ramblings were interrupted by Squire Aidric knocking on the door to hand them a letter.

'Just arrived by messenger from York, Sir,' he said.

Walt thanked him and sat down and read the letter while Katherine waited patiently for her turn. It was from William, he tended only to write once a year now and bring them up to date with the news of York. They had not seen him and Freda since Walt received his knighthood.

Most of the letter was routine well-wishing, and news of difficult times. Not much corn to deal in times of famine, so the prices were very high. William hastened to add that this did not mean that they were better off, but generally it was harder to maintain their lifestyle and they needed to make savings in many areas.

Including letters, Walt thought wryly, *they used to be twice a year.* He continued reading that Uncle Hugh was now very frail and taking little interest in the business. Freda was well but still no signs of a child. Then he came to a part he found interesting.

'Listen to this Katherine.' He read out,

'Mark has gone. It happened about two months ago. Ingrid came to us one morning in a state of distress. She said that Mark had not come home the previous night, and she has found much of his clothing missing. He had not been to work the day before but missing a day was not unusual for Mark so I had not been concerned. I tried to reassure Ingrid that it was just one of his drinking sessions and he would probably be back by nightfall hungry and broke. Ingrid said that she was sure this was different, because as well as the clothes, he had found her hiding place for their savings. He had taken it all, his horse and her horse had also gone, hers to be used as a pack animal she supposed or maybe to be sold. She was convinced she would not see him again. Although very upset she told Freda, that on top of his drinking and womanising along with unnatural behaviour with some of his drinking cronies, this was the final betrayal and she intended to get over him and look to the future.

Ingrid has since taken to coming to work in the office. She performs tasks previously done by Mark, only to a much more satisfactory standard. Now she has accepted that she will not see him again, nor forgive him, she is a much happier person than before. We have assisted her with a petition to His Holiness the Pope, for an annulment of her marriage to Mark on the grounds of his unnatural behaviour making it no true marriage. Our priest has advised us that this is one of the few reasons which may be accepted by the pope. Of course this needed to be accompanied by a generous donation to his church. A copy of the notice has been posted publicly and now she just has to wait for the Pope's decision. We are assured that the priest's recommendation and our donation should have the desired affect.'

Ignoring the remainder of the routine news in the letter he turned to Katherine.

'So what do you think of that?'

'Poor Ingrid, she is so naïve. Using her horse as a packhorse indeed? It is most likely packing one of Mark's strumpets. However, that is the best news I have ever heard from York. Let us hope the poor girl does not get mixed up with another such scoundrel.' Katherine replied.

'She has Freda to guide her now and she should be able to assess users.' Walt summed up.

Katherine could not resist a sarcastic comment. 'Are you sure about that?'

Walt felt himself redden, as he hurriedly pushed the letter over to her. 'Here read it yourself, I have to go out and give some instructions to David Reeve.' With that he left the room quickly, seeking to hide the guilt that he still felt for the way he had used Freda.

The reeve declared he was despondent about the loss of yet more sheep to thieves and the pestilence. Walt was worried on several counts. The value of his diminishing flock was high for slaughter, but prices would be lower for fleeces this year due to the poor quality. There had been no letup in rainfall, and insufficient feed to properly sustain the flock over winter. He could not afford to allow more to be stolen, or to sell too many for slaughter, despite the high price they would fetch. He needed to breed more if he was to remain in the business and safeguard their future.

'Bring the flock closer to the manor and use the shepherds to keep a sharp eye, Reeve, and get them to report to Sergeant Guddal the moment they see anything suspicious. He will know what to do. Use the old barn behind the mill if you need shelter for lambing. I will have Guddal post a sentry out there.'

The following morning, having bid a loving farewell to Katherine and the children, he returned to Horton to prepare for his next venture of protection for anyone who he felt would value his services. Although he was allied with Gilbert, on many of these ventures he usually preferred to work separately. Gilbert did not have his powers of persuasion and tended to jump too quickly into a violent reaction to the first refusal, resulting in serious harm to the victim. This was not good, because a farmer who could not work or make more money, could not afford protection. Quite separately he was concerned that Gilbert would soon be responsible for someone's death, and he did not want to be there when that happened. That may mean losing the goodwill of the other conspirators.

When he and Aidric arrived at Horton they were met by Sergeant Heddon, to whom Walt gave his latest bad news. 'The Earl of Lancaster has arrived at Newcastle with his men and is waiting there for the king to join him.'

'He may have a long wait,' replied the sergeant. 'It is believed that the king has no intention of leaving London despite his promise to the earl. Almost as an afterthought he added. 'There is also a messenger here for you, Sir. He would not leave his message, said he would wait for your return.'

'Do you know where he is from Sergeant?'

'Wouldn't say, Sir, but I suspect Scotland by his speech.'

'Right Sergeant, give me an hour to get settled in my quarters and then show him up.'

'Yes, Sir.'

Walt and his squire rode on through courtyard, while the sergeant ordered the drawbridge over the moat raised and gate closed behind them. They passed their horses to the groom and made their way to their private quarters in the keep, to change from their travelling clothes into loose indoor robes. Walt asked Aidric to join him in the feasting hall when he was changed. The hall was the only room in the castle impressive enough to receive visitors. Horton castle was quite small by comparison with many other castles. It was essentially a moated stone manor house for which a previous owner had gained permission to crenelate and fortify from Edward Longshanks about twenty-five years previously. There was little evidence of the last occupant, Sir Guiscard de Charron, or his knights and squire. Walt wondered if they had been killed along with their employer at Bannockburn. Sir Guiscard's wife Alice and her daughter had certainly cleaned the place out when they left, unless robbers had finished it for them during the time it was unoccupied.

Walt finished changing and went downstairs to the feasting hall, which took up most of the second floor. He arrived to find Aidric already there, and asked him to call the messenger in. The messenger introduced himself as Ian Mackay. Walt returned the courtesy. 'Good afternoon Mr. Mackay,' he said formally, 'I am Sir Walter Radulf and this gentleman is Squire Aidric Johansson. You have a message for me?'

'Yes, Sir Knight, but it is for you only,' he said, glancing at Aidric as he fished into his coat and produced a sealed parchment.

'That is an acceptable precaution Mackay, but my squire is to be trusted. Have you need of refreshment while I read this letter?'

'Maybe a little ale, Sir, if I may?'

'Aidric, would you see the servant and have ale brought for our guest?'

Aidric opened the door and shouted for a jug of ale and three tankards. Walt smiled. His squire did not want to leave the room in case he missed something. He waited patiently until the servant had delivered the jug of ale and departed. Aidric poured them each a tankard of ale and sat down next to the messenger, opposite Walt, who was now opening the letter, the seal on which he had recognised from the letters he had received regarding his father's death at Bannockburn. He guessed that this meant the time had come for him to earn his protection. Walt moved to the end of the long table, where the two would not be able to see the letter, spread it out. *Thank God it is written in French,* he thought, as he began to read.

Edinburgh 20 August 1317

To Sir Walter Radulf,

Congratulations young Walt, on being awarded your knighthood.

I have heard of the movements of Lancaster. He is no threat to me without Edward's force and my intelligence says he is still in London and has no intention of moving.

I have a more pressing matter I would wish you to attend to.

I have received knowledge of two representatives from the pope who are travelling north. First they will meet up with Lewis de Beaumont, the Bishop elect of Durham. They will travel to Durham to witness the installation of the new bishop, before completing their journey. It is also my knowledge that these two are carrying a letter for me from the pope. On arrival in London they were received at court by King Edward before proceeding

north. I suspect treachery, and would know what the contents of the letter are, before it reaches me.

I will delay receiving the emissaries until I receive your message with a copy of the letter they are carrying.

I leave to you, how you achieve this, and the nuncios should be unaware that you have seen the contents. In recognition of the dangers you face there will be ample reward for a successful mission.

R de Bruce, King of Scotland.

Walt carefully folded the letter and looked at the messenger.

'Do you require a written reply?'

'No, Sir Knight. My master said the only reply he wanted was a result from his request in the letter.'

'Do you know what is in this letter?'

'No, Sir.'

'Good. You may leave today, or in the morning, as you wish.' He turned to Aidric.

'Have cook give this man food for his journey before he leaves, whether it be today or tomorrow.'

'Farewell, God be with you,' he said as the messenger left, and to Aidric he said, 'come back and see me when you have seen to the messenger.'

Well, Walt thought when alone. *You have got to earn your money now Walt Radulf.* He folded the letter and put it inside his robe. He would destroy it later when he was alone.

Walt sat in quiet thought until Aidric returned and sat down, reclaiming his tankard of ale. Walt looked up from his thoughts and said. 'Do you know who the letter was from Aidric?'

'I saw the seal, Sir, but I guessed the Scottish king, mainly because the messenger is Scottish.'

'You guessed correctly Aidric.'

Walt went on to briefly explain what he was required to do, after which he said. 'This is dangerous work Aidric. If you wish to have no part I will understand.'

'I am your squire, Sir, I do your bidding.'

'If we are brought to justice that excuse may be good enough for the soldiers but not for a squire, Aidric.'

'Where you go, Sir; so do I, unless you order me otherwise.'

'Alright Aidric, we have no time to lose, tomorrow we ride for a meeting with Sir Gilbert. You may be party to that meeting but remember this. No mention of the letter; or how I came by this information.'

Walt dismissed Aidric and sat again in thought. He had a plan, but he needed Middleton to help him execute it. Not for the manpower but to cause a diversion as to the reason for the attack, which he decided must take place before the bishop elect and the papal nuncios reached Durham. He realised the seriousness of what he intended to do. He knew that the bishop elect, intending to take up residence at Durham cathedral would have all his possessions with him, which would include a small fortune in jewellery and silverware. This was the part that he knew would appeal to Middleton, and throw suspicion away from his real reason for the attack. He would point out to Middleton that the nuncios were of equivalent status to ambassadors and it would be too dangerous to hold them as hostages or rob them. He would be responsible for their safety and getting them away without cause for serious complaint. He would say he expected a share of the subsequent spoils from the robbery to allay suspicion. Providing there was no killing he was convinced they would get away with it. The county was still in rebellion and no king's men would come for them. Yes he thought it was a good plan. He just needed to convince Middleton; whose greed he was sure would do the job for him.

Noon the next day saw him and Aidric at Mitford Castle, having their meeting with Sir Gilbert de Middleton. As expected Middleton was eager to partake in the raid, and insisted that he should provide the bulk of the men required to overcome the papal party. He said Walt would only need a few men to escort the nuncios and their servants away and put them on their way to Durham.

Wanting to stress the need for minimal violence, Walt said 'Gilbert, it is important that we carry this off without any deaths. Remember that Lewis de Beaumont is somehow connected to Queen Isabella and we must be sure that no harm comes to his person. We should not display colours and try to remain anonymous.'

'You worry too much Walt. Nobody is going to die, you take care of the pope's cardinals and I shall see to the bishop's wealth. We can lie low for a couple of weeks and if there is no danger I shall send a messenger to Horton and you can come and select your share of the loot. I doubt anyone will put a force together to challenge us; Beaumont was not the monk's choice, he was foisted upon us by the queen and all objections were overruled.'

'Very well then, let us get on with our plan,' Walt responded.

They resolved to get some men to Durham and further south to make discreet enquiries as to the progress of the party.

They next needed to decide on a good place to ambush the travellers. This was left for Walt to organise, Middleton not liking to waste his time travelling into dangerous areas unless there was some immediate gain.

Walt and Aidric returned to Horton, and next day set out south dressed inconspicuously, still as knight and squire but without displaying colours.

They travelled south to Darlington and then turned north again to slowly follow the road leading to Durham, the route they knew the two cardinals would have to follow. They passed through the small hamlet of Woodham, and rode slowly towards Rushyford studying carefully the lie of the land around them. Passing a large wooded area on their left they soon after came upon the ford over Rushyford beck. Beyond that was the small hamlet of Rushyford and a crossroads. Walt turned back and went for another look at the woods. He determined that they were not congested with undergrowth, and would be suitable to hide a body of horsemen. Riding on through the ford he turned left at the crossroads and they rode for a while, south of the beck and parallel to the northern edge of the forest. Walt eventually found the spot he was looking for, a shallow section of the beck with gently sloping banks where horsemen could easily cross. 'This will do fine,' he said.

Aidric knew exactly what his master was thinking, and the two were soon hatching a plan for their ambush. All they now needed was better intelligence as to the day the papal party would be travelling the route, and to ensure that they were in the area beforehand, but not too long before.

They hastened back to Mitford to consult with Gilbert de Middleton, stopping off for one night at Syhale where Walt fondly and none too gently hugged his pregnant wife, and an overjoyed Jeanne, with a nod of agreement from Katherine, whistled Aidric away to the privacy of his cottage for a couple of hours. Aidric never spoke of marriage and Jeanne never pressed him on the subject. She was afraid he may not be inclined to a domestic life, and did not want to broach the subject for fear of losing him. She had never been so happy as when she was in Aidric's company, and she would wait for him to decide on matters such as marriage, and not jeopardise her position by being pushy.

That night in their solar, Walt told Katherine what they were about to do. She responded with shocked words. 'Walt you are putting your life in danger. Even the local rebels may object at robbing and endangering the lives of men of the church.'

'Nobody cares for the bishop elect; he is not Northumberland's choice but an interloper positioned by the queen. Nobody is going to get hurt Katherine. Middleton will deal with the bishop while I will look after the pope's emissaries, get sight of their letter and see them safely on their way.'

'What will you do afterwards if there is a hue and cry?'

'Hole up at Horton Next the Sea until it quietens down.'

'And if it does not quieten down?'

'Then I will take the first opportunity to flee to Scotland and seek shelter from Bruce, who was the beneficiary of this venture.'

'You trust him that much Walt? I hope your trust is justified, because that is surely where you will end up.'

'I will see you again after the raid and before I go to Horton, do not worry so much, it will all turn out right in the end. Please do not speak about this to Jeanne or Daisy, I know they worry about their men but I will keep them safe, trust me.'

'Oh Walt, how can you make such promises when you don't even know if you can keep yourself safe.'

'No more talk now Katherine; let us make love a little and go to sleep.'

'Oh come on you idiot, how can we make love a little, surely it's all or nothing with you?'

***

The next morning, Walt and Aidric left early for Horton.

As soon as he arrived in Horton, Walt made plans for a possible siege. He knew that he would not have to counter any large military force, but did not want to end up fighting his friends. He believed they would feel the same, but may think it necessary to put on a show of indignation at his actions. He drew up a long list of provisions he would require to maintain his garrison at Horton under siege conditions for six weeks. By that time he thought most, if not all, of his assailants, would have got fed up and gone home.

He sent Sergeant Heddon with two men and a horse and cart to Newcastle. He did not want to buy local and tip people off that he was laying in stock for a possible siege. The sergeant was given a list of goods and told to go to a Newcastle wholesaler by the name of Richard de Emeldon, who was well known to Walt. He gave him some money and a note to say he would be good for any balance if that was not enough.

All he now needed to do was to sit and wait for news from Middleton's spies in the south, monitoring the slow progress of the party, who seemed to be making little more than around fifteen miles a day depending on the frequency of inns for their overnight stays. It appears that the pope's cardinals cherished their comfort and would not consider a night outdoors. They made detours if there was not an inn on their direct route. Walt determined that they would not need to detour from the route he had reconnoitred as there was an inn at Rushyford and Ferryhill, after which Durham was only around thirteen miles.

Finally a messenger arrived from Gilbert de Middleton and handed over a sealed parchment, in which Gilbert had written.

To WR

We should set out in two day's time to be north of Darlington not later than Thursday the twenty-fifth of August. We should meet in the woods that you suggested for the ambush. At this time I have calculated that we should be a day or two ahead of the papal party.

I strongly suggest taking the road to the west at the Rushyford crossing and coming around to the wooded area by using small tracks from the rear to avoid people seeing a large body of soldiers heading over the ford and into the woods.

GM

After reading the note Walt smiled and addressed the messenger. 'Tell your master we shall be there as he suggests. Go to the kitchen and get some refreshment before you leave,' he added as he dismissed the man.

As soon as the messenger was gone, Walt laughed and handed the note to Aidric.

Aidric looked at it and handed it straight back. 'Sir, you know I cannot read French, English and a little Latin, but never French.'

'Sorry Aidric, I forgot. Shall I read it to you?'

'Yes please, I want to know what amused you so.'

Walt read the note, seeing Aidric smile as he heard the content.

'Sir, he has just repeated the plan you put to him after our reconnaissance.'

'I know, Aidric, he likes to believe he is in control of everything and that only he could make such a plan.'

Judging the distance from Horton to be around fifty miles, but allowing extra time for the westward detour, Walt determined to leave on the twentieth.

So far so good, he thought later in the day, when Sergeant Heddon returned to report that he had acquired all the provisions he had listed from Newcastle. The money was insufficient but Richard de Emeldon had accepted Sir Walter's promissory note.

After an early rise on the twentieth of August, Walt set forth with his squire, Sergeant Heddon and ten men, leaving the remainder to look after the castle, under senior trooper Botolfe Best. They had an uneventful journey to Rushyford, turning west at the crossroads to follow the route Walt had previously reconnoitred, and skirting south and east again along small farm tracks until they came to the rear of the wood. After a check of their surroundings to the north and south within the wood, they determined that they were first there, and settled down to camp in a small glade around one hundred yards in from the road, leaving sentries nearer to the road and at the back of the wood to look out for Middleton's party. His men were given instruction that there should be no shouting. Talking should be in low tones and there must be no fires. Their food would consist of bread and cheese for the next two days, with water or a little ale for refreshment. Any man who got drunk would be flogged, after first being gagged to ensure he did not shout. Dusk was approaching when the sentry came in to report that Sir Gilbert's party were arriving from the west as agreed. Walt was surprised to see he had at least twenty men with him. Their intelligence told them that the nuncios party had only six escorts so it seemed like a battleaxe to crack a nut from Walt's viewpoint. It was his understanding that Middleton would rob and run, and that Walt would quickly escort the cardinals away from the area acting as some sort of robber come protector of their persons.

They had concealed a scout a couple of miles down the road towards Darlington during the hours between sunrise and sunset. As soon as the quarry was spotted he was to ride and warn them so they could set their trap.

The next day passed without incident and they settled down for another night in the woods.

***

At an inn in Darlington, the papal party were sitting down to their evening meal. The Bishop elect, Lewis de Beaumont, his brother Henry Beaumont, Earl of Buchan, Cardinal Gaucelin D'Eauze and Cardinal Luca de Fieschi, the pope's two nuncios were seated in an exclusive area separated from the rabble by a rush screen. They were all in a jolly mood and the wine was flowing freely, as they took their not insubstantial supper. The cardinals expressed their pleasure at the thought of seeing Durham Cathedral on the morrow, and witnessing the bishop's enthronement later in the week.

The two cardinals had talked privately in their chamber on the previous night when Cardinal Gaucelin had expressed his surprise at the bishop elect's lack of Latin. 'How could the pope have chosen such a man?' he asked.

Cardinal Luca was convinced that pressure had been brought by the English queen, and told of the gossip he had heard whilst they were at Edward's court. 'Beaumont is brother to Isabella de Vesci, a close friend of the queen, who was determined it would not be her husband's choice. Queen Isabella is now virtually estranged from Edward, disgusted with his behaviour with his new favourites the Despenser family, but determined to use her still considerable influence, when it suits her.'

Thinking back to their last evening's conversation, Cardinal Luca was amused by the idea of Lewis's lack of Latin. He thought, *the ceremony should provide some amusement to the congregation, especially other priests and monks.*

He was brought back to the present by the interruption of the sergeant at arms in charge of their small escort. He came to report to the earl that he had heard reports of groups of soldiers of unknown origin in the area of Rushyford.

'Perhaps we should revise our route to Durham, Sir' he suggested to the earl.

'Nonsense,' interrupted Lewis de Beaumont loudly, before his brother could respond. 'If they are soldiers they will be attached to one of the knights or barons of the area responsible for maintaining order. We have nothing to fear from soldiers.'

'With respect, Sir,' the sergeant offered, 'I am told that many of the soldiers who are supposed to uphold the law only do their masters' bidding and usually to their own gain.'

Cardinal Gaucelin pointed out that following the installation of the bishop at Durham they had an important mission to Scotland on behalf of the pope and nothing should unduly delay that.

'There,' shouted Lewis already the worse for wine. 'Any deviation of our route could mean delaying the enthronement by a day. You have nothing to fear from soldiers in Northumberland. Did your informant say anything about recent robberies in the area, Sergeant?'

'No, Sir.'

Sir Henry had heard enough. 'We continue tomorrow on the original route and keep a sharp lookout. It is only around three or four hours from here to Durham which will give us a good rest, before the early start on the enthronement day of my brother as bishop.'

The cardinals had no idea if they should be afraid or not after the decision was made. They were more worried about delays reaching Scotland than the bishop's inauguration, which was a sideshow to their true purpose here. Another cardinal could perform that service if they could not, but they were in agreement on one thing. They did not want to miss the fun.

***

It was around four hours after sunrise on Thursday the first of September and raining, as was the weather routine on most days this year. The sentry from Darlington came galloping into the wood to tell Sir Gilbert that their quarry was on the way. A detachment of men were sent to hide up towards the ford, to cut off escape in case they tried to make a run for it. Another party would emerge from the wood behind them and the third group would emerge when they were level with their position and take them by surprise, hopefully disarming them before they had chance to offer resistance.

They waited silently and patiently. Some of Sir Gilbert's men were positioned near the ford as the forward block, and others in the woods to emerge from the rear. Walt was at the actual ambush point with his men. He had a feeling that he had been manoeuvred into that position during the planning stage. He was sure that Gilbert was not frightened of the guard fighting back. More likely he was worried in case someone was killed during the initial attack, and he did not want to be blamed for murder. After around an hour had passed, Walt caught sight of the ecclesiastical party approaching. He passed the word and called for absolute silence and no action until he signalled by dropping his arm. They saw the party getting closer, with three escorts to the front followed by the two cardinals leading a pack horse. Behind them were the earl and his brother Lewis de Beaumont. Behind them were three more escorts, one of them leading a pack horse, and the other two escorting a peasant, driving horse and covered cart. All the approaching men were wearing their sheepskin capes, with heads bowed inside their hoods to avoid the inclement weather.

Walt indicated silently to his men that he and Aidric with four troopers would take the rear escort and the earl, while Sergeant Heddon and his five should take the front escort. Walt wanted to be where the earl was to ensure that he had no chance of putting up resistance. The very last thing he wanted was the death of a noble. He did not expect any resistance from the churchmen.

The party was drawing level; everyone knew exactly what they had to do. Walt raised his hand and waited until they were exactly opposite their position. The instant he dropped his hand the troopers ran out from the forest simultaneously. There were no warning shouts, just total surprise. Walt trusted the others to do the job they were trained for, as he made a beeline to his target the earl. Before the man knew anything was wrong he had been pulled from his horse and held at sword point. The three escorts at the rear had dropped their weapons and were also off their mounts and being quickly tied, as were the escorts at the front. Walt noticed Gilbert's men galloping in from the rear brandishing swords and wondered at the childishness of the display when it was virtually all over. He wondered no more as they drew level and one of them took a great swipe at one of the earl's guards, who was about to have his hands bound. The guard was caught across the throat and almost decapitated. Blood spurted over all in the vicinity as the man collapsed dead to the ground. Walt was furious.

'What the hell did you do that for you oaf,' he shouted.

'Sorry, Sir, I thought he was trying to escape,' the soldier shouted back as he wheeled his mount to pull up alongside Gilbert.

'A mistake,' said Gilbert, 'I will deal with him when we get back to Mitford.'

Gilbert's other ten men from the ford had now joined the party and Gilbert had taken control of all the horses, including the pack horse and the covered cart belonging to the bishop elect. The earl was tied and put back on his horse with his feet tied underneath its belly. His brother was similarly tied. Gilbert and his men then prepared to leave with their prisoners to Mitford Castle.

Walt was horrified. 'What the hell are you doing Gilbert, we are just supposed to rob them not kidnap them.'

'You can do what you like with yours Radulf. My two will be held for a fine ransom.'

'Don't be a fool Gilbert you will hang for this, if you kidnap them.'

'We will hang anyway since your man killed the guard.'

'My men killed nobody.'

'You were here Radulf; that is enough.'

With that Gilbert de Middleton gave the order, and he and his men rode away with their loot, all the horses from the guard, and their two hostages.

Walt was left with two very frightened cardinals, their mounts, a pack horse and five bound guards.

'We have been well and truly double crossed and implicated in a serious crime now, and I will see that no blame is attached to you men. If there is any blame it is mine.' He said to Sergeant Heddon, but in his mind he thought, *I should have paid more heed to Katherine's warning,* as he made a quick decision on what to do next.

He stripped the two cardinals of all they carried including any documents. They seemed very agitated at this move, but out of fear they did not resist. He then took from them their expensive scarlet cloaks and their pack horse. He asked one of the cardinals to say a prayer over the dead guard, and then out of earshot of the prisoners, he told Aidric to take four men and escort the cardinals to Horton castle. 'Ride hard,' he said. 'When you stop for a rest, ensure the prisoners are secure and guarded at all times. Do not mistreat them, and lose them at your peril Aidric. I will be there sometime tomorrow.'

The prisoners were released from their bonds and given the choice of taking their comrade with them or burying him. Without a spare horse for the body, they opted for burial, but nobody had a shovel. They scraped a shallow hole with their shields, which immediately filled with water, dragged the body of their comrade into it and with the help of some of Walt's men collected enough stones to cover him as a protection from animals, until maybe someone could return and do the job properly. With this task completed they were set free without their weapons. Walt, with Sergeant Heddon and the remaining men, set off with the cardinals' pack horse and headed for Syhale. Arriving at Syhale village around noon the following day, Walt took the documents the nuncios had been carrying and put them into his coat, saying to Sergeant Heddon. 'Tell Lady Katherine I shall be home later. You may then visit your lady friend at the mill, if you so wish. Be ready to ride with me to Horton in the morning with your men.'

'Yes, Sir,' the sergeant replied with a wide grin, as he hurried off to rejoin his men.

Walt quietly led the pack horse to the small wood framed wattle and daub dwelling next to the church. He hitched the animal to a rail and knocked on the door. Father Livio expressed surprise at the unexpected visit from Walt, but politely invited him in.

Once inside, and taking some refreshment offered by the priest, Walt broached his difficult request. 'Father Livio, I am about to ask you for a great service. To be honest I must say that knowledge of what I am to show you could be most dangerous. One item at least is a letter from the leader of your church to King Robert de Bruce. I fully intend that they be returned to their rightful owners and would just have knowledge of their contents, without the messengers being aware of any tampering. If you do not wish to be involved I will go away and trouble you no further.'

107

'What is it you expect me to do, my son?'

'Just translate the letters for me and copy out some of the important parts in their original Latin. I swear that no person shall ever know you did this for me. I dare not attempt it myself as I fear for the accuracy of my translation, due to there being much ecclesiastical and political content.

'No one will hear from me either my son,' he said wryly. 'You had better give them to me.'

Walt gave the priest the four documents.

Father Livio first looked at the two that were not sealed. 'These are just letters of introduction, proclaiming the two cardinals as the pope's nuncios or ambassadors. Now these two are sealed, I am going to have to be very careful if they are not to know we looked.'

'They think they are being robbed or held as hostage. When I give back the letters as worthless to me, I hope they will not look too closely.'

The priest took one of the letters and went to the fire where there was a kettle of water steaming from the beverage he had just made. He gently softened the wax seal evenly so as not to cause it to run. Then he got his most worn knife with an extremely thin sharp blade and gently eased it under the sealed edge of the parchment. He worked the knife gently across until he had separated the seal. 'That was easy; the trick now is to get it together again to look complete.'

He allowed the seal to harden slightly before opening the letter and reading it. After looking at the letter for a few moments he said. 'This is a letter from Pope John in Avignon, demanding that King Robert de Bruce come to an arrangement with King Edward and cease his war. He is threatening the excommunication of all of Scotland if his terms are not met.'

'Can you please copy that for me, as it is in Latin?'

'Certainly, do you want me to look at the other one?'

'Yes please.'

Father Livio then repeated the procedure to open the other letter. He looked shocked when he read it.

'What is it, Father?' Walt asked.

'I thought the first letter with the threat may have been a bluff to try to bring Bruce to heel, but this letter is a Papal Bull, decreeing the excommunication of Scotland from the Roman Catholic Church. The cardinals have been sent prepared for a refusal.'

'I bet the poor buggers do not know what they are carrying. I would not like to be in their shoes when King Robert reads this lot.' Walt said.

'Do you think he will harm the messengers of the pope?'

'No he would not do that, but he may frighten them a bit and chase them out of the country.'

'There is no need to copy the excommunication letter, I will just tell him the contents, but the other one I need copied and translated, as it sets out some conditions for peace which he must agree to. I know Bruce speaks French and some Latin, but I am unaware of the extent of his Latin. If it is at my level he would find some difficulty, and may not wish to bring a translator into his confidence.'

Father Livio nodded, took down his quill and ink, along with a piece of parchment from a shelf and began to copy the letter.

Two hours later after carefully resealing the two letters, he handed them to Walt who on examination had to agree that they did not look as if they had been tampered with.

He thanked the father and pressed a gold florin into his palm. For the parchment, he said. Father Livio smiled and blessed him as he rode off to the manor.

On arrival, he handed the horses to Will Foster, instructing him to remove the load from the pack horse, but not to open it. He was to get it loaded on again at dawn, ready for departure. Heading over to the house he saw the back door open as he approached, and Katherine waiting with outstretched arms. He stepped through the door and they hugged each other tightly. He thought he could feel the little bump on her tummy, although still tiny.

'I can feel my son,' he said, 'you said you missed your first moon in September so it can only be two months, he must be a big lad.'

'Oh Walt, you imagine it. Have we not got enough sons, this one is going to be Isobel.'

'No it is going to be John.'

'Do you always have to choose the boys' names?' she asked.

'You chose Hugh and James, it's my turn.'

Katherine gave up. She had Annie serve him some rich soup and a goblet of wine and sat looking at him until he finished.

Walt locked the door and said, 'Come on wife; let us retire for a little loving.'

Without question, Katherine called into the kitchen to inform Jeanne that they were retiring early as Sir Walter was exhausted from the long and arduous journey.

Once undressed and laid on the bed, Walt took Katherine's hand, gave it a gentle squeeze and said quietly, 'you were right about Middleton.'

'Oh my God, Walt, what has happened?'

'He deliberately had one of his men murder one of the guards to implicate us all in a capital crime and he has kidnapped the bishop and his brother for ransom.'

'He's mad Walt, what about the cardinals, and your share of the proceeds?'

'I have got the cardinals; they should be at Horton now with Aidric. I have got the information from their letters and I will give them back to them tomorrow along with their pack horse but minus their valuables. It must look like a robbery to throw suspicion away from the documents. As for the proceeds from the bishop's party, I do not believe he had any intention of sharing anything except the blame. I only have the cardinals' pack horse with whatever it carries and their fine robes. '

'Then what will you do?'

'I shall see them safely on their way to Scotland, leaving them sufficient money to complete their journey. The king's men will definitely be after Middleton. He probably killed the soldier as a warning what will happen to the bishop and his brother if the ransom is not paid. What he thinks he will do after the ransom is paid, I have no idea.'

'I meant after you have seen the cardinals on their way.'

'I have got siege stores at Horton. Middleton is going to attract all the attention with his hostages so I will sit tight and see what happens. I don't think anyone will try to invade me. If things get too dangerous I will make a run to Scotland.'

'How will you know when to run?'

'My friends will warn me before an assault is made, if they hear of such orders. Don't worry, I have it under control.'

'As it may be the last time I will see you for a long time I think we had better make the most of tonight Walt, and I want a bit more than a little loving.'

When dawn came and Walt was awakened by the sound of the cockerels crowing, he felt as if he had not been asleep at all. He was still exhausted from his night of blissful passion with his wife.

Katherine felt him stirring and grabbed him as he was about to get up. She pulled him onto his back and straddled him. 'You are not getting away that easy Walt Radulf.'

'Oh God, have mercy.'

'It is not God you should be asking it is me, and I am not letting you leave without some credits for the time you will be away. Also, remember not to invoke the Lord's name for personal gain. You could bring a terrible curse on our house.'

She leaned over and kissed him, gave a cheeky wriggle and Walt was lost again.

It was mid morning before he finally got away. The household was not used to them rising so late and there were a few nods and winks passing around the servants. Before he departed Walt took Jeanne aside to assure her that Aidric was in good health.

Outside he found a mounted Sergeant Heddon and his troopers waiting for him, holding his saddled horse and the packhorse. He did not ask them how long they had been waiting so as not to promote more amusement.

On arrival at Horton, Walt unpacked the cardinals' pack horse to find little of value except a pair of silver, gilded goblets, and a carefully wrapped ornate gilded crucifix, which Walt guessed was a present from the pope to the Scottish king. There were also a goodly amount of gold Italian florins in their purses along with some silver pennies. He helped himself to the florins and the goblets, but left the crucifix, feeling it sacrilegious to take such an icon, and the pennies, to provide for their food on the journey. Any more they needed would have to come from an appeal to the church for help. He decided also to keep the scarlet cloaks and give them some rough brown ones for the remainder of their journey. He had the cook pack their horse with some bread and cheese for their sustenance until they found an inn for the night. He then picked up their purses, the brown cloaks and their letters and went to find them.

Entering the room where they sat with Aidric, he asked, 'what have you told them?'

'Nothing, Sir,' his squire replied.

Walt handed over their purses and the cloaks. The cardinals looked in the purses, and at the brown cloaks, then back at Walt with an accusing look.

Walt shrugged and said. 'It is a robbery, what do you expect. Here you can have your documents back, I see from these two that you are the Pope's Nuncios.' He threw all four documents onto the table. 'These bits of paper are of no interest or value to me, take them.

They eagerly grabbed at them, and secreted them in their robe where he had taken them from. They picked up the two dowdy brown cloaks and gave them a disgusted look, but did not reject them.

One of them asked, 'are you going to ransom us now?'

'No, I would not kidnap envoys of the pope. I have merely helped you on your way, and will see you safely to the border so you are not troubled again in Northumberland. Consider the items I have taken as payment for the escort.'

'You have taken the Pope's crucifix,' one asked in horror. 'That is a gift from His Holiness to the Scottish king.'

'No, your crucifix is still safe in your pack; I would not steal such a religious item.' Turning to his squire he said. 'Aidric, you have not given them their waterproofs, they are going to need them, it is pissing down again outside.'

The two men took the heavy sheepskin hooded capes, nodded silently, and followed Sergeant Heddon when he beckoned them from the doorway.

Walt had given the nuncios an escort of Sergeant Heddon and four men, to see them to the border at Berwick. He told the sergeant to be wary not to get captured on his return. 'If on your return, the way to the castle is barred, or we appear to be under siege, then take your men to the manor and tell them not to speak of their actions, if you want to stay free.

He watched with Aidric as they rode away. As yet there was no hue and cry about the actions of the previous day. They just had to sit tight and wait to see what would happen next.

Walt returned to his quarters and took pen and parchment to write a note to Bruce.

Horton Next the Sea. 3 September 1317
Sire,

112

The Pope's nuncios left this place today bound for Edinburgh, with my escort as far as Berwick. You will find inside this package a complete copy of the Latin message from the pope to you. The outer part of the sealed note is addressed to Robert Bruce., without reference to Your Majesty's title. A summary of the Latin content is that the pope is imposing a set of conditions for making peace with King Edward. Failure to accept these conditions will result in the Excommunication of Scotland from the Catholic Church.

The nuncios are also carrying another document. This is a Papal Bull declaring the Excommunication of all of Scotland, should you not agree to his terms for peace.

WR

He folded his letter with the copy of the Latin terms from the pope, sealed them and addressed it to, **His Majesty Robert de Bruce, King of Scotland**.

The message was then enclosed in an outer packet as was the usual manner, sealed and addressed to Allan Stewart at Yetholm. He entrusted the valuable letter to Squire Aidric to deliver, as quickly as he could.

Four days later Sergeant Heddon returned from Berwick after escorting the nuncios to the border. The sergeant reported that there was still no word of any action regarding the robbery or kidnapping.

The day after that, Wednesday, Aidric returned to confirm the delivery of the letter to Bruce's man in Yetholm, and this time there was news of the robbery, which he relayed to Walt. 'I called at the manor on my return journey, to advise Lady Katherine and Jeanne that we are well. Lady Katherine told me that she has heard from her father that enormous ransom demands have been made by Middleton, for the release of the bishop and the earl. It seems that they are going to be in captivity for some weeks while sufficient money, silver and gold is gathered together to meet his demands. The good news is that all the attention is on Mitford where the prisoners are held. There is no talk about an assault on the castle; nobody has the stomach for that. There has been no mention of your name yet, Sir, and no mention of this place.'

'Give them time Aidric, I am sure that having dealt with the ransom and Gilbert de Middleton, they will get round to us. Maybe we will be able to visit the manor a few times, the danger will come when the ransom is paid, and the prisoners released. The earl and the bishop will be vengeful.'

'What do you intend we should do if they come for us, Sir?'

'We will have warning, I am sure. For those who wish to come with me, we will make our escape to Scotland.'

'Will we be safe in Scotland, Sir, as English soldiers?'

'With me Aidric, you will be safe, I assure you, and you are no longer a soldier, you are my squire.'

For the next three weeks there seemed to be no interest in the men at Horton castle. Most of the men stayed in the castle, but Walt and Aidric would visit the manor a couple of times a week and stay overnight. On days other than their visits, Walt would allow Sergeant Heddon to check on the welfare of his troopers under Sergeant Galeron, and pay a visit to the mill.

Katherine was grateful for the regular visits, but she noted that the men still took the precaution of not using the same days or times for each visit. She knew that Jeanne and Daisy also looked forward to the visits.

Early in December, during one of his visits, Katherine told Walt that she had heard that the ransom had been collected from various sources, with much treasure being taken from the cathedral. She believed there was to be an armed escort to convey the ransom in a cart to Mitford castle in the next few days, but she could not find out the actual day.

It was agreed that Walt and the others would suspend visits until the ransom situation was settled, after which they could again review their options.

Two weeks later, on the fifteenth of December, the occupants of Horton Castle were disturbed by a dozen horsemen gathered across the moat shouting to be let in. Walt was called and his advice sought. He recognised a sergeant from Middleton's troop of soldiers, and told him to advance alone across the drawbridge when it was lowered. When the sergeant arrived he was brought into Walt's quarters, where he and Aidric interrogated him as to his reason for seeking refuge.

The sergeant told them that the ransom had been delivered that morning, but during the handover of the prisoners, Gilbert de Middleton and his brother John of Belsay, who was with him, had been tricked by the Sheriff, whose men had gained access to the castle. All within had been arrested and conveyed to prison, firstly to Tynemouth, although he believed the Sheriff would probably move them to his main prison at Newcastle the following day.

'How come you and these men are here?' Aidric asked.

'We had been sent out the night before reiving cattle for Sir Gilbert. We saw something amiss as we approached the castle so we abandoned the cattle and came here for safety.'

Walt decided to accept the men at Horton, but wished to check each man as they came in.

'You are to go outside Sergeant and call your men to approach the gate, one at a time to be let in. Do you understand?'

'Yes Sir,' the sergeant replied, as he stuck his head out of the gate and called the first man through. Walt looked at each one and nodded his acceptance, whereupon they would fall in and wait for instructions when the exercise was completed.

The sergeant was mystified as to why Walt wanted to see each man as he was sure that he did not know any of them. He was to be proved wrong, Walt had reason for his scrutiny. The last man to approach obviously knew what was going on, and looked very nervous.

'State your name?' Walt demanded staring directly at the man.

'Harry Dodd, Sir.'

'Well Harry Dodd, you are the man who killed the unarmed guard at Rushyford. What have you to say about that?'

'I was obeying the instructions of Sir Gilbert, Sir. He said I was to kill one of the escorting soldiers.'

'Did he say you were to wait until he was disarmed and a prisoner before killing him?'

'He just said I had to kill one, Sir, whatever happened.'

Walt called over Squire Aidric and Botolfe Best.

'Take this man to the dungeon and chain him,' he instructed. To the man who was being led away he added. 'When and if the sheriff's men come, you can tell your excuses for murder to them.'

Dodd was led away, grumbling that he was only obeying orders. Walt turned next to Middleton's sergeant.

'Have you or your men any problem with that decision Sergeant.'

'No, Sir' came the quick reply.

'You will take your orders from me, my squire or Sergeant Heddon while you are with us, is that understood?

'Yes, Sir.'

'Very well Sergeant, we have collected all your men's names, now I must have your name if you are to serve with me. You are still to be in charge of your section, but you will take direct orders from Sergeant Heddon when required. Do you understand?'

'Yes, Sir, my name is Richard Wilson.'

Walt instructed Sergeant Heddon to have them stable their horses and show them to their quarters.

Two days later, Sir Hugh Delaval's Squire Elfric arrived at the castle asking for Walt. Having been admitted and made welcome in Walt's quarters he broached the reason for his unexpected visit.

'Sir Walter, I have been sent by Sir Hugh, to warn you that the sheriff is getting together a force to take your castle, and to bring all within to justice. Sir Hugh thinks you have two days at most before they will be at your gate.

After the squire had partaken of some food and refreshment, Walt asked him to convey his gratitude to his father in law, and sent him on his way. Immediately following Elfric's departure, Walt had Sergeant Heddon parade all the men.

'The time has come for us to leave this place, he told them. 'I am for Scotland. Whoever is with me take four paces forward.'

Aidric took more; he walked over and stood by Walt's side. All the Syhale men stepped forward but there was indecision among the Middleton men.

'Have you explained the situation to them Sergeant?' he asked Heddon.

'Yes, Sir, but they are worried about their treatment by the Scots.'

'It is your choice men but you see the faith my own men have in my ability to parley with the Scots.'

'What about Dodd, Sir?' one of them asked.

'Dodd stays here.'

That did not seem to bother them, and he assumed that maybe Dodd was not very popular. After a short discussion among themselves, they all stepped forward.

Walt was satisfied, and told them that they should prepare to leave immediately. He asked Aidric to see the cook, and arrange for each man to be given a bag of dry rations to keep them going for a couple of days. Walt also ordered a pack horse to be loaded with as much non perishable food they could pack. He then told the groom to prepare his and Aidric's horses. There was no need to take the castle staff with them. They were only paid servants and would hold no interest for the sheriff's men.

Walt sat down while the preparations were in hand, and wrote a short note to the Sheriff explaining the reason that he had left Dodd in the dungeon, and where he might find the key. In case any of the servants saw fit to try to release him, he addressed, folded and sealed the note, before giving it to the groom, who he trusted as an ex soldier to do his bidding.

'Hand this only to the sheriff or his deputy,' he instructed.

Walt had his personal small hoard of gold florins secreted about his person with a small quantity of florins and silver pennies in his leather purse, tied around his waist. Dressed only in his chainmail armour, carrying his helm shield and sword, with heavy coat, rain cape and groundsheet rolled behind his saddle, he rode out with his squire and his troopers.

They headed west, where they would lie low on the English side of the border, nearest to Yetholm, whilst he sought out Allen Stewart, to get a message to King Robert de Bruce requesting asylum. It was unusually warm for December, but it was not long before the rain capes were needed. Walt fervently hoped that 1317 would see the last of this interminable rain which they had suffered long enough.

When the men realised that Walt had a definite destination and a plan, they soon lost their worried frowns, and settled into their journey. They were now convinced that all they needed to do was to wait in Scotland until the fuss died down, and they would then be able to return home.

The journey was to take them two days, avoiding all areas of population wherever possible. Their progress was not a pleasant one. The weather was foul, with frequent rain and some torrential downpours. They had no tents for protection, only their sheepskin capes, or coats and groundsheets. Overnight camping was a miserable affair with no fires being lit, not just for fear of attracting unwanted attention, but for total lack of dry kindling. On the second night they camped in a wooded area just over a mile from Kirk Yetholm, where Allan Stewart lived.

Walt waited until just before dusk, and asked Aidric, who had been before and knew the way, to take him to see Bruce's man.

Allan Stewart was not surprised to see them. News of the kidnapping had travelled fast, he told them, and he had expected a flight to Scotland when he had heard of Middleton's arrest.

'Did you know the two Middletons are to be taken to London?' he asked.

'No, we thought they were at Tynemouth gaol or Newcastle,' Walt replied.

'They have kept his soldiers in Newcastle to be tried. Where are you camped?'

'Just the English side of the border about a mile east of here.'

'Tomorrow morning, bring your men to the village and I will take you to a better place, where there are some barns you can use for shelter for yourselves and your horses. You will be able to light fires to cook, and if you have some money, buy food. You will be safer this side of the border. I will send word to the king, and he will probably send an escort for you. It will take a few days, maybe a week or more.'

Walt and Aidric thanked the Scot, gratefully accepting hospitality in the form of morsels and a tankard of ale each. With their immediate hunger satisfied, they set off through more rain, to bring the good news to their men in the forest over the border.

***

At Syhale, Katherine was discussing the food purchases for the next week with Jeanne when there was a knock at the door. The visitor proved to be a glum looking Squire Elfric.

Katherine invited him inside and offered him ale. Without acknowledging her offer, he walked over to the corner where Tilly was playing with the four children. Walter, the eldest was now seven, and the youngest James two years old in August. The weather was much too cold for them to play outside so Tilly was obliged to keep them amused indoors. They were playing a game of stall keepers, where they pretended to be selling things on the market. There was lots of laughter coming from the corner. Tilly was a good nursemaid and well practised at keeping them amused on these cold days. Elfric greeted each of the boys by gently ruffling their hair. He then turned to Tilly, saying quietly, 'Tilly, why do you not take the boys into the hall, and play a game of chase with them?' Tilly, noting his sombre demeanour, guessed that he wanted a private word with Katherine without the boys listening, and took her cue. 'Come on boys, let us go into the hall and play chase.'

The two youngest jumped up eagerly, but Walter and Alex complained that it was too cold in there with no fire.

Katherine went to the cupboard by the door and fetched out woollen over shirts which she gave to Tilly, who put them onto the children, and took them into the hall to run around, with the eldest two still protesting.

After the children had left, Jeanne who had poured ale for Elfric, despite his lack of response to her mistress's offer, retreated to a seat in the corner where she hoped she would not be noticed. Uncaring about Jeanne's presence, Katherine ensured all three doors were closed before bidding Elfric to take a seat at the table. She waited patiently until he had sat down and took a sip of his ale.

'What is it Elfric?' she asked with her mind whirling and thinking of the dreadful things that may have come to pass for Walt.

'The sheriff's men were sent for Sir Walter this morning my Lady.'

As Katherine reacted with horror, he hurriedly continued. 'I warned them yesterday and they had all left hours before the sheriff arrived.'

'Where have they gone Elfric?' asked a worried Katherine.

Jeanne who had so far listened in silence could no longer contain her worries. 'Is my Aidric with him?' she asked as she walked over to stand by her mistress.

'Yes Mistress Jeanne, also the eleven men of Middleton's who joined him. They have gone to Scotland and are likely to remain there until Sir Walt deems it safe to return.'

'Let us hope that the trust he puts in Bruce is now justified.' Katherine said, reaching for the comfort of Jeanne's hand. They had become more than employer and employee over recent times, and were now firm friends. After all Jeanne was to be wife to her husband's squire one day. She had no doubt that it was only a matter of time before the two were married.

'I think we shall not see them again until the spring' Elfric opined.

Katherine thanked him for the information, and after finishing his ale, he headed back to Delaval.

Katherine had no idea how it would ever be safe for Walt to return, and thought Elfric's suggestion of spring merely a sop to diminish her worries. After some thought, she came to a decision. 'Jeanne, we shall have to tighten our belts again. There is barely enough money for wages left for the next six months. Savings must be made. The prior's tithes can wait.' *We will only pay tithe on this demesne* she thought. *The tithe for the rest of the estate can wait; we cannot possibly anger the prior more than we already have.*

'I am willing to work for my food and lodgings only' Jeanne put in.

Katherine gave her a hug. 'No need for that yet Jeanne. We must manage without our men folk to scavenge for us until lambing. After that the fleece fair at Tynemouth, if God is willing, and if we have finally got rid of this pestilence of the animals, and if the summer is fair for crops, we will be solvent again with enough money to last the next winter.'

'There are a lot of ifs in the hopes My Lady,' Jeanne said formally.

Katherine took the same route she always did when she needed hopes fulfilled. 'Tomorrow is Sunday Jeanne. We shall all get dressed in warm clothes, including Tilly and the children and go to early morning Mass, where we can pray to God, with the help of Father Livio, for our salvation.'

'Will that be before breaking our fast?' Jeanne asked, practically.

'Yes Jeanne. What is prayer, if God does not see us making some earnest sacrifice to his glory?' *Besides,* she thought. *I shall have another mouth to feed in the summer.*

Jeanne gave up. There was no swaying Katherine when she was in one of her religious moods. Early morning mass it would be then. She opened the door to the hall and called in Tilly and the children. Tilly took the idea of early mass in her stride, but the older two children started to complain again, until Katherine became quite cross and they both received a sharp clip around the ear. 'There, complain about that if you want another one.' Katherine said as they went quiet, holding their ears, but determined not to cry and show a weakness to a woman, even their mother.

Tilly watched and thought. *Already they try to be men; they will be strong like their father and be masters of their household.* It did not occur to Tilly that the master had not put in an appearance for some weeks now. As far as she was concerned the estate ran to his wishes even when he was not here. Her mistress, she knew, would do everything her husband required of her, even in his absence.

The next morning, as planned, they all rose at dawn and headed for the small church, where a pleasantly surprised Father Livio conducted mass, and joined them in a prayer for a better year. When they got home again, Katherine took quill and parchment and wrote a letter to her brother in law, William, in York. She thought that it was his right to be aware of the situation and the danger to his elder brother. She did not paint a bad picture but told him truthfully what had transpired, omitting some of the detail about theft, or borrowing of papal letters. Having sealed her letter, she called Galeron and asked him to organise a messenger to deliver it to William in York.

=====

CHAPTER 5

Escape to Scotland

The morning after meeting with Allan Stewart, Walt and his squire led his mounted troop of twenty-seven men into Kirk Yetholm as instructed. At last there was a let up in the inclement weather, which cheered the troopers. He was surprised that the villagers seemed to display little interest in having a large party of English soldiers in their midst.

They were shown to two large barns, and invited to take up temporary residence. The accommodation seemed weatherproof, and was certainly a great improvement on their previous night's location. Walt noticed that at one end of both barns, which were built of stone, at the apex of the roof there was a smoke hole, and below next to the wall was a stone fire area with irons above for hanging kettles or pots. Walt selected two men who he knew had cooking skills and allocated one to each barn. He and Aidric would be together in one, with Sergeant Heddon and their most senior soldier Botolfe Best in the other. The remainder he would share between the barns, except for Cethin Gwyn and his Welsh colleagues, who he wanted with him. Middleton's men would be mixed between the two to encourage integration, and discourage plotting. Middleton's sergeant, Richard Wilson, was detailed to Walt's barn. *Better to keep an eye on him*, thought Walt.

'Where can we obtain cooking pots and other supplies?' Walt asked Allan Stewart.

'You will find everything you need in the village. Pots, food, ale, wine; all is available to you from local merchants.' With that, the Scot left them to it and strode off towards his house.

Aidric waited until the Scot was out of earshot before expressing his thoughts on the subject. 'You know what I think? This village makes a living out of fugitives from all sides, and they probably sell the same cooking pots over and over again. Let us get the food unloaded from our packhorse and store in this barn. I shall control it and distribute it as required, with your approval, Sir.'

'As long as they don't sell the same food over and over I shall make no complaint. Come Aidric, collect a couple of helpers and we shall go shopping. Tonight the men will eat a good potage, if the ingredients are to be found, accompanied by fresh bread.'

Once they were in the hands of the merchants, it soon became apparent that Aidric's speculation about the village industry had been correct. They were offered new cooking pots at somewhere around double the normal price or second hand pots at the price they would expect to pay for a new one. Food prices were expensive but not doubled, which was a relief to Walt, who was funding this expedition. All in all, they found all their needs, and looked forward to an improvement in their diet from today. There was a general feeling of wellbeing amongst the men now, and Sir Walter was totally accepted as the leader by Middleton's men.

Over the days that followed, Sergeant Heddon could not take them outside training, even in the brief periods when the rain ceased. The villagers had their limits of hospitality, and the line was drawn at Englishmen doing overt military training in their Scottish village. He did what he could indoors by ensuring discipline was strict; and that they spent time making sure their uniforms and weapons were kept in good order. He had taken responsibility for the well being of the horses, and set up a rota of men to guard and feed the animals, which were confined to a nearby paddock.

After ten days, Walt was beginning to wonder if the village had some sort of trade agreement with their king, to ensure maximum profit from each group of refugees. He was glad he had plenty of money secreted, and made a point of only ever producing a little at a time. He was not worried about his own men who depended on him, and he had Aidric to watch his back. His main worry being, that the villagers should not think he had endless supplies of money and begin to raise their prices.

The prices certainly did rise when Walt went to buy some food to give his men a special treat for the Christ's Mass celebration. They celebrated separately in their barns, not feeling they would be welcome in the tiny Kirk at Yetholm. Allan Stewart thoughtfully arranged for a priest to attend and lead them in prayer.

It was on their twelfth day, and the first of the New Year, just after they had broken their fast; that a small party of Scottish soldiers arrived under the command of a knight and his squire. As soon as he saw the knight, Aidric smiled and stepped forward to greet him.

The knight laughed when he saw Aidric, saying, 'you again, do you like Scotland that much you must keep coming back?'

Walt recognised the knight as Sir William de Middleton, and stepped forward as he dismounted, holding out his hand in greeting. The pair firmly grasped each other by their forearms.

'I have come to take you to the king, Sir Walter, what say you to that?'

'We are happy to have your protection, Sir William, and eager to meet your king. This time you are collecting horses and troopers. I am much indebted to you for escorting my men to safety following Bannockburn, and here you are again leading us from danger. I wish also to express my regret on the fate of your brothers, who I am told are to be transported to the king's prison in London. I fear all will not end well for them.'

The other men had by now gathered outside the barns, curious as to what was taking place. Sir William cast his eye over them and soon spotted Sergeant Heddon and Botolfe.

'Another two Bannockburn veterans I see, are all these men yours Walt?'

'No some are your brother's men who escaped the trap. They were on another mission when it was sprung. They came to me for help and I accepted them, apart from one who was a murderer. He was left behind for the sheriff.'

'Well, can you and your men be ready to move in one hour?'

'Certainly can! Where are we to go?'

'To a village called Currie, south of Edinburgh. The king has a military camp there and he wishes to grant you audience following your arrival.'

'Sergeant Heddon, get the men ready to travel within the hour.' Walt ordered. Of Sir William he asked, 'how long a journey is it to Currie?'

'Two days, you will need some food for the journey, and we shall be sleeping rough tonight. We should arrive before nightfall tomorrow. We are expected, so there will be accommodation, probably tents, for your men, and something a little better for you and your squire.'

Walt thanked him and instructed Aidric to take a man to the village and procure dry rations for today, and for breakfast and midday tomorrow. They were all ready to move, well within the hour, with their food on the packhorse and a pause in the rain, welcomed by all. Allan Stewart came to bid them farewell, and Walt thanked him for his help and handed him an Italian gold florin, which he noted, was accepted without comment.

Mid morning saw them well on their way. They had by now been travelling for over an hour, with the two knights and their squires at the head of the party, followed by Sergeant Heddon. Sergeant Wilson rode at the rear of the troop, now standing at twenty seven men since the addition of Middleton's fugitives. Behind them were the small party of five Scottish soldiers and their pack horse, carrying a barrel of ale and some horse feed. *Presumably to make sure none of our men get lost on the way,* thought Sergeant Heddon.

Aidric riding behind his master, and alongside Sir William's squire, introduced himself and learnt the man's name was Ian Ferguson. They were soon chatting amiably and swapping tales of adventure and combat.

They headed due north as the terrain and tracks allowed, and it was just after midday that they rested near the hamlet of Earlston. Until this time, the soldiers in the rear had kept strictly in their separate groups. Having moved off the track into a clearing and dismounted to eat and drink, a number of them became curious and began hesitant conversations with others who they had only ever seen as enemies before. However, before they could become better acquainted, the rain began again, their rest time was over, and they were ordered to remount and continue the journey. The next time they were able to talk was at dusk when they halted in some hills that the Scots told Sergeant Heddon were called Lammermuir Hills. The terrain consisted of rolling moorland heights and shallow glens, with some forests on their sides. The moorland parts were very open and bitterly cold. The Scots were better prepared than some of Walt's party for travel in early January. The English soldiers from Mitford were wrapped in cloaks and their rain capes. Their heavy fleece lined coats were still at Mitford castle, where they had been unable to return. Walt determined that he would have to procure some warm woollen coats for them as soon as practicable. *The traders at Yetholm missed an opportunity there,* he thought. There had been no warm clothing available for sale. *Maybe they enjoyed seeing the men shiver?*

Fortunately, Sir William led them down through a section of forest, to a shallow glen that afforded them a little shelter from the biting wind, with the rain having held off so far. There was a swollen burn in the glen which provided fresh water. They settled down to eat, drink, and find themselves a convenient spot to place their groundsheet. Soon everyone was settled and previous conversations were continued. Introductions were made and they generally got on well, and as soldiers do when not actually fighting, they deplored the politics of war, and expressed their wish that the border could be agreed, and each left to get on with their own lives. A great simplification of a complex situation, but they eventually went to sleep after a few tankards of ale from the barrel on the Scottish pack horse, believing they had solved the problem, and it only needed their respective kings to be made aware of the solution.

The next morning they were up at dawn, and there were no objections to grabbing a few oat biscuits, and getting on their way immediately. Fortunately there was again no rain, but there was still a bitterly cold, teeth chattering wind. They rode non stop until midday when they had some bread and cheese, and a sip of the last of the ale, to slate their thirst. The journey began to improve a little as the track was now quite well defined, and tended to stay more along the glens with only short distances that were fully exposed to the elements. In the late afternoon they came in sight of the camp at Currie.

It was a large tented camp and the local commander came out to meet them. He indicated an area of tents, and told the Scots soldiers to escort the Sassenachs there, and see them billeted. Walt told Sergeant Heddon to go ahead, and that he would come and see they had all they needed later, after he was settled in his billet.

Sir William and his squire turned their mounts towards the village and called for Walt and Aidric to follow. They rode across a fairly deep ford over a burn that Ian Ferguson told Aidric was called Leith Water.

Sir William chipped in with a comment. 'They have plans to build a bridge here.'

'I see no need of a bridge' Walt responded.

'Now there are only a couple of feet of water. You should see it after heavy rains or in the spring when the snow thaws. The village can be isolated from the southern road for weeks' Sir William advised.

'But it has been raining,' Walt responded.

'Not so much as it has further south,' Sir William commented.

'Be awhile yet afore we have a bridge, nay money.' Ian Ferguson added laconically.

Sir William led them into the village, where Walt was to share a room with his squire, in an annex built onto the inn to provide for the extra need of the military, and profit of the innkeeper. Sharing suited both of them fine, neither was comfortable with the idea that they might be sleeping alone in the land of the traditional enemy.

Sir William said he would leave them to their own devices, but they may want to see that their men are catered for. 'No arrangements have been made to feed them. You will need to see our quartermaster for that. You and your squire should use the inn and pay the innkeeper.'

'What happens tomorrow?' Walt asked.

'I have no idea; that will be the king's decision. You just sit tight until you hear again from me or receive a message from the king. I think you can reckon on being here until the spring. It's too cold for fighting now.'

'Are there restrictions on our movements?'

'You and your squire can use the village and go to the camp to see your men. Your men will be confined to the camp for at least one week, until the camp commander assesses their demeanour. They may then be allowed to the village. We do not want a border war breaking out here; please make them aware of the rules when you visit, to arrange their sustenance.'

Walt and Aidric rode across the ford and back into the camp towards the area they had seen their men directed to. As they picked their way through tented areas towards their goal, they observed that there must be many thousands of men camped in the glen to the south of the Water of Leith. They passed enclosures of cattle, sheep and swine, also many pens containing fowl. 'Reived from our northern counties, no doubt,' commented Walt. Everywhere they looked there were cooking fires. The whole encampment appeared to be covered in a haze of smoke. They saw smiths beating steel for

127

weapons and making arrowheads, whilst fletchers were at work on the flights with goose feathers. Men sharpening their swords and cleaning armour. These activities seemed to be repeated everywhere they walked through the massive camp.

They found Sergeant Heddon supervising two soldiers who had been designated to look after the horses. The sturdy garrons were confined to a paddock area and fairly immune to the cold with their thick coats. The sergeant assured him that the tents were satisfactory and the men settled in, but hungry. He had already located the quartermaster, who said he would provide some dry rations and arrange for the men to be catered for longer term, on the receipt of suitable payment. Walt had already prepared for this and ensured that some of his secreted money was in his purse. Winter or not, he would have to find some way to let his men earn some money or come to some agreement with the Scottish king. He was certain he did not have enough to last until spring. Leaving Aidric with the Sergeant he made his way to the quartermaster, who took more of his precious gold florins, and said that would be enough for one month.

He returned to the Sergeant and gave him first the good news about the food, and then the bad news, that the village was out of bounds until the camp commander said otherwise.

This task completed, they returned to the inn and Aidric handed their horses to the ostler, taking their saddle bags and groundsheets into their room. The room was very basic. There were two stools, one small table, water ewer and basin, pisspot, and two palliasses with blankets. Dropping their saddle bags, they went directly into the tavern for supper.

The next morning saw Walt bargaining with the quartermaster for eleven second-hand sheepskin coats for the Mitford men. After much bartering which started poles apart, they eventually reached an agreed price, and more importantly, one that Walt could afford. He collected the men and paraded them at the quartermaster's tent, where they were given the best fit available. Nobody complained if the coat was a bit tight or too long. They were grateful for the warmth of the thick fleece lined garments.

Arriving back at the inn, he found Sir William and his squire chatting to Aidric whilst waiting for him to return.

Sir William greeted Walt saying, 'put on your mail, warm coat and make yourself presentable. Bring your sword and shield, no need for your helm. I have already ordered your horse to be made ready, and your squire's, we are to be presented to the King.'

Walt noticed for the first time, that Aidric had indeed already tidied himself up, and was ready to travel.

'Where are we going?' he asked.

'Edinburgh, it is less than an hour's ride.'

As Walt left to make ready, he wished that he had some of the fine clothes that had been left at the manor when he took residence at Horton. Nevertheless, he was sure he could make himself look presentable with what he had. Half an hour later, the four of them were on the road to Edinburgh.

Walt and Aidric were awestruck by the imposing sight of Edinburgh Castle standing majestically on the rock, overlooking the city. When they approached more closely, it was to see that much of the outer defences were destroyed.

'Did that happen when you took the castle before Bannockburn?' Walt asked.

Sir William laughed at the suggestion and replied, 'no, the King ordered the defences dismantled so that if the English were to retake it, they would no longer be able to lord it over the city with strong defences.'

A bit like sticking your sword in your own foot, thought Walt, but he made no comment.

They wound their way up the narrow track to arrive at the castle entrance, where the gate was opened when Sir William was identified. Inside the courtyard a man came to take their horses, and they were shown into a long room and told to wait.

After about half an hour a page appeared and called for Sir Walter Radulf. Walt looked at Sir William, who said, 'I am only your escort; it is you he wants to see.'

Walt followed the page out of the room and up a winding staircase, where they came into a rectangular area with several doors leading from it. The page knocked on one of the doors and a voice shouted for him to enter. He stepped inside, bowed, and then held the door open and ushered in his guest, stepped back outside and closed the door.

Walt was not sure what he expected, perhaps a man wearing a crown sitting on a throne. The man in front of him was sitting on an ordinary chair, to one side of a warm fire. He was dressed as a knight would be, but bareheaded. He looked much as Walt had remembered him from his brief introduction in Galloway, with his father, over twelve years ago. A little older looking he thought, but still an imposing figure.

Walt took a pace into the room, then noticing two sturdy guards standing in the shadows, he sensibly laid down his shield, unbuckled his sword, laying it alongside and bowed deeply in obeisance to Robert de Bruce, King of Scotland.

The king acknowledged his obeisance and spoke. 'Get up young Radulf and take the chair opposite me; I would speak with you about a number of matters.'

Leaving his sword and shield where they were, Walt took the seat as suggested, and sat quietly waiting for the king to speak, not knowing the protocol with kings.

Maybe the king was expecting him to start the conversation, because he opened with. 'Well then, tell me why I have the pleasure of your company in Scotland.'

Walt was surprised that he did not know of the circumstances of his flight, but he went over again the waylaying of the cardinals, Middleton's kidnap of the bishop and his brother and the murder of the soldier; the subsequent capture of Middleton and his men, with the exception of the ones who escaped to join his own troop, and the message that the sheriff was coming to arrest him. He also told him that he had subsequently learned that the Middleton brothers were to be taken to the king's prison in London.

'That is much as I heard it told. I just wanted you to confirm the account for me. I have further news of Sir Gilbert de Middleton and his brother Sir John of Belsay, which will make you glad that you chose your moment to flee.'

Walt felt a cold shiver down his body as he anticipated what the king would say next. King Robert continued. 'The two of them have been sentenced to death; I have no news of the sentence having been implemented.'

'Sire, what of the letter I copied from the cardinals?' Walt asked respectfully.

'That was capital work Sir Walter. The cardinals arrived here one day before your letter. I had no intention of seeing them until I had received your intelligence. After I received your letter, I still made them wait another few days, to steady my temper before receiving them.'

The king paused and Walt waited for him to continue.

Following a moment's thought the king continued. 'They were shown in to my throne room for a formal interview. Firstly, I did not like their lack of suitable obeisance to my majesty, as king of Scotland. Secondly they presented me with a letter, which they said was written by the pope. The letter was addressed to Robert de Bruce. Which Robert de Bruce I asked? You, Sire, they said. I told them that Bruce is a common name in Scotland, and there must be many named Robert Bruce. I was insulted by the lack of proper recognition of my position. I told them they had obviously come to the wrong place, and bade them leave my land immediately by the most direct route.'

'So they did not present the second letter?' Walt asked.

'This was also addressed to someone called Robert Bruce, instead of to His Majesty Robert de Bruce, King of Scotland.'

Walt felt he wanted to burst out laughing at the audacity of the king, but decided to hold a stern countenance, as the king appeared to take the matter most seriously.

The king looked at him closely and then himself, roared with laughter. 'Come on Radulf, I know you find hilarity in the tale, you are allowed to express laughter in my presence, as long as you laugh with me, and not at me.'

Walt let his feelings loose, and laughed heartily at the scene he imagined when the cardinals were ejected.

He thought that now the king was obviously in good humour, this would be a good time to approach his financial difficulties.

He waited a moment for the king to regain his composure and then put his question respectfully.

'Sire, apart from myself and my squire, I have my sergeant and twenty six troopers in your camp at Currie. I am given to understand that there is unlikely to be any action until the spring. When I left Horton in haste I had only limited funds available. I have purchased warm clothing for Middleton's men, and feeding for one month for all of them and their horses. I do not have sufficient funds to purchase for them all for another month. Can I give these men into your service to be given some paid work, so that they may buy for their own needs? I place myself, my squire and men at your disposal.'

The king replied without hesitation. 'You and your men have provided me with a great service already. Have no fear; I shall have the quartermaster refund your payment for feed, but not for the clothing. It may be April or later, before I have further need of you and your men. You may approach the camp commandant and enquire of any tasks he wants done. I am sure he will find plenty to keep them occupied when they are not doing their training.'

At that point the king stood up to signify that the audience was at an end. 'Buckle on your sword and pick up your shield, I will come out with you to greet Sir William and see once again the brave soldier, who is now your squire. It took some courage for him as an English prisoner to demand an audience with the King of Scotland. It was because of his courage that I agreed to see him. Otherwise you may never have got your men back home after Bannockburn.'

Walt followed the king out of the room and down the winding stairs to where the others were patiently waiting.

The three immediately rose from their seats and made obeisance.

The king acknowledged them and walked straight to Aidric. 'Aidric Johansson, congratulations on your promotion to Squire.'

'Thank you, Sire,' mumbled Aidric, astounded that the king remembered his name.

That was it. The king gave instructions to Sir William regarding the refund of the food payment from the quartermaster, and employment of the soldiers. He then bade them all farewell, turned on his heel and headed back up the stairs.

'That was a long audience,' Sir William said, fishing for information.

'Yes it was,' replied Walt not wishing to discuss his private meeting.

They were escorted back to the village where Walt was resigned to settling in for the next three or four months.

***

In Tynemouth, Prior Gregory was keeping up with all the developments regarding the kidnapping. He knew that the Middletons had been rewarded with the most cruel and humiliating punishment in London. He would see no more of them, but why had they not caught Radulf at the same time? In his mind it was total incompetence on behalf of the sheriff and local barons and knights, that they had not organised a simultaneous trap for Sir Walter at Horton. Maybe it was because he had not detained the cardinals, but escorted them on their way after robbing them of a few insignificant items. The robbery worried him as well. Middleton seemed to have gained all the spoils while Radulf had the scraps. He was sure there was something he was missing but he had no idea what.

It did not occur to the prior that despite his intense dislike of Sir Walter, the man had many friends in the area, who would warn him of such traps, or that Sir Walter may have been more interested in the cardinals' reason for their journey than their wealth.

No matter, thought the prior. *Radulf was mixed up in a raid that resulted in robbery, kidnap, ransom and murder. If I get my hands on him he will hang or I am not Prior of Tynemouth.* What specifically annoyed the prior was that Radulf had escaped with a sizable party of men, yet nobody had seen which direction they took, or knew where they had gone. He ground his teeth together in frustration. *Rebels, all of them,* he thought, referring to all of Northumbrian gentry.

Still, things were not so bad after all. His old enemy was on the run somewhere and it was only a matter of time before he had him. He could wait. This year, next year, sooner or later his opponent would make a mistake from which he would not be able to run away.

He was devastated, when only a week later, he heard that the sheriff was no longer interested in Sir Walter. Convinced that there had been collusion to allow his antagonist to escape, he stormed about the priory unable to contain his frustration. For over a week, both monks and nuns kept away from him as much as possible, so foul was his temper, despite the warning he had received from the bishop. The prior's New Year had not been a good one and he wearily wished for improvement. *Any setback for the haughty Radulfs would help,* he thought.

***

Katherine had also suffered some disappointment in the New Year. On the first day of January she had taken Galeron as escort, to pay the traditional visits to the villeins, bearing small gifts. Knowing the hardships many were suffering due to the continuing famine she had determined to give food to each family, according to their needs. These tenants were the poorest, who were allowed to strip farm on the Radulf demesne for a small rental. They received no wages and were obliged to provide labour when called upon; mostly during times of ploughing and harvesting, otherwise they must make their living from their small holdings and a few sheep they were allowed to mark and run amongst the estate flock. They generally lived in two roomed timber framed wattle and daub dwellings. One of the rooms was a byre into which they would bring their few ewes to lamb and shear, and their cow for the winter, to keep the animal warm and help to provide some warmth for the tiny dwelling. They would as likely have no animals left now, with all being either eaten or stolen. In the other room they lived slept and cooked, on the small central hearth with smoke hole above.

Katherine knew that vegetables were in short supply and highly expensive, but had ordered her cook, Emma, to obtain all on the list she had made. She had used some of their reserved flour to have bread baked for each family, and had an old ewe butchered and sectioned to provide a basis for a good potage. All these were bagged up according to the size of the family, marked accordingly, and slung onto a packhorse, along with a keg of ale. Once all was ready she decided to call upon Jeanne first.

Because she knew that she would be away most of the day visiting, Katherine had given Jeanne leave to visit Aidric's holding to ensure that his housemaid was keeping the place in good order and looking after the home and the domestic fowl. The land was being overseen by the estate reeve who visited to check on the farm serfs. She knew that Jeanne would be alone and fretting for her beloved, and although she had the day free from her duties at the manor, Katherine was sure that she would appreciate the visit, as she had seemed reluctant to take the liberty when granted it, saying she was sure the serfs had things in hand.

They found Jeanne busy with the hens, replacing the straw in their nesting boxes. 'What are you doing cleaning the fowl when I gave you a day of rest? That is work for the maid' scolded Katherine good humouredly.

Jeanne looked up from her work. 'I know, My Lady, but I have to keep busy, to keep my mind free of the plight of our menfolk.'

'Perhaps you would like to come to the manor after I have finished my rounds, or if you wish to ride with us you are very welcome. Maybe I should not have condemned you to a lonely day here? You must object a little more forcefully next time Jeanne,' she said, laughingly.

Jeanne, noticing Galeron's obvious amusement with the conversation replied formally. 'Yes, My Lady,' before adding. 'Would you like to step inside into the warm and take some mulled ale, whilst I attire myself in more suitable clothes for visiting, and saddle my horse?'

Galeron interjected before Katherine could reply, 'you go in My Lady; I shall saddle Jeanne's horse whilst she changes.'

Katherine took Jeanne's present, an elaborately crocheted snood for her hair, and followed her inside, where Jeanne called the young servant girl to warm some spiced ale over the fire in the centre of the room, before disappearing into the only other room to change her clothes.

After a small mazer of warm ale to keep out the cold, the rest of the morning was spent visiting villein farmers and distributing the bags of food, which were all most gratefully received. Katherine noted that they were home again soon after midday. Whenever Walt had undertaken this duty alone, it had always been dusk before he returned, and the worse for ale, to boot.

After returning to the manor and partaking of their midday meal, Katherine left Jeanne in the company of Emma, and called upon Galeron's services again to escort her on a visit to her parents. Arriving at the Delaval pele, they were met by Watson, the groom. 'Sir Hugh and Squire Elfric are not back yet. They are still visiting the tenants, My Lady' he said.

'Well I am sure my mother will be here,' responded Katherine, knowing her mother no longer travelled, unless in her carriage, and certainly not in this cold winter weather.

'Oh yes, My Lady, and Master Richard' the groom responded.

Oh, My God, thought Katherine, *Richard is going to be out of sorts, being left as nursemaid to our mother, whilst father and Elfric go around greeting and supping ale.* Katherine handed her horse to the groom. 'Look after Trooper Galeron when you have seen to the horses Watson. Take him to the kitchen and have cook give him a tankard of ale.'

Katherine walked up the steep outside stone staircase to the first floor entrance, saw only the cook in the kitchen, and so ascended the spiral stone staircase to the family room above. There she found her brother Richard, sitting in his father's chair with his body slumped over the table and his right hand gripping the handle of an empty ale tankard. 'Richard, wake up' she shouted. There was no response, so she took the tankard from his hand and proceeded to shake him vigorously by the shoulders.

Richard awoke in ill spirits. 'What the fuck do you think you are doing you stupid cow? Cannot a man have a few winks after ale? Because you are a bloody Radulf now, does not mean you have to treat your brother so roughly.'

'Richard, you do not speak to me in the language of a drunken tavern brute, I am your sister and desire some respect. Why are you so drunk and alone so early in the afternoon, where is Mother?'

'Mother is in her solar resting, she said I was no company for her.'

Katherine left him to sleep, drink, or do as he wished. He was not in a fit state to talk and she well understood why her mother had taken to her solar.

Another flight up the stone spiral and she found Isobel sitting before a small fire, embroidering. She was accompanied by her handmaiden, who since her illness was constantly by her side to assist.

Seeing Katherine, Isobel immediately despatched the servant to obtain beverages for them both, before holding out her arms to greet her daughter.

'What need was there for Richard to remain behind to attend you Mother, have you had another bad turn?'

'No,' he was drunk before they set out to visit the tenants. Your father was furious and ordered him to remain at home. I asked Cecily to help me to my solar, Richard was too drunk, and I did not wish to remain and listen to his blasphemous and foul ranting after Hugh had departed.'

'I thought all that nonsense was behind him after Father sent him away to learn manners and chivalry?'

'Oh it was the drink talking. He was going on about Saxons and Norse occupying land that should be Norman held. His old lament, ever since Freda rejected his advances. No need to worry, Hugh will sort him out when he returns. It was just the ale talking' Isobel concluded.

Katherine was not so sure; she had not liked her brother's attitude at all. *Still,* she thought, *Father will put him in his place when he returns and Mother tells him of his behaviour. If she tells him. She has always been soft on Richard.*

Katherine spent an hour with her mother before taking her leave. Passing through the family room, she found Richard sound asleep and snoring loudly. Ignoring him she continued to the kitchen to pick up her escort who was being entertained by some appreciative maidservants.

On the way home another thought worried her. *I wonder if Father has discussed the situation of the Syhale deeds with Richard?* Without realising, she uttered her next thought aloud. 'My God, I hope not.'

'Is something wrong, My Lady?' her concerned escort asked.

'Just me thinking aloud, Trooper Guddal, please forget it.'

Katherine put her concerns behind her and determined on a sunnier outlook for the New Year. *With testimony from the pope's envoys that Walt did them no harm, feeding them and escorting them safely to the border to continue their journey, the sheriff should look favourably on his plea. Also the bishop should testify that he had no part in his kidnap,* she thought.

====

CHAPTER 6

A treasonable return

Things began to happen at Currie earlier than Walt expected. Just over a week into March of 1318, King Robert de Bruce gathered his forces, which included Walt and his troop of mounted infantry. They were not given an objective but were marched south east towards Berwick for two days, before halting in the forest several miles away.

Walt could not believe they were going to make a frontal attack on Berwick. They would not succeed with such a plan he was sure. Not being privy to the king's military strategy, he discussed the situation with his squire, and they agreed they would just have to wait and see.

Around midnight on the seventeenth of March, they were ordered to move forward to the edge of the forest, nearest to Berwick. There was little moonlight, and movement was difficult and slow. They halted at the edge and were told to sit tight and keep silent.

Dawn was beginning to break when Walt noticed a small party heading across the open ground towards Berwick gate. He nudged Aidric and said quietly, 'they will never get in unless there is treachery afoot.'

Watching carefully they could just make out the party arriving at the gate and, surprisingly, disappearing inside.

'They have been let in' Aidric whispered.

At that moment a figure came out of the gate under the arch and waved a burning torch. That was the signal for a company of Scottish soldiers to run silently across the intervening space and disappear through the gate. Half an hour later they were all signalled to advance. When Walt and his men arrived, the garrison had already surrendered, having been completely taken by surprise. The surrender was so complete that nobody escaped to raise the alarm.

Walt was summoned to the king's presence an hour after dawn. King Robert told him that he now had a campaign for him. 'We are going to press on to the south and take more ground. To the east Wark castle has been captured from the English. Now I am dividing my forces. Half will head west for Harbottle Castle, and the others south beyond Mitford.'

'Who am I to go with, Sire?'

'You Sir Walter, are to command a company of men from the force riding towards Mitford. You will have eighty of my Scottish mounted infantry with their captain, plus your own men, to surprise and capture Mitford Castle. You shall be my Governor of Mitford Castle from that point onwards. The remainder of my force will press on southwards so do not fail me.'

A shocked Walt did not quite know how to respond. After a moment's hesitation, during which time the king glowered at him expectantly, he recovered his wits, quickly realising that he had no option but to comply, and hope for a way out later. 'Thank you, Sire, this is a great honour and I apologise for the delay in my response. I was momentarily surprised that you placed such trust in my loyalty.'

'Trust, and eighty of my men,' replied the king cynically with a nod to his aide, who responded by calling in a Scottish knight unknown to Walt.

'Sir Walter I present your second in command, Captain, Sir Arthur Kerr. Now away with you both, and do my bidding.'

Walt recognised that in order to be sure of surprise they must leave immediately, before news spread to Mitford of the loss of Berwick. He knew that he would need to engineer a way to gain admittance through deception to take control. Even lightly defended, Mitford was still a formidable fortress.

They departed after brief introductions, depending on the men gaining some comradeship during the two days of travelling.

Arriving in the forest near to Mitford in the afternoon of the second day, Walt had determined to take the castle in the early morning, but quickly decided on a change of plan, when they found they had more than one hour left before dusk. Concerned that waiting may give time for word to precede their arrival, he decided to act immediately. He did not know who was occupying the castle, but hoped there would be some of the original troop there, who would know him and his men from his visits to Sir Gilbert.

He explained his plan to Kerr. 'I shall advance with my troop and ask for shelter, and the opportunity to surrender to the sheriff's order. They may have already heard about Berwick but most unlikely to know of my involvement. You remain here with your men, and as soon as we are admitted we shall signal for your advance and hold the gate until you arrive, at a gallop I hope.'

It sounded like a good plan, but the commander of the eighty Scottish soldiers did not trust him, and thought they may enter the castle and betray them. The only way he would agree, was if Walt left behind some of his men as hostages and took some Scots. He demanded that one of the hostages be Squire Aidric, knowing the closeness of the two men.

Walt was exasperated by the mistrust, but if he was to succeed he would have to go along with the idea. He had seven of his own men pair up with seven Scots and told them to exchange tabards. The Scots were not keen on the idea, but Walt pointed out that to gain entry the men must all appear in Radulf colours. After a little grumbling, the clothing was exchanged, and Walt set forth with Sergeant Heddon, seven of his own men and seven Scots. The remaining Scots, along with Aidric, the Syhale and Mitford men, were to wait for his signal and make all haste to the gate as soon as they received it.

Walt ensured that Sergeant Heddon and his own men were to the fore, as they rode casually towards the castle gate. They approached the castle without being challenged. Walt deduced that the castle must be operating with a skeleton staff for the wall not to have a continual lookout. They halted about twenty-five yards from the curtain wall which was part way up the motte and before the bailey, where there was the barbican and main gates to the inner ward and keep. The curtain wall was severely damaged from a previous battle and had never been successfully repaired. There were no gates here, but Walt did not want to appear aggressive by riding directly up to the bailey. He called out, 'hello the castle.'

There was no response.

'Hello the castle,' he called again louder.

This time, there was an answering shout, and a man appeared on the battlements atop the bailey.

'Who are you, what do you want?' He shouted.

'Sir Walter Radulf and his men, returned to accept the order of the sheriff to surrender.'

The man turned and shouted first to someone below, and then to Walt. 'Advance to ten yards from the gates to be recognised.'

Walt urged his horse forward at a walking pace until they were nearer the gates.

'Stay there,' the man said.

The gate opened a small amount, and a man came out and approached them.

Walt recognised the man who walked up to him and looked him and his men over, as Sir Gilbert's squire, Robert Shaftoe. Looking away towards the woods and seeing nothing that gave him concern, Shaftoe asked, 'where are our men that came to join you before you fled from Horton?'

Walt had to think quickly, he had not expected this. 'Sergeant Wilson and his men are with us but are camped some distance away. They refused to come until I sent someone back to say it is safe.'

'Sounds like them' the squire said. 'They ran when the sheriff tricked Sir Gilbert, had they assisted us, he may have escaped.'

Walt shrugged his shoulders. 'They did not tell me that.'

'They would not be likely to, would they?'

'How is it that you were not arrested with Sir Gilbert?' Walt enquired.

Robert Shaftoe gave him an unfriendly look and replied. 'I did not betray him, I was arrested, but released after it was shown that I was away on my master's business at Newcastle at the time of the kidnapping, and only returned as the arrests were being made.'

Walt decided to move the situation on a little. Things seemed to be going to plan so far. 'So, what is the situation here, can you keep us until the sheriff comes for us?'

'No need. The sheriff no longer has any interest in you. On their return from Scotland, the pope's nuncios told him that you helped them to escape kidnapping, and guided them on their way. They did say you relieved them of some small items, but considered that as payment for your help. They also confirmed that it was the soldier you left for the sheriff, who killed one of the earl's escorts.'

Walt's mind was reeling. He was between the devil and his accomplice. If he took the castle he would be once again a wanted man. If he did not, the Scots in his party would raise the alarm and try to do it themselves, and the others would kill Aidric. He had no choice, he had to continue with the plan, to stay alive and safeguard his men's lives.

'Well we have been riding all day to get here, can we come into the castle and rest for the night. I have money to pay for food and lodgings.'

Squire Robert seemed to light up at the prospect of money. Walt immediately grasped the situation. 'If money is a problem, maybe I can be of help. If you are low on food due to shortage of funds, I can help you resolve that, providing there are not too many mouths to feed.'

'We are only ten men. The castle is now in the hands of a knight, Sir Bertram Monboucher, but he has not taken possession. We are supposed to be caretakers, but we have received no pay for a month. Money and credit has just about run out.'

Walt waited no longer. 'Let us go inside then and improve your miserable lot with some fresh provisions in the morning.'

Without further question the squire turned and walked quickly to the gate, shouting for it to be opened and the soldiers admitted. Walt gave Sergeant Heddon a nudge as they passed through the gates into the barbican and out of sight of anyone on the ramparts, the sergeant hung back and made the agreed signal to those waiting in the forest.

***

In the forest, Captain Arthur Kerr was beginning to lose patience. He had seen the man come out from the castle to speak to Walt and they seemed to have spent a long time talking. The Scot was still suspicious of treachery and ordered Aidric brought to him.

'Do you know that man talking to your master?' he asked.

'Sorry Captain, it is too far away to be sure, but I think it is the late Gilbert de Middleton's squire.'

'If that is the case, what the hell is he playing at? Surely they know each other, why is he not already inside?'

'Maybe Squire Robert still needs to be convinced it is safe to admit them.'

The Captain grunted and said, 'if we get no signal in the next few minutes we go anyway.'

Aidric protested, 'Sir, if we go too soon we could cost them their lives. We don't know how many are in the castle and what their reaction may be.'

One of the soldiers watching the castle pulled on his captain's sleeve. 'Sir, something's happening.'

They all concentrated on the tableau in front of the gates.

'Mount up now,' the Captain ordered.

They saw the gates open and the squire pass through, with the rest of the men positioning themselves to follow. At the rear they saw the awaited signal given by Sergeant Heddon. The Captain immediately gave the order to charge, as he gave his horse the spurs and galloped forward, followed by his company.

***

As the last man, Sergeant Heddon was passing into the gate, there was a frantic shout from the sentry atop the barbican. Squire Robert turned and shouted to the sergeant to shut the gates quickly. Too late, he realised that Walt's men had positioned themselves inside the gates and were making no effort to close them. He looked at Walt with an expression of abject betrayal and hatred on his face.

Walt said. 'I think squire; that you will find I am in command of Mitford castle now, on behalf of His Majesty Robert de Bruce, King of Scotland.

The squire gave him a malevolent stare. 'You are a traitor to your king Sir Walter, and you will lose your head for this.'

'My king has done nothing for me or mine for many years, and your late master lost his head for a rebellion, which you also joined, or have you forgotten? You will not lose your head to these men approaching the gate, you have my word. You and your men may stay and join us or go. You have until tomorrow morning to decide. Any action against me or my party will be put down mercilessly.'

The Scots and the remainder of Walt's men galloped into the castle. Sergeant Heddon and his men closed the gate behind them.

Walt introduced Squire Robert to the Scottish captain, explaining that he was the squire of the late brother of Sir William de Middleton, who the captain knew well. With the tension eased somewhat, he ordered Squire Robert to call all his men together, as he wished to address them. Behind him, he was amused to see, that the priorities for some of his men seemed to be getting their tabards back from the Scots.

Walt repeated his offer to all Squire Robert's men, except the servants, such as cooks, groom and the like. They were told that they worked for him now and that they had no option.

The following morning Squire Robert and his men expressed their wish to leave. They were searched before they left and relieved of any money in their purses. The price of freedom, they were told.

Captain Arthur Kerr had been given money for sustenance by Bruce. If that was not enough, they would have to go out and forage for their needs, he had been told. They were a strong party and there were no militia in this area that could resist them. Walt discussed this with the captain, and they decided that Walt would take a party out the next morning to purchase necessities. Following that they would decide according to their needs whether to buy or forage.

For now, Walt decided, they must pool the food they had brought with them, and get the cook and the servants to combine it with any supplies remaining in the castle, to produce a meal for tonight and breakfast for the morning.

***

March at Syhale proved to be normal for the season, with strong winds. Because there had been little snow over the winter the land was not water logged and the winds soon dried it out. They were able to do spring ploughing and get the land prepared and seeded. David Reeve reported that the remaining sheep were free of disease and all ewes due to lamb. The news gave Katherine great encouragement and she said a private prayer to thank God.

Not wishing to ride herself, she had sent Galeron with the reeve to visit all the tenancies and ensure that they were all taking advantage of the opportunity to plough and plant. They subsequently reported back that all was well. Katherine was desperately worried about reivers taking advantage of the first good news for three years. She knew they did not have enough protection if they were raided for lambs. She ordered Galeron to take some of his men, and under the guidance of David Reeve to build a large fenced area in the meadow, where they could keep watch easily and corral the sheep for lambing. She used some of her scarce funds to arm some of the labourers with bows, and put them with the soldiers as night guards.

Thus far all was well, and Katherine delighted in telling a sceptical Jeanne that it was as a result of their sacrifice to almighty God at early morning mass in January. Jeanne thought, uncharitably, why she didn't pray years ago after the first failed harvest, but she said nothing, merely smiled and nodded agreement.

Katherine's pregnancy was now plain to see, and Jeanne guessed she would have been about two months gone at the time of her prayers. She now understood why her mistress had wanted to make the sacrifice of early Mass before breakfast. Once again, a sceptical Jeanne wondered if she had been praying for a successful birth, or for it to go away. As soon as the thought entered her head, she was ashamed; she knew that Katherine's adherence to Christ would never allow her to pray for such a sin.

It was her brother Richard who brought the news of Walt to Katherine, telling her that he was holding Mitford Castle with a party of Scots. He had always been respectful since his drunken outburst on New Year's Day, but today although respectful, she could not but notice a satisfied smirk on his face, as if saying. *I told you so.*

Nevertheless, Katherine collapsed into a chair with relief, and called for Jeanne. When she heard the news, the pair of them hugged each other with joy, before realisation of the situation sank into their minds and joy turned to sadness.

Embarrassed, Richard could only try to mutter trite words of encouragement that fell onto deaf ears. Afraid of seeming uncaring and risking another telling off from his father, Richard announced his departure.

Katherine pulled herself together enough to thank him for coming, and ask to be kept advised of any further developments. Jeanne stood up and suggested she make them both a chamomile beverage to calm their nerves.

Alone again and sipping their chamomile, the two women, pleased that their men were safe at Mitford for the moment, began to take stock of the situation.

Jeanne was the first to say what they were both thinking. 'How can they be safe under a Scottish flag in England?'

'They could hang for this' Katherine said, sadly.

Jeanne replied 'they have to catch them first; we don't know how many they are in the castle. There is no army up here to get them out unless the king brings one.'

'Do you think we will be able to see them, I am really missing Walt,' Katherine said.

'And I Aidric, but I doubt they will come here. It would be too dangerous. If they did they would have to come with a strong armed party, and that would put us in jeopardy as fellow conspirators. They would never want that.'

Katherine thought through the situation for a while then replied. 'Let us wait and see. They will be missing us as much as we miss them. They will think of something. You will see.'

***

News of the taking of Mitford Castle by the Scots, under the command of Sir Walter Radulf, soon spread throughout the land. Further south at the king's court, it was considered unimportant, and just another minor irritation from the Scots. 'Probably a good thing that there should be this type of disruption and raids in Northumberland anyway,' commented the Earl of Lancaster who was effectively running the country. 'They are a rebellious lot who need to be taken down some. It will make them more cooperative, when the king's rule of law is restored.'

The king however, was more interested in the Scottish occupation of Berwick. This was his border bastion and as such reflected directly on his ability to control his borders. Something would have to be done about Berwick.

Some of the Northumberland knights and barons were against Sir Walter's action, not because he had occupied Mitford, but because he had involved Scots. The castle, although in poor condition, would not be easily taken without a large force and the necessary engines to breach the walls. It was concluded that there were no garrisons strong enough to take Mitford without heavy losses, and probably none with the will to try, and there were no siege engines in the area.

Sir Walter still had many friends in the area, many of whom were also a little too friendly with Scots. Bruce was conducting guerrilla raids and not generally occupying the land so they would have to give up sooner or later. Until that time came, or they received a direct order from the king, the High Sheriff decided, they would ignore the occupation.

=====

CHAPTER 7

Desertion and isolation

At Tynemouth priory the news about Mitford was like music to the ears of Prior Gregory. *The fool has done it now,* he thought. *It is only a matter of time before I can get my revenge. When he is caught they will bring him here to Tynemouth Prison, if I have my way.* He spent the next few hours supping ale, and speculating on his best course of action, to ensure that his hated enemy received the maximum punishment. He knew that the actual trial would be certain to take place elsewhere, but he would find ways to ensure the evidence against Sir Walter was maximised. There was no doubt in his mind that his old adversary would hang.

The prior was now going through a period of good grace and good will to all. The monks and the nuns of Tynemouth priory were grateful for his good humour, but suspicious of the reasons for such a happy prior.

***

At Mitford, relations with the Scots had remained very much on a formal basis, and especially since their captain's distrust over the capture of the castle, there had been little fraternisation. There only remained a respectful and businesslike relationship for the purpose of discipline and good order.

It was on Friday the fifteenth of April, that Captain Kerr told Walt that he intended to take his men on a foraging expedition, for livestock and other foodstuff. He had paraded all his men in the castle courtyard and split them into four troops. He did not shout his orders but talked to each troop commander in turn, before marching over to Walt and asking him to get the cook to bank up the fires for a banquet when they returned.

After they had departed, Walt called Aidric and Sergeant Heddon. 'I have a strange feeling about this foraging; he has taken all his men. When we took over the castle he went to great lengths to ensure that there was no way we could betray him and lock him and his men out. Now he takes them all for an expedition better done with about twenty men. I know he has split them in four troops, but I believe that was just for our benefit. Why did he speak quietly to each troop leader? He always shouted all his orders before.'

'Do you think they are not coming back?' Aidric asked.

'That is exactly what I think, Squire. I also think it was planned like this, and that my friend Bruce found us an embarrassment in Scotland, and this was a good way to get rid of us and make us useful to him at the same time.'

'You mean we have been abandoned? How will we hold our position now?' Sergeant Heddon asked.

'Who's going to take it off us? Nobody around here has a troop of more than around twenty men and they are too busy trying to protect their own lands to worry about us. One that has, like Sir Henry Percival, is not going to venture with them out of Alnwick. Besides, if the Scots have gone, we shall hoist the Cross of Saint George, and I can claim we are looking after the castle for the king now.'

'You can try that one but I doubt it will work, Sir.' Aidric responded.

The Scots did not return at nightfall, as Walt had predicted. They were now on their own. Many of the men expressed the view that they preferred it this way and felt more secure than before.

Walt agreed with this sentiment. Food and supplies would no longer be such a problem. The Scots had taken nothing with them that was not theirs so they had plenty of food for tonight, and would be able to eat well. Tomorrow he would review their situation again. Without enemy in the castle, it opened up new opportunities for various actions. It did not occur to Walt that the men he was now calling enemy were only that morning allies. Such was the pragmatism of Northumberland life on the borders during the Scottish wars.

The following morning, Walt called Aidric and Sergeant Heddon for a discussion on their tactics. He opened with, 'I have a mind to visit my wife, gentlemen, and how would you feel about visiting your womenfolk?'

His two subordinates looked astonished. 'Is it not too dangerous, Sir, what if we get caught?' Aidric responded.

'We will not get caught because we will not go together, or on the same day. I will leave tonight at dusk; it is only twelve miles, if I ride hard I will be there in around an hour, as darkness falls.

I shall call at the mill, and tell your Daisy you are well Sergeant, before continuing to the manor. I will leave early in the morning before sunup. All I ask is that you stand by to open the gate quickly when I return. I do not want a situation where I may be pursued and find myself locked outside. If the pursuing party were to be so big, and so close that you dare not open the gate, or could not chase them away, then you may lock me out.'

Aidric responded as if he had received a personal insult, by the suggestion that he may leave his lord locked out of his own castle. 'As you said before, Sir, nobody around here has a troop that big, so that will not happen.'

That day, four of them went on a foraging trip under Sergeant Heddon. They returned with two small pigs, an old ewe which would do well for potage, and a bag full of chickens.

Walt sent another two to the nearby village to purchase bread and fresh vegetables, using some of his precious cash resources.

In the late afternoon he went to the stables to inspect his trusty garron. The animal looked to be in fine condition, and the groom reported that horse feed was still plentiful, especially now the Scots had left. He asked the groom to have his horse saddled and ready before dusk this evening.

Later when he departed, he skirted the nearby village, and picked up a little used track south towards Syhale, he was in his own territory, and knew the area like the back of his hand.

***

Katherine was taking her supper with Tilly and the children. Jeanne, also invited to join them, was being treated more like a family member by Katherine as the days wore on. Katherine found great comfort in Jeanne's optimistic approach to life; she was like a soul mate, always seeming to come up with similar ideas. Katherine and Jeanne had the eldest two children sat next to them, and on the other side of the table was Tilly with James on her knee and Hugh sat alongside with a box on the bench to raise him to the correct height. James could feed himself, but Tilly had two bowls of mutton potage, one for herself, and a smaller portion in another from which she was feeding Hugh.

There was a good fire burning in the fireplace, and a kettle of chamomile beverage keeping warm in front of it. Those around the table were busy, either chattering or paying attention to their meal, and took little notice of a small disturbance in the kitchen. Cook and the others girls were always getting excited about something or other, which would result in the odd squeals of delight, or loud laughter emitting from the kitchen area.

Katherine, Jeanne and the older children were sitting with their backs to the fireplace and the door to the kitchen. It was Tilly, on the other side of the table who let out the wild shriek of delight that startled them.

'What on earth is the matter Tilly?' Katherine asked as she turned to look in the direction of the kitchen door that Tilly was pointing to.

'Oh my God,' she said, as she saw Walt coming through the doorway. She leapt out of her chair; and despite her now not unnoticeable swollen figure, made record time to the doorway and threw her arms around him. She was irritated that she could no longer reach easily round his waist because of her condition. This did not worry Walt, as he took a firm hold on her, and kissed her with passionate feeling. He gently released her and then went to each of the children, giving them a great hug and a kiss. He turned and saw Jeanne standing, looking forlorn and waiting for him to say something. He walked across to her, and to everyone's great surprise, especially Jeanne's; he put his arms around her and gave her a big friendly kiss.

'Sir Walter!' She exclaimed with genuine shock. 'What will Lady Katherine think?'

'That was a present from Aidric, to say he is fit and well.' Walt told her.

Katherine laughed aloud, and reassured her that she understood, it was just a kiss being delivered.

'It would be nicer if he could deliver it in person,' Jeanne said, looking at Walt hopefully.

'He soon will, Jeanne, he soon will,' Walt assured her, 'and he already has my permission for any suggestions he may make.'

Jeanne's face lit up like a beacon, as she withdrew with embarrassment.

Walt walked around the table again, giving Tilly a hug and a chaste kiss on the cheek, so that she did not feel left out.

Greetings over, he then sat down with them, and Annie brought him a bowl of potage and a tankard of ale. She had such a glow on her face that Katherine wondered if he had kissed all the servants in the kitchen as well. *Oh my,* she thought, *he is feeling fruity, and here is me, with my swollen belly. Perhaps he would rather have Annie or Tilly.*

After they had finished their evening meal, Tilly took the children to bed, whilst Katherine asked how long he would stay.

He explained the situation, telling her that it was only safe to stay the night, and leave early in the morning. He told them that he had visited the mill and advised Daisy of the plans for visits. He, Aidric and Sergeant Heddon would alternate their visits. The visits must be on irregular days in case of traps but would usually be at night. Walt explained about the circumstances of their occupation of Mitford.

Katherine listened quietly, before replying. 'Bruce used your predicament to his own advantage, as he will always do Walt. So how long do you expect to remain as Governor of Mitford Castle, in defiance of the king?'

'So far, nobody has shown any interest in our occupation of Mitford, and now the Scots have gone they will probably not bother us. We shall sit it out, however long it takes, until we have some guarantee of immunity from prosecution. In the meantime we have raised the cross of Saint George above the keep.'

'It will need more than that my dearest, for you to get out of this new predicament. Have you got money for food?' Katherine asked.

'Not much left, how are your finances?'

'I think we will just last until we sell the fleeces and some old ewes for mutton. Take a ewe with you for potage when you leave.'

'The sale of the wool went well last year so same again, take all the wool from our tenants, as we shall not have the Middleton fleeces any more. Thank you for the ewe, we have been foraging for some food, but it worries me, as the people in this area are our friends. You can tell anyone who complains that we will pay later. I know what I took and from where' Walt instructed.

With Tilly now upstairs with the children, they were interrupted by Jeanne, who sought permission to retire and give them their privacy.

'One important request first Jeanne,' Walt asked. 'Please ensure that you awaken us at first light.'

'You can be sure I shall not fail you, Sir,' Jeanne replied, as she bade them goodnight.

Katherine watched her leave, and then kissed her husband fondly. He allowed himself to be led docilely by the hand, up the stairs to their bedchamber.

In the privacy of their room, Walt took her again in his arms and kissed her properly, until her heart was thumping as if trying to escape her chest. He gently undressed her and caressed her swollen belly. She took his hand and held it against it.

'Feel it kicking?'

'Yes I can feel him, he feels very strong. I think he is trying to escape.'

'Here we go again with the him. It may be a her.'

'Definitely him, he's already wearing his riding boots.'

'That's enough of that; you will have to wait and see, only a couple of months now Walt. Come, get undressed and come to bed, I'm getting cold.'

Once in bed they caressed and cuddled. Katherine could feel that Walt was seriously aroused. She no longer wondered how he could fancy her when she looked like a fat sow; she had had four children before, and that had never put him off, besides, she was feeling very warm and receptive, and she knew exactly what to do to satisfy both of their desires.

As they lay exhausted following their lengthy love making, Katherine turned slowly towards her husband. She caressed his face lovingly, leaned over and kissed him.

'My God Katherine, not again,' Walt moaned. 'I am done in.'

'I just do not want to sleep yet Walt, please talk to me for a while. You come home, we go to bed and make love, we sleep and you leave. Do you know what that is like for me Walt?'

'The same as it is for me I imagine Katherine, but what would you have me do? You know I dare not risk staying longer, and you coming to Mitford is not even to be considered.'

'That is not what I mean Walt. Can we talk about our situation and how we are to get out of it?'

He turned toward her and kissed her gently on her soft lips. 'At this time my dear, I can see no way out of my predicament. I am unlikely to be pardoned, and at worst I shall lose my head, at best, spend the rest of my days in the king's prison in London. I shall find out soon if I have any friends left in the north. I think the sheriff is sympathetic; he is not making any move towards ousting me.'

'Father says that he is sounding out knights who have the king's ear.'

'He will have a difficult task, to find knights who are not known as rebels but would risk exposure by helping me.'

Katherine was not to be outdone, 'what about Baron Percy of Alnwick?'

'The baron is favourable to rebels, but will want to keep low because it is said that he plots with other barons for the removal of the Despensers from the king's court.'

'But maybe he knows others who have influence with the king.'

'That maybe, but little gets to the king without first passing through the Despensers' hands. Now my dearest, may I have my sleep?'

'Soon,' she replied as she pulled him closer and gently ran her hand down his belly.

Walt gave in. 'Come on then, take what you want of me wife, and afterwards we shall sleep.'

Jeanne came at first light to awaken her master as instructed. She had to knock many times on the door before gaining a response.

'What is it?' came the sleepy reply from Katherine.

'First light, My Lady. It is time for Sir Walter to arise and break his fast.'

'Go away Jeanne, it is too early and we are tired.'

'I cannot do that, My Lady, the Master gave me strict instructions that he was to be awakened at first light.'

'Oh, my God Jeanne, do you always have to be so bloody efficient? Walt, wake up,' and again louder, 'Walt, wake up.'

Jeanne heard a loud groan, followed by some quiet muttering beyond the door. 'Sir, are you awake now?' she called.

'Yes Jeanne I am awake. Now bugger off and make ready for my breakfast, I shall be down in two shakes of a lamb's tail.'

Walt was not down in two shakes. It was over half an hour before he appeared. 'No bloody porridge this morning Jeanne, tell Emma, I want bacon, eggs and anything else she can put with it. I need strength for my journey.'

He looks more tired than when he dismissed me last evening, Jeanne thought. *And I wager I know why.*

After eating a hearty meal of bacon, eggs and pig's blood sausage; he collected his horse from the groom and galloped off to the north, and Mitford.

Katherine did not put in an appearance until mid morning. Jeanne bade her, 'good morning,' with a knowing smile. Her mistress made no comment, ate her breakfast and immediately sought out Tilly and the children who were outside in the yard, having been up on time to see their father off.

====

CHAPTER 8

The prior seeks revenge

Throughout the remainder of April things continued to go well, and all at Syhale had their hopes up for a successful shearing towards the end of May or early June. So far this year the weather had returned to a normal spring pattern and all were hopeful that they had seen the end of the persistent rainfall of the last three years.

Following Walt's first tarriance there had been a visit by Aidric on Saturday evening, returning Sunday morning to Mitford at first light, the last day of April.

Before seeking out Jeanne at the manor, he had visited his own small farm to ensure that his serfs were maintaining the land in good order. Sir Walter's reeve was paying regular visits to give instructions but he still wanted reassurance. After satisfying himself with the outcome, he hastened to the manor to see his beloved.

Not wishing to compromise Jeanne's reputation by taking her into his home unaccompanied by a chaperone, where they would be observed by their servant and any nearby field worker, Aidric rode with her to the old barn, where they could be alone. He was disappointed to find the barn in a poor state of cleanliness due to cattle having been housed there over the winter. With the dim light entering through cracks in the boarded walls, they managed to clean a corner and find some straw to spread under their groundsheet. Aidric stood in front of her on the groundsheet and slowly dropped to his knees. He took Jeanne's hand gently in his own and looked into her eyes.

'Jeanne Jensen, will you honour me, by becoming my wife?' he said.

Jeanne had been expecting his proposal, after Sir Walter had let slip that his permission had been sought, but she was not going to spoil Aidric's day. She looked suitably surprised, but could not conceal her delight, as she fell on top of him shouting. 'Yes, yes, a thousand times yes, I thought you were never going to ask me.'

'Thank you for honouring me dearest Jeanne. Tonight when I return you to the manor I shall pay a visit to Father Livio. We are in no position to hold a celebration at the moment, so we will just have the service, and celebrate in better times. Whoever is free to attend the service may do so. I will ask the good father if it can be arranged as soon as possible and conducted when I next visit.'

When Jeanne had finished agreeing with everything he said, Aidric turned to her and with mock seriousness he continued. 'Jeanne, you must ask your mistress to get someone to clean this place out.'

'For what purpose should I say that I was here to see the need, and why should I be interested?'

'Do you think she doesn't know where we go? Just ask her, you will see.'

'You ask her then.'

'Alright, now come here and let me show you how much I have missed you, I don't know when I will be able to make another visit.'

'Are you trying to hurry me up Aidric?'

'No my dearest Jeanne, that is the last thing I want to do, take as much time as you like and enjoy it.'

The following morning Aidric had an early breakfast in the family room with Jeanne and Katherine. Tilly was still upstairs getting the children dressed.

Aidric put down his porridge spoon, turned to Katherine and said. 'Lady Katherine, would it be possible that you could ask the reeve to have someone clean out the old barn down near the mill, please?'

Jeanne choked on her porridge, and Katherine, without any hesitation and with serious countenance said. 'Of course Squire Aidric, it should always be cleaned after use in order that the next occupants have a clean floor for bedding their horses down. I shall speak to the reeve immediately after breakfast. How did you know it was dirty?'

Aidric and Jeanne stared at each other, wondering what to make of her answer, and what to say next, when Katherine, unable to contain herself any longer, burst into laughter.

A seriously embarrassed Squire Aidric made haste to bid them both farewell, and departed for Mitford, leaving Jeanne to tell them her news in her own time. He came to the ford by the mill and saw that the occupants were up and about. Young John West was working in the mill race. The water had been diverted and he was busy clearing river weed from the wheel. He called a greeting as

Aidric approached and dismounted. Inside, Aidric found Daisy busy clearing away their breakfast bowls, and Henry West finishing off some hot beverage. He said good morning to Henry, and walked over to shake his hand. Henry did not display his normally cheerful attitude and only grudgingly held out his hand. Daisy came around the table and gave Aidric a kiss on the cheek, and asked when she may see Nicholas.

Aidric whilst still facing Daisy and sensing a strained atmosphere, let his eyes roll towards Henry and said. 'Soon, probably in a few days, but I can't say when.'

'Would you come into my private room a moment please, Squire, I have a little something I would like you to take to Nicholas.'

'Of course,' Aidric said following her into the room, where she closed the door behind them.

'What is it Daisy? Is something bothering you?'

'Henry West asked me to marry him.'

'And what was your reply?'

'Oh, Squire Aidric, you must know my reply was a firm no. I love Nicholas and no other.'

'Henry had no business asking you, without having first sought permission of Sir Walter, and he should know that.'

'I told him that as well. He has been moody ever since. I think you noticed his miserable demeanour when you greeted him. I am afraid that if he does not accept my answer and get on with his work as before, it may become impossible for me to remain here.'

'I will speak to Sir Walter, and he will surely have a solution when he comes next.'

'Thank you, Squire, now here is a packet of oatcakes I baked for Nicholas. Please give him my love, and please do not tell him about Henry, I would not want to worry him.'

They moved back into the kitchen, where the grumpy Henry was moving sharply across the room, towards the mill room. Aidric wondered if he had been listening at the door. He bade them both a cheery goodbye, receiving only a suspicious look from Henry and a grunt in response.

**

Henry Miller went into the mill room, thinking to take his mind from the recent events by milling some corn. He had no sooner entered than he noticed that the main shaft was not turning, and remembered that he had sent John out to clean out the weed from the mill race. Walking outside he saw the lad had just climbed out and was lifting the sluice gate to allow the water back through the race.

He called his son over and told him what had transpired, and how he thought their jobs may be in jeopardy, as a result of that woman's tale telling. Convinced that she had forgotten about her stupid sergeant, he had thought to make himself master of the mill. He was now feeling most resentful, about both her refusal, and the words he had heard through the door to Daisy's private room. *That bloody squire would tell his master, and they would lose their jobs. It was not his fault, how could he ask permission when the lord was not here.*

John, having listened quietly without interruption, said. 'Father, we know that they come at night to see their family. Her sergeant has not yet been, maybe he is not allowed to leave the castle. What if Sir Walter were to be caught? Who then would think of us, or your small error of not seeking permission to court Mrs Miller?'

'I think you have it, Son. I have heard that the prior of Tynemouth has vowed revenge for some one time insult. I have an idea of what we can do. You go out and close the sluice gate again. Wait until the water is down and the wheel stopped then open it. I will be inside with an iron bar applying goose grease to the wooden shaft and millwheel cogs. When the wheel suddenly takes off again the bar will be obstructing the cogs, and there should be sufficient damage to put the mill out of action. We will claim it as an accident, and I shall ride hastily to Tynemouth, to seek the carpenter to make the necessary repairs. Whilst there, I shall make sure that the right ears know about the clandestine overnight visits to the manor.'

'Father, the mill could be out of action for weeks if you break the cog.'

'Worth it if we can get the lord of the manor out of our way.'

The plan worked. A cog was broken on wooden pinion which drove the large crown wheel attached to the vertical shaft driving the millstone.

Daisy was beside herself at the disaster, but had to accept that it was a careless error, due to poor communication between father and son.

As expected, Henry was despatched to Tynemouth to bring the craftsman who could make a new piece. Once there he quickly located a carpenter who could undertake the work, but spun out his stay until the morning, to allow time for a visit to the priory. 'To attend mass and pray for a successful repair,' he had told the carpenter who had been willing to leave the same day.

Prior Gregory had attended evening mass and was leaving the priory church to return to his quarters when a man approached him from the congregation. He called quietly. 'May I speak with you privately, Prior, Sir?'

Annoyed at the interruption to his routine Prior Gregory replied abruptly. 'No. You must see my clerk in the morning and make an appointment.'

'It's about Sir Water Radulf, Prior.'

Prior Gregory stopped in his tracks, and turned to face the man. Seeing his attire, he immediately judged him to be a person of no importance. He asked him in an abrupt manner.

'And who might you be?'

'I am Henry West, employed as miller at Syhale manor, Sir.'

Prior Gregory felt a leap of optimism. Maybe God was going to reward him at last. 'Come with me Henry West,' he said, leading him to his private quarters.

Once seated in his quarters, and his new found friend plied with a tankard of ale, the prior asked. 'Well, what is it you have to tell me?'

'Sir, I have discovered that Sir Walter and his accomplices make regular visits to their womenfolk, travelling at dusk or dawn. They always come down through the forest and over the Seaton Burn ford, by the mill.'

'Why would you want to betray your master like this,' the prior asked, suspecting some sort of trick to get money out of him.

'The old miller's widow and I would be wed, but the master has forbid it, and he will likely now use a breakdown of the mill to force me and my son to be replaced.'

'How much reward do you expect for this information?'

'Only as much as you think it is worth, Prior, Sir.'

Prior Gregory was satisfied. The man had a grudge, and that was a good enough reason. He went to the door and called a novice to find Brother Cornelius.

When the treasurer arrived he indicated he should bend close and whispered his instructions.

Brother Cornelius left, to return around fifteen minutes later with a small canvas purse drawn together with a string.

Prior Gregory took the small purse, and tossed it onto the table in front of Henry.

'There you have two gold florins. Take it as your reward for your information, but beware. If you cross me you will rue the day you were born. Now go and speak to no one about this visit. Do you understand?'

'Yes, Prior.' Henry replied, unable to believe his luck. He had saved his job, probably got the widow, so would soon have the mill. Unable to comprehend so much money in his hand at one time, he thanked the prior profusely, as he backed out of the door with head bowed, and left in haste before his benefactor could change his mind.

As soon as he was alone with the prior, the treasurer asked what the money was for.

'Just write it up as priory expenses; you think of something, it's your job,' the prior snapped. He was not going to tell Brother Cornelius his business.

He knew exactly who the right man for this job was. Brother Saul, his scribe and close associate for all things secret. He walked through to his office but he was not there. He shouted for Brother Richard who always seemed to be hanging around somewhere, he wondered sometimes if he listened at doorways. The novice appeared from the shadows as usual and was asked to fetch Brother Saul immediately to the prior's private quarters.

When the scribe arrived, Prior Gregory told him that he had a secret mission. 'Go into town and fetch me the man known as Badger, you know where to find him, and I want him immediately. Tell him he will be paid, and don't come back without him.'

One hour later Badger, a known local gang leader and sometime robber, was ushered into the prior's quarters, where he was given lengthy instructions and warnings by Prior Gregory. Under no circumstances was the prior's name or the priory to be linked with this project. He was to recruit at least four others and the task was to capture Sir Walter, although his squire or his sergeant from Mitford would also be useful, if either could be captured at the same time. They were not to target them unless they first had Sir Walter. There would be no money without him.

Badger looked uneasy about the dangers of such an adventure, but the prior soon won him round with the promise of substantial rewards, and advised them of the best place for an ambush.

'Be sure to keep well away from the manor to avoid an encounter with any of Radulf's troopers,' he said. 'Detour around the southern side of the estate both on your way and afterwards on your return, and deliver the prisoner to Tynemouth gaol. The governor will be expecting you.'

'What about horses for me and my men?' Badger asked.

The prior replied impatiently, annoyed because he had not thought of that himself. 'Go now and round up your men ready for travel. I will have Brother Saul bring five horses saddled to the inn. He will wait for you there. Make sure your men are suitably armed; remember the man you are to capture is a knight.'

'We will have him before he knows we are there,' the rogue bragged as he turned to hurry back to town.

'He must be alive; there will be no money for a dead knight. I care not about the condition of the others, but the knight must be taken to the gaol alive,' the prior shouted after him, as he passed through the door.

Prior Gregory congratulated himself on his swift actions. It was still Tuesday and not yet midday. With luck his men would be in place well before dusk and ready to catch any night riders. He just hoped the idiots did not catch the wrong man and spoil it all by showing their hand too soon. They would just have to lie low and wait, however long it took.

On his return to the mill on Tuesday with the carpenter, his apprentice and their cart, carrying suitable materials and tools for the job, Henry explained to Daisy that he had considered it too late after locating the craftsman to return the same day. He made no mention of mass or the priory.

***

Following an uneventful return to Mitford, Aidric first sought out Walt, and explained about his visit to the mill and the uncomfortable atmosphere there. Sir Walter gave the response that Aidric expected.

'She is not going anywhere. She is my mill tenant, and has the knowledge to run it, she only requires paid labour to operate it and carry sacks of corn and flour. The situation cannot continue. That woman does not need any more grief in her life, leave it to me, I will think on a solution. Have you seen Sergeant Heddon yet?'

'No, Sir.'

'When you see him give him Daisy's wishes, but say nothing of this matter, or he will not think for his own safety and probably make a rash decision.'

Walt dismissed Aidric to go and greet his friend, but not before he gave him a dig in the ribs and said. 'Well, did you ask her then?'

Aidric nodded, 'she said yes, and we are to be married quietly on my next visit. We agreed to have our celebration when everyone could join in at a later date.'

Walt was pleased for him, but thought. *I shall have to see what can be done for a wedding feast.*

The next day was the first of May, and still no representation from any authority to demand he vacate the castle. *Surely they have not forgotten about me,* Walt thought. He began to daydream about a peaceful handover of the castle and living at Syhale again, when he was interrupted by Sergeant Heddon.

'There are two men at the gate to see you, Sir.'

'Do they have names Sergeant?'

'John of Unsworth, and William of Washington, Sir.'

'I have never heard of them. Both the places mentioned are far to the south of here. Do you know what they want?'

'No, Sir they said they had a private delivery to be given only to you.'

'Get Squire Aidric to join me here, and then get three men to go to the gate with you. Have the watch scan the surrounds carefully for any other hidden men, and then if all is clear, let them in and close the gates immediately behind them. Ensure that they are disarmed and bring them to me with their delivery.'

The sergeant left to carry out his orders.

Aidric arrived and Walt told him of the situation, asking him to stand guard behind the door in case of treachery.

After a short time had elapsed, the two men were ushered into the room by Sergeant Heddon. One of them was carrying saddlebags over his shoulder and he stepped a pace forward.

'Sir, I am John of Unsworth and I am a messenger from King Robert of Scotland.'

Walt pointed at the other man, 'and you?'

'William of Washington, Sir, I am his escort.'

'Well he's here now and safe. Sergeant Heddon, take William away and give him food and drink.'

'Now John of Unsworth, what have you for me?' Walt asked after the escort had left with the sergeant.

The man walked forward and dropped the saddlebags on the table, and then stepped respectfully back to his original position.

Walt opened one of the bags and looked inside. It contained a large quantity of gold florins. He opened the other one and there were more gold florins and a sealed parchment. He opened the parchment knowing by the seal that it was indeed from Bruce.

He saw that it was a declaration that he was being paid two hundred marks for services rendered. He was instructed not to pay the messengers, as they would be paid twenty marks for the delivery when they returned with his signature of receipt.

Walt pulled over his inkwell and quill, and signed his name on the bottom of the parchment. He asked Aidric to fetch a burning candle or lamp. This done he resealed the parchment and handed it back to the man, with the question.

'What are men from Sunderland area doing with Bruce?'

'We were captured at Bannockburn, Sir; we have no family alive so we stayed to work in Scotland. We are useful to carry messages in England, and not suspected here because of our northern accents. The king pays us well for such dangerous missions and we have been so sustained during the poor years of famine.'

'Where are Bruce's armies now?'

'He was into Yorkshire, Sir, as there was little left for plunder in Northumberland, He is now returning to Scotland and avoiding any confrontations, to concentrate on getting his spoils back to Scotland.'

'So I see. Aidric take this man to Sergeant Heddon where he may take refreshment with his friend. When they are finished, see them off the castle grounds.'

164

Walt waited until they were gone and tipped the money out onto his table. There was now no longer any such coin as the mark in England, but the value was often used for accounting purposes as a hangover from Saxon times. *Two hundred marks being the equivalent of one hundred and fifty pounds, which in anybody's reckoning is a great deal of money,* he thought. *How much of this has been contributed by Northumberland, and Cumberland?*

Putting aside such thoughts, he quickly piled the French and Italian florins into respective piles on his table and did a quick calculation. Due to the higher value of the Italian coin he soon established that there was in fact a little more than stated. Bruce had been generous with his count.

All this money put a different light on things now. He had enough money to sustain them in the castle for a considerable time, and to give some to Katherine to help out with the wages until the fleeces were sold.

He would resolve the mill problem on the next visit to Syhale and at the same time take the money for Katherine.

Walt decided to take some of the money out of the saddlebags and secrete it away here in the castle. He took his time studying the room, sure that there must be a place here that past masters of the keep had used. Taking his dagger, he went carefully around the room, checking for signs in the walls and floor. He finally found a slab in the floor in a dark recess at the end of the room underneath a storage chest. Careful examination showed that the crack around the edges of this slab looked cleaner than the others. He tried to lift the edge with his dagger, without success. He brought over the burning lamp that he had used to seal the parchment. Casting some light on the cracks showed that there appeared to be some small metal catch. He inserted his dagger and pulled the catch. It would not move. He tried pulling it the other way and it slid back about half an inch. Trying his dagger under the end of the slab he now found it possible to lift it. He was getting quite excited about his discovery. What if there was treasure within, which Gilbert had hidden and been unable to collect. He gingerly lifted the slab until he had it fully open, and he could look inside the space beneath, which was around two foot square and two foot deep. There was a canvas bag inside which he lifted out. It felt like coins. It was more lovely Italian florins and plenty of them. Middleton no longer had need of his hoard so he put

165

them back, and resolved to take all the money from Bruce to Katherine at the manor. For safety he crammed the saddlebags into the hole as well, before closing the slab and sliding the lock.

Time to talk to Sergeant Heddon he thought. He sent a servant to locate the sergeant and invite him back to his private quarters for orders.

Sergeant Heddon was in a good mood. He had received the oat biscuits which Daisy had sent and was biting on one of them gently, whilst thinking of the delights of Daisy. Any thoughts of Daisy's incapacity due to losing her hand did not cross his mind. As far as Nicholas Heddon was concerned she was a magnificent woman, hand or no hand, and now, after receiving his orders, was an ideal opportunity to ask Sir Walter for permission to ask for her hand in marriage. Only second in his thoughts as he followed the servant upstairs, came the question of why his master wished to speak privately with him for routine orders.

Once in the room Walt told him to sit. 'Sergeant Heddon, what is your opinion of Botolfe Best as a soldier?'

'I think he is a very fine soldier, Sir.'

'How do you think he would be as a sergeant?'

'He is an independent thinker, Sir, which does not mean he can't follow orders, but that he has the ability to improvise when the situation demands. What are you considering, Sir? Do you think I am not up to the job anymore as a result of my wound? You know that it does not affect my horsemanship, and I only have a slight limp when walking.'

'Stop' Walter interrupted before he could say anymore. 'Hear me out Nicholas. How would you like to be my miller?'

The sergeant was much taken aback, *what is going on*, he thought. *First, he seldom, if ever, calls me Nicholas. Second, miller where? Daisy is his miller. Perhaps he does want to get rid of me.*

He replied tentatively, 'I don't understand, Sir, miller where?'

'At my estate mill of course, where did you think?'

'What about Daisy, Sir? Is she not the miller?'

'Daisy is the tenant and I would like you to be the miller if you will agree.'

Nicholas Heddon could hardly believe his ears, and had to ask Walt to please confirm his understanding as to what was being asked of him, before replying.

'Sir, you are offering me my dream, and now I feel guilty after such generosity by asking if yet another dream may come true for me.'

'Spit it out then,' Walt said, having a very good idea what was coming next.

'May I have your permission, Sir, to ask Daisy Miller for her hand in marriage?'

Walt smiled and replied, 'Does the lady in question know you are asking for this privilege?'

'It was her idea, Sir,' the Sergeant said a little sheepishly.

Walt laughed loudly, 'Wonderful, we are all in agreement then. Just make sure you retain control of the breeches. That is a strong woman you are to wed my friend.'

There was still something worrying the sergeant that he needed to understand.

Walt, seeing the frown appearing on the sergeant's forehead knew what was coming, and forestalled his next question. 'The present miller and his son are leaving. They are to seek work elsewhere. They will be gone by Friday. I shall arrange for you to go to the mill at the weekend to take up your post as miller.'

'I know little about milling, Sir.'

'No matter, Daisy is the expert on the job, you provide the strong arms. Daisy will find you a lad from the village as a labourer. Say nothing to Botolfe Best. I will promote him after you leave. I will go to the manor on Thursday and deal with matters at the mill while I am there.'

With matters at the mill settled, he would as planned take the bulk of the cash to Katherine. She would need it. She needed, among other things, to consider schooling for the two eldest boys, starting with Walter. Tynemouth priory could not be considered so another would have to be found. He decided that he would take Aidric with him on Thursday as he was carrying such a large amount of money. The two of them together was probably putting Aidric at unnecessary risk, so he determined that they would not ride together, but that Aidric should track him as he did not want to risk both of them being surprised in an ambush.

***

Wednesday night was clear with no cloud and stars all resplendent in the night sky. Walt decided to set out next morning in the early hours. He set a candle of uniform length burning, marking its side with a notch at a point he knew would be reached in around six hours. He instructed his guard to wake him when the candle had burned to that point.

He was duly awakened some two hours before dawn. After refreshing his face with some cold water, he collected his saddlebags with the money and went to collect Aidric, who was ready and waiting with a couple of oat biscuits and a mug of warm ale. After quickly downing the light breakfast, they saddled their own horses, had the guard let them out of the gates, and headed for Syhale. Aidric hung back until Walt was just out of sight, and then picked up his trail. He noticed that Walt had been riding at a steady canter so he did the same to match his speed and avoid falling too far behind. Out of wooded areas the moon was so bright that visibility was almost as good as daylight. He reckoned they should arrive at the mill around dawn.

Walt was enjoying the ride in the clear moonlit night air. He found it refreshing and invigorating. He had covered two thirds of the journey and he was now riding over some high ground following an old barely used trail. Once on the other side of the hill he would see the forest to the south which he would pass through, and then down the gentle slope to the burn and the ford below the mill. *Nearly there,* he thought to himself as he approached the forest section.

As Sir Walter was approaching the forest trail, a sharp pair of eyes was watching from the edge of the forest. As soon as Badger was certain of his quarry, he hastened back to set his trap.

Entering the forest, the moonlight was not so bright, being shielded by the trees, but the trail was still clearly defined and Walt continued at a canter, musing to himself on what he was going to say to Henry West and his son, and if he should give them any pay at all considering the elder West had disobeyed the code of conduct, in relation to the marriage of employees. *What if - ?*

He got no further with his thoughts. He experienced a massive slap across his chest and found himself flying from his mount. As he fell, his head thumped heavily against a tree and despite his wearing a standard trooper's steel bonnet, he was barely aware that men were rushing at him, before he lapsed into unconsciousness.

The rush of men out of the trees to seize the fallen knight startled his horse, which bolted back the way he had come. Two of the men were about to take to their horses to give chase but Badger shouted.

'Leave the bloody horse, let's get this bastard tied up quickly before he wakes up, and thrown across behind me. Sooner we get back to Tynemouth the happier I will be. We have got what is wanted, and will get our payment. No need to risk our lives for the sake of a horse.'

With Walt tied hand and foot, and secured behind Badger's saddle, they headed off to the ford. Having crossed the ford they rounded the mill, to head for the track west past the old barn. The sun was rising and there was a woman outside the mill putting out feed for poultry. She looked up curiously as they passed but nothing was said. They carried on along the trail.

Aidric following on behind heard the short shout when Badger stopped the man from chasing the horse. He warily quickened his pace to close the distance to his master. As he was about to follow the trail into the trees he saw a loose horse galloping towards him, turning quickly he waited for it to approach, spurred his horse and galloped alongside, leaning precariously out of the saddle to take the reins of the runaway and slowly bring it to a halt. He recognised it as Sir Walter's horse and noted that the saddlebags were still in place. Placing one hand under each bag and checking the weight confirmed they had not been emptied, besides there had not been time. He knew that Sir Walter must have been unhorsed by accident or some surprise trap, and maybe hurt, or he would have heard sounds of a fight.

Leading his master's horse Aidric decided to proceed with caution, there was no point in him getting caught, and he would not be able to help that way. He proceeded towards the trees at a canter, and once in the forest trail slowed to a walk. Dawn was now breaking, but under the trees it was much darker and although the trail was easy to follow, it would not be easy to see unexpected obstacles. He was riding with his sword drawn in his right hand, and his reins and those of Sir Walter's horse in his left. He was about half way through the short forest section of the trail when he suddenly perceived something different in front of him. He reined in saying quietly, 'woah,' then edging his horse gently forward he realised that it was a rope, stretched taut across the trail between two trees. He saw instantly what had happened and knew that his master was probably unconscious and a prisoner. He moved across to the right and with one swipe of his sword severed the rope. He then proceeded to the end of the forest trail and down to the ford. There was no sign of any horsemen ahead. Passing through the ford and up to the mill he saw Daisy outside. She was calling the men from in the mill. When he got there Henry West and his son had joined her.

Daisy called out to him. 'Five men just rode down the west trail with a man trussed across one of their horses, I don't know who it is, and I thought it was maybe you or Nicholas.'

As she shouted she realised that Aidric was leading a horse. She clasped her gloved hand to her mouth and then shouted, 'Oh my God, is it Nicholas?'

Aidric shouted to Henry West to give Daisy a help up on the horse he had with him. He moved forward slowly and reluctantly, saying, 'If it is help you need to send for, surely it would be better if I went.'

An impatient Aidric yelled at him to do as he was bade immediately, whist waving his sword at him to emphasise the point. Henry got the point, and Daisy was soon mounted. Aidric led her off around the back of the mill, out of earshot of the Wests.

'Daisy, you are on Sir Walter's horse. It is him they have captured. Now ride quickly to the manor. Make sure Lady Katherine takes the saddlebags from your horse. Tell her that five men have Sir Walter, and ask her to get Galeron to send two men down here to catch up with me on the west trail from the mill. Tell him to ride with three others to the village and then having joined the road which leads to Tynemouth, head west and then north around the western perimeter of the estate. They will meet the gang heading south. But they must hurry or we will have to give chase south of the village, and lose the element of surprise. When you have delivered your message, stay there. Do not go back to the mill.'

Having seen Daisy off towards the manor, Aidric headed out past the old barn and along the western trail towards the southern boundary of the estate. It was getting quite light now, so he could see well in front of him where the ground was open. Shortly after the barn he topped a rise and saw the horsemen ahead. They were about half a mile in front of him and just nearing the top of the next hill. He counted five horses as Daisy had said, so they had not left any rear guard. He waited until they had disappeared over the rise and then spurred on to a gallop to make up ground while he was out of their sight. Coming to the top of the next rise where they had disappeared, he slowed and approached with care until he could see the trail. He could see nothing down the hill, and at the bottom, the trail entered a small wood, beyond which he could not see. He took a chance and galloped again until he reached the edge of the wood, where he slowed to a canter. The light was good enough now for him to see any traps with ropes, but he did not think they even realised he was following them. Emerging from the wood he suddenly reined in. He had nearly ridden straight into them. They were only around one hundred yards away. He could see the man with Sir Walter's limp form across the back of his saddle, but hanging down one side as if about to fall off. One of the men had dismounted and was pushing him further over the saddle and helping the rider to secure him to prevent him from sliding again.

Aidric smiled to himself. He was willing to bet that his master was no longer unconscious, and the sliding off was engineered to cause delay. *We shall have them soon,* he thought. He was sure that Galeron would spring a surprise somewhere around the southern end of the estate. It would not be far now, around another mile, before they would turn south. He noticed that the men had now got going again, and was preparing to start forward himself as soon as he could do so without being seen, when two Syhale troopers came galloping out of the woods to join him.

***

Galeron and his three troopers rode west to the village and past the church. They were travelling at a gallop and hoped to reach a place of his choosing, to await the arrival of the kidnappers and take them by surprise.

Galeron knew that there was only one place on the southern route just outside the Radulf demesne that would provide them cover, and fortunately it was at the village end of the trail, which gave them time to get set. The chosen place was a peasant farm which straddled the track, with outbuildings on either side which would provide ideal cover for his men.

171

A LAND APART – REBELLION

***

Badger and his band continued on their journey, oblivious to the fact that they were being followed. Badger was thinking of the reward he would get from the prior for having captured the knight. Things were going well, they were about to turn south towards Syhale village and Tynemouth. Nobody would know they had their prisoner; they had only seen one person, a dim looking woman feeding chickens at a mill. The woman and the mill meant nothing to Badger; as the prior had not thought it necessary to explain the significance, on the basis that the less Badger knew, the safer for him and the priory. Their progress was slow; the stupid knight had nearly slid off a while ago. They had to heave him back into position and push him a little further over so his head was hanging further down as he kept sliding off feet first.

Head further down was just what Walt had hoped for. It meant that his hands which were tied together at the wrist could now just reach the saddle girth strap. He found that he could manipulate the strap loose from the buckle, so that now if he gave a good tug on the strap it would unbuckle, and when he let go it would slide through the buckle leaving the girth, he hoped, loose enough for the saddle to slip around and the rider fall off. He now had to wait for the rescue mission, that he was confident would come, and choose his moment.

The party were approaching some farm buildings, after which they would soon turn onto the road to Syhale village and Tynemouth. Badger reminded his men to keep a watch for trouble, but as they neared the farm they saw only what was to be expected. There was a woman collecting eggs into a basket from nesting boxes at the back of a chicken shed, a man heading out south towards the village with an ox cart and a young girl of voluptuous proportion and a low cut bodice, sitting on a milking stool, milking a cow which was tethered to a rail and eating hay from a rack. As they passed, the girl stood and waved to them. All eyes turned to the right, whilst from the left out of a barn appeared Galeron and one of his men, who were almost upon them before Badger's men realised they were there. When they did, and turned to their left to meet the challenge, two more appeared from the right. In the general melee that ensued, Aidric and his two were galloping in from the rear to join the fun, while Walt chose this moment to loose the girth from its buckle.

Badger attempting to wheel his horse, to address the challenge he could hear galloping in from the rear, suddenly found his saddle slipping, and he fell ingloriously to the ground.

The troopers of Syhale soon had Badger and his men under control, with no injuries to themselves, and only a couple of minor injuries to two of Badger's men. Aidric had made straight for Badger's horse, where he had cut his master free. Walt, to the surprise of his captors slid from the horse and grabbed the fallen Badger by the neck, hauling him to his feet. The troopers soon had the Tynemouth gang trussed, Badger's horse re-saddled, and them all draped over the horses, with hands and feet tied together under their bellies.

The farmer with the ox cart had turned around, and headed back into the yard, his wife took her basket of eggs inside, and the milkmaid sat down and continued her milking.

Aidric walked over to Badger, now tied across his saddle, with his head held up by Walt who had a firm grasp on his hair. Aidric prodded him with his sword.

'Who are you, and who sent you?' Walt asked his prisoner.

'I am known as Badger and nobody sent me. I was trying to catch rebels from Mitford for reward.'

Another sharper jab of the sword, this time drawing some blood, and Aidric waved the point of the bloody sword under Badger's nose. Walt followed this with a further question.

'Who told you where to set your ambush and when rebels might be passing?'

'Honestly, Sir, nobody told me. I guessed a likely route.'

'Tell me then Badger, why are you riding priory horses?'

'How did you know they are prio-?' Badger realised he had been tricked and shut his mouth.

Walt turned, reached underneath the saddle of Badger's horse and unbuckled the girth strap again. He gave the unfortunate Badger a push and he and the saddle slipped around and hung under the animal's belly. He called Aidric to look.

'See here, under the saddle, the brand mark of the priory.'

Aidric looked, and looking meaningfully at his men, said 'so it is, Sir. I would wager that they are all priory horses, what say you lads?'

173

With that the grinning soldiers undid all the girths and tipped the gang unceremoniously, under the bellies hanging only by the rope tying their wrists to their ankles. Having confirmed that the horses were indeed all priory horses, Walt knew exactly who was behind the forest ambush.

He took Galeron and Aidric to one side to speak privately, after telling the men to saddle up the horses again and tie the prisoners on as they were before.

'Galeron can you and your five men get these ruffians to the constable in Tynemouth, without letting them escape.'

'Of course, Sir, but what do I tell the constable?'

'That you caught them thieving just north of Syhale, after complaints from local farmers, that they had been seen trying to drive stock in the area. After you caught them you found they had some gold florins, which you did not think could belong to such men. On examination they were also found to be riding stolen horses. There is surely no other way that such men would be in possession of priory horses.'

'Yes, Sir, which farmer shall I say made the complaint?' Galeron replied smiling.

'The farmer here at this farm will testify that he saw them in the area, and reported them to you yesterday.'

Walt reached under his coat to his purse and gave Galeron three florins. The ruffians had been in such a hurry to get out of the area, they had disarmed him but failed to search him for his purse.

'You hold onto the florins, hand them to the constable and say you got them off Badger the ringleader.'

Galeron nodded his understanding and left for Tynemouth with his men, and the prisoners trussed uncomfortably face down across the saddles of the priory horses.

***

As soon as Galeron and the other troopers had left with the prisoners, Walt hurriedly asked the question that most concerned him. 'What of my horse, Aidric, did you find him?'

'Yes, Sir, he was startled and galloped back towards me. You need have no worries. Daisy rode him back to the manor with the

174

message for Galeron, and your saddlebag will be safely with Lady Katherine.'

'Good man,' responded Walt, with a friendly hand on his squire's shoulder. 'Let us away home now, to our womenfolk.' At a signal from Aidric, one of the troopers dismounted and offered his horse to Walt, whilst he then swung up behind Sergeant Galeron. The sun was up now, and when they arrived south of the manor, it was to find the track guarded by two of their troopers. They greeted them, and passed by to the manor house. Katherine and Daisy appeared from the house as they approached; they had been keeping watch in both directions and spotted them as soon as they turned the corner past the guards.

'Thank God, you're safe,' Katherine said, running to his horse and taking his hand before he could dismount.

Walt gently disengaged his hand, dismounted and kissed her.

'My God woman, when are you going to have my son?' he asked. It was late May and Katherine was well due to give birth. After his recent adventure he worried that, had he been taken, she would worry about him to the neglect of her own welfare. Deciding to take no further chances he called for Annie Foster, the house servant.

'Annie, I want you to go to the village, and bring Widow Elton, the midwife. Lady Katherine will deliver my son any day and we must be prepared. Tell the woman she will stay here until it happens. No excuses. Do you understand?'

'Yes, Sir,' the girl replied and hurried off to the village immediately.

Katherine began to object, but Walt raised his hand for obedience, and she closed her mouth before saying anything, knowing that he was right, and that her pains were imminent.

Will, the groom appeared to take their horses and the trooper regained his, whilst Walt and Aidric went inside and a delighted Jeanne appeared with Ursula, bearing tankards of ale and bowls of hot porridge for them both. Aidric took the ale and porridge from Jeanne, putting them down on the table.

'Ale and porridge first Jeanne, you always get your priorities right,' he said taking her in his arms and kissing her lovingly.

'Who were those men who took you, Sir?' Daisy asked.

'Ruffians from Tynemouth whose leader is a man called Badger, the same name the Tynemouth innkeeper told me, for the man who

175

thought he had stolen Agnes's coffin all those years ago. They would not say who hired them, or where they got their information from about my movements, but they were riding priory horses.'

'I believe it may be my fault' said a shocked Daisy. 'On Monday the mill cog was broken, and I allowed Henry West to go to Tynemouth to bring a craftsman to make another. He did not return until Tuesday morning. The carpenter said that he told him he could come right away on the Monday, but Henry said he wished to attend Mass at the priory church.'

Aidric interjected, 'I was sure he had been listening at the door when Daisy complained to me, now I know he was. If he could have Sir Walter out of the way before he could discipline him, it might never happen.'

Walt looked to Daisy. 'Who is at the mill now?'

'The two Wests the carpenter and his apprentice.'

'Alright Daisy, you stay here. I will go with Squire Aidric and sort them out.'

Walt and Aidric had Will saddle their horses again, and rode the short distance to the mill, arriving to find the carpenter and his apprentice outside working on the carving of the large pinion wheel. This was being carved out of a single piece of oak, to form the cog and about two foot of shaft, which would then be connected to the iron axle shaft from the water wheel. The carpenter had taken all the surplus wood away to reveal the rough shape with his adze, and was now carving with chisels to get an accurate and smooth finish.

As they arrived, the carpenter stood and was about to greet them and ask their business, but Sir Walter put his finger to his lips and shook his head. The man sat quietly, back on his stool. Walt and Aidric dismounted and tied the horses to the rail.

'Where are the Wests?' Walt asked the carpenter quietly.

'Somewhere inside the mill, Sir,' he replied, realising that he was talking to somebody important, by their dress and the quality of their mounts.

The two of them walked into the mill house. A look into the milling room proved fruitless, and they had walked through the main room to get there. They were not in their own sleeping area so there was only one place left, and that was Daisy's private solar. Walt walked over to the closed door and drew his sword, followed by Aidric, likewise armed. He opened the door quickly to reveal Henry

West, lying on Daisy's bed as if it was his own, and his son sorting through a chest and examining its contents, presumably looking for her cache of money.

Both men leapt to their feet with surprise when Walt and Aidric entered the room.

'Would you like to explain, just what you are doing in my mill tenant's bedchamber?' Walt asked.

'Sir, I share this room with Daisy now, since we are to be married' a startled Henry replied.

'This gives your son the right to sort through her belongings does it?'

'He was looking for something I put away in the chest just yesterday.'

Walt put away his sword and Henry's expression changed from startled and afraid to one of relief and cunning. He believed his explanation had been accepted. Sir Walter held out his hand to him, and he stepped across the room to shake it. One moment his hand was taken and then Walt turned his body sharply and pulled on Henry,s arm. Henry found himself propelled forward and over Sir Walter's shoulder. He flew across the room, crashed into the wall and slid down to the floor in a dazed heap. His son John was also taken by surprise; he had never seen such a quick action before. He stepped forward towards Walt to find the point of Aidric's blade at his throat. 'Do not do it' Aidric said. John West froze with fear.

Walt told Henry to get up, which he did, painfully, whilst holding his shoulder. The father and son were then lined up against the wall, and Aidric stood, by brandishing his blade while Walt searched them. He recovered a small amount of money, and a small dagger from Henry. John had nothing on his person. They then took them through to their bedchamber and told them to pack their sacks. They watched as each item was packed and relieved them of any money they tried to pack away. Then with the two of them standing in the main kitchen, Walt spoke to them. 'You thank me and Daisy Miller, by a catalogue of betrayal, treachery and sabotage?'

'No, Sir -' Henry West began.

Walt shouted at him angrily. 'Shut up unless you want to bounce off another wall.'

'You asked Daisy Miller to be your wife, and when she refused you, she was pestered and insulted with the view to scare her into submission. Asking for her hand without my permission is against the law, and I could have you flogged for that alone.'

You and your son sabotaged the mill in order that you could go to Tynemouth to see the prior, and attempt to bring about my arrest to save yourself from punishment. We come here and find you making free with my tenant's bed, and your son searching for her cache. Now tell me why I should not thrash you both, and have you thrown into gaol?'

'The prior would not let us go to prison, he paid father for his information and–.'

'Shut up you fool,' screamed Henry.

Walt smiled, and thanked the young man. He decided to check the contents of their sacks again. Picking up each one, he tipped them out on the floor and examined each of the articles, dropping them to one side as he was satisfied. There was a wooden box which contained a few candles, a flint and striker. Walt was curious; the box seemed very heavy but was not made of oak. He tipped out the candles and fire lighting items onto the floor and examined the box more closely. He shook it but nothing rattled. Telling Aidric to stand guard over the two men he took the box outside to the carpenter and asked him if he had seen such a box before.

'Not only have I seen one, Sir, but I have made a number of them myself, there is a compartment in the bottom.'

'Can you open this one,' Walt asked.

The carpenter took a small awl, and pushed in two small almost invisible pegs on the inside of the box. He tipped it upside down, and a false base fell out followed by something wrapped tightly in cloth. Walt scooped up the cloth and removed from it a quantity of silver groats and gold florins, which he pocketed, believing that the florins were most likely Henry West's reward from the prior for his betrayal. He replaced the cloth, now wrapping a handful of iron nails from the carpenter, and false base in the box. Thanking the carpenter, he gave him a shilling for his trouble and went back inside.

Throwing the box down in front of the men, he said nothing of his discovery, but was pleased to see them exchange sly smirks, as he told them to put their stuff back into the sacks and be off his land by the shortest distance, which was appropriately west, past the old barn. He advised them strongly against going to Tynemouth. The prior would be angry that his plan had failed and his men were in prison. Seeing them would only add to his anger, and he would want his money back. With their sacks over their shoulders the sorry pair headed away along the track, followed by a farewell shout from Walt. 'One more thing, if I catch you on my land again, there will be no more threats, I will kill both of you. Now go, and quickly.'

The carpenter and his apprentice watched curiously as the pair trotted off down the track away from the mill, occasionally looking back fearfully as if expecting to be chased.

Walt smiled, as he thought of their surprise when they would later realise that he had taken their treacherous gains.

Returning to the manor, Walt and Aidric handed their horses to the groom, before going inside to find an expectant Daisy waiting for news.

'They have gone, and they will not be back if they value their lives.' Walt told her.

He continued to tell her briefly the situation that they had discovered on their arrival and that as far as they could tell the Wests had not managed to steal anything of significance from her.

Daisy was not concerned about this, as she was certain that her cache was too well hidden, and that if they had found it they would no longer have been searching, but already on the run. She did however voice another concern.

'Sir Walter, I thank you from my heart for your help, and you my good friend Aidric, but how am I now to manage the mill alone?'

'You will not be alone Daisy. Tonight I shall send a trooper with you to stand guard until morning. In the morning your new mill operator will report for duty. Then you and he can discuss the employment of a lad to help.'

'Who is to be the operator, Sir? How will I know he is suitable?'

'Trust me Daisy you will know; now off you go home. Aidric will detail the trooper to accompany you. I will arrange for your friend Sergeant Heddon to visit you tomorrow. You may tell him of the treachery of the Wests, but it is your choice if you tell him of your personal worries regarding the operation of the mill, as myself and Aidric will say nought.'

Walt could see that Aidric was eager to have some time with Jeanne, and told him that he was returning to Mitford as soon as the midwife arrived, but if he and Jeanne wanted to make their arranged pledge with Father Livio, he was sure that Lady Katherine and one of the servants would agree to witness the ceremony.

A grateful Aidric hurried off to find Jeanne and visit the priest to arrange the ceremony for the next morning.

Katherine expressed her disappointment at Walt's early return to Mitford and assured him that the money he had brought would be safely stowed away as soon as the servants had retired.

'You just look after yourself, dearest, and I shall come home to see our new son as soon as I dare. News may have got around that I was at large so I shall keep my head down until it is deemed safe again.'

'There you go again Walt, with our new son. You cannot know that.'

'Do you want to wager on it?'

She gave him a playful push in the chest. 'Be off with you and stop teasing me.'

***

The wedding ceremony was a quiet affair, with the only guests being Lady Katherine, the maid Annie Foster and Aidric's close friend Sergeant Galeron Guddal.

After the church service they returned to the manor, where they and the servants who had not attended drank a toast to the newly married couple before returning to their duties. Aidric and Jeanne retired to their smallholding for a couple of hours alone, before he would have to return to Mitford. Arriving at his cottage, Aidric picked up his new wife and carried her through into the bedchamber of their single story home and lowered her gently onto the bed.

'Are you happy Mrs Johansson?' he asked.

'Never happier' she replied, pulling him down on top of her.

They lay there for several minutes, just comfortable with holding each other and revelling in their joy. Eventually Jeanne rolled him off, and sat up to remove her kirtle, while Aidric, taking his cue, and never slow to respond to Jeanne's needs, rapidly divested himself of his clothing.

'We only have a couple of hours Aidric, let us not waste them,' Jeanne said, pulling him back onto her, and kissing him with great anticipation of the joys to come.

***

Prior Gregory had taken Thursday's midday mass, and he was in his private quarters awaiting news of his plan to arrest Sir Walter. He thought that they should have caught him by now, and at any moment there would be news from the town that they had arrived and his enemy was incarcerated in the gaol. *I must not appear too eager*, he thought; *after all it was nothing to do with me, just some public spirited citizens doing their duty for their king.*

He poured himself another goblet of fine wine, and sat congratulating himself on his ability to grasp a situation and turn it to his favour.

Brother Richard knocked on his door and told him the constable wished to see him.

'Good' he replied, 'saddle my horse, I will go right away.'

'No, Prior, the constable is here, and wishes to see you.'

'Well what are you waiting for you dim monk? Show him in,' he said, with a definite smirk on his face.

Brother Richard ushered the constable into the room and closed the door, staying outside himself, where he put his ear to the door but could not hear clearly through the thick oak panels, until he suddenly heard a loud shout by the prior: 'What!'

He quickly backed away from the door and after a short time the constable came out and hurried away. Brother Richard nervously entered to ask the prior if there was any other service he needed. He was greeted by a scream of rage, followed by the hurled goblet of wine, and any other items to hand on the prior's desk. The monk beat a hasty retreat, rapidly pulling the door closed behind him whilst hearing objects striking the inside. He ran through the priory to catch up with the constable, ostensibly to see him respectfully off the premises. In reality he desperately wanted to know what had transpired in the prior's office.

'Is the prior alright Constable? I thought I heard him shout' he asked innocently

'I don't know why he is so upset, I only told him that we had some thieves in custody and we had recovered his stolen horses.'

'I see, it was probably a shout of surprise and anger as I don't think he knew the horses had been stolen, Sir,' Brother Richard replied, with a wry smile.

There was not much that got past Brother Richard. Walking back past Brother Cornelius's office he was called in.

'What's the shouting about Brother Richard?'

'He is in a terrible rage, and should be avoided for around a week, I would think Brother. It is even worse than the treasury incident.' Brother Richard headed towards his quarters determined also to keep out of the prior's way as much as possible.

=====

CHAPTER 9

A proposition is made

Walt was relaxing in his private chamber in the keep at Mitford castle, reflecting on his current situation, and the year past. It was December 1318, and soon the Christ's Mass festivities would be upon them. He would have to take care over his visiting then, as the prior would expect him to try to be with his family. On the other hand, the prior may consider his options and decide that he had better rein in his ambitions, after his previous abortive attempt at capture, and his subsequent embarrassment. Whichever was the case, he would have to be careful and ensure that lookouts were posted when he was at home. Generally since the failed attempt to capture him, he had much freedom to come and go at will, exercising only the basic security precautions of travelling at dusk or dawn when there were few people about, and keeping off main routes.

Walt's highlight of the past year had been on the twenty first of May, when Katherine had presented him with his fifth son John, only a couple of days after he had insisted the midwife stay at the Manor, before he had returned to Mitford. On their next meeting she decreed that she was not having any more babies, as they were always sons, and the Lord had obviously decided that Katherine Radulf should have no girls. Walt could only think of the expense of the education for five sons. Girls were cheaper, until they got married, and then they wanted a chunk of your wealth for a dowry. In the long term, he thought, boys were probably the better investment. *I will need to find a few more landowners who may need my protection to pay for them*, he thought.

The mill had been repaired the week following its sabotage and the craftsman paid. Daisy Miller had been overjoyed when Nicholas Heddon showed up on the Friday morning while it was still being repaired. He had shown her his discharge paper from Sir Walter, and needed to say no more, as she had recalled Sir Walter saying that she would approve of the replacement operator. She knew immediately that she had no need to ask him what he would do now. The pair had found a labourer within the month. He was anxious to move into the mill on a permanent basis rather than leaving each evening to his accommodation at the manor. Daisy suggested that he and the new youth take up residence in the chamber originally added for the Wests, until they were married. He realised that he was taking a risk leaving Mitford on a permanent basis, but no longer in uniform, and with the local gentry now taking little interest in Mitford, it was a risk worth taking. It was not as if they had all suddenly decamped from the castle. Nobody would be bothered by a miller, and he would keep away from Tynemouth.

Walt had also decided there was one more important thing that had to be done that year, and with Katherine having given birth in May, he had resolved to risk exposure and seek a place of education for young Walter, who was now eight years old. Tynemouth Priory was out of the question for obvious reasons, so he had decided to go on a visit to Alnwick Abbey to speak with Abbot Stephen, who had officiated at his dubbing ceremony. The visit had been fruitful, the Abbey had a number of teaching monks, and Walt had soon agreed a mutually satisfactory arrangement for young Walter to join the students last September. The boy had already completed his first term and was now about to come home for Christ's Mass, a different arrangement than Tynemouth, who kept the boys over that period and only sent them home for the New Year. If all went well, young Alex would also be there in two years' time.

With nobody seemingly bothering about his occupation of Mitford any longer, Walt had been able to pay more attention to the affairs of his estate and was pleased that the weather was greatly improved this year, resulting in a good harvest, justifying the extra acreage they and their tenants had planted. The sickness in the livestock had also passed and they had a good shearing with just enough fleeces to send to Tynemouth market to allay any suspicions of tax avoidance, whilst the bulk went to Blyth for shipment to the Low Countries via the good graces of Jon Monek in Bishops Lynn. *I shall increase the Tynemouth sale next year to avoid suspicion, or maybe sell at Newcastle, thus bypassing the prior's jurisdiction altogether. I must inform Katherine of these possibilities in case I have to flee,* he determined.

Bruce's money had been a boon to help them invest in crops, replace stock lost through pestilence, and tide them over most of the year until the harvest, and fleeces were sold. Replacing stock had been difficult due to shortage of animals, and many of the replacements were of poor quality, but he hoped to improve them by feeding and good husbandry.

Raids into Northumberland by Scottish regulars had been sporadic, but he and his favoured friends had been left alone. Bruce was obviously keeping his agreement. There had been other raids by reiving gangs, but they were generally ill organised, and presented no problems for the troopers at Syhale. Sometimes a detachment had to give chase when the raid was on an outlying yeoman tenant, and the reivers had already left by the time word got to the manor. Walt made a mental note that more soldiers were needed at Syhale. He thought, *too many are tied up with holding this castle against nobody. I will have to take some of them out on some expeditions of my own, and make other reivers aware that it would be better to leave my lands alone, and those tenants under my protection.*

He brought his mind back to the present, and determined that he must ensure that he and Aidric were not away from Mitford at the same time over Christ's Mass, whilst both should have an opportunity to spend time with their loved ones. He decided that he would go home on Christ's birthday to attend mass with his family and friends, followed by a modest banquet. He would return before dawn the next day to allow Aidric time with Jeanne. As there was to be no banquet that day, he would have all day to enjoy her company.

Two weeks later, Christ's Mass had passed without incident as family and close friends celebrated modestly, still cautious after the difficulties and privations of the famine years, and vividly aware of how quickly God could punish them, for taking him and his gifts of health of body and crops for granted.

The winter passed into 1319. As soon as the weather improved Walt brazenly began operating his protection and enforcement business again, from Mitford castle. With sections of his militia, he would ride out wearing no colours, and always ensuring he was a good distance away from Mitford, usually at least three days' riding before operations began. They lived off the land and slept rough during the operation, leaving horses light of loads to accommodate their booty for the return journey. They would survey farms and buildings as they rode through unfamiliar territory, looking for signs of wealth. If the signs were good they would approach the owner and offer him protection from marauding thieves or Scottish reivers.

Acceptance of their protection would involve a fee in advance, which would go into Walt's saddlebags. Rejection would be met by dire warnings that there were plenty of reivers about, and without payment they could be of no help in recovering stolen stock or valuables. If there was still no acceptance, they would ride on, noting any signs of opulence in the house or amount of stock. The place would then be visited on the return journey and a cow or a few sheep picked up for their trouble. They would not visit the same place again and constantly had to look for new areas to operate, often far south of Durham. Their success was due only to the general lawlessness of Northumberland, and the disinterest of the crown in getting to grips with the problem, because much of it was put down to the Scottish raids.

Walt did well, until he heard that the king and the Earl of Lancaster had settled their differences and were embarking on an expedition with a large force to retake Berwick. Such a force may travel up the coast or indeed it may come past Mitford. When that happened he determined to lie low with the gates locked, and hope the king showed as much interest in him as he usually did, which was none at all.

His act of lying low paid off. Nobody paid any heed to Mitford castle, and the king's army did not even pass near as they headed for Berwick, where they laid siege in early September. It was on the seventeenth of that month that Walt heard that the king and his army had abandoned the siege, and were making all haste to York, as a Scottish army had penetrated in the west from Galloway and was threatening that city. The king could not afford to let York fall as his wife Queen Isabella was staying nearby, and would provide a prime hostage for the Scottish king.

York did not fall, but Edward, under pressure from the Scottish raids, proposed a truce which was accepted by Bruce. With the armies again withdrawn from the scene, Walt was able to continue his life of part time running his estates, and part time freebooting, still in a friendly alliance with the formal enemy, the Scots.

Of the resultant profit made from such escapades, he retained only enough at Mitford to take care of one month's supplies and pay for his men, who were well paid for their loyalty. The remaining money went with him on his visits to Syhale manor, to be put away in the family vault. He was aware that there would be a day of reckoning, and was only surprised that no one had as yet forced him from the castle to answer for his treachery. His main concern was that if he were to go the same way as Middleton, his wife and family should be provided for. *Who knows how long these troubled times will last,* he thought. England and Scotland had been at war as long as he could remember, and probably still would be when his sons were his own age.

When he was home last Christ's Mass, he had been pleased to find that young Walter was happy with his tuition at Alnwick Abbey. He had a tutor, known to him as Brother Daniel, who he said was very strict, but made his lectures most interesting. He had complained about the food, but so had Walt when he was at Tynemouth. They were never going to get home cooking from monks. Now they were nearing the end of the year again, he would have to enrol Alexander. At least it was taking some of the pressure off Katherine and Tilly, who were kept busy enough with the younger ones.

***

Towards the end of 1319, improvements in yields from the estates saw the family accounts again in sound order after the previous year's investment. Early in the following year, Walt determined to end his freebooting ways and concentrate on increasing the yields from his crops and livestock. He was aided in this decision by Katherine, who, in the privacy of their solar, when they retired after family celebration for the New Year of 1320, made it quite clear that she did not approve of his lifestyle. Having prepared for bed, Walt was about to take her in his arms when she placed her hands on his shoulders, holding him at arms length. She spoke quietly but earnestly as she faced him, so as not to disturb their sons. 'Walt, you cannot remain for much longer at Mitford. Father has heard talk of plans to have you surrender or be evicted. I would urge you to give up freebooting in all areas, so as not to alienate what friends you have remaining. You are going to need all the goodwill available, to get away with your past deeds, and still keep your head. If you will not take heed of my words for yourself, please consider me and our sons. I beg you give it up.'

Expecting his anger at her open disapproval of his lifestyle, she was pleasantly surprised when he acquiesced, by drawing her gently to him and whispering in her ear.

'Your will is mine my dearest, I have been giving the situation much thought in recent weeks. I know nothing about plans to take Mitford but freebooting is over; upon my word. Now can we go to bed as a husband and wife should?'

Katherine had no doubts as to Walt's sincerity, as he playfully pushed her onto the bed, where they indulged each other's wildest passions, as if newly wed.

The next celebration on the Syhale estate was the wedding of Nicholas Heddon and Daisy Miller in July of 1320. Protocol did not call for a banquet in the hall, but Walt made sure that there was a first class hog roast, and plenty of ale and mead supplied for an open air fest with minstrels and dancing, on the manor meadow. Aidric and Jeanne were invited by the newly married couple to share in their celebration, as circumstances had so far prevented them from having their own reception.

Walt had made a generous donation to ensure there was plenty of everything. The wedding ceremony was conducted by Father Livio, who subsequently and joyfully joined in the celebrations, as only a priest like he could do. As usual one of the troopers escorted him back to his small home afterwards, because he was deemed too unsteady on his feet to manage alone.

During all this time they had only seen Walt's Uncle Adam twice, once at each of the last two Christ's Mass celebrations. They had received only one letter from William, who expressed joy that the famine was finished, and his business was back to normal. Freda sent her love, and reported that there was a well connected young man with interests in the grain business showing an interest in Ingrid.

Walt had made a couple of visits to Clennell with escorts, where he had picked up his rents from Simon. Tenants who had been in arrears were now beginning to gradually reduce their debts and Walt had returned to Syhale with full saddlebags.

'Folk over there know nothing of my occupation of Mitford' he told Katherine, on his return.

'I should think they have worries enough within their own area.' she said.

'I thought to try Harbottle, but Simon assured me that de Umfraville was not in residence, as the castle is in need of much restoration, so we are still no further forward with our permission to build our fortified home at Bytilsden.'

'Not likely now, my dear. Umfraville is certain to know of your disgrace. There can be no further thought of such actions until your present situation is resolved,' Katherine opined sadly.

Alexander had been enrolled for schooling at Alnwick Abbey, and had now joined his brother. Walt, now satisfied that his family affairs and finances were in good order, began to think how he might extricate himself from his current position. At the moment he saw little option but to sell up and flee to Scotland with his family. He knew that this option would result in massive losses as he would be offered minimum value for his lands under the circumstances. Just to surrender to the sheriff was out of the question. He remembered vividly what had happened to Gilbert de Middleton and his brother John. No, he would have to wait awhile, maybe something would crop up. He knew he had plenty of friends in the area; otherwise he would not have held the castle for so long.

Katherine, like Walt, knew that their days of being together on a regular basis could not last. The king had his truce with the Scots; there were not so many raids, and those mostly by reivers. It would not be long, she was sure, before the High Sheriff received instructions from the monarch, and turned his attention to Walt's occupation of Mitford castle.

In the spring of 1321 the truce had generally held for the last eighteen months. Katherine was glad that they had amassed a good deal of wealth. She may need much of it for lawyers to keep him alive, if and when they took him. She knew now that there was no if, it was just a case of, when.

Walt having given up his freebooting existence, needed to distance himself from that life, whatever his future was to bring. His family, he hoped, were secure financially and from the point of view of his land at Syhale. He hoped that over time memories might be dulled regarding some of his excesses, but already only four months into the year he was getting bored with the dull routine. Since his promise to Katherine he had gradually reduced freebooting activities. She had been most aggravated that he did not desist immediately and her displeasure was reflected, to his dismay, mostly in the bedroom. With few reasons to exercise the men outside the confines of the castle grounds, he was finding it difficult to keep them occupied, and could sense their restlessness. There was only so much training you could do within the castle walls, and not a very large castle at that, considering the outer curtain wall was long ago destroyed, leaving the remainder of the castle atop its motte. Much of the inner bailey was occupied by the keep, and wooden structures against the curtain wall to house horses and animals for food and provision of milk. There was also a smith who fashioned shoes for the horses and basic armaments when required. Cooking for the men was done in another of these huts.

Walt realised he could not abandon the castle and take his place back at Syhale, because that would lead to certain arrest as soon as word got around, and he would have no bargaining power. He was also acutely aware of the loyalty of his men, and needed to consider their future wellbeing.

He was letting the men go out for odd days in small groups under supervision of Aidric or Sergeant Best to make purchases for the kitchen as a way of relieving boredom. So far they had always returned with no absentees. He determined that if nothing happened by the end of the year, he would have to attempt to open negotiations with the sheriff.

According to Hugh Delaval, the king was again at loggerheads with many of his earls and barons, over his favouritism to the Despenser family, since he promoted Hugh Despenser to Chamberlain three years ago. It was rumoured that he undertook drunken orgies with them and practiced perverse acts, much to the annoyance of the queen.

Such distractions, Walter hoped, would keep his mind away from such trivialities as removing one rebellious knight from one of his smaller castles.

***

Early November of 1321, things finally came to a head. During his long weekend at Syhale, Sir Hugh Delaval had visited Walt soon after his arrival on the Thursday morning. After some initial small talk, he expressed a wish for a private conversation. Walt led him into the feasting hall and ensured the doors were shut and the bolts secured.

'Well old friend, what is it of such importance that you wish to tell me?' he asked.

'I had a visit from Sir Robert de Umfraville, Earl of Angus, this week.'

'What did he want? I hope his manners are somewhat better than his father's,' Walt replied. 'Is he going to allow our pele at Bytilsden?'

'He wanted me to speak to you about Mitford.'

'Go on,' said Walt cautiously.

'Well it seems he and others have received notice from the king that they must recover the castle into his name. They have been given some assurances by the king as to your welfare, and would like to meet with you, to discuss the terms of your relinquishing the castle to His Majesty's care. They were at pains to point out that the king had no wish to attempt to take the castle by force, as he knew of your friendship with influential people in the area and wished the northern rebellion to fade, and not be fanned into flame again.'

'Who do you mean by others?'

'Sir Ralph de Greystoke; and Sir John de Eure, Sir John being the legal governor of the castle that you occupy.'

'Who the hell is Greystoke? I have never heard of him.'

'He is a knight from Cumberland, who has the king's ear, I am told.'

'Has the king's ear, or the Despensers' ear?'

'The king's I am told, but I doubt much reaches the king without the knowledge of the Despensers.'

Walt pondered the situation for a while before replying. 'I will agree to meet them at Mitford, but they must come without escort and present themselves at the gate for my satisfaction. They must also bring with them some document which clearly states their permitted scope of negotiation with regard to my personal welfare.'

Hugh looked at his friend sadly and said, 'I don't see what alternative you have Walt. You have secured your estate here for your son, through Katherine and me. At worst you could lose the rest of your lands as punishment.'

'Also my life,' said Walt sourly.

191

'You must wait and see what they offer. You have many friends, and if you are betrayed we will all fight for your cause.'

'I do not recall much fighting to save the Middletons.' Walt retorted sharply.

Hugh gave him a hurt look and replied. 'Nobody liked the Middletons, even their friends.'

'Tell them to come next Wednesday morning, eighteenth of November,' Walt said decisively.

Hugh nodded, and business completed, they returned to the family room where his father in law stayed for some food and ale, before returning home. The moment he was gone, Katherine had wanted to know what it was all about. Walt persuaded her to wait until they retired, when he would tell her in the privacy of their solar, where he was back in her good grace, since convincing her that freebooting was of the past. He wanted a little more time to think before telling Katherine his plans, and suggested she retire and he would follow shortly.

The first thing he did was to call in Sergeant Galeron and arrange messengers to visit members of his family to arrange for them to visit urgently on the Tuesday the twenty-fourth of November. He was not meeting the knights until next Wednesday, and he was sure that he could delay any handover for another week, giving himself time to set matters in order with his family. That task done, he left Jeanne to lock up and retired to join Katherine.

She did not take the news well, and was not reassured by promises of security for Walt's welfare. Walt assured her that he would carefully peruse any document they produced, and ensure he obtained a copy. She was still not convinced, but nevertheless could see no alternative, but to try this avenue of escape from their current predicament. She did not want to think about the worst outcome, and forced herself to accept Walt's optimistic view, but to his chagrin, not his amorous attentions.

'My mood is sad and not conducive to lovemaking,' she said curtly, in answer to his advances.

Walt turned grumpily away and sought to sleep.

He departed the following morning for Mitford, still out of sorts, after a chaste kiss from his wife.

***

After his master's return to Mitford, Aidric noticed his unusually morose attitude but thought it wise to wait. Sir Walt would confide in him when he was ready, he knew.

Walt wandered around the castle all day, sometimes speaking to one of the men, sometime sitting alone in thought, but still looking glum.

The following morning, Walt rose early, and having broken his fast, he sat at his desk, still upset from Katherine's refusal of his favours, and thinking through what he had to tell the men, and what their response may be. Not another rebuttal, he hoped. He had determined how he should address them, but was at a loss to understand how they may respond. He had resolved to take a positive view whatever the outcome, when Aidric knocked on the door of his private quarters and entered. 'The men are paraded and waiting, Sir, apart from four keeping lookout on the battlements.'

'If the gates are secure and there is no-one in sight from the battlements, have them come down to join us. This will not take long.'

Aidric called and received assurance that there was nobody in sight and the four sentries joined the parade.

Walt explained the situation to the men, telling them nothing about any suggested arrangement for his person, but he did tell them that handover of the castle would be subject only to a promise that none of the soldiers or his squire would be arrested. He told them that any man who did not trust him to look after their interests was free to leave now, but all who stayed would either remain in the employ of his family, or continue to be employed until other posts were found for them.

'Discuss it amongst yourselves, and any man who wishes to leave should report to my squire and be gone by midday.' Walt told them.

With that, he turned on his heel, and returned to his quarters.

Half an hour later, after a brief knock, Aidric appeared in front of Walt's table.

'The sentries are back on duty and the remainder of the men are going about their duties, Sir.' Aidric reported.

'Is nobody going?' Walt asked.

'Only me, Sir,' replied Aidric seriously, to a look of shock and consternation on Walt's face.

Aidric continued with a cheeky smile. 'It's my time off, Sir, to go and see Jeanne tonight.'

Walt had to laugh. 'You would jest with me you rascal at such a serious time? What if I forbid you to take time off to pursue your marital activities?'

'I will be back at first light on Wednesday, to be here when you receive your visitors.' Aidric replied, ignoring the threat. 'You will not receive them alone, Sir. I insist you have adequate bodyguard and that they are disarmed.'

'Thank you Aidric,' Walt said, 'now go and issue the men with a barrel of ale, and tell the cooks to use whatever rations they want until Wednesday. Give the men a banquet, they deserve it. I will review the situation again after the meeting.'

Time passed very slowly for Walt, until Wednesday morning, when he was awakened by Aidric reporting for duty and asking if there were any specific orders.

'Yes, I want you to double the sentries on the battlements, have a number of men busy practising with swords in the courtyard, and some indoors making noise to appear as if they were many more. Ensure that the Smith and the Fletcher are working, tipping and adding goose feather to our arrow shafts, and there is general air of industry and efficiency, such that our visitors may think we talk from a position of some strength. As you suggested, the visitors must hand over any arms on arrival, and you may pick two men to join you as my bodyguards during the meeting. Now off with you and leave me to prepare.'

Walt took breakfast in his chamber and then proceeded to trim his beard and attire himself in his formal uniform, with tabard displaying family colours. He buckled on his sword, laid his shield on the table to his left and sat down behind it to wait. He had arranged three chairs in a row about six feet from his table and facing him. He would have two of his bodyguards standing, one at each side of the visitors, and Squire Aidric standing alongside him.

It was nearly midday, and Walt was beginning to wonder if something had gone wrong or maybe there was treachery afoot when after a brief knock, Aidric poked his head around the door and announced that the visitors were in sight, and there were only three of them.

'Good.' Walt responded. 'Due to the time of day, I want you to ask the cook to ensure that there is sufficient food to satisfy our guests' hunger at the conclusion of our meeting.'

'What if the meeting produces no satisfactory outcome, Sir?'

'Then we shall still feed them. They are gentlemen, and so are we Aidric. Rest assured, they have not made this effort to leave without satisfactory outcome on their behalf, and it is my duty to ensure the outcome is satisfactory for us. You and the two bodyguards will bear witness to the negotiation, and you Aidric, are free to raise a question when I ask you for comment. Now go and greet our esteemed visitors, I shall go to the roof of the keep and watch from there, and I shall be here behind my table again before you get them to this chamber.'

Aidric left to greet the guests, and Walt exited his quarters by the spiral stone staircase leading to the roof of the keep. Once there he crossed to the side overlooking the barbican. He had a clear view from there of the battlements on the outer wall, his men patrolling them, and the preparations he had ordered for the visitors' arrival.

He saw a troop of soldiers practising swordplay. He noticed that they were taking no chances, and were not using practice weapons but their own battle prepared swords. He hoped there were no injuries as they appeared quite vigorous in their simulated combat.

The gate was opened, and the three visitors rode through and dismounted, their horses being taken, hitched and watered by a soldier. Without being asked, the visitors handed over their swords and daggers and held out their arms for inspection for other weapons. After a thorough inspection, Aidric was satisfied that they had no concealed weapons, and proceeded to escort them, past the various industrious activities on display, to the keep, closely followed by the other two guards.

Walt was back in his seat before they arrived, and as they entered he bade them good day and indicated they should take the three chairs arranged in front of his table. Sir Robert de Umfraville, one time Earl of Angus, took the centre chair, presumably indicating his seniority, even though his earldom in Angus had been seized by Bruce, on his right sat Sir Ralph de Greystoke and on his left, Sir

John Eure of Castle Ward Northumberland. They sat silently, waiting for Walt to open the meeting.

The two guards had taken their positions on the wings, either side of the row of chairs and stood at ease, with their hands resting on the hilts of their swords.

Walt stood and walked around the table, followed quickly and nervously by Aidric, thinking, *this was not in the plan,* as Walt approached the three visitors. 'Good day to you gentlemen. We have not previously met, but by your colours, I assume you, Sir, to be Sir Robert, and you Sir John. By my default, not knowing your colours, Sir, you must be Sir Ralph. I am the errant Sir Walter de Radulf, who seeks to treaty with you for the handover of this castle to another governor.'

The three men stood in respect as Walt approached. He grasped the forearm of each in turn and bade them welcome. He enquired if they would like some water, ale or other refreshment before they got down to business. They each requested a cup of water to wet their dusty throats.

Walt nodded to one of the guards who, after a nervous glance at Aidric to receive his approval, left to order the drinks.

The three visitors retook their seats, and Walt returned to his chair behind the table with Aidric standing at his shoulder.

'Well gentlemen, as soon as you have your refreshment, we shall begin our discussion. I thank you all for coming. Sir Robert, I hope your demeanour is more convivial than your father's, the last time I met him in the company of my own late father, at Harbottle. We were seeking his permission to construct a fortified tower at Bytilsden, and were once again refused without good reason and in bad grace.'

Sir Robert de Umfraville looked uncomfortable when he answered. 'First I offer my condolences for the loss of your brave father at Bannockburn, secondly, I would like to apologise for my late father's attitude, and assure you that I shall look upon the matter in a different light when this current business is resolved and behind us.'

Walt thanked him and turned to John de Eure. 'Well Sir John, some of the men I have with me had been originally put into this castle by your father and served under Gilbert de Middleton. They fled to join me after Gilbert's kidnapping of the bishop, and murder of one of his men.'

John de Eure slowly stroked his beard before replying. 'If I recall correctly Sir Walter, you were also involved in that escapade.'

'If you study the statement made by the pope's emissaries on their return to England, you will see I offered them only help and assistance with their onward travel to Scotland. Also, that neither I nor any of my men were involved in the murderous attack on the bishop's guard, and that, by the bishop's own words.'

'Then why were you there at all?' Eure asked.

'To protest at the imposition of a bishop over the man elected by the monks of Durham, and maybe relieve the wealthy gentlemen of the burden of carrying too much treasure. Not to kidnap or kill.'

'And how much of that treasure did you take?'

'None, Sir John. As soon as I realised the intent of Middleton, I concentrated with my men on the safety of the pope's emissaries, leaving the scene to escort them to safety. I wanted nothing to do with kidnap and he had taken a superior force.'

Walt then turned to the third man. 'Sir Ralph, we have not met before, may I ask what your interest in this matter is? I believe Greystoke to be in Cumberland.'

Sir Ralph smiled, 'you are correct in your belief Sir Walter. You probably did not know but our fathers were acquainted. At the moment I have taken this task on behalf of another acquaintance, a friend of yours and your late father, who does not wish to be openly involved, but wishes to ensure that you get a fair hearing and resolution to your dilemma.'

Walt wanted to ask him who this benefactor was, but knew it would be useless with others present. He resolved to attempt a private word at some other time.

The soldier returned with a large tablet, upon which was placed seven earthenware cups and a large ewer of water. At Walter's indication he placed it on the table.

Aidric poured out four glasses for the guests and Walt, and with a dark look at the man who had the temerity to bring seven glasses, picked up the tablet and placed it on the floor behind. He then handed a glass to each of their guests and took his place again at Walt's shoulder.

Walt took a sip of his water and proceeded, 'well gentlemen, what is it you have come to offer me?'

Sir John began by an explanation of how the offer was formulated. 'It seems that the king had sent a messenger to the High Sheriff of Northumberland in Newcastle, asking him to resolve the problem without bloodshed. He had no wish to fan the flames of rebellion in the area any more than necessary. He recognised that your family had many powerful friends in Northumberland and generally very few enemies of power. The sheriff contacted me and Sir Robert among others, to find a way to solve the problem of Mitford Castle. Sir Ralph was brought into it by some friend of yours, who for reasons of his own wishes to remain anonymous.'

'So what have you to offer? Have you brought a document to set out your offer?' Walt asked.

'Not yet, we need to agree to the terms. Our suggestion is this: you surrender Mitford castle and your person to the sheriff at a time to be agreed, and you have our word that you will get a fair hearing, and receive the king's favour in this.'

Walt gave a sarcastic laugh. 'What is that supposed to mean? Could it be that the king will only hang me but not draw and quarter me? What about my family and my estate? And what about my soldiers who are loyal subjects, and only do my bidding?'

Eure looked uncomfortable. 'I can promise that your soldiers and your squire will be allowed to go free, without let or hindrance, to pursue their lives as they will. As for you, you will have to place yourself in the hands of the sheriff to face trial in a king's court for robbery and possibly treason.'

Walt replied angrily. 'treason means a hanging, so there can be no surrender. I did not choose to be placed in charge of this castle. After fleeing to Scotland from the robbery, I was a virtual prisoner of Bruce, and placed in this castle, along with these men and a strong detachment of Scots to make sure we did not hand it over. I have been a prisoner of my own unfortunate circumstances, unable to hand over after the Scots departed, until I could do so without being called a traitor. You will note that the flag of Saint George flies from our keep and not the Scottish Saltire. I saw this meeting as my opportunity, but it seems not. I fear we are all wasting our time gentlemen.'

Greystoke spoke up. 'Could your men give evidence that you were brought here by a larger force of Scots and forced to take the castle under pain of death.'

'Of course they could, but I don't want them hauled into court.'

'Supposing you wrote out the circumstances as you told us, and we had your men sign as verification. The document could then be passed on to the High Sheriff and submitted to the court,' countered Greystoke.

'Yes I suppose that would be alright, but what about my land?' Walt said.

Eure took up the argument again. 'We could do nothing about that, only to assure you that any land registered at this time to other members of your family will not be touched and no members of your family persecuted in any way.'

'What about my money?'

Eure answered, 'any money that is in your possession on your arrest will be held by the crown until completion of your trial. Any fines in excess of this amount will be realised from sequestered land. None of your family will be approached to take on your debt.'

Walt made up his mind. This was the best he would get. If his family were alright and his men were safe, all he had to do was to get away with his life, and there was now a good chance of that.

'I will agree to those terms, on condition that two copies of this agreement are written out, detailing on whose authority the Sheriff can make such terms, and signed by the three of you and the Sheriff. I will write out two copies of the circumstances of my taking possession of Mitford Castle and have it signed by all the men.'

The three visitors looked at each other and Greystoke spoke first. 'Who did tell the Sheriff he had the power to make a deal?'

The other two shook their heads and shrugged their shoulders.

'So this is all pointless and we have made no progress at all.' Walt said, disgusted.

Eure was not going to give in so easily after making such good progress. 'That is not so, the Sheriff assured me he had court authority, and I will ensure that he states whose it is on the document and attaches his seal to such a statement.'

Walt decided to look on the positive side of the situation and said. 'very well, you get the two identical documents drawn up and brought here for signature. I will have my document ready. After signing, one copy of each is to be retained by Sir Ralph de Greystoke and the other by me, to present to the court on my indictment.'

This was agreed, and they all breathed a sigh of relief as they rose from their chairs to shake hands on the proposed deal.

The guards were dismissed, Walt and Aidric escorted the visitors to the feasting hall, where the cook had made a commendable meal, and laid on wine in fine pewter goblets. Walt was relieved he had not used the silver. It may have been recognised by someone.

Following a lengthy meal and a sufficiency of wine, the three emissaries stood up to leave and Walt sent a trooper to have their horses brought to the courtyard.

It was agreed that Walt and his men could move freely until the handover date to be agreed, and there would be no harassment or arrest, providing they did not attempt to flee the county. It was likely that the sheriff would have men watching for unauthorised movement Eure pointed out. It was arranged that they would meet again at a similar time the following Wednesday to finalise the agreement.

After his visitors had departed, Walt returned to his quarters and put pen to parchment, to detail the circumstances under which he became the occupier of Mitford castle.

Whilst writing his detailed account, he stressed that they were there under duress to take Mitford from a superior force of Scots, who had remained until April 1318. Since then he had occupied the castle on behalf of King Edward, awaiting approach and instructions for handover. He had incurred no costs for the state, administering the castle and troops from his own funds. He added that these actions were attested to by all his men as witnesses, although they had no choices in any of the decisions made. He then listed their names with space alongside for each man's signature or mark. At the foot of the document he added his own name and signature along with his seal. He then set about writing an identical copy for Greystoke as they had agreed.

Later, at dismissal parade, Aidric read out the statement to the men. Walt then asked them if anyone disagreed with the account. There was no dissent, so he continued to ask if all were willing to sign as witness to these occurrences. Having also received no opposition to this suggestion, he told them about the arrangement for the handover of the castle, and the security he had obtained for their futures, whereby they were to be absolved of any responsibility for the holding of the castle on Bruce's behalf.

'Until further notice,' Walt said; 'you will carry on with your duties as normal. My squire will fill you in on details as the need arises. If you will now follow me to my quarters you may sign these documents as we have agreed.'

Once in his quarters, Walt arranged the two identical documents side by side on the table, with inkpot and quill to hand. As each man made his mark, or signed as indicated against his name, he was thanked and given a small bonus of a silver penny.

The men saw in this document a testimony that they were in no way to blame for what happened, and Walt saw a possible way to keep his neck out of the noose. He was still not convinced by the promises received, but recognised this as possibly his only chance to come out of the situation with his head still on his shoulders.

The last man to sign was his squire, after which Walt bade him sit down.

'I have until next Wednesday morning to set my affairs in order Aidric. That is when the knights return for my final decision. If you have no objection I would like to spend some of this time with my family, but I would feel more secure if I knew that you were in overall control here. I do not want anything to go wrong in the short time we have left. I strongly suggest that all the men are confined to the castle. Talk outside of what is underway, or any drunkenness or misdeed could jeopardise the agreement and the men's own freedom as negotiated. If you wish some time with Jeanne, I will endeavour to be back by Sunday morning so you can leave and return on Tuesday evening.'

Aidric waved his hand, in a sign of dismissal of the suggestion. 'After the handover I will have all the time I need with Jeanne, Sir. You come back on Tuesday evening. Have no worries, I will look after things here.'

Walt felt a lump in his throat. 'You are not only a first class squire, Aidric, you are indeed a true friend and this action will not be forgotten.'

'Thank you, Sir, will that be all?' asked Aidric.

Walt dismissed him, and prepared to leave for Syhale manor. He packed everything up including his armour; he would not need that again for the foreseeable future. He had his armour loaded onto a pack horse and after sorting out sufficient money to keep the garrison for another two weeks, he packed the rest into his saddlebags. Any money found here when he handed over would be confiscated, and he wished to keep that to a minimum. If they ran short he could always bring a little back from the manor.

***

Katherine was worried. She knew that today was the day the knights were to go to Mitford, and discuss the terms under which Walt would be allowed to hand over the castle into the king's hands by way of the High Sheriff.

Annie was just clearing away the breakfast things and Tilly was engaged in getting the children ready to take them for a walk. It was a bright sunny day, albeit there was a chilly November breeze blowing and they had to put on their warm coats. Tilly intended to take them for a walk to the mill, where she could have a little chat to her friends Daisy and Nicholas, if they were not too busy. She enjoyed going to the mill for the occasional visit but it was never easy with the children as she had to keep a sharp lookout at all times to ensure that they kept away from the millrace. She dare not contemplate the consequences of returning to the manor with one less than she set out with.

Katherine watched them donning their warm woollen coats, and as they were leaving she said, as if having read Tilly's thoughts, 'if you are going to the mill, take care to keep them away from the millrace and do not let them out of your sight Tilly.'

'Yes, My Lady,' responded Tilly as she ushered the three children through the door.

Katherine followed her out as she needed to seek out the reeve to discuss the day's work on the estate. She knew that it was unnecessary as David Reeve would already have everything in hand, the bailiff would have seen to that, but Katherine was looking for any excuse to keep busy, and her mind off Walt's predicament until he came home at the weekend, if he came home at the weekend. Perhaps she should have told Tilly to keep the children at home to help distract her from her worrying thoughts. She found the reeve, and as expected, he had everything under control.

Walking back to the house she saw Jeanne riding up the lane towards the manor. Nowadays Jeanne lived at the farm she shared with Aidric, where she also, had just been checking with her reeve that all was in hand with the workers there, before coming to perform her housekeeping duties. She approached and dismounted, handing her horse to a stable boy and walked into the house with Katherine. She was about to go through into the kitchen to check supplies and make a shopping list with cook, when Katherine took her by the arm and said.

'Jeanne, the shopping list can wait awhile, please sit with me for an hour and keep me company, I have never felt so alone. I think it is the worry of not knowing what is going to happen, and I am not sure I can wait until Walt comes at the weekend.'

'I am sure he will try to get some news to you My Lady, as soon as he can. I am also worried about Aidric's future so I know exactly how you are feeling.'

Katherine placed her hand over Jeanne's and gave it a gentle squeeze. 'Call me Katherine when we are alone together Jeanne.'

'Yes My Lady,' responded Jeanne, and they both simultaneously burst out laughing. The laughter broke their aura of gloom and brought about a slightly more optimistic feeling.

'You are right Jeanne; I wager they will send someone with word before nightfall. Now you had better go about your duties, to be sure we have sufficient food and stores for the coming days.'

'Yes Katherine, My Lady,' said Jeanne, correcting the address as she realised that acknowledgment of orders was better treated formally. This caused them both to laugh again and Katherine saw her off to the kitchen with a friendly wave of her hand.

After midday repast Katherine made up her mind to visit her parents, to enquire if her father had heard any rumours about the outcome of the meeting at Mitford. She asked Sergeant Galeron for an escort and set off directly to Seaton Delaval pele.

Arriving at her parents' home she found her mother to be still in poor health and her father showing signs of worry and strain from looking after her. Nevertheless they both welcomed her enthusiastically, asking if she had any news of Walt.

Katherine's disappointment at their lack of any useful news was obvious. Her father took her in his arms and gave her a comforting hug.

'I am sorry my dear, we have not heard any news other than to confirm that a meeting did take place' he said gently.

Katherine decided to remain for the duration of the afternoon and keep her mother company. She was dismayed to find that Isobel was now taking regular potions, for the relief of pains in her joints, and could not negotiate the stairs between floors of the pele without the assistance of a servant. Sometimes she would try, and get stuck half way, then have to call for help. She told Katherine that Hugh got very angry when she attempted to negotiate the narrow spiral stairs alone. Katherine agreed with her father, and scolded her mother for putting herself in danger, when there was always help at hand. She understood that her mother hated having to be dependent on others, and was much saddened by the situation.

As the day drew to a close, Katherine left her parents' company for a quick canter home with her escort, before darkness fell. Arriving at the manor she handed her horse over to Will, to be told by him that Sir Walt was home this past hour. Rushing inside, and feeling guilty for being absent when he arrived, she found him playing with the children in the family room. He came across to greet her, and she threw her arms around him with great enthusiasm and kissed him lovingly.

'What happened?' she asked anxiously, 'I did not expect you so soon.'

'Well, the men are to be released at handover and I am to be arrested and conveyed to gaol where a decision on my future trial will be made. They have intimated that I have the king's favour such that I shall keep my head, but will make no further promise.'

'You could be in for life,' said a horrified Katherine.

'Hopefully it will not come to that, it seems I have a powerful but anonymous friend in Northumberland, who is looking out for my interest. Although the fact that he wishes to remain anonymous suggests that he has fear of being branded a rebel himself.

It would appear that the king had already given the order for the banished Despensers to return. He is set to take the fight to the rebel barons, including the Earl of Lancaster, with whom he has again fallen out. My informants tell me it could get very nasty and I am better out of sight in prison, and hopefully out of the king's mind until the dust settles. They are sure there will be many hangings and beheadings of rebel barons and knights, with me being included if I do not take this early opportunity.'

'How long are you home for?' Katherine asked hopefully.

'Just until next Tuesday evening, then I must return to Mitford for the meeting and viewing of the written conditions of my arrest. At this time I assume I will be told when that will be.'

'Will you go and see the boys at the Abbey before you return?'

'Yes I think I will do that tomorrow. I would also like to see the abbot and give him a little extra cash to ensure their protection, and show my goodwill. When I return, I will donate all my remaining time to you, and our other three sons here my dearest.'

Walt's ride to the Abbey the following day was uneventful. He passed to the west of Alnwick castle and gave some thought to visiting Baron Percy, but he dismissed the idea as too dangerous, even if Percy was still holding him in favour, he could bring trouble on his head by turning up openly. He rode on over a bridge and along the northern bank of the river Aln. The ground rose onto a long promontory which jutted out on the north bank of the river causing it to wind around its end. On this high ground was a small cluster of buildings which comprised the Abbey, and beyond towards the end of the promontory were more buildings housing a Carmelite Priory.

Abbot Stephen was pleased to see him, and even more pleased to receive the extra cash. *When was a monk not pleased to receive extra cash?* thought Walt wryly.

The difficult part of the visit for Walt would be explaining to young Walter and Alexander that he may be away for a few years, and they would be unlikely to see him when they came home this Christ's Mass.

Abbot Stephen took him to another room with a table and some chairs, and bade him wait while he summoned his sons. After some fifteen minutes his boys were ushered in by their tutor Brother Daniel. The two boys walked quietly over to the table, said, 'good morning Father,' and took seats quietly opposite to him. Brother Daniel also bade him good morning and took a seat at the end of the table.

Walt returned their greetings and turning to Brother Daniel, asked for his report on the boys' behaviour and progress. The monk responded enthusiastically with a report of behaviour as good as could be expected from boys of their age, and of their willingness and ability to learn all he could teach them. 'Most satisfactory' he concluded.

Walt thanked him and continued. 'Now Brother Daniel, I have matters to discuss with my sons that I would do in privacy. Could you please leave me alone with my boys, and tell me where they should report to you when we are finished?'

Brother Daniel looked a little disturbed at being excluded from the meeting, but rose and said they should return to their classroom on conclusion.

After the monk had left, Walt called the boys over to him and took one under each arm for a hug. He asked them to return to their seats, and please listen carefully and he would answer their questions afterwards. He took a deep breath and began.

'Walter and Alex, you know you are both dear to me, as are my other sons. Soon you will be coming home for a few weeks over Christ's Mass, to stay at home before returning in January for further tuition. I must tell you now, that it is most likely that I will not be there when you return.'

He saw Walter about to speak and held up his hand for silence, continuing.

'I have to go away on business with the High Sheriff. He in turn may want me to go to London and see the King. The king may insist that I stay for a while as his guest, so I could be away for a long time. You must not worry, your mother will look after things while I am away, and you will continue to carry on with your studies. Your mother will send one of our soldiers to escort you home for the holy days, and she will give you further news at that time.'

Walter was the first to speak, being the eldest and clever enough to know that there was something wrong with his father's casual explanation of absence.

'What is it you have done to upset the sheriff and the king, Father, that they would take you away for such a long time?'

'Quite a lot Son, but it is not to be discussed now, and please ensure neither of you repeats any of this conversation to the monks. Your mother will tell you more when you are home later. Now tell me boys, how is it here? What is Brother Daniel like?'

Alex decided it was his turn to speak and piped up. 'He is very strict. If we misbehave we get the stick on our arses.'

Walt smiled; he did not disagree with discipline for his boys, provided they suffered no long term harm.

'Well then I should assume that you both have quite a few red lines on your backsides.'

'No, Sir.' They both piped up in unison, with Walter continuing. 'You heard Brother Daniel Father, we are quick learners, especially when not learning results in sore arses.'

'What is the food like?' asked Walt, remembering the apology for food served up at Tynemouth when he was a scholar.

'A bit boring but generally wholesome and tasteful, not as good as home,' Walter replied.

'Good, I am satisfied you are getting along well boys so let us go to your class and hand you back to your teacher.' Walt said, striding towards the door with the boys following.

Outside the door he stopped and said, 'that is as far as I know the way; you had better lead now Walter.'

Both boys laughed, and Walter took the lead to a nearby building and stepped through a doorway into a small room with only six desks arranged, three each side and a table at the front. In the centre of the room was a stone circular fireplace with a smoke hole in the roof above. There was a small fire burning, just enough to prevent the room from freezing, Walt judged. Four of the desks were unoccupied and at the table sat Brother Daniel. Walter and Alex took up their places at two of the empty desks.

'Have you only four students?' Walt asked of the monk.

'We have gone through hard times, Sir. These other two are from the castle, otherwise there has been nobody these past three years. We are hoping that things will return to normal soon and some more young men will come. We have a larger classroom but it is too cold for a small number, and we cannot afford the wood to heat it when we have so few students.'

Walt told him that he had left a donation with the abbot, and hoped it would be of help. Brother Daniel thanked him without enthusiasm, and Walt wondered if donations ever got as far as firewood. He thanked the monk, bade farewell to his sons, and sought out the abbot to say his farewell.

Abbot Stephen wished him well with his troubles, and advised him not to lose heart whatever came his way.

As he rode away, Walt wondered if the abbot knew something he did not? On his return journey he felt totally miserable at the thought that he may never see his boys and his lovely Katherine again, after next week. He began to think about his future following his surrender, and what were the advantages and disadvantages.

In his favour he would have: the testimony by the men as to the circumstances of his taking Mitford, his guarantee of fair treatment, the king's favour for handing the castle back without duress and his chivalry towards the pope's envoys. Many friends, both known and unknown, and he would not be short of money for bribes.

Against him he had: his actions against the bishop and the cardinals, flight to Scotland, joining with Bruce to take Mitford, robbing and freebooting during most of the years at Mitford, and some enemies, not least being Prior Gregory. Most of all was the unpredictability of the king.

All in all, Walt decided that he would be lucky to keep his head, but he was not intending to admit that to his wife and children. He was thankful that he had the foresight to send messengers to summon William, his Uncle Adam and Simon Clennell. It would be a rush for William all the way from York, but he had told the messenger to ride hard, to allow his brother as much time as possible. Stressing the urgency he had also made it clear that it was likely to be a farewell banquet, and that where possible, they should be accompanied by their wives and offspring.

Knowing all was in place, he set about enjoying what could be the last days of his freedom for a long time, or maybe for ever. Most of all he tried to make up to Katherine for all the time he had already been away. He wanted to give her enough love to last her for ever if that was possible.

Katherine, on her part, still loved him as much as when they first married but had to admit secretly, that she would certainly need the rest when he went back to Mitford next Tuesday night. She had not forgiven Walt for continuing his illegal foraging long after he had promised to stop, but the thought of punishing him just made her feel so guilty, that she instigated their next lovemaking, in spite of feeling completely drained of energy. Walt was not so engrossed in his own lust that he did not notice her exhaustion. He kissed her and laid her down gently on the bed. 'Let us rest tonight my dearest,' he said. 'You may wake me in the morning if you so wish, but I will make no more demands until you have slept.'

Katherine felt her guilt rise again. Had he read her thoughts? She put her arms around him, returned his kiss and promptly fell into a deep sleep.

By Sunday they had satisfied most of their lust and steadied down, realising that they could not live only for each other, at the expense of their children, and their other responsibilities.

Katherine spent some time stitching gold florins and silver pennies into Walt's clothing. Not too much in case it was taken, but enough to be of help if the opportunity arose to offer bribes for an easier passage of time. She showed Walt where to unpick to retrieve the coins and ensured that the material was thick enough around the coins for them not to be easily detected by handling the garment.

All too quickly, Tuesday came and the first to arrive were William and Freda, who had ridden up from York and spent the previous night in a hostelry in Tynemouth. He told Walt that it was common knowledge in Tynemouth that there was to be a handover of Mitford Castle, and surrender to the sheriff, but nobody knew when, so many had dismissed it as rumour.

That was not good news to Walt, who immediately had in his mind a vision of Prior Gregory rubbing his hands with glee.

Early on the Tuesday morning Walt had ridden down to the mill, and invited Nicholas Heddon and Daisy to their family banquet. At the same time he had made a request to them for use of the mill, for a private meeting for him and a few friends after the midday repast. Daisy agreed they could use her parlour and she would have the lad ensure there was a fire going and the room was nice and warm.

By midday the others had all arrived as summoned and they assembled in the great hall. All had brought with them their wives and children as requested. The only children missing were Walt's own two sons Walter and Alexander who were at Alnwick. The cooks had done them proud and they had a very enjoyable if not slightly overcrowded meal. Nevertheless everyone enjoyed themselves.

After the meal Walt called the menfolk together and they left the women and children to chatter on in the hall while they walked down to the mill and settled in Daisy's parlour. The lad brought them some refreshment, and Walt thanked him and told him to go to the manor and see the cook who would give him a treat. The boy was quickly away and they could get down to business.

In the room with Walt was his brother William, his uncle Adam Radulf and his son Matthew, his father in law Sir Hugh Delaval, his brother in law Richard Delaval, his uncle Sir Simon Clennell, and finally his trusted Squire Aidric Johansson who had been summoned from Mitford and temporally replaced by Sergeant Galeron Guddal who was to remain there until relieved.

Walt opened the meeting by thanking them all for coming, several of them from some considerable distance. He continued, 'you may or may not know, that I have agreed to meet with three knights at Mitford on Wednesday. We have negotiated some terms for my surrender of the castle, and my person into the king's hands, by way of the High Sheriff at a time to be agreed. Subject to them bringing the written terms of my surrender, it could be on Wednesday or at some later date. I imagine it will be sooner, rather than later.'

Walt paused to let this sink in to those who may not have known about the arrangement, like William and his uncles Adam and Simon.

William was the first to speak. 'Who are the knights who you negotiated with?'

'There was not much negotiation for my part Brother, more a take it or leave it. Under the current circumstances, having assured the safety of the soldiers, I took it. It seems that at least I am to keep my head. The knights in question are Sir Robert de Umfraville, Earl of Angus, Sir Ralph de Greystoke and Sir John de Eure.'

'What is this to do with Greystoke?' asked Simon. 'Surely his demesne is in Cumberland.'

'Yes Simon,' Walt replied. 'Those were also my thoughts, but it seems he is acting on behalf of a powerful benefactor of mine who wishes to see me treated fairly, but for political reasons wishes to remain anonymous.'

'What is it you want us to do?' asked Hugh getting to the point of the meeting.

'I will have two documents on my person when I am arrested. One is the terms of my arrest, and the other a testimony signed by all the men stating that we were under duress when occupying Mitford castle. A copy of each of these documents is to be retained by Greystoke to hand to my benefactor for safe keeping. If anything goes wrong it is he you should approach in the first instance. I do not expect any of you to bring unwanted attention to yourselves, we are in troubled times, but I would like to be able to join you all in a banquet again at some future date.'

They all assured Walt that they would work towards his early release and make approaches to the negotiators, when and as appropriate.

Walt continued, 'God and my gaoler willing, I shall be writing to Katherine and we will arrange a way of keeping in contact through her. Aidric here, who you all know, will arrange any messengers required. It may be some weeks before I am able to contact you, as I think it likely I shall be transported to the king's prison in London.'

There was a groan of dismay from all concerned at this suggestion. High in their minds was the fate of Middleton, after he was transported to London.

William suggested that he ensure the document promised life, limbs and sanity, not just keeping the head.

With a promise to help all they could, and generally keep their ears open and their mouths shut, he asked them to use Aidric as a sounding board for any actions, as he would always be privy to the latest news from his confinement. With that last comment, Walt bade them all return to the manor, where they could take beverage and be merry. There would be more food in the evening, he told them, for those who wished to remain for the night.

As they all left the mill, Walt held Aidric back as he turned the key in the lock and handed it to him, with instructions to give it to Nicholas or Daisy, but advise the mill lad, in case he wished to return early.

Now walking behind the main group, after a few paces, Walt turned and said quietly to his squire, 'you know that you are my main man back here at the manor now, Aidric. You will find that I appreciate your loyalty, and you shall be rewarded over the coming times accordingly. Anything you hear you can discuss freely with Lady Katherine. She will be in receipt of my letters, if I may write. Anything she asks you to do, please comply, it is likely to be at my request.'

'Yes, Sir,' replied Aidric, he needed to say no more.

Walt knew he could rely on his judgment. 'You hurry on now Aidric, Jeanne will be waiting, and I think my brother wishes to speak with me.'

As soon as William saw his brother was alone he took him to one side. 'Walt.' He said, 'I am coming back to Syhale with Freda.'

'There is no need, Katherine can manage. She has plenty of friends.'

William looked hurt. 'Walt, we are family and there are bound to be difficulties with the control of serfs for a woman, no matter how determined she is.'

'William, if you so wish, then so be it, and we shall all be very grateful, but what about your business?'

'We have a steward now who is most efficient, and Ingrid is highly competent in overlooking the accounts. She seems very fond of Cuthbert, that's the man I mentioned in my letter and now our steward. Unfortunately Ingrid would never be able to marry without first having her marriage to Mark annulled by the Pope.'

Walt put his hand on his brother's shoulder and looked him in the eyes. 'I could not wish for a better brother than you William, but you must be sure your business is safe in York.'

'Have no fear Brother, I will not neglect my business and will make frequent visits to York, to satisfy myself of its wellbeing, and also of Ingrid's good health and security.

At that point Freda appeared. 'Has he told you?' She asked Walt.

'Yes Freda, he told me, is it your idea to return?'

'Of course not, but William discussed it with me, and I agreed it was the correct course of action. Walt, you should know that I would not be presumptuous enough to try to make decisions on my husband's behalf.'

Walt looked at William and they both burst into spontaneous laughter, while Freda on her part could feel her blood rising, and knew that she was visibly blushing.

'That is settled then,' said William. 'You can tell Katherine, and unless she objects, I shall return alone to York tomorrow to explain to Ingrid, and close up my house. I shall retain one servant to maintain the house in good order, and have Ingrid look after my interests while I am away.'

Katherine did not object. She looked forward to the company and the authority that William would be able to bring to her orders for the workers, especially their bailiff, Turstan Gathergood, who had a tendency to question her decisions. This annoyed her, but she did not complain as he was generally most efficient at his work, and well thought of by the reeve and the serfs.

The afternoon continued as if it were a normal happy family gathering. As dusk began to fall, Walt bade them all farewell, and went to the family room to say a sad goodbye to his three sons and Tilly. After a quick farewell to his tearful staff, he mounted his horse for the journey to Mitford with Aidric. He was to be accompanied as far as the mill by Katherine, who insisted on riding the short distance alone with him. Arriving at the mill she turned to the left along the track to the old barn.

'Katherine, what do you think you are doing, what about Aidric?' Called Walt, but he still followed her.

'I told Aidric to go straight to Mitford and relieve Galeron, and you know well what I am doing Husband,' she said.

'Katherine it is cold, nearly dark and the barn is bound to be in bad order and dirty,' he called. Katherine was now some twenty yards ahead of him.

When Walt caught her up she was afoot, and Walt was surprised to see that the doors looked in good order, even though they had not been used for some years. He dismounted and followed her inside, leading his horse as she had done. Walt saw that there was a rail on the left to hitch the horses, and troughs with hay and fresh water. Over the other side was spread a large groundsheet with a lamp burning on a wooden box. Also on the box were two goblets and a gourd of wine.

Katherine took him in her arms and said, 'Walter Radulf, you don't think I was going to let you go without a very special goodbye do you?'

At the manor, Freda had watched them leave with a sadness in her heart. She knew exactly where they were going. It was with her that Katherine had conspired to get the place ready in the morning, before midday. Nobody had missed Freda and William for an hour while they went to get the place ready, and took advantage of the situation themselves for a little reminiscence. Katherine had ensured the building was kept in good order, all the time Walt was away. The old barn would always have a place in her heart, just as it did for Freda.

***

Walt awoke late the following morning. He shouted for Aidric to demand why he had been allowed to oversleep. Slowly, as he wakened properly, the previous night came back to him. The private paradise he entered with Katherine, their heartrending farewells, and his difficult ride back to Mitford. The moon was nearing the end of its third quarter, and he had only starlight to guide him, and sometimes not even that when the heavens clouded over. Progress was very slow, and he took a couple of wrong tracks, after unwisely overriding his horse's instinct for direction. Eventually he capitulated and let the animal have rein and find its own way, which it did with some confidence albeit very slowly.

By the time Aidric arrived in his quarters, Walt's temper had evened, after recalling the memories of the night before. 'Good morning,' he said to his grinning squire.

'You had a good long goodbye then, Sir,' Aidric responded.

Walt, seeing his grinning face, breathed a deep sigh. 'I suppose I am the only one in the household who did not know what to expect last night' he said.

'Oh no, Sir, only your brother and his wife, and whoever they may have told, and I think I might have mentioned it to Jeanne.'

'So everybody then,' retorted Walt.

'Probably, Sir, but now I think you should prepare yourself, have breakfast and make ready for your visitors later in the morning.'

Their guests arrived earlier this time, and were there a good hour before noon. Having been shown up to Walt's private quarters, they lost no time in getting down to business, and immediately produced the surrender agreement for Walt's perusal.

Walt read through it carefully and could see no problems. It seemed quite clear that his person was not to suffer any torture or execution. He looked for the authority and saw it was signed on the king's behalf by his Chamberlain Sir Hugh Despenser at a date prior to his banishment. Walt looked from the document to Greystoke whilst holding a questioning finger against the signature.

Added after the Despenser's seal, and signed by the High Sheriff, Sir William Fenton, was the clause regarding the freeing of all his

214

men, and reference made to their testimony regarding the taking of the castle.

Ralph de Greystoke explained that the main part of the agreement had been written and signed in London earlier in the year before the banishment of Hugh Despenser from office. He assured Walt that the document was valid. It would take too long to have another drawn up and could jeopardise, or delay, the whole surrender agreement and anyway, Hugh Despenser would be back in office any day soon. He insisted that the High Sheriff had authority to decide the men had no case to answer, under the circumstances.

Walt had to trust the document, he now had little option. He took his quill and signed. After asking Aidric to bring a candle and sealing wax, he applied his seal. He checked the second copy of the document and repeated the process.

Taking one copy of the surrender document he folded it with a copy of the men's testament and handed them to Ralph de Greystoke, the others he folded together and slipped inside his tunic.

'Well gentlemen if we are to be finished with our business, and you can tell me when I am to hand myself over to the sheriff, I would be grateful.'

Greystoke stood and offered his hand. 'The sheriff will be here with a small party tomorrow morning to take possession of the castle, and to escort you to Newcastle, where you will be his guest in the king's prison there, until further instructions are received from London. You will not be bound, but you will be put under oath not to abscond whilst travelling with the sheriff.

Walt took Greystoke's hand and shook it enthusiastically. He then offered his hand to the others, and invited them to join him and his squire in some good ale, wine or uisge, whichever they preferred.

====

CHAPTER 10

Surrender and skulduggery

With his guests departed and the castle occupants now relaxed, Walt retired early in the evening after the signing. He intended to have a good night's sleep to prepare for what the morrow would bring. It was not to be; he slept only fitfully and was laying awake, waiting for dawn to break on the Thursday morning. In his mind he was going over all the things he should have done but had forgotten. He should have thought more of any difficulties Katherine may have, and was grateful, but a little resentful, that it had been his younger brother who had reminded him of the difficulties which might be experienced in running an estate over a lengthy period by a woman alone, without a dominant male of the family on hand. Women in his family tended to have more importance attached to their role and somewhat greater freedom than many in the county. He had forgotten to take account of that, especially as she would have to deal with the likes of Prior Gregory from time to time. She may have difficulty drawing labour from outside the demesne at busy times; also there was the business of the soldiers. There would be too many of them for Katherine. He had already discussed what should be done, but someone must put the plan into operation. He decided he needed to speak to Squire Aidric on that matter; he could liaise with William in the event he was not allowed visitors in the prison.

Once he had swilled his face with cold water to wake up, he dressed and went to seek the cook and demand some breakfast. While the cook was making breakfast porridge, he wakened Aidric and asked him to come to his quarters as soon as he was dressed.

A short time later Aidric arrived, to find his master sat at his table with a hot steaming pan of porridge on the table and two bowls and spoons.

'Sit down Aidric and help yourself to porridge, I wish to discuss one or two things with you.'

'Yes, Sir,' Aidric replied, taking the seat opposite and helping himself to a good helping of the hot and sticky oatmeal preparation.

'After the handover we will have too many soldiers for Syhale, as we have already discussed. We will also have three Sergeants, Guddal, Best and Wilson. The total needs to be trimmed to around twenty to twenty five maximum for the defence of Syhale. We don't need more than two sergeants, and I would prefer we keep Guddal and Best. Try to keep all our own men and the best of the new men to make up the new troop. Make sure you keep that Welshman Cethin Gwyn and his four colleagues, unless they want to be discharged. Keep all the extra men until they can be found other posts, or accept a discharge payment. You will need my brother William for this to ensure all is done legally; I don't want my wife getting into any trouble. William is returning to York but will be back within the week, and he will take charge on my wife's behalf. Do you understand that Aidric? Take all orders regarding the estate from my wife, or from my brother William.'

'I understand, Sir and I wish to express my pleasure that Master William will be there to give his valuable help.'

Walt grinned. 'Alright Aidric, don't overdo the forelock tugging, it does not become you. Go down now and wake the men. Get them fed, and then get them to clean up their barracks. After that, get them into clean and tidy order, ready to parade for the handover to the High Sheriff. I will ask him to inspect them to show that we are a disciplined unit and not the rabble we have been made out to be by some.'

Without further question or comment Aidric left to obey his orders. Walt took the two signed documents he had been left with the previous day, and wrapped them into a linen envelope. He sealed the fold with wax and taking his quill, wrote boldly on the linen. *Private papers belonging to Sir Walter de Radulf of Syhale.* This envelope he placed inside a waxed canvas wallet to protect his precious documents from damage from rain or damp. Taking a large canvas bag he then began to pack clothing he thought he might need, and be allowed to take to his prison. He dressed himself in good clothing befitting a man of his status but suitable for a long journey on horseback. The canvas wallet containing his precious documents he slid into a pocket inside his cotehardie. He made another bundle containing his dagger, sword and shield. Armour and helm was tied into a third bundle. Aidric would take the latter two with him to be kept at Syhale.

217

Opening the door, he called for Aidric. Whilst waiting he took down his warm winter riding coat from the hook by the door and draped it over the chair. When the groom saddled his horse for the journey, he knew that there would be the rolled up canvas groundsheet and cape fixed behind the saddle, and his bag of essential clothing and personal belongings would also fit comfortably strapped behind his saddle.

Aidric arrived in the room and immediately took in the situation. Without waiting for Walt to speak, he moved the bundles containing armour and weapons to the door, and called for a soldier to help him take them to the stable and strap them to a pack horse. Walt was grateful that Aidric's experience and knowledge of his needs so often led him to act instinctively in his interests. At that moment he had been sitting at his table, looking at his few possessions in three bundles and feeling, along with the great lump in his throat, a sense of utter despair. Soon he would be separated from his soldiers, who had served him faithfully for many years, and be taken away as a prisoner to Newcastle, and who knows where else, or for how long, or when, and if, he would see his family again? *I really am in the shit this time,* he thought. *If only I had paid more heed to Katherine's misgivings about Middleton.*

Walt was still sitting with his head in his hands when he heard footsteps running up the staircase outside his quarters. He immediately sat up straight and brushed his light hair back from his eyes. He felt ashamed for his moment of weakness. What would his father think if he was watching from above? *Pull yourself together Walt,* he told himself. *You are being selfish. You are only one, where your loved ones are many, and have more reason to grieve than you. They did no crime, but their husband, father, brother and friend is being taken from them.*

Aidric entered and was pleased to see that his master had shaken off his previous melancholy.

'Sir, there are riders approaching.'

'Thank you Aidric. Take this bundle of clothing down and have it fixed behind my saddle. Have the men paraded, and have Sergeant Best bring them to attention when the Sheriff enters the castle. I will come down and invite him to inspect the men, and then I would like you to accompany the sheriff and me to this room where we will conduct our short business.'

After Aidric had left to obey his instructions, Walt had a final look around the room, smoothed down his jacket and strode purposefully out, and down to meet Sir William Fenton.

The castle gate was opened and the sheriff galloped through in style, with a small party of ten men. They pulled up opposite the paraded men, who had been brought to attention by Sergeant Best, who in turn made a commendable show of saluting Sir William, with a flourish of his shiny sword. Walt invited Sir William to dismount and inspect his men. He was heartened when the sheriff showed him some respect by accepting.

Following the brief inspection, Walt ordered Sergeant Best to show hospitality to the escort, while he would take the sheriff to his private quarters for the formal handover.

Sir William showed no hesitation in accompanying Walt, even when it was plain that Squire Aidric was also to be present. Once inside, Walt invited the sheriff to be seated and took his own position opposite. He noisily and self consciously cleared his throat. 'Sir William, this is not a procedure with which I am familiar, perhaps you may advise me what is to be done next.'

Sir William produced a parchment from his saddlebag, which he had brought with him to the room. He spread it out for Walt to read, saying, 'I think this handover document will satisfy your requirements. It contains briefly the elements of the other two documents you have in your possession. There is only one copy, which will be retained by me after signature.'

Walt read the document carefully. It stated clearly that in accordance with previous agreement the High Sheriff, on the king's behalf, was accepting the voluntary handover of Mitford Castle from Sir Walter de Radulf, on the understanding that all the men under the said Sir Walter at Mitford be free to go about their business without hindrance.

Further to this, that the said Sir Walter was to be treated with respect as a gentleman, and that no harm should come to his person, other than imprisonment according to the king's pleasure. This in accordance with a document authorised by the king's chamberlain Hugh Despenser.

This was more than Walt expected and taking his quill and inkpot he signed without delay. He turned the document around, and Sir William signed below him and invited Aidric to sign as a witness.

Aidric was unsure about adding his name to a document that may be read by unknown others; nevertheless he stepped forward and nervously signed his name.

Sir William looked at him quizzically and Aidric said. 'Aidric Johansson, Sir.'

The Sheriff appended the name beneath the illegible signature.

Aidric feeling embarrassed and inadequate said. 'I do read, Sir, but my skills with the quill and ink leave much to be desired.'

Walt changed the subject to save face for Aidric. 'Well, Sir William. May I take your hand to seal this agreement?'

They both stood and gripped each other's forearms firmly. Walt stepped around the table intending to lead them out of the room but Sir William raised his hand to stop him.

'Sir Walter, would you not wish to offer your guests some refreshment now the business has been concluded? We have less than half a day's ride to Newcastle and I thought that your squire could see to marching your men away, to wherever it is you have arranged for them to go, while you and I rested awhile. We have only one of my men coming as escort to me; the remainder will stay in the castle until relieved by the next legitimate commander.'

Embarrassed, Walt apologised, and asked Aidric to organise some light food and some ale and wine before leaving with the men for Syhale. There would be no problem with Walt's horse being prepared, as the groom was a local employee who would remain as long as he was needed by his new masters.

Once alone and supplied with food and beverages, Sir William looked directly at Walt and said. 'I knew your father and respected him as a knight and a warrior. How did you get into such a situation?'

Walt decided it would be stupid to lie but even more stupid to tell all the truth, so he gave the Sheriff his edited version, which tended to diminish some of his own responsibility for events, without trying to plead innocence.

The Sheriff then asked him about the welfare of his family, and confirmed his fears that he would most likely have the bulk of his lands sequestered. He hoped that Walt had made provision for his family, and was complimentary to him, when he was told that all was in order for their welfare.

After a break of about an hour, the two set off with their escort for Newcastle, the Sheriff and his man to continue their duties, and Walt to gaol.

Arriving in Newcastle at the castle keep which was now used as a gaol, the sheriff departed and left the escort to hand over his prisoner.

Walt was led into a square and dismal room with only narrow slits to the outside providing what little light there was. The escort told him that his horse would be stabled and fed in case he required it for a continued journey. The gaoler instructed him to place his bag of possessions on the table, where he searched through it and satisfied himself that there were no prohibited items. Next he searched Walt and found the documents inside his jacket. 'What are these?' he asked.

'They are documents to be presented in my defence when I appear in the king's court.' Walt replied.

'Then you won't need them here.' The gaoler responded, stuffing them into Walt's bag with his clothes. 'You will get them back when you move or go to court. If you need other clothes, you ask and I will get them for you. Your topcoat you leave here also, you have no need of it until you are moved.'

He then called for a guard who escorted Walt to a cell. The cell was about eight foot by six foot, with a dirty looking palliasse on the floor, and a bucket in one corner. There was no chair or table. The door consisted of an iron grill, so he would have no privacy. At the end of the cell, high in the wall, was a narrow window which had no curtain or covering against the elements. Lying on the palliasse was a small pile of blankets, which he supposed he should be grateful for. As the guard locked the door and departed, Walt arranged his blankets on the palliasse and lay down to rest, trying to adjust his eyesight to the almost dark conditions of his miserable space.

Walt's depression returned. Was this to be his life from now on? It was almost as bad as being a pig in a sty. He could not imagine years of living like this, and prayed for the king's court to be convened sooner, rather than later, to decide his punishment. Then at least he would know what to expect.

***

News of Sir Walter Radulf's imminent surrender to the High Sheriff had leaked out, and during his journey to Newcastle under escort; there were small knots of people, inquisitive to see if he was being transported in chains. Most of the way the onlookers were relieved to see he was free to ride normally, but as they got closer to Newcastle there were more who were disappointed that he was not bound and hooded. One of these, standing in the shadows and wallowing in his own good fortune, was Prior Gregory of Tynemouth.

At last, God has answered my prayers, he thought. Some loose tongues, among those with knowledge of the arrangement for Sir Walter's surrender, had made the prior aware that there was some sort of agreement, which was supposed to protect him from the excesses of the king's justice. He did not know who the keeper of such a document might be, or even if it existed. If there was such a document maybe the prisoner was carrying it on his person. He knew he had to find out, whatever the cost in bribes. He was not going to let this chance of a final revenge pass him by.

On his return to Tynemouth, the prior once again asked his fellow conspirator, Brother Saul, to go into Tynemouth and seek out a suitable rogue who would be willing to bribe a prison guard in exchange for an agreed fee, preferably someone without close ties in Tynemouth he stressed. He knew Badger himself was still incarcerated, and even if he wasn't he would be unlikely to want further involvement with the prior, as he had denied him when he claimed he was acting for the priory in his effort to capture Sir Walter. He had taken the harshest sentence of ten years hard labour, and this only because the prior admitted asking him to gain information for the possible arrest of any of the rebels, and claimed a possible misunderstanding with regard to the horses. Without this statement Badger would have surely hung from the gibbet. Badger's accomplices were flogged and thrown into prison at the king's pleasure, which would probably be at least until the next Eyre, which could be a year or more under current circumstances.

The prior's statement had not endeared him to the High Sheriff, who at the time had seen it as unwarranted interference in his business, and a criticism of his failure to recover the castle. He had made no secret of his displeasure with the situation, resulting in Prior Gregory now wisely deciding to be a little more circumspect in his actions, and hopefully avoid any further displeasure from the Sheriff.

Brother Saul eventually turned up with a man called Henry Park. He claimed to be a member of Badger's gang but the prior had not seen him before. He took Brother Saul aside and whispered.

'Are you sure about this man? I have never seen him before. There is a great deal of money involved here. Has the man got family in Tynemouth?

'Only his parents, Prior, he has no dependants. He lives by his wits, theft and deceit is his forte' whispered the monk.

Prior Gregory made an annoyed ticking noise between his teeth, and said. 'I suppose he will have to do,' in a voice now loud enough for the man to hear.

Henry Park smiled; the monk had told him there was much to be gained from this enterprise, and nothing to be lost.

Prior Gregory dismissed Brother Saul and took the ruffian to his private office. Inside he directed the man to a seat with a gesture as he said: 'Henry Park, the work I am offering you requires a deal of cunning and the ability to negotiate a price for an object which I require. Do you understand?'

'Yes Sir, you want me to buy something for you but nobody is to know it is for you.'

'Something like that Park, but it is not in a shop and not for sale in the normal manner.'

'You want me to steal it?' Park interjected enthusiastically.

'That would be the ideal solution, if we could be sure you were not caught, but I fear it is not a practical one. No Mr. Park, I want you to bribe someone to give it to you.'

Park responded eagerly. 'I can do bribing, Sir, how much must I offer, and who must I bribe?'

'The guard at the reception of Newcastle keep prison, the one who has responsibility for storing prisoners' personal effects.' the prior replied.

'What if he will not take the bribe, Sir?'

'He will take the bribe. You will start at an Italian gold florin; this is worth about six months of his wage. If he declines, offer a French gold florin, about double the value. I do not expect that I shall have to go above that. I will give you silver pennies as well, so you can make offers above the Italian coin before moving to the French.

Everything you save above the value of the Italian florin you may keep, in addition to your reward for completing the task.'

'What if he does not take the French florin,' Park asked slyly.

'Then you must return to me and we will see what is to be done next. You will still be paid, but not as much as for success.'

A few more minutes were spent haggling over Park's payment for the task, before he agreed to the prior's offer, and asked for details of what he was to get for the prior.

Prior Gregory leaned over the table and spoke in a low conspiratorial voice. 'There is a prisoner in the cells named Sir Walter de Radulf.'

Before he could continue, Park held up his hand. 'No prior, I am sorry; I want nothing to do with it.'

Prior Gregory's rage was instantaneous. 'Have you been wasting my time man, I will see you punished for this.'

'No, Sir, it is just that Sir Walter's friends and family are bad ones to cross. They would hunt me down as they did Badger, and maybe even kill me, then your money would be of no use to me.'

'What if I increase your reward?'

'I could still be dead, Sir.'

'Suppose I was to send you to another county with sufficient money to buy a smallholding, and a document to verify you as a freeman of the city of Durham by the name of Mason? You could say your ancestors helped build Durham Cathedral,' he chuckled, 'or anything else you want to have built.'

Park did not respond to the prior's attempt at humour, but after some further negotiation a deal was struck, whereby Prior Gregory promised sufficient money for two years' wages, which would enable Park to take a lease on a few acres of ground if he so wished. The resulting payment was to be three French Florins and a horse. Prior Gregory was not a happy man, he was sure he was being cheated, and he was also sure, that he would find a way out of paying all Park demanded. He had a sudden flash of inspiration as he turned to Park and said.

'I will give you some money now. You must buy some better clothes; you cannot turn up at the prison looking like you do, they will as likely lock you up as a thief. You will receive your document and full reward after you have successfully completed your task.

You must also leave the district as soon as you have been paid off, without staying another day or speaking to anyone.'

'How can I explain my leaving the district, Sir?'

'Who do you have to tell, friends or family?'

'Only aged parents, Sir, and a couple of friends'

'Well then, after you have been paid and given your freedom, just tell them that you have work as a messenger, and you are off to the south with despatches for the Earl of Lancaster on the orders of your lord. Once you have left the area, you become Arthur Mason. Is that understood?'

'Yes, Sir,' replied Park.

The prior opened the door and called loudly for Brother Saul, who was hiding around the corner. He had been doing his best to listen at the door, and scuttled around the corner when he heard the prior's chair scrape as he stood to walk to the door and call for him.

'There you are,' said the prior, not surprised that Brother Saul appeared so quickly. He would wager that he had been listening at the door, not that it mattered, he thought. *Brother Saul would have much further involvement to come in his plan.* 'I want you to escort Master Park from the priory and purchase him a horse, see Brother Cornelius on your way out and tell him you have my authority to take money for the purchase. When you have completed these tasks come back to see me.'

Brother Saul could not see why he should purchase a good horse for Park, when there was an old nag in the stables due for the knackers' yard. Ignoring the prior's instructions he had the nag saddled for Park, before escorting him from the premises and instructing him to waste no time in doing the prior's bidding. He then went to Brother Cornelius and obtained sufficient money to purchase a good mount from the town market as a replacement.

Several hours later Prior Gregory was again sat at his desk and this time it was Brother Saul who had been summoned again. He sat facing the prior nervously wringing his hands. Had the prior found out he had disobeyed him regarding the purchase of the horse for Park? The prior studied him quietly for several disconcerting moments before he said.

'Brother Saul, how would you like to be my Deputy Prior to supervise the running of the priory in my absence?'

Brother Saul looked at his superior in astonishment. 'How can this be, Sir? Is there such a post?'

'There has not been one at this priory for a long time, but I am recreating it for you, as a mark of my gratitude for your loyalty.'

The prior watched and saw that the idea was having the desired effect. A smile had appeared on Brother Saul's usually miserable features, and he sat up straight and there was a definite puffing out of his chest as opened his mouth to reply, only to produce a strange croak from his suddenly dry throat.

Prior Gregory waited and watched with some amusement as the monk fought to control his nervousness.

Brother Saul at last found his voice and said uneasily. 'I thank you Prior; you will not regret your trust in me.'

That worked, thought the prior, *he seems to think that he has grown in importance. He probably thinks the position will help him to be my successor, although he would have no chance of becoming prior in the ensuing ballot. The fact that he feels important is sufficient for my needs.* The prior looked directly at the monk and continued. 'Brother Saul, when the man Park, has finished his task and collected his freeman document and reward from me, I want you to be the one to organise his exit from the area. You should recruit a suitable person from Newcastle, where Park is not known, to assist you as his escort out of the county, after he has completed my task and received his reward. You will provide for his safety with all the gold he will be carrying. No need to tell the recruit where you are from or your name, just make certain he knows who he is to guard until he is satisfied they are out of out county, and be sure he knows that Park will be carrying gold.'

'How long should we stay with him then, Sir?'

'At least until he is out of the county and you and the guard are satisfied that there is no one else around who could rob him,' he paused slightly and continued, 'and despatch his soul to heaven. Do you understand me Brother Saul?'

'Yes Prior.' Saul suddenly understood why he was promoted to Deputy Prior. He now felt tricked. He would have to be careful and ensure he found a suitable guard for Park. Nothing must come back to him or the priory.

'One more important point Brother,' the prior added, as he showed him to the door. 'You must leave the escort in town when you return, and wait until Park hands over my package and receives his reward, before you accompany him into the town and pick up your Newcastle ruffian. Whatever he takes from Park is his reward, including the freeman document and he also, must not return to the county.' Brother Saul was less than enthusiastic about the idea of some third party ruffian profiting from this enterprise, but had no intention of conveying his misgivings to his superior.

***

Squire Aidric rode into the manor grounds with the troop of soldiers from the castle, to find Katherine, Jeanne and others waiting for them.

Katherine looked disappointed that Walt was not with them. She had nursed a forlorn hope that the sheriff might make a detour to let him say a final goodbye.

Somewhat mollified by the knowledge, provided by Aidric, that he had not been put in chains, but allowed to ride freely on his own word that he would not escape, she nevertheless worried about her husband's wellbeing.

'What happens when they get to Newcastle? Will he be fairly treated? Will he remain there, or will they send him to London?' She trotted out the questions in quick succession.

'My lady I do not know what they will do, or what the whim of the king may be; but I do believe we should send somebody to keep an eye on him, wherever he is sent, and report back any difficulties, to determine what help we may be able to give.'

Katherine seized on this idea with enthusiasm. 'Who do you suggest Squire?'

'It has to be me, My Lady. I am his squire and I can read and write well enough to send and receive messages, although my penmanship is in need of improvement. If you give me sufficient money for a month, and some for messengers, I will advise you where to contact me when the master's place of confinement is confirmed. I can also try to make contact with him and see to his needs.'

Overhearing this conversation, Jeanne did not look too pleased with the idea of losing her husband, over what was likely to be an extended period. She knew that it was no use appealing to Aidric, his loyalty to Walt was unshakable, and she did not want to make him choose, because even though she had no doubt about his love for her, she knew under such circumstances she would lose.

Katherine gave no thought to her friend Jeanne's feelings, as she thanked Aidric gratefully, for doing what she considered was his duty anyway. After all Jeanne would be safe and they would have each other for company.

Aidric was ready to set out the next morning, travelling lightly, with his immediate needs packed in saddle bags, or along with his cape and groundsheet in rolls behind his saddle. He wore the warm riding clothes of a man of his station, carried his sword and dagger but no armour. He had been given a letter of introduction by Katherine, stating his identity and position.

'Be very careful how you use this Aidric,' she said. 'You must seek out a Northumberland or northern knight, and be sure of his politics, before you broach the subject of help for Walt. Do not involve hotheads, just a sympathetic ear. There must be no talk of escape, or this could finish him, do you understand? You may also use the letter to show to his prison guards, as proof you have right to enquire after his health, or visit him.'

Having put Katherine's mind at rest that he would be careful, Aidric mounted and rode off to begin his duties at Newcastle, which he knew to be the first destination for his master.

***

Henry Park had purchased some clothes with the money the prior had given him, and in accordance with his instructions, he told his parents that he may be travelling a lot from now on, as he had taken work for a knight, as a messenger. Knowing that his parents would be proud he had such an important job, and that it would not be necessary to tell any others, he was in a hurry to get to Newcastle and complete his task. He could not imagine any guard who would not be swayed by the amount of money the prior would pay for a bit of parchment.

Henry's journey was much slower than planned due to the worn out nag provided by Brother Saul. It was dusk when he finally arrived, and he cursed the useless animal the monk had given him. The first thing he would do when he was paid and out of this God forsaken county, he promised himself, would be to purchase a good horse.

Unsure how to begin, he stood outside the gaol entrance, thinking what he should say to the guard inside. A well dressed man of stature, on an expensive looking horse rode up, hitched his horse alongside Henry's, and walked purposefully into the main door of the prison. Henry took his opportunity and followed him at a discreet distance, but close enough, he hoped, to hear any conversation.

Inside the man called assuredly to a guard who was sat behind a heavy wooden counter. 'God be with you soldier,' he said with the confidence of status. 'I am told you have a knight here by the name of Sir Walter de Radulf.'

'Yes, Sir,' replied the guard respectfully. 'He is his Majesty's prisoner, who wants to know.'

'I am his Squire, Aidric Johansson and I enquire after his welfare.'

'Too late to visit now, Sir, no visits allowed after dark, Sir. Come back tomorrow three hours after sunrise, and maybe you can see him.'

'What of his possessions? Was he allowed to keep them with him, for his comfort?'

'Only what he stood up in and anything else he needs is in his cell. His other possessions are safely stored through that door behind me, and will be returned when he is released or moved to another place.'

Aidric thanked the soldier and as he turned to leave, passed a man coming into the room, who was vaguely familiar. He could not rightly place him, but alehouses in Tynemouth were at the top of his speculative list.

Henry, having heard how amiable the soldier seemed, decided to use similar tactics. 'God be with you soldier, I am told you have Sir Walter Radulf here in confinement.'

The guard looked the man up and down. Clean clothing, he thought, slouches and speaks like a peasant, so he is a peasant.

'Go away, I just told one man there is no chance of seeing him until tomorrow,' the guard said impatiently. He followed that with a disapproving look at Henry.

Henry held his ground and said quietly, after looking around to ensure they were alone.

'I do not want to see the prisoner soldier, nor have I any interest in him. I do have interest in making you an offer of gold you cannot refuse.'

The soldier's eyes first lit up with avarice, and then turned slowly to a look of cunning.

'What do I have to do, and how much?' he asked.

'You have to let me have a document from Sir Walter's possessions in your store.'

'Not possible, you would have me in prison along with Sir Walter if I were to do that.'

Henry could sense that they were entering a phase of negotiation, as the cunning was apparent in the soldier's attitude.

Seeing that he still had the guard's attention, he asked. 'When they collected the items from the prisoner did they put them into a box and make a list of each one?'

'They put them into a box but no list was made.' The guard replied.

'In that case nothing can be missed can it?' Henry said triumphantly.

'How much?' The guard enquired without further ado.

'Two shillings,' Henry offered hopefully.

The guard laughed. 'I will not get off my arse for two shillings.'

'But that is more than two week's wages.'

'Not nearly enough for what you want. This is for some gentleman, and not you, so there is more money to be had,' the guard said, craftily adding, 'Anyway, you have no idea how much I earn.'

Henry offered an Italian gold florin, and with still no acceptance from the guard he began to bargain with silver pennies. He was sure it would be wrong to offer the French florin, as the soldier would surely want both and that would eat into his own bonus.

He got to six shillings, which was the equivalent of the French florin, and insisted he was now out of funds. When the guard seemed still undecided, Henry thanked him and turned on his heel to leave. These tactics proved to be correct, for the guard immediately agreed to the Italian florin plus the six shillings in silver money.

'Wait here' he said as he took a large key from behind his counter and entered the storeroom. He returned with a canvas wallet and opened it to reveal the linen package, sealed with wax and confirmed in ink, as the private papers of Sir Walter de Radulf.

'Is this what you want?'

'Yes,' said Henry, trying hard to conceal his excitement. He handed the money to the guard, and exited the gaol with the wallet in his hand before the man could change his mind. Stuffing it into his saddlebag, he mounted his horse and made tracks in the darkness towards Tynemouth. The sooner he got this over with, the happier he would be.

Aidric at this time was settling down for the night in a local Newcastle hostelry and hoping he would be able to see Walt in the morning.

On the Friday morning, he presented himself to the guard at the entrance, and was led into a room where a senior prison guard asked him what he wanted.

Aidric stood to attention and said politely, not being fully aware as to the social position of a senior prison guard, but not wanting to jeopardise his request by upsetting the man: 'My name is Aidric Johansson; I am Squire to Sir Walter Radulf. I respectfully request permission to visit him, and attend to his needs. I bring some small comforts from his wife, Lady Katherine.'

'Then open your parcel, and let me see what you have brought,' the guard replied.

Aidric opened the parcel and displayed some shortbread biscuits, and a silver chain with a pendant in the shape of a cross. He explained that it belonged to Lady Katherine and she wished her husband to have it to hold when in prayer.

The guard saw no problem with such a gift to the prisoner, but Aidric was required to relinquish his sword and dagger. A second guard was called in to search Aidric for concealed weapons. Once satisfied that he was clear, the second guard took him and his parcel to a small empty room, with one small slit of a window, through which a narrow beam of sunlight illuminated a small table in the centre with a stool on either side. Aidric was told to sit down. He took the stool facing the light, so that his master would not be inconvenienced when sitting in other stool.

Aidric looked around the room whilst waiting for his master to be brought from his cell. He could see very little except the area around the table where the light fell. He could imagine that as the sun moved around, the area of light would diminish due to the narrow opening, until there was barely any light at all, even when it was still daylight outside. The place was cold and smelt damp, with overtones of a persistent smell of urine. Aidric shuddered. He did not envy his master in such a place, without his home comforts.

The door opened, and Walt was ushered in by two guards. One of them indicated that he should take the empty stool, and moved to stand alongside the door, the other guard left the room and Aidric heard the bolt being thrown on the outside. He reached across the table for his master's forearm, and they gripped each other firmly. Whilst maintaining his grip as if he did not want to let go, Walt leaned across the table and clapped Aidric on the shoulder with his left hand.

'Thank you for coming Squire,' he said quite formally.

Aidric immediately picked up on this formality, realising that it would be better for all concerned if strangers saw them only as knight and his employee, and not the intense friendship that they felt for each other. Not knowing what the future held, Walt was signifying that it was unwise to give potential enemies leverage over either of them.

'Do you know when you are to be tried, Sir?' Aidric asked formally.

'No I do not Squire, but I believe my sojourn in this place to be only temporary, until the sheriff receives instructions from the king, or his chamberlain.'

'How often may I visit you, Sir?'

At this question the guard stationed inside the door interrupted with the answer. 'Every day mid morning to mid afternoon for up to half an hour, except on Sunday, Sir.'

'Thank you guard,' replied Aidric, picking up his small bundle and opening it on the table. 'Shortbread biscuits that Lady Katherine says you like, and her small silver cross, which she wishes you to wear about your person that you may join with her spiritually in prayer.'

'Thank you Squire,' Walt said. 'Lady Katherine takes much comfort from the power of prayer. If she is praying for me, I am sure to see Syhale again. She would not allow God to deem otherwise, but don't tell her I said that,' he added hurriedly.

Aidric felt he should laugh at Walt's little joke, but only managed a weak smile. This was not a place for laughter. They continued making small talk until the guard came over and told them that their time was up for the day.

Aidric bade his master goodbye, promising to ride to Syhale with news for Lady Katherine, and be back again for a further visit on the morrow.

***

Henry Park arrived at his lodging clutching the valuable documents inside his coat, and close to his chest. If the prior had paid so much money for them, what would he be prepared to do to him if he was to lose them? The idea did not bear thinking about.

He crawled onto his grubby palliasse still in his clothes, keeping his dagger to hand. Supposing that guard had him followed with a view to recovering the documents? He would not feel comfortable until he had handed them over to the prior, received his payment and was far from Northumberland.

Brother Saul had also been to Newcastle, and watched Henry Park enter and leave the gaol. He had already decided that there would be no second escort for Park. The whole idea was preposterous. The man would know he was a monk, and surely connect him to the priory under the prior's ill-thought plan. Besides, if anyone was to profit from Henry Park's misfortune it should be him, and not some alehouse thug.

Brother Saul had a much better idea in his mind, which he was sure would be more beneficial to himself, and a reward for all his hard work. Saul had been a thief and a vagabond, before being obliged to give his life to the priory by becoming a monk, to avoid certain death under the law. He foresaw a possible chance to escape his incarceration in the dreaded priory, if circumstances were favourable to him.

Priory Gregory had not been to sleep since Brother Saul had returned to report the deed done, and now he was nervously awaiting the arrival of Henry Park, who he was sure would be there soon after morning mass.

As expected, shortly after mass, one of the young novices approached Brother Saul, to announce that there was a man at the door to see the prior.

'Good morning Master Park,' Brother Saul said, noticing that Park had arrived on horseback, and was obviously packed for a journey immediately afterwards, as indicated by the baggage roll behind his saddle.

Park grunted a reply and followed the monk to the prior's office, where he produced the package with a proud flourish, and dropped it on the desk in front of Prior Gregory.

Looking pleased the prior said 'good work my man. How much did you have to pay him?'

Henry Park's eyes flicked down to the left as he lied. 'There was no bargaining with him Sir, I had to part with it all.'

The pleased expression immediately left the Prior's countenance as he snapped. 'Were you stupid enough to let him know your strategy and give away how much you were carrying?'

'Oh no, Sir, we bargained, and he kept refusing until I told him there was no more and he could search me if he did not believe it.

The prior did not believe him. 'I have a good mind to make you turn your pockets out.'

'Sir, you may if you wish but I am telling you the truth.' Henry was not stupid enough to appear in the prior's office with a French florin in his purse.

Prior Gregory gave up. He was never going to prove he had been cheated, and he knew he had what he wanted, or did he have it? He made a grab for the parcel and excitedly pulled the package from the wallet. He took one glance at the writing declaring it to be the property of Sir Walter de Radulf, before impatiently breaking the seal to pull the documents from their wrapping. Holding the two documents in his hand he cast his eyes over each in turn. There was promise of leniency signed by the chamberlain, and the deposition from the soldiers. This was better than he expected and a broad smile spread itself across the prior's fat podgy face.

Without further ado he produced a document declaring one Arthur Mason to be a freeman of the land. He had signed it Lewis de Beaumont, Bishop of Durham, and sealed it with a seal which was sufficiently indistinct as to make it unrecognisable. This and a leather purse containing gold florins he handed over to Park.

Henry Park could not read, so had to accept the document as true. As far as money was concerned he was not so gullible. He opened the pouch and looked up at the prior.

'You said three French Florins, these are two Italian coins. If you want me to keep quiet you had better keep to our agreement prior.'

Prior Gregory was not perturbed by this insolence. He calmly tipped the coins out and replaced them with the French Florins demanded. Henry Park was surprised and happy that the prior had capitulated so easily, he had expected more difficulty. He knew he could not expose the prior, without making his own part in the plot public, and the prior must know this also. It worried him a little, but the thought of more money than he had ever had before, in his hand, soon overcame his doubts.

After indicating that the meeting was over, the prior gave a little nod to Brother Saul, who led Henry Park back to his horse, where Park was surprised to see another horse saddled and prepared for an extended journey hitched alongside his own.

'I am coming with you,' Brother Saul declared.

'Why? I would rather go alone.'

'The prior has decreed that I am to escort you from the county, and see that you are not molested.'

'Will it not look a little odd for me to be leaving in the company of a monk?'

'I shall be accompanying you at a distance, to raise alarm if for any reason I believe you to be in danger. I have another accomplice who will watch you more closely,' he lied. 'Do not try to lose me, or you will be deemed to have broken the prior's agreement and you will never see your new life.'

Now Park was worried, he was not a brave man, and decided to go along with the rules in the hope that once out of the county, the monk would take his leave and that would be the end of it.

Several days passed before Park crossed the border into Cumberland, and evening was approaching when the monk caught up with Henry on a lonely trail. 'This is far enough, I am turning back now,' he said. 'There is an inn around five miles back where I can stay. I wish you good fortune for your future Henry Park.'

He moved his horse towards Park's, and held out his hand to clasp the scoundrel's forearm, and bid him farewell. Henry Park relieved that he was finally to be rid of the shadowy figure, willingly proffered his own arm for the ritual. Brother Saul took Park's wrist in a firm grip, while at the same time bringing his left hand holding a long dagger out from a fold in his cassock. He quickly stabbed, with great force, under Park's ribs and upwards. Before Park realised what was happening he had withdrawn the blade and stabbed him a second time. Park was in no position to defend himself, he was already dying in the saddle. Brother Saul held on to him, took his rein and walked both horses slowly off the trail and into the trees. Once there he allowed Park to slide off his horse and fall to the ground, whereupon Brother Saul dismounted to check that he was dead. He was not; Park was weakly attempting to get his own dagger out to defend himself, his stumbling words coming quietly.

'You are a man of God, what-.' He got no further.

Brother Saul stood on the wrist holding the knife while he quickly drew his own dagger across Henry's throat, opening up from side to side with a deep gash. With one last gurgle, Henry's lungs were filled with blood and he was no more. The monk made the sign of the cross over him, and muttered a short hypocritical prayer.

Brother Saul then turned his attention to the main reason for his being there, to recover the money and also the document giving freedom to the fictitious Arthur Mason. He searched the person and the belongings of Henry Park, until he found what he considered to be all the money and the precious document. Without further ado he decided to get on his way before someone should come and discover his misdeeds. He took Park's heavy riding coat, hood, hose and cotehardie. As an afterthought, he took the saddle roll containing Park's groundsheet, and these he fastened behind his own saddle. Saul pulled off his hooded robe and struggled to pull it over the lifeless body. He climbed into the breeches and donned the cotehardie, both a little too large for him, finally slipping into the warm riding coat. *Much warmer than my thick woollen robe,* he thought. He opened the document and smiled. *Well Arthur Mason, you had better get a move on, before you are discovered.*

Leaving the body and Park's nag in the trees, he retraced his steps to the last crossroads. Terrified that someone would see him, he took the first available road to the east. It would take him in the right direction, but he had no idea of the terrain, except that he was certain it would be inhospitable. It was getting dark and he needed somewhere to shelter for the night. There had been a sudden drop in temperature, and the wind had risen. He put his horse into a canter in order to reach the next village before dark, he hoped. As darkness fell there was still no sign of a village, but seeing a light in the distance he assumed it must be a small farm or crofter's cottage, and decided to seek hospitality and overnight shelter.

The track was barely visible now and the light did not seem to be getting any nearer. Brother Saul was feeling cold. Even his thick winter coat and hood could not keep out such a wind. *Surely I must soon reach that light and shelter.*

It came as a complete surprise to the brother when his horse, still at a canter in the near darkness, stumbled and fell. He found himself catapulted from the saddle, and waited with horror for the expected thud, and whatever the consequences as he hit the ground. When that did not immediately arise, he quite suddenly became aware of his situation, and screamed in terror as he visualised himself falling over some high crag, and being dashed to pieces at the bottom on jagged rocks. The thought was so intense that Brother Saul lost consciousness and his night turned truly black.

The monk was not unconscious for long, and came around to searing pain in his legs and right arm. He tried to move but soon gave up as the pain intensified. His right arm hurt and he could not lift it. His face felt wet and sticky and there was a strange taste on his lips. He was cold and miserable, but at least he was sheltered from the worst of the wind. He managed to move his head around but could see very little, except that damned light that he had been chasing. Now other thoughts began to go through his mind. Was he being punished for his dastardly deeds? Had God put the light there to lure him from some high crag? He began to pray and plead forgiveness for his sins. Somebody would surely find him in the morning he thought. Slowly, out of exhaustion, he drifted off to sleep.

Brother Saul awakened at dawn. He was shivering, and in great pain. He now realised that he had broken his right arm and both his legs. He moved his head around to where he thought the light had come from, but could see nothing except the other side of a valley which looked like mainly bleak moorland; if there was a dwelling there, it must be small or nestled in bushes so as to be difficult to see in the daylight.

He was horrified to find that he was on a small ledge, around twenty feet down from the top of a short crag. Turning his head a little confirmed that he was further from the bottom than the top. He realised that in his condition he had no hope, unless he was rescued by a passing traveller. He listened, but heard nothing, he shouted as loud as he could, 'Help.' There was no response. He lay there, thoroughly dejected, and wondered how he had got himself into such a situation. Why had he not paid a vagabond to do the deed as the prior had suggested? He knew the answer. It was because he wanted the money for himself, and the freeman document as his escape from the priory. Now they were all lying on a ledge somewhere in Cumberland. He thought he heard voices somewhere above, and tried to shout for help, but only small ineffectual croaks emitted from his throat.

The day wore on and as Brother Saul's pain became more intense, he began to pass in and out of consciousness. In his periods of awareness, he tried again to shout for help but nothing came.

In the afternoon he sensed some great shadow above him. At first he thought it was an angel, until his eyesight focussed correctly, and he realised it was a buzzard, and then he saw its mate. He screamed in forlorn terror, but no sound came out, he suffered unbearable pain and his heart seemed to give an almighty lurch, after which he lay still as his world went black.

***

The two poachers were sat by their small fire. They were poor men who had no work, and poached on the fringes of the estates, mainly taking rabbits, and rarely venturing into forested areas where deer were to be found. Where there was good game, there were also the baron's game keepers and their hounds. Punishments were severe if caught poaching and could even mean death for taking a rabbit with some lords, and definitely for a deer. They knew they were in an isolated area, but were still taking a chance lighting the small fire to cook a rabbit and warm themselves a little. They had one old mule between them, on which they carried their small canvas shelter and their hunting bows. Tomorrow they would head back down the trail to the west until it met with the main road. There was nothing to the east, another half mile and the trail ended at a ruined cottage.

There had been a moment of panic earlier in the evening, not long after they had lit the fire. They were both convinced that they heard a loud shout from the west, and thought they had been spotted by keepers. They threw a damp groundsheet across the small fire for a few minutes, until they determined that it must be some animal, whereupon they had uncovered the fire and allowed it to burn up.

Now it was dawn. They should be on their way and get back to their village with their haul of rabbits, enough to feed their families for some time, and a fine basis for an ongoing potage. Stowing their canvass shelter and booty on the old mule, they set off along the track, down the valley, up the other side, across the top of the crag where the track ran close to the edge for about twenty yards and onwards towards the road junction.

Arriving at the junction they were about to turn south towards their village of Penrith when one of them looked to the right. 'Look at that,' he said to his companion. There was a loose horse, with reins hanging, quietly grazing at the roadside.

'We should see if the rider is about,' the second man said.

Having ascertained that there was no rider in the vicinity, they took the horse with them, whilst discussing what they should do with it. They sensibly decided that they should hand it to a person of authority, such as the constable. If they kept it, they could be hung for stealing, as no one would believe it could be theirs. If they gave it to the constable, there may be a reward.

Ernest Constable questioned them as to where they had found the horse. He examined the animal and noted that it had a slight limp, and its right foreleg was bleeding about the knee.

'This horse has had a fall,' he said. 'Are you sure you saw no rider?' Both men shook their heads in the negative.

'Well there is a rider somewhere, probably hurt,' the constable said. 'I will organise a search party immediately, and one of you is to come along to show me exactly where you found the horse.'

The older of the two poachers elected to accompany the constable, while his young companion headed off home with their mule and their catch. The constable soon had a small group of villagers together and a horse and small cart in case there was a wounded man to bring back. The searchers and the old poacher rode on the cart as the constable led on his horse.

On reaching the road junction, the poacher indicated where the horse had been found. Ernest Constable sent two searchers to scour the bushes for one hundred yards along each side of the main road. He then turned his attention to the small lane leading to the east. He looked carefully at the damp earth of the road and saw a number of prints. Some he recognised as human footprints leading out of the lane alongside some hoof prints. Turning to the old poacher he said, 'Did you come out of this lane?' the man looked shifty and reluctant to answer.

'Answer me man,' the constable said angrily. 'I am not interested in what you were doing up here. If I was, I would have taken your bag from your mangy mule, and let your family starve.'

The poacher quietly affirmed that they had indeed come down the lane. After a further examination of the earth on the lane, the constable said. 'A horse went up here carrying a rider and returned with a limp and without a rider.'

'How do you know, we saw no one,' the poacher said.

'There are a set of hoof prints going up the lane, larger than your mule and a set returning. The returning set are shallower prints suggesting that the horse is no longer laden. The set leading up the lane suggest the horse was at a canter and the returning ones show signs of lameness. Come we will follow the hoof prints and see where they lead.'

The constable headed off up the lane, signalling the horse and cart to follow with the poacher who rode next to the driver.

As they approached the crag top there was a flurry of sound, which resolved into beating wings, as two startled buzzards suddenly appeared above the crag edge and flew high to circle until it was safe to land and continue their grisly task.

'Well I think we have found our rider.' The constable said in a matter of fact voice.

A rope was quickly anchored to the cart and the driver sent down to make it secure to the body below. The driver climbed back to the top and they then hauled up the body of the unknown man and laid him in the cart.

The constable decided to search him to see if he could uncover any identity, other than being possibly a monk, by his tonsured crown. The man's face was a mess, having been severely disfigured by the buzzards. Where his eyes should have been were now just two bloody holes. They had also made a start on other exposed parts like his hands and feet. Ernest Constable was intrigued, he was not wearing a monk's apparel, and why would he be riding at a canter along a road he probably did not know, and probably at night. He ran his hand under the coat, and came to a leather belt with a scabbard containing a long dagger. He unfastened the belt and took the dagger from its scabbard, it was covered in blood.

Running his hands over the somewhat loose cotehardie, he realised that the man was wearing some type of harness beneath with a sizable pouch attached. Taking his own dagger he slit the fastening cords of the cotehardie down the front and removed the pouch. Having ordered the driver and the poacher to begin making their way back to the road on foot, to advise the other searchers that the rider had been found, he opened the pouch and discovered the sealed parcel. He laid the parcel to one side, delved into the pouch again and was astounded by the four French florins he found along with a number of silver coins. Enough to keep a man for two or three years, he thought. Packing it all together again he mounted his horse, took the reins of the carthorse, and headed down the lane after the others. *I will have to give this my attention when I am alone, and not distracted,* he decided.

He caught up with the other two who were just around the corner, the carter being reluctant to be parted from his rig. The pair climbed aboard and the carter resumed his duty.

When they reached the road junction, it was to see the searchers waving excitedly and holding a horse. They led the constable to the area where they had found the body of Henry Park. It was obvious to the constable that the man had been brutally murdered. It was soon also obvious that he had no money at all on his person, and was clothed in a monk's habit.

Examination of the area showed that there had been two horses here and one set of hoof prints looked remarkably similar to those he had seen on the lane. He had the body of the unknown man loaded onto the cart alongside that of the other, and headed off to the village, where the constable paid the searchers for their help, and gave a little extra to the old poacher for bringing in the horse.

There was more to be found out about these strange occurrences and Ernest Constable was the man to do it. He was determined to get to the bottom of this little mystery. He noticed that the horses were both branded the same and a cross was involved which probably meant they belonged to the church. He would have a look at the contents of the parchment envelope tonight and see what that would bring. Tomorrow he would have to find the coroner and go through it all again, *probably be in trouble for bringing the bodies in*, he thought. *But then he could not leave them to the buzzards, certainly not a man of God, if he was really a monk? But which one was the monk, the one with the tonsured crown or the one in the robe?*

The constable despatched a messenger to Carlisle, with an urgent request for a visit by the coroner. He needed a coroner's report before he could bury the bodies, and he did not feel qualified to speculate on who was who. Once he had the report he would set about finding the owners of the horses and perhaps solving the riddle.

After his evening repast, the constable dismissed his servant and sat down with a tankard of ale to study the package he had taken from the dead man at the crag. The document within, a certificate of freedom, was supposedly signed by the bishop of Durham, for one named Arthur Mason, so it would probably mean a journey across the Pennines to investigate. He would keep the horses safe until March. He had no intention of undertaking such a trip so close to Christ's Mass, and certainly not until the winter weather was past.

***

Aidric continued to ride once a week, on a Sunday, from Newcastle to Syhale to report on his master's welfare to Lady Katherine. Otherwise he would pay a daily visit to Walt, to ensure he was being looked after, and fed correctly. Following his first return from Syhale, he reported to the reception office to find a new guard at the post. He had once again to go through the formalities of arranging his daily visit, accompanied by a suitable remuneration to oil the wheels of officialdom. This annoyed Aidric, and he asked where the previous guard was. The guard smirked and replied.

'It seems he came into a sudden windfall, Sir. He did not turn up for work yesterday and rumour has it, that he bought a horse and has run away. Let us hope for his sake that he has enough money to get far enough away. If they catch him he will be flogged, and most likely sent to Ireland; or some other godforsaken place to serve his time.'

Aidric nodded his understanding; he was not interested in the guard's chances of evading capture. He gave the matter no further thought, and headed off towards the inner door to the cells, where he would be admitted by another guard and taken to Sir Walter's cell, as had been the practice following his fist visit, when they had used a separate room. The guards had now given Walt a stool, so one of them could be seated whilst the other squatted on the palliasse. He could never get used to the smell of stale urine that permeated the prison, but Walt did not want to discuss it, saying that he no longer paid it any heed, and it was no worse than the yard of most taverns. Aidric knew he was just putting on a brave face, and did not pursue the subject further.

On the last Sunday before Christ's Mass, Aidric was at Syhale to report to Lady Katherine on her husband's wellbeing. He had some startling news for her, and deliberately waited until others were out of the way before broaching the subject.

When they were alone he said softly. 'My Lady, I am afraid I have some unpleasant news for you.'

A shocked Katherine took a grip on his wrist like that of a vice. 'You told me he is in good health so what can it be Aidric. Is his trial set?'

'No My Lady, he is to be sent to London, to the king's' prison there.'

'The Tower,' Katherine said with horror, 'when?'

'Immediately after Christ's Mass, My Lady. They want to complete the journey before the winter is too harsh.'

Without further thought, Katherine gave him a set of orders to make arrangements for her, William and Freda, to stay in Newcastle over the week of Christ's Mass. 'I don't want him to be moved without saying goodbye,' she said.

'They may not let you see him over Christ's Mass, My Lady.'

Katherine gave him a haughty look. 'They are prison guards not earls, and they have not met Lady Katherine Radulf yet,' she said dismissively.

On his return to Newcastle, Aidric carried out Lady Katherine's instructions, and henceforth, until just prior to the period of Christ's Mass, he visited his master at regular intervals and reported to his mistress each Sunday.

After the first couple of weeks, Walt reported that apart from the nauseating smell, which he had become accustomed to, things were as well as could be expected, the food was good enough for pigs, but adequate, and he had been allowed books, parchment, quill and inkpot. He told Aidric that he had written to Baron Percy at Alnwick, explaining his predicament and impending move to London, with the forlorn hope that his old acquaintance may be able to offer some help. Aidric took Walt's letter for delivery to Baron Percy, promising that he would return before Walt left for London.

Katherine arrived in Newcastle, along with William and Freda, on Wednesday the twenty-third of December, and they took up the lodgings, as arranged by Aidric, at an inn deemed suitable for gentlefolk. That same afternoon, as soon as they had deposited their bags in their chambers, they headed for the Castle Keep to visit Walt.

William, knowing that Katherine was likely to antagonise the guard if she began by making demands, persuaded her to let him make the initial approach. He walked cheerily into the reception area leaving the ladies outside; bade the guard a 'very good afternoon' and held out his hand in greeting. The guard automatically put forward his own arm with open hand and found he was now holding several silver pennies. He closed his hand and looked questioningly at William.

'William Radulf, brother of Sir Walter, along with Lady Katherine Radulf, and my wife Freda Radulf. We are here to visit my brother.'

'Sorry, Sir, his cell is small and only one visitor is allowed at any one time, and only one per day.

William sensed that more could be achieved if the right bribe was offered. He looked around and ascertained that they were still alone before saying. 'If I give you the same amount for each of us may we come to an arrangement where we have half an hour each?'

The guard agreed readily to the extra bribe, whilst William cursed himself for being unnecessarily generous, but decided to try to extend his privilege. 'If only one of us comes they have one and a half hours and for two, three quarters of an hour each. Agreed?'

The guard agreed, but pointed out that it would only work when he was on duty, and he was away on the day of Christ's Mass. They agreed that Katherine was to visit first, followed by William and finally Freda.

On the eve of Christ's Mass, as usual Katherine was first in to see Walt. She came out looking very shocked and unhappy. An anxious William asked what was wrong.

'They are taking him to London on the twenty-sixth,' she said miserably. 'I knew that he was going soon, and tried to put it out of my mind, but the reality has now thrust itself upon me, and I want to wake up and find it all a bad dream.'

'It is unusual for such a mission to set out on a Saturday.' William observed. He made an instant decision and said, 'I will go in now for a short time and I will say my goodbyes today. After that Freda can see him for a short time to say goodbye, and then you can have the rest of the time today with him, in case we should be unable to see him tomorrow.'

Katherine thanked him for his thoughtfulness, and he departed to see his brother while she and Freda engaged in quiet conversation on a bench outside the keep.

William was soon out again, and Freda passed through the outer door to be escorted to Walt's cell. 'I have fixed it with the guard for you to return when Freda comes out,' he told Katherine.

'Hello little cousin and sister in law,' Walt said, as Freda entered his cell. He saw tears welling up in her eyes and drew her into his arms to comfort her. 'Are you happy with my brother?' he asked.

'Oh yes, very much so, but I am unhappy about your uncertain future in prison in London. Also Walt, I can never forget that you were my first love, and I shall always hold you very dear.'

'Shush,' he replied, giving her a hug and a light kiss on the lips. 'I hold you dear as well Freda, but now you must be like the sister I never had.'

'I know,' she said, 'and you know that I would never deceive William. I am truly his wife and have grown to love him dearly. We have been unable to have any children yet, and may never have. I fear I may have been too badly injured at that awful time when we were raided. We have tried all the potions known to the physicians, to no avail.'

Walt expressed his sorrow for her childlessness, and urged her not to let William stay at Syhale too long if it would damage their business in York.

Freda assured him there were no problems there, and they would stay only as long as they were needed to assist Katherine. Walt kissed her again and she took her leave, wiping her eyes in the reception room, before going outside to call Katherine.

Katherine spent the rest of the time holding Walt, and alternately hugging and kissing him. She willed herself not to cry. She did not want to upset him; after all it was him who was in prison not her. Eventually, the guard impatiently told her that she had overstayed her time.

The following day the three of them attended Christ's Mass in the newly built St. Nicholas church near to the keep.

After Mass, they headed straight for the gaol, for a further attempt to see Walt. As expected it was a different guard, and he was adamant that there was to be no visiting today. William explained that they had travelled from Syhale to bring Sir Walter's wife, Lady Katherine to say her goodbye, on this last occasion before he was to be transported to London on the morrow. Eventually, after a bribe of six silver pennies, he agreed to allow Katherine around fifteen minutes with her husband, but only her and no others.

Walt was surprised and pleased that they had allowed Katherine another visit. There was no sadness in the visit. Katherine was now fully reconciled to the fact that they may have to spend some considerable time apart. *We have no longer any worries about money,* she thought, *thanks to Bruce and improved productivity of the land, the children's education was all in hand*. The contribution gained from Walt's various unsavoury activities, she chose to erase from her mind.

'You will be fine with William and Aidric there to attend your needs and resolve any problems.' Walt said.

Katherine did not respond.

'What is it my dear? Is there something you are not telling me?' Walt asked.

'William will be there, but not Aidric. I have instructed Aidric to follow you to London and see that you are properly treated.'

Walt was surprised. 'What can Aidric do about my treatment, except maybe get into trouble, and end up being locked up?'

Katherine was not going to yield. 'He can visit you in prison and see to your requirements. He can send a message to me to tell me all is well.'

'Alright,' Walt conceded, 'but only until I am settled and we know something of the terms of my imprisonment. Then I shall send him back to his wife, and his duties to the manor which are also his duties to me.'

This agreed, they shared a passionate kiss, to the sound of an impatient guard rattling his keys to be rid of her, before the sergeant at arms could catch him illegally allowing visitors.

***

On the twenty-sixth of December 1321, soon after dawn, a small party set out from Newcastle Keep gaol to begin their journey to London. In charge of the prisoner's escort was Sergeant John of Eddeworth, with three other guards under his command, all from London. Walt with wrists bound in front of him, and ankles tied together with a length of rope, was mounted on a poor excuse for a horse, which the sergeant doubted would complete the journey. When he expressed his misgivings, he was told by the governor, gleefully, that should the prisoner try to make a run for it on such a horse, he would have no chance.

This did not please the sergeant, as he knew that such a poor mount would slow the progress of them all. He had been sent with his men from London to bring this prisoner to the Tower, and the sooner he was out of this northern hellhole and returned to civilisation, the better. *My God*, he thought, *the bastards can't even speak proper English.*

The sheriff had made plain that his prisoner was a man of rank, had given his word not to escape, and therefore should not be chained. He had said nothing about rope. The sergeant had never lost a prisoner, and was not going to start now.

Walt was wearing his heavy winter riding coat, with his cape and a canvas roll containing his belongings fixed behind his saddle. His face was dark with anger, not because of being tied with rope, but because having been allowed to check his few belongings before rolling them up, he had discovered that the precious documents for his defence were missing. He had demanded to see the sheriff, but to no avail. The guard who was here on his arrival was nowhere to be seen. There was nothing to be done but get on the aged horse, and go with his escort. He wondered idly who was riding his own horse now.

Outside the gaol, in the shadow of a building, William stood with Katherine and Freda. They were waiting quietly without drawing attention to themselves, and watching. As the small party disappeared down the street and around the corner, the two ladies were seen to wipe a tear away from their eyes.

====

CHAPTER 11

The priors woe and the king's prison

Prior Gregory was a greatly worried man. They were now into the January of 1322, and there had been no sign of Brother Saul, since he was sent to see Henry Park out of the county. The prior was also concerned that he had taken two horses from the priory. Park was supposed to have bought his with the money he was given. Had Brother Saul decided to accompany him out of the county himself? He was afraid to make too many open enquiries. What had become of the man? Was he wrong to put his trust into such a devious fellow? He could not believe that the good brother had absconded, when he thought he may have a chance of one day becoming prior. He had ascertained from Brother Cornelius, that Brother Saul had indeed been given money for the purchase of a horse. Brother Cornelius also told him that he had been advised by the stable hand that Brother Saul had taken another horse, an old nag, as well as his own, from the stable. The prior was furious, but afraid to question further in case he made the treasurer suspicious of his actions. He could only return to his quarters and brood over his impending problems.

What if the man he had told Saul to hire in Newcastle, to take care of Park, had killed them both and taken the money? What if the monk had not hired another, and been caught trying to do away with Park? What if the monk had absconded with his money? Who was the second horse for, Park or the hired assassin? Worst of all, was the thought that Park may be riding a priory mount, and carrying his forged document. He remembered the last time robbers had priory mounts, and how it had taken some quick thinking to get him and the priory out of that situation. Prior Gregory tried not to think about it all, his mind was whirling with possibilities, each one more worrying than its predecessor. His only solution was to keep busy on priory matters, which involved more contact with his monks and more difficulties trying to rein in his bad humour, which was continually simmering just below the surface of his thoughts. The prior was indeed feeling very sorry for his predicament, and tried to cheer his thoughts by repeatedly telling himself. *Things can only get better, when news comes of the demise of the rebel Radulf.*

***

Walt and his escort were close to London. As he had expected, his horse had become lame on the way and the sergeant had to part exchange it for a replacement. This had put his escort into some difficulty with money, as replacing a horse was not in the sergeant's remit. Walt had taken the sergeant to one side and offered him money, to help with the lodgings and food for the journey. Sergeant Eddeworth took it gratefully, promising to recover the money against his invoice for the horse on reaching London. He also looked upon Walt in a friendlier manner, and removed the rope from his wrists, but not that which joined his ankles together. *At least,* Walt thought, *riding was now more comfortable.*

From time to time during the course of the long journey, Walt had caught a glimpse of Aidric. He was not worried by this. His escort did not know Aidric, and Walt knew that his squire would not do anything stupid, as he was aware that Walt had given his word not to escape. He did after all, find it comforting, that somebody he would trust with his life was following, and keeping him under observation. The journey was generally uneventful, but mostly tedious with the weather being mainly dry but very cold. With regular stops for one or the other guards needing to empty his bladder, because Sergeant Eddeworth did not regulate their intake of ale during their long midday repast, they only managed to cover around thirty miles each day, with the exception of the first of January when they remained at their inn in Nottingham with none of the escort except for the sergeant fit to stand on their feet, let alone to travel, through overindulgence in ales and spirit. Walt was sorely tempted to abscond but kept his head and enjoyed the day's rest. The inns at which they stayed were generally of a poor standard, probably due to the limit on expense imposed upon his guards. He always had to share accommodation with the sergeant, but the man accepted his word and he was not bound. The two men built up a degree of respect for each other, and Sergeant Eddeworth confessed he did not like Northumberland, but was intrigued by the hard life the people there appeared to suffer. Walt would readily answer his questions, but would shy away from any political discussions. He could never be quite sure of his guard's motive for engaging him in conversation.

One small diversion demonstrated that life was also not always peaceful and harmonious in the south. They had the capital in sight and had stopped at a tavern for food and refreshment. Walt was sitting on a bench with his guards when Sergeant Eddeworth suddenly sprang from his seat, and accosted a man about to enter the tavern. The ensuing fight seemed serious and two of the guards eventually managed to separate them. The sergeant accused the man of being responsible for the death of his brother. Eventually, on being reminded by Walt that the party was on the king's business, and that it would be better settle such differences another day, Sergeant Eddeworth allowed the man to proceed, albeit with bad grace on both parts, as they vowed to lay in wait for each other at some future time, when the matter would be settled once and for all. The sergeant retook his seat, and Walt sat quietly making no further comment or question, but he thought. *That was the only bit of interest in an otherwise boring journey.* After a period of silence the sergeant took Walt to one side. 'Sir Walter, with respect, I would beg you not to speak of this episode. It would not go well for my future if my superiors were to learn that I had neglected my duty to become embroiled in fisticuffs.'

'I saw nothing to suggest you had done any such thing, only the ale dwindling in my tankard,' Walt replied.

The sergeant smiled and ordered them all a refill. With ale consumed, the sergeant ordered them to their horses. Walt mounted and waited for the sergeant to order his ankles bound again. The order did not come and none of the other three guards moved to bind him. He looked to the sergeant, who just nodded and moved off signalling them to follow. Walt wondered if Aidric had witnessed the sport at the tavern.

Approaching London, the road passed through a tangle of crude dwellings, with a stench of sewage. The people were dressed in rags, with many begging at the roadside. The sergeant rode up alongside Walt, leaned across and said. 'You do not want to be caught in this area after dark. They are all thieves, drunkards or sick with the pox, denied access to, or thrown out of the city for various reasons. They would slit your throat as soon as look at you, if they thought they could get away with it.'

'Why do they not have the militia clear them away?' Walt asked.

'They do, but unless they hang them, they just keep coming back. They will eventually have another clear out, but a month later they will begin to put up their shacks again.'

It was on their tenth day of travel that they entered the city through a massive gate, that the sergeant told Walt was called Aldgate. Here his escort was required to pay a toll to enter the city. Just after entry they passed by a large priory, causing Walt to think of Prior Gregory's probable delight at his current predicament. Walt was amazed by the size of the city, *much bigger than York,* he thought. They rode on through narrow overcrowded streets with drainage gullies running down the centre, which reminded him of the Shambles in York. The streets they passed through were rubbish strewn and smelly but not as bad as the Shambles. They were travelling through cramped and obviously poor areas. The streets began to improve a little as they neared their destination. Eventually the sergeant pointed ahead, to a huge fortified structure which he said was bounded on three sides by a deep and wide moat and on the fourth by the river Thames.

'You see before you, The Castle of London,' Eddeworth stated. 'Prison, and home of the king's personal guard company, and sometime home of the king, when he feels threatened and wishes to retreat behind its impenetrable walls.'

The sergeant proceeded to explain their route and the names of the places they encountered. Skirting the outer walls, they approached down Tower Hill and turned toward the river and the west entrance, Middle Tower. Walt was in awe at the scale of the defences, the massive walls with towers built into them at strategic points. The guard in Middle Tower inspected the sergeant's papers and waved him and Walt through. The other three guards were dismissed at this point with Walt and his sergeant escort continuing into the castle.

It was early afternoon as they crossed the stone bridge which spanned the main part of the wide moat, and rode onto the wooden drawbridge lowered from another tower that the Sergeant told Walt was called Byward Tower, because it was next to the accommodation which housed the wardens. This tower, in addition to controlling the drawbridge was equipped with a portcullis and massive oaken doors, reinforced and studded with iron. Walt was astounded by the scale of the place, as Eddeworth continued to explain. 'Beyond is the Bell Tower, so called because it accommodates a bell, which could be rung in case of emergency to signal the raising of the drawbridge and closing of portcullis and gates.'

Walking their horses now, they passed the Bell Tower and turned to their left into another entrance, which Walt realised was part of another layer of defensive wall, inside the one through which they had just passed.

'This entrance is called the Garden Tower,' explained the sergeant, as they passed under another massive portcullis and a further set of substantial gates. 'There are many towers here and several have some accommodation for various categories of prisoners. I am to deliver you to the London Tower, where I shall hand you over to your gaoler, and we shall probably never see each other again.'

Walt was not keen on the word never; in the context of him not seeing someone again, but he remained silent and still somewhat overawed by the complexity of the castle, which they seemed to call a tower, but was in fact many towers, especially as they left the Garden Tower to cross into an open space of a green. He took the opportunity to look around and could see that there were many towers built into that inner wall of various shapes and sizes. In the centre of the area was a large square keep, which was obviously the last line of defence, in the unlikely event of the outer two defences being breeched. Walt's mind was racing as he tried to take in the splendour of the defences, and pondered the chances of ever having something so grand to defend against the Scots in Northumberland.

A shout from the sergeant brought him back to reality. He looked around to see a stout man come out from a room, alongside the tower to which they were heading. A groom followed him to take Walt's horse, but the sergeant waved him away, explaining that the horse was his, and he had to deliver it to his officer after handing over the prisoner.

Sergeant Eddeworth turned to Walt. 'Sir Walter Radulf. I would like to introduce you to your gaoler, Sir Osbert Lancaster. Sir Osbert is the head gaoler for London; he will see you to your quarters and introduce you to your prison guards.'

Sir Osbert noticed that Sir Walter was not in any way restrained, and deduced that the knight must be an honourable person held in some regard by his captors. He decided to go easy on this one, who was to know what powerful friends he had. The land was in constant turmoil and this man's friends could be in charge tomorrow, but he would still be here with a different set of prisoners. A rebel today may be his master tomorrow was Sir Osbert's pragmatic view of life. He quickly decided on his course of action, and stuck out his hand to welcome Walt as if he were receiving a guest into his own home.

A surprised Walt readily grasped his forearm and squeezed firmly. He then turned to bid his escort farewell. The two men wished each other good health, and Sergeant Eddeworth departed on foot, leading the two horses, having unloaded Walt's baggage roll onto the ground.

Sir Osbert indicated that he should pick up his baggage roll, and follow him into the outer office of his quarters, where he was asked to unroll his possessions for inspection.

Walt did as requested, and the gaoler went through them to check there were no weapons. Satisfied he looked at Walt to tell him he may roll them up again, and take them with him to his cell. Seeing that Walt's face appeared to redden with rage; he took a pace backward and asked. 'What is it Sir Walter, is something wrong?'

Walt immediately pulled himself together. His anger had boiled up again when he thought of his missing papers, and he did not want the man to know that he had lost some important papers for his defence.

'No Sir Osbert, I had a moment's anger because some letters from my beloved wife seem to have been lost during my sojourn at Newcastle gaol.'

He was no longer sure of the veracity of the agreement signed by the Lord Chamberlain, after hearing that the Despensers had been banished from the country by Earl Thomas Lancaster, and no longer held influence. His document was probably worthless, from the moment he received it, even if they were to return as had been rumoured.

'Carelessness or devilment on somebody's part, no doubt,' said Sir Osbert sympathetically, referring to the missing letters. He turned and looked directly at Walt. 'Come, follow me and I will take you to your quarters.'

Quarters sounds rather grand thought Walt, thinking of the confined cell at Newcastle, as he was led out of the office carrying his roll of personal belongings.

Sir Osbert opened the door leading into the London Tower, using a large key from a ring of others, on a chain attached to his belt. The door opened into a room in which there was a table and chairs. Some of the chairs were draped with items of clothing, and there were trenchers and cups on the table, which still bore remnants of a meal. A guard, who was lounging in one of the chairs as they entered, sprang to attention when he saw Sir Osbert, and reported that all was well.

'Where are your colleagues?' Sir Osbert asked.

'Upstairs Sir: delivering food to the prisoners in their cells. I only have two on my floor and they are fed.'

'Good. This is Sir Walter Radulf. He is a political prisoner, and is to be treated with respect. He has not yet been tried, and is here at the king's pleasure. He is to be accommodated under your supervision, and I will leave you to take him to his quarters and explain the rules here.' He turned to Walt, 'this man will be one of your guards, and his name is Matthew. There will be two others who you will become acquainted with, named Geoffrey and Fredrik. There are others who work on other floors, who you may see from time to time but will have no direct responsibility for you.'

With that Sir Osbert turned on his heel, and left Walt with the guard.

Walt, not wanting to get off on the wrong foot, said to the guard. 'How do I address you?'

'You can call me Matt,' the guard replied, 'and I shall call you Sir Walter, as is befitting. I suggest that you ask the others the same question, and address them as Guard when asking. Pick up your roll and follow me.'

Walt followed Matt into a corridor at one end of which he could see a spiral staircase leading upwards. They ascended to the first floor, and entered a curved corridor along which they walked until the guard stopped outside a door on their right. It was a heavy wooden door with a rectangular grilled opening in the upper half, allowing the guards to look into the cell. Matt took his key bunch, selected a key and opened the door, giving Walt his first view of what was to be his home for his foreseeable future.

It was better than Walt had expected, and much better than Newcastle. The room was only around six foot wide inside the door but around ten foot long to the outside curved wall, where it had widened considerably. The facing curved wall had a stone window seat and a splayed window glazed with parchment. The parchment being opaque did not let in much light but could be opened, revealing the iron grill on the outside. There was a heavy blanket which served as a curtain, and could be pulled across inside the widow, when required to retain warmth. At least there was some light in the room, he thought, he would be able to read and write near the window, or sit in the window seat if it was not too cold.

Walt passed his eyes around the remainder of the room. In the right hand corner of the room he saw a commode. Other furniture included a sturdy oak chair and table, a bed with a mattress, linen sheets and thick woollen blankets. There was a wooden box for storing personal items and a stand with a washbasin and ewer. Most importantly there was a fireplace with logs and kindling, and another chair.

Walt dropped his roll on the bed and asked Matt. 'Am I allowed visitors?'

'Yes, one hour a day but not Sundays,' the guard replied.

'I am expecting my Squire Aidric Johansson to visit me soon. Will he have any difficulties?'

'Not now you have told me his name. I will add him to the visitors list at the Byward Tower. He will be booked in there, and escorted to this tower, where a guard will bring him to your cell.'

'What is the routine here?' Walt asked.

'Guards will rouse the prisoners soon after dawn. You will be given a breakfast after time is allowed for you to dress. Midday we bring food and again in the evening. In that box you will find a bowl and mazer. Your food and drink will be served into them. It is up to you to keep them clean; your linen sheets will be exchanged every three months. The cloth to dry yourself with, you must wash yourself in your bowl. Each morning after breakfast your door will be opened for you to empty your commode bucket, and fetch water in your ewer. I or another guard will show you where and how.'

'Can I have writing materials? I have a quill but require ink and parchment.' Walt said.

'If you have money I can get such things for you,' Matt replied promptly.

'Thank you. Apart from the routine of emptying the commode and fetching water, am I to remain locked in my cell?'

'There will be periods of exercise where you will be allowed out onto the green under supervision. They will take place when a guard has time to supervise you, and you are to restrict your exercising to the area of the green. Any wandering will result in loss of that privilege. I will leave you now to settle in. The next guard you see will be Geoffrey who will bring you your evening meal. Make sure you have your bowl and mazer ready, he won't want to hang about when he has meals to deliver.' Matt departed, locking the door behind him.

Walt unrolled his bundle, and folding his clothing into neat piles he placed them in the box. His heavy coat and cape, he hung on a hook on the wall behind the door. He took out of the box a pewter mazer, wooden bowl and a spoon, all of which he placed on the table in preparation for his evening meal. He was starving, they had not stopped at midday as his escort was keen to hand him over and be off.

After he had organised his clothes, he inspected his bedding. It all looked clean, except the blankets smelt a little musty. He unfolded them and draped them near the window where they might air a little. After opening the wooden frame with the parchment panes, he was not sure how long he could stand the fresh air, as it was now cold and draughty. Before laying down his bottom sheet he inspected the mattress, which he was pleased to find was not a straw palliasse, but stuffed with horsehair and much more comfortable than he had experienced at Newcastle. These tasks completed, he sat in his chair and began to make a mental list of his requirements to make life more acceptable during his confinement.

Materials for writing, books, tinder box, candles in case they did not provide enough. He saw only one in a holder on the table. Perhaps he could purchase a rug for the floor, if he was allowed. He would try to speak to the next guard when his food was served. First he needed to enquire, when and if, he was allowed to light the fire.

It was getting dark when the guard arrived with a steaming cauldron of potage carried by a servant. The door opened and the servant poured a ladle of potage into the bowl on the table, while the

257

guard doled out a lump of bread from a sack he was carrying, and then picked up a jug which he had placed in the doorway. Walt noticed that they had stuck a burning torch into a bracket in the corridor outside. The guard said curtly, as he poured ale into Walt's mazer, 'I am called Geoff, Sir Walter, and I am one of your guards. If you want light, take your candle now and light it from that torch. You had better close that window; if it blows out I will not be back again.' With that the pair of them left, locking the door behind them after Walt had hurriedly lit his candle, and remained silent, after sensing that the guard's impatient demeanour did not invite questions. First he closed the window, as advised and pulled the heavy curtain across, then he sat at his table and hungrily wolfed down his bowl of passable mutton potage, and the fairly generous chunk of bread. His mazer had been filled to the brim with ale, and he soon supped that as well. Afterwards he put the slightly aired blankets on the bed, and washed his bowl and mazer in the basin ready for morning. For want of anything else to do with the dirty water, he emptied it into his commode bucket, as advised by Matt, who had seemed quite amiable. He decided not to risk lighting the fire, and incurring a possible penalty.

The next morning he was awakened by a guard, banging on doors with some hard object and shouting. He got up, used his commode, and freshened himself up with some water from the ewer. After a short wait the door was opened, and a different guard entered and said in a friendly way, 'good morning Sir Walter. My name is Fredrik; call me Fred if you wish to address me. Now pick up your commode bucket and ewer, and follow me,' he instructed.

Walt was led out of the tower, with another prisoner, and taken out of a doorway leading straight onto the ramparts, along a short distance and down into a room, within which there was an open sewer where they were instructed to empty their buckets and swill them out with the remaining water in their ewers. Fred told them the sewer ran underground into the river, but to discount any idea of escape by that route as it was barred at the river exit, and he believed there was a sump.

When this task was completed he led them out of the building to a nearby path, and told them to put down their buckets and follow him. They walked out of the inner courtyard, the way Walt had entered, through the portcullis at the Garden Tower, turning left around a tower, the guard said, was called Wakefield, and then a good walk to another tower where the guard told them to enter and fill their jugs from the well within. Fred remained outside while they entered and approached the well. As soon as they were out of earshot, Walt turned to his fellow prisoner and quietly introduced himself.

'Sir Walter Radulf, rebel.'

The man shook his hand and replied, 'Sir Dai Tudor, Welsh.'

'Do you mean they locked you in here just because you are Welsh?'

'Pretty much so, if you are Welsh you are seen as a rebel anyway. I was Constable at Caernarfon under the old king. I made some careless observations about the young prince's antics with that Gaveston boyo, that his father had banned him from associating with, and to the wrong people. When the old king died, and the prince took over, he brought Gaveston back to court, I was arrested and I have been here ever since.'

'How long have you been sentenced for?' Walt asked.

'Have not had a hearing yet,' he replied.

Walt was horrified. 'You've been here for fifteen years? You should have been tried, it is the law.'

'Listen my friend, the king's fortunes at the moment are rising. He has defeated many of his main enemies, and now has Lancaster on the defensive. He is showing a ruthless disregard for the law in the treatment of his enemies. There are many being hung drawn and quartered. Now is not the time to shout for justice because there is none. I shall keep my head down, I am happy to be forgotten for a few years more.'

They were interrupted by the guard coming into the well room, and shouting at them to get a move on. With their ewers filled they retraced their steps, picked up their commode buckets, and were returned to their cells.

Arriving in his cell, Walt was surprised that Fred followed him in, and made himself comfortable on the small chair next to the fireplace.

'Well, did you get to know your neighbour then?' he asked.

Walt answered cautiously. 'We did introduce ourselves, but I know little about him, and he nothing about me.'

Fred looked oddly at him. 'He probably told you he has been here fifteen years without trial, and advised you not to make a fuss about getting a quick trial.' Looking at Sir Walter's expression the guard knew he was correct. He continued, 'listen to his advice Sir Walter. Now is a bloody time for those who have crossed the king. Better lay low and hope you are forgotten like Sir Dai, until quieter times. You probably do not know that the constable who governs all at the tower is Sir Henry Plantagenet, a relative of the king. Keep your head below the parapet I say, Sir Walter.'

A servant entered the room carrying a cauldron of porridge and a jug. He doled out porridge and beer into the respective receptacles on the table, and departed without comment.

Walt sensing that now was a good time to ask Fred his questions, plunged in while he had the opportunity. He asked about the fire, more candles and other items of interest to him.

'You can have most anything you want within reason, you have not been found guilty of any crime,' Fred told him, 'providing you have the money to pay; you may have a manservant to carry out such tasks as you did this morning. You would also need to pay an administration fee for him to have a pass to enter the tower at limited times. You may have the fire lit day and night if you buy the fuel. You may arrange with a visitor to bring things in to you, but best you sort it with me or Matt beforehand, so there are no complications.'

'What about Geoff?' Walt asked.

'He is a miserable bastard. He will say no, or you will have to pay him handsomely for the smallest concession. Stick with me and Matt. We will help, for only a small consideration.'

'What if Geoff objects to privileges you or Matt have sanctioned?'

'That will not happen; we three guards have an agreement. Also we clear all such concessions with Sir Osbert, and he seems to be kindly disposed towards you. Now you should get on, and break your fast before the porridge gets cold.'

Walt was not about to upset any applecarts so he thanked Fred, and promised to take his advice. The porridge was nearly cold anyway, and he determined to get the fire lit and some method of hanging a pot over it to heat food or boil water.

His midday meal of bread, cheese, raw onion and ale was brought by Matt, who gave him the news that he had a visitor waiting down in the guardroom, when he was ready to receive him. Walt asked that he be brought up immediately, and greeted Aidric warmly when he was shown in. The door was left open by the guard, and he could be heard walking away down the corridor. Nevertheless the two thought it prudent to speak quietly.

Walt told him everything he had learned about the dangers of demanding a trial, and the comforts he could buy. Aidric went down to the guardroom and came back with parchment and ink. The two then made a list of items for Aidric to bring on the following day. He told Aidric which guards he could make arrangements with, and went to his jacket to get some of his secret coins.

Aidric held up his hand to stop him. 'I have been given plenty by Lady Katherine. Save yours for emergencies, Sir.'

Finally Walt told him of the missing documents. He was certain they must have been removed from the gaol at Newcastle.

Aidric's memory returned to the strangely familiar face he had passed when he was leaving the gaol at Newcastle after requesting a visit to Sir Walter.

He told Walt about the memory, and his feeling that he had seen the man at some time, probably at an inn in Tynemouth.

'Prior Gregory!' said Walt, grim mouthed. 'Aidric you must try to contact the other signatories and get an affidavit from them about the contents of the missing document. The knight from Cumbria may be difficult as you will have to track him down.'

It was decided that Aidric would first look to Walt's comforts, and arrange for a servant to attend. When this was done he would leave at the weekend to report to Katherine, and contact the knights who had signed the document.

Walt's immediate requirements for comfort were met by the Friday, and as planned, Aidric left to report to Katherine and try to locate the knights. He returned to London one month later, to report that John de Eure had died, Umfraville was somewhere in France, and he had been unable to locate Greystoke, but he was also believed to be in France.

'It seems,' Aidric reported, 'that there is a great popularity with foreign parts among many knights, barons and earls at the moment.' Aidric continued quietly, 'also, all your lands, with the exception of your demesne and my holding, have been taken into the king's hand, but I am sure that one of your letters will contain the full details.'

Walt smiled grimly, thinking what the guards and Sir Dai had told him. Well at least he had letters from Katherine, William and his eldest son Walter to read, even if they did contain some bad news.

'I will write replies for when you next go to Syhale. Maybe you should stay in London for a while, until the weather improves. For now Aidric, see if you can get me a nice rug for the floor. Everything else is going well; I have the servant and all my needs are catered for, I even have soap. Oh! And I would appreciate your daily visits, and before you come tomorrow find me a bible to read,' he added, as Aidric was taking his leave.

***

In Penrith, Ernest Constable was eager to solve his little mystery. The worst of the winter had passed; it was nearly the end of March. The coroner had found that the man murdered in the woods was probably one Arthur Mason, murdered by an unknown monk, found wearing his clothes and with a freeman certificate. The monk also had an unusual amount of coin for a monk, and an extra saddle roll containing items that could be from the other horse. The monk's death had been ascribed to misadventure.

The monk, identified as such by his tonsure and the sandals he was wearing, had been found otherwise clad in hose and coathardie, which were obviously too large for him. The cotehardie was caked with dried blood in an area where the monk had no wounds. This area of blood matched the wounds found on the other dead man, found wearing a monk's habit, but still wearing his riding boots. The monk had presumably retained his sandals because the boots were obviously much too large for him, or he had thought someone was coming and panicked before he could remove them.

Collating his evidence in his report, the coroner summarised that the unknown monk had murdered one Arthur Mason, stolen his clothes, money and certificate, only to subsequently meet his own end by misadventure.

Armed with a copy of the coroner's report, and the knowledge that the certificate was signed by the bishop of Durham, and the horses appeared to belong to some religious order judging by the brand which was formed around a cross, *it is now time,* thought the constable, *for me to pursue my enquiries.* He handed control of his company of soldiers to his deputy, chose a reliable man as his escort, and following the clue he had from the document, they set forth, leading the two recovered horses. The horse that had been found lame had recovered, but it was fortunate that they were being led as the other old nag would probably not have withstood the journey carrying a rider. They were headed for Durham to seek audience with the bishop, who had apparently signed the document found on the dead monk. The constable also had with him the money found on the monk and the dagger. Rolled up behind his saddle was the riding coat he suspected had belonged to the dead man in the woods. *Oh yes,* he thought. *I will get to the bottom of this. I can't have such behaviour going unnoticed in my jurisdiction. Somebody else is responsible or knows something about these deaths.*

Three days later after some hard riding on winding trails across the Pennines, the two men arrived in Durham and sought a suitable inn with an ostler, and stables for the horses. Once the two mystery horses were in the care of the ostler they set off towards the cathedral, which could not be missed because of its height and grandeur. They had no idea where the bishop resided but were sure they would find out at the cathedral. Once there the constable left his horse in the care of his escort, whilst he entered the building with a feeling of awe, from its magnificence. He approached an elderly priest and politely enquired about procedures for an audience with the bishop. Disappointingly, he was to learn only that the bishop was away and not expected back until the next day. Having left his name, authority and place of lodging, he was assured the priest would arrange an audience, but not to expect it for a few days as the bishop was very busy.

Ernest Constable attempted to stress the seriousness of the matter, but the priest was not to be swayed. The frustrated official rejoined his escort, and the pair retraced their way back to the inn to wait until they were summoned.

Three days had passed before a messenger came to summon the constable to the bishop's residence for an interview. This time, as the messenger was on foot, he accompanied the man alone. Once in Bishop Beaumont's presence, Ernest Constable introduced himself, and gave the bored looking bishop an outline of the situation. It was only on mention of the document bearing his signature, that the bishop suddenly showed an interest.

'Have you got it with you?' he asked.

Ernest produced and unfolded it with a proud flourish, 'yes, My Lord Bishop, and here it is.'

The bishop pulled it across the table, took one look and pronounced it a forgery. 'That is not my seal, and not my signature,' he said. 'So who is using my name?' He scrutinised the document closely, and then suddenly called in his scribe. 'Bring me the last letter from Prior Gregory,' he said, 'and my box of scrolls regarding his priory.'

While the scribe was gone, he asked the constable to describe the monk again, in as much detail as he could, including his habit.

This the constable did, as well as handing over the carefully wrapped bloody dagger he had found on the monk, he also handed over the French florins and the silver coins the monk was carrying, but held back the Italian florin, in case he was not compensated for his troubles.

After what seemed like an age, where the bishop said nothing, but drummed incessantly on his desk with his fingers, the scribe returned with a letter, which the bishop unceremoniously snatched from his grasp and studied closely.

'Who wrote this letter, the prior or his scribe?' he demanded.

'It could be either,' the scribe replied.

'Then find me something private that only Prior Gregory would have penned,' he ordered.

After a further tedious wait, during which he studied some scrolled report written by Bishop Kellawe, his predecessor, his sour demeanour improved enough to allow a slight smile to reach his lips.

The scribe returned with a further document, which he insisted was in the prior's handwriting.

The bishop did not need to look twice. He was entirely satisfied that the document made out to one Arthur Mason had been written by Prior Gregory. His features transformed from that of ill humour to a satisfied smile.

Ernest realised that he now had the bishop's full attention and pressed home his advantage.

'Then there is the matter of the horses the murdered man and the monk were riding, My Lord Bishop' he said.

'What about the horses?' the bishop asked, now eager to hear more.

'Well, My Lord, they have an unusual brand mark below the saddles, which involves the symbol of Christ's cross and a small t under the left extension and a p under the right.'

'Do you have the horses here Constable?'

'They are stabled at the inn where I am staying, My Lord.'

'Then bring them to me Constable, today, immediately,' he said irritably.

Ernest Constable hurried out of the office and back to the inn where he told his escort to hurry and get the two horses saddled with their own tack, and be ready to return to the bishop's palace within half an hour. As soon as his escort left, the constable relaxed with a tankard of ale, and thought through the little cameo in the bishop's office. He had certainly rattled the bishop's cage, so to speak. Ernest was now certain, that his guess that the horses belonged to some religious order was correct. He had deduced from the bishop's reactions to the document that some prior called Gregory was the forger. All he needed now was to find out where that prior was.

An hour later they were back at the bishop's residence, and advising the same priest they encountered previously at the Cathedral, that this time the bishop wished to see them and urgently. The priest looked dubious, but decided it would be unwise to risk annoying the bishop, and left to give him the message that two men were here with some horses.

This time they did not have long to wait, until the bishop came hurrying into the courtyard along with the priest. Ernest Constable loosened the girth strap on one of the horses, and slid the saddle forward a little until the small brand was visible. The bishop took one look. 'Are they both the same?' he asked.

'Yes, My Lord,' replied Ernest.

'Very well Constable, I will take care of these horses now. I thank you for your interest and bringing the information to me. This is now a church matter, and you can go home happy that I have it in hand.'

Ernest Constable was about to object that it was a matter of murder and fraud, but he changed his mind when he saw the frantic warning signals he was receiving from the waving hand of the priest, standing slightly behind the bishop. Instead he said, 'certainly I understand, My Lord Bishop, but could you please give some consideration to our costs of looking after the animals and bringing the evidence to you.'

The bishop grunted, and as he turned on his heel to stride away he said to the priest, 'you see to this Father Wilfred, that old nag looks half dead anyway.'

The good father duly compensated the constable fairly generously, after negotiation, during which Ernest casually slipped in the question. 'Who is Prior Gregory?'

The priest replied unthinkingly, 'Prior of Tynemouth Priory, Sir Constable.'

'Thank you,' Ernest said, neglecting to mention that he had already extracted some money for their expenses from the monk's hoard. *Well after all,* he thought, *we still have to visit Tynemouth Priory before we return home.*

Bishop Beaumont was not finished with the matter either. He instructed Father Wilfred to pay a visit to the priory at Tynemouth, and gave him some specific instructions.

'You are to visit the hospital under the pretext of concern of your bishop. I will give you a small donation for you to make to the hospital. You are to give it personally to the prioress, Mother Rachel. Also to legitimise your visit, you may administer prayer and Christian counselling to the sick on my behalf. The main aim of your visit is to secretly gain intelligence from the good prioress as to any unusual happenings regarding disappearing monks or horses, before, or around the time of Christ's Mass. Make the questions diplomatically as part of normal chatter, I do not want the Lady Prioress to realise she is being interrogated.'

The bishop subsequently gave Father Wilfred a small purse containing an Italian florin for the hospital, and some silver pennies for any expenses, bade him a good journey, and sent him on his way.

Meanwhile, Ernest and his soldier escort headed back to the inn, where they collected their bundles, paid the innkeeper, and set off for a hard ride to Tynemouth, and another inn for the night.

Early the next morning saw Ernest attending Mass with his man at the priory church. Following the service the priest, singling him out as a stranger to their church, approached and bade him welcome, asking his business in Tynemouth.

'I am a merchant from Cumberland,' he said, 'looking to do business here later in the year at your wool fair.'

'Have you not got enough wool in Cumberland?' the priest asked quizzically.

'Not to buy but to sell,' said Ernest, laughing. 'I hear prices are good here.'

He engaged the priest in conversation, by praising the fortifications of the priory, and the majesty of the buildings. They began to talk about the hospital, and the good work the nuns do. Ernest skilfully swung the subject gradually around to the monks, and innocently asked the prior's name.

'That would be Prior Gregory' the priest replied.'

'Well, your Prior Gregory is to be congratulated Father. This seems a well run priory and I have seen some beautiful horses being exercised this morning when I entered for mass. They must be very valuable. Do you have them marked?'

'Oh yes.' replied the priest. 'They are branded with a cross and t p for Tynemouth Priory.'

'That's just as well. So you can identify them should they stray?'

'That does not happen normally, but some months ago we lost two, and a monk. We believe the monk may have disturbed the thieves, and been abducted with the stolen horses, and murdered somewhere,' the priest contributed, to the delight of the constable.

An elated Ernest commiserated with the priest, and nodding to his escort to follow, walked away towards the priory, where he requested an interview with the prior, with reference to a missing monk, now announcing himself as the Constable of Penrith, in Cumberland.

He was astounded by the speed at which he was ushered into the prior's presence.

'What's this about a monk?' the prior shouted excitedly.

Ernest told him about the discovery of the body below the crag. He decided not to mention the other body at this stage, and described the monk in as much detail as he could remember.

'What brought you here?' the prior asked guardedly.

'The brands on the horses.'

'Horses?' the Prior snapped. 'Was there someone else involved?'

'Yes some rough chap found dead nearby, and obviously robbed as he had no money or papers on him.'

'And they left the horses?' the prior mused. 'Strange, but it bears out my theory that the horses were stolen and the good Brother Saul

267

was murdered trying to recover them. Well there you are, Constable, your case is solved. Where are the horses?'

'I have made arrangement for them to be delivered to you shortly Prior. I thank you for your cooperation.'

With that he left the priory with his escort, paid his innkeeper for the night's lodging and the pair happily headed off to Penrith. He had indeed solved his crime, but not in the way the prior thought. He would have liked to be there when the prior was confronted, but knew he would be wiser to be out of the county.

**

There was plenty of activity at Syhale Manor in the spring of 1322. The land was being prepared for sowing of crops, and the sheep were quartered in the meadow and in the process of lambing.

William and Freda had been a huge help to Katherine. Freda giving her good conversation when they were alone together, and not always reminding her of Walt's plight, which would only serve to depress. Katherine was a practical woman, and knew that her friend was deliberately avoiding the subject because Walt was also still dear to her, even though she was obviously now deliriously happy with William.

Katherine had received a threatening letter from Prior Gregory saying that he had authority to sequester her land in the name of the king. This forced her hand into activating the transfer deeds prepared by Walt, to place his demesne into her father's ownership, whereas she would now be the tenant but still responsible for the tithes. She dared not challenge the prior as she had no idea who may have given him such authority.

Handling the transfer of the property through the priory was out of the question so Katherine asked William if he would take the signed and witnessed document to the sheriff's registration office in Newcastle. Dates on the document had been left blank for completion at the appropriate time. She dated it for the day before Walt's arrest.

'We may need both copies,' William volunteered. 'I shall ride first to Alnwick and retrieve the second, and you can date it likewise. Are you going to tell Walt?'

'I think he has sufficient concerns already with his confinement, no need to worry him unnecessarily. There is no problem; my father will deed it back to us as soon as Walt is released.'

If Walt is released, thought William. But keeping his thought to himself, he replied, 'you would as well give me a letter for Baron Henry.'

'Yes I will do that immediately William, and after the registration is complete, I shall write to the prior to advise him that I am not the owner of the land. Let him find out for himself who is, I care not if he is aggravated.'

Three weeks later, after the deeds had been successfully registered William again, had proved a great help when Prior Gregory had attempted to increase her tithe payments by an unreasonable amount, by way of revenge for being outmanoeuvred, presumed Katherine.

William pointed out to the prior in a letter, that Sir Walter's extended Syhale estates, which had been taken into the king's hands and administered locally by the prior, with the exception of those given by way of compensation to the bishop of Durham, were no longer the responsibility of young Walter or Lady Katherine. He would have to collect his tithes directly from his tenants. The tithes for the demesne remaining, and owned by Sir Hugh Delaval would be paid directly by Lady Katherine as a tenant, but should be proportionately reduced, and he was prepared to go to law to achieve this.

It had also transpired that Walt's land at Bytilsden; also forfeit, was still to be administered by Sir Simon Clennell, on behalf of his Majesty. His uncle Adam had now become a knight tenant of the king, and the prior would likely collect his tithes as well. This situation should be held until after Walt's trial when a decision would be made on the final distribution of the land, although there was no certainty. It was in the king's hands, and he could grant some or all of it to others on a whim, as he wished.

Katherine had paid the tithes due for her demesne and no more. She had been careful to get a receipt signed by Brother Cornelius, the treasurer. She liked Brother Cornelius and had found him most sympathetic to her plight. He had accepted the money and written out her receipt without any further reference to other monies previously demanded.

Katherine, a little surprised by the lack of reference to her supposed debt, boldly asked the monk if perhaps the prior had made other arrangements to collect his tithes from the tenants. Brother Cornelius gave an answer that left her with no solution, and only more questions. She wisely decided to keep silent and discuss this with William on her return.

'What exactly did he say?' asked William when she told him about the monk's remarks.

'He said that the prior had greater things to worry about at the moment, and muttered something about horses and a missing monk, which I did not hear correctly. When I asked if he could repeat the sentence he declined, muttering that he had said too much already.'

'All the same, we should keep our ear to the ground when we visit Tynemouth. Some tittle-tattle may get out of the priory from time to time.' William said.

Later when alone with Freda in the great hall, Katherine could contain herself no longer. It would soon be April and nothing from Walt since that first visit by Aidric to say he was comfortable in his prison room. Surely the weather must be good enough now to allow for Aidric to return for the second time with letters and news. Freda sympathised but said that it was still early in the month, and it would take Aidric a week to ride from London, at least, without changing horses. They carried on talking about the children. Young Walter was now twelve and he was spending one day a week over at Alnwick castle receiving the rudiments of weapon training and duties of a knight. This would continue alongside his education at the abbey until he was sixteen, when he would move to the castle full time, as his father did at around that age, when he moved from Tynemouth Priory to Horton to be trained by Sir Geoffrey Wiles, then a knight in the service of Sir Guiscard de Charron. Horton was now derelict but Geoffrey Wiles was serving under Baron Percy at Alnwick, and this was convenient for young Walter's knight training. Alex was still learning at the abbey, as yet too young for formal knight's training.

Their third son Hugh, now eight years old, was practising on his pony with a small lance. Botolfe Best had rigged him a small target on the quintain, and one of the men, with the smith, had fabricated some small plates for armour. He would play all day if allowed and was quite proficient at striking his target whilst galloping past.

Katherine realised that she needed to get the boy to the Abbey for his education, but was reluctant to leave Syhale to make the arrangements with the Abbot. Until Aidric had been with his report, she would not take the chance of being away when he arrived.

They were interrupted by Tilly, who had brought the three boys through to say goodnight to their mother. Each boy took his turn to kiss Katherine and their aunt Freda, starting with the eldest Hugh, then James, now six years old and John four. Katherine was proud of her boys. They were fine young men, they made her happy and were a great comfort in the absence of Walt, but sometimes, as this evening, she needed the company of a sympathetic adult of equal standing to whom she could bare her feelings.

***

Aidric arrived in Tynemouth at dusk. Tired and not wanting to continue to Syhale in darkness, he made straight for an inn that he knew was previously frequented by Badger and his gang of cutthroats. If he was to stay the night in Tynemouth he may as well kill two birds with one stone, by trying to pick up whatever gossip was going in the tavern, whilst he ate, and relaxed with a few ales before retiring. There may be something to be heard about the disappearance of Sir Walter's documents, which both he and his master were certain would involve Prior Gregory, and some rascal from Tynemouth, and therefore by default, such people as visited this establishment. The inn was not as comfortable as the one he normally stayed at with the family, but he was keen for information. He had experienced a dreadful journey, with gales and sheeting rain on many of his days travel. He knew he was three days behind schedule after having to make detours to the nearest bridge, when fords were in flood and too deep or dangerous to cross. On one occasion his detour was much further than expected when a bridge - had been swept away by the power of the water. *I should have paid heed to Sir Walt, who advised me to wait until April to travel,* he thought as he handed his mount to the ostler.

Having settled his horse and taken possession of his palliasse and bed space, Aidric descended the rickety ladder from the communal loft for evening repast, with his saddle bags slung over his shoulder. They only contained letters but they were as valuable as money to

271

the family. His small amount of remaining money was in his purse, tied safely beneath his cotehardie. Whilst he was eating he cast his eyes over the occupants of the tavern. There were plenty of locals drinking around the bar, and at nearby tables. He noticed one group, some of whom he was sure were associates of Badger's gang, and one in particular he was certain of.

With his meal finished, he picked up his empty tankard and walked over to the nearby trestle and opened with. 'Terrible weather, I have been travelling alone for the last twelve miserable days, and would be pleased if I could join you gentlemen for some amicable company before I retire.' He received five unfriendly stares, but before they could respond further he continued, holding out his hand. 'Who is for having their tankard refilled with ale?'

All of the men at the table either took a large swig to empty their tankard, or immediately pushed the empty vessel towards Aidric to be refilled, whereupon he obligingly grabbed the tankards by their handles in both hands, along with his own and swung them round to the bar for the innkeeper to replenish, and return to the table. As he pulled up a stool to join them, he noticed that the one man he was sure he recognised was looking at him with interest. 'Did you not work for Sir Walter?' he asked suspiciously.

Aidric laughed. 'You have a good memory, Sir, but that was a long time ago. The bastard dismissed me after Bannockburn, said I was responsible for his father's death in the battle, and should not have come back alive. I went to London to get away from his wrath, and what should I see there but a small cavalcade with a prisoner being taken to the king's prison in the tower. And who was that unfortunate prisoner?'

All five of them roared with laughter at the thought of the hard done by employee seeing his former tormentor being taken to such a notorious prison. At this point the innkeeper placed six tankards of ale on the table and they all toasted. 'To the lord of the manor chained to the wall in his cell,' they mocked.

After a further round of ales, the tales were running fast. One man called Wedge, for some unknown reason that Aidric did not pursue, began relating tales of his old boss Badger, who was still in prison along with others of his men. After some further conversation, when Aidric asked if he had been a member of Badger's gang, he said yes, there was only him and a chap called Park, who had escaped prison, as they had both been ill with the fever when Badger and the others were arrested, so were not involved. 'Funny thing,' Wedge continued. 'Just before Christ's Mass, Park went off to Newcastle, on a private matter. When he came back he told me he had been given a job as a messenger in a southern county, he said he was leaving and would not be coming back. Jack Wilson said he saw him talking to a monk outside the priory before he left, and was sure the monk had set off in the same direction afterwards. I thought he must be mistaken, what would a monk want with Henry Park who never even knew the way to church.'

Everyone roared as if he had made a great joke. *Maybe it was if you knew Henry Park,* thought Aidric.

Wedge rubbed his chin, and continued. 'Maybe there was something to it, there have been rumours of a missing monk, but nobody at the priory speaks about it.'

Aidric bought them all a refill, and left them well the worse for ale as they all bade him a cheery goodnight.

The next morning Aidric rose early, broke his fast, paid his bill, and set out for the couple of hours' ride to Syhale manor. He was pleased to find that it was no longer raining, and the wind had dropped to a gentle breeze. Unfortunately the rain had not long stopped and the roads were still a quagmire of rutted mud which his horse had to carefully pick its way through. He made slow progress until he eventually came to the track leading up to the manor. Sir Walter's father had laid much broken stone on this track over the years, and the going for the last half mile was much easier.

He rode straight to the rear of the house and dismounted outside the stables, where Will Foster came out and greeted him calmly as if he had only been away for the night.

'Good morning, Sir, will you need your horse again soon, or can I unsaddle, rub him down and feed him?'

'I may need him again soon Will, please do as you suggested, but be prepared to re-saddle at short notice.' With that he turned and walked to the back door of the family room, carrying his saddlebags, and knocked boldly.

Jeanne opened the door, and roused the whole household with her squeal of delight, as she threw her arms around Aidric, and covered him with kisses.

'Oh my dearest Aidric, how I have missed you,' she said as she finally released him to report to Katherine, William and Freda, who waited with quiet dignity until the two of them had finished their over exuberant greeting.

'Sorry for the delay, My Lady,' Aidric began.

'Never mind apologies Aidric, just tell us about Sir Walter, how is he? Have you brought letters?'

Aidric opened his saddlebag and took out a pile of letters for Katherine and William. He pointed out that Sir Walter had dated them all, and they needed to read them in the correct order for them to make sense.

They all agreed to read the letters in privacy later, wanting first to hear all the news from Aidric.

He told them of Walt's conditions in his cell, and how they were regularly improving. He told them, in case Walt had mentioned it in his letter, about the missing documents and their suspicions that Prior Gregory was involved. In return Katherine told him of her own difficulties with the prior, and how they had resolved them for now. She said she was also sure that something was going on there, as she had never before known the prior to be so easily distracted from the pursuit of money.

Aidric recounted his conversation with the man at the inn, and determined to pay a visit to the priory before he returned to London, to see what more he may learn. He knew he could talk to the sisters in confidence, and maybe Brother Cornelius.

With some questions of his own he needed answered, Aidric asked Jeanne how she managed their small farm, if she was here all the time while he was away.

'I am not here all the time,' she replied, 'but I am still the housekeeper and have some daily duties here. Lady Katherine has loaned us a trooper experienced in farming, he fills a post as would you, to assist the reeve to see that the serfs do my bidding whilst I am here at the manor.'

'I am indebted to you Lady Kath –,' he began.

'Nonsense,' she interrupted, 'it is the least I can do when Jeanne is kept here so much and you away in London, attending to Sir Walter. Now you can go to your holding, and have the soldier take you round so you can inspect his management in your absence. Take Jeanne with you, I have no need of her for a few days. I am going to

Alnwick Abbey to make arrangement for young Hugh to begin his formal education.'

Aidric and Jeanne thanked her for her consideration and took their leave. Katherine prepared to go to her solar to read her letters in privacy, and write a reply to add to the pile she had already written for Aidric to take back. Some of the things she had asked in her letters would probably now be answered in Walt's, but she was not going to change any. She had dated them so he would know which to read first, as he had done with his. Picking up her letters she saw that William and Freda were also eager to read their smaller pile. She gave them a cheery wave and said, 'William, are you able to accompany me to Alnwick tomorrow?'

'Of course I can sister in law, might I suggest that young Hugh rides with us to get sight of the place where he is to be lodged for the next few years?'

'Certainly, that seems a good idea, perhaps Freda would like to come along, and if we set out early we can later spend some time in Alnwick and lodge the night at an inn, returning the following morning.'

With the excursion settled, they set off to their solars to read the letters from Walt, Katherine alone, and William together with Freda.

After Katherine had quietly read the letters, and shed more than a few tears in the process, she put the most recent two letters aside. These were the ones where Walt was saying that he had settled in at the tower, and the guards were friendly and helpful. These she would read to the younger boys and take them with her to Alnwick for Walter and Alex to read.

That evening, after all had gone to bed, Katherine went quietly down the stairs. After ensuring that the doors from the kitchen and the back yard were barred to prevent entry, she then went into the closet and opened the panelled section to reveal the small iron doorway to their vault. Crawling inside with her candle, she took her key and opened the chest within. Having removed what she considered enough money to pay the fees at the Abbey, and an advance for Hugh to begin at the earliest time the abbot could accept him, she carefully locked the chest and the iron door, replaced the panelled wall section and rearranged the hanging coats and the boots on the rack below as she had found them. She removed the bars from

275

the doors, so the staff could gain entry with their keys in the morning, and returned quietly to her room.

***

'Come in,' called Bishop Beaumont in answer to the knock on his door.

A timid looking Father Wilfred entered the room and bowed to the bishop.

'Well, what kept you so long, Father? You can ride to Tynemouth and back in a day and it is now the third day since I told you to go.'

'Yes Your Excellency, but when I arrived, Mother Rachel had taken to her bed with a fever, and I was obliged to wait until she was feeling sufficiently recovered to grant me an audience.'

'Was there no one else you could talk to?' asked the bishop irritably.

'Yes My Lord, and I did, but you told me specifically that I should give the donation to Mother Rachel.'

'Well then, stop being evasive and tell me what you learned,' the bishop said sharply.

'My Lord, I spoke to Sister Amelia the nurse. I just asked in an innocent manner if there was any interesting gossip. I knew that if there was, the good sister was the one to ask. I was pressed to be sure not to repeat what I heard as the prior had previously been very angry when he found out about the talk, and forbidden them to pass around such nonsense, as he called it.'

'For the Lord's sake,' shouted the bishop. 'I am not interested in the prior's anger; I want to know what the nonsense was. Get on with it man, before I lose what little patience I have left.'

'My Lord, they have lost a monk and two horses since Christ's Mass, and the prior was a more than normally happy man after receiving a rough looking man clutching a folded canvas wallet. Tavern gossip suggests that this man has also disappeared.'

'You went into a tavern?'

'No my Lord, but Sister Amelia talks to workers who come to help at the hospital, gravediggers, and merchants delivering food and the like. Sister Amelia knows everything that goes on in Tynemouth.'

'Thank you Father. Which came first, the loss of the horses and the monk, or the man with the canvas wallet?'

'The man with the wallet, My Lord.'

'You have done well, did you hand the donation to Mother Rachel?'

'Yes My Lord and I ministered to the sick as you instructed.'

The bishop dismissed the good father, and sat quietly considering what he had just heard. Put together with the information from the Penrith Constable, it was clear that some definite dishonest acts, probably including incitement to murder and fraud, had taken place under the control of Prior Gregory. Whilst he was considering his next action, there was a further knock on the door. 'Come in,' he shouted, annoyed at the interruption.

The door opened and Father Wilfred returned to the room.

'What is it this time?' The bishop exclaimed.

'I forgot to tell you, My Lord, while I was there I saw that constable from Penrith nosing around. He came out from early mass and headed for the prior's house.'

'Do you know what he wanted?'

'No, My Lord.'

'And you did not think to find out? No do not answer that, just get out of my sight,' he shouted.

After the hurried departure of the priest, the bishop returned to his thoughts. This put a different light on the subject. The constable would now know as much and probably more than he did. He had to act, and act decisively; he could no longer treat this as a purely internal matter. He would take his findings to the sheriff and let him take responsibility. In the meantime, he called his scribe, and wrote two letters, one to Prior Gregory stating that he wished him to attend a meeting at his office in Durham immediately. The other was to Brother Cornelius the treasurer, telling him that until further notice he was to take the position of Acting Prior, and was to show this letter of authority to Mother Rachel and any other, who he thought needed to see it.

Having signed and sealed the two letters, the bishop sent for a messenger. The man was instructed to hand the appropriate letter to the prior, but to retain the other until he saw the prior ride away from the priory. He could then hand the second letter to Brother Cornelius.

***

Prior Gregory was nervous as he approached Durham. Why did the bishop wish to see him so urgently? It could only be two things. At best, a promotion to an abbot, or at worst, he had found out that Brother Saul was missing, and wanted to know why his disappearance had not been reported.

What he did not expect when he entered the bishop's office was to see the High Sheriff flanked by two guards standing to one side of the room. He was surprised but not immediately alarmed, until the bishop spoke. 'Good day to you Prior Gregory, you will no doubt be pleased to hear that we have knowledge of your lost horses, the whereabouts of your missing monk, and the man under the name of Mason, who he murdered.'

Prior Gregory felt his head whirling and dizziness overcoming him. He shook himself in an attempt to bring his senses under control, and had opened his mouth to begin to protest his innocence, when he realised what it was that the bishop was waving in front of him. He had no difficulty recognising his own handwriting, and his clumsy attempt at the bishop's signature. Prior Gregory lost control of his legs as his whole body began to shake with fear at the realisation of the presence and purpose of the sheriff and his men. He slumped semiconscious to the flagstones.

At a nod from the sheriff, the two guards sprang forward and lifted the quivering prior from the floor. They clamped manacles on his wrists in front of him, with a chain linked to a further chain between manacles they clamped to his ankles. The chain between his ankles was just long enough for him walk, taking awkward short steps. A rope was tied to the wrist chain, and this was held like a lead by one of the guards.

The bishop spoke as the prior was dragged to his feet and manacled. 'We are not sure what you have been up to, but we do know it involved bribery, forgery, a lot of money, and theft of church property. I have the money here, and the horses which were stolen. It may go better for you if you were to tell me what it is all about.'

The prior was tempted to come clean, as he knew that the bishop had no love for the man who had helped to rob him, but self preservation made him hold his piece. From the documents he had stolen, he knew that the sheriff was a friendly conspirator in the effort to avoid Sir Walter receiving the full force of the king's law. Better admit what he thought they knew when in court, than be charged with interfering with evidence for the rebel's trial.

'I have nothing to say until I am taken before a court.' The prior said defiantly, after realising that they knew nothing of the real reason for his actions. By the time they got him to court, he would have some explanations for the unfortunate deaths of two nobodies, and the theft of a couple of horses.

The bishop thanked the sheriff for his attendance, thus indicating that the audience was at an end. At a signal from the sheriff, the guard tugged on the rope and propelled Prior Gregory forward and through the door, the prior walking with a strange shuffling gait, due to the restriction of the chain between his ankles. Bishop Beaumont requested that the sheriff stay a moment, and when the prisoner and his guards were well away, he asked the sheriff to close the door and indicated the chair opposite his own. He poured two goblets of wine and toasted their success over the prior's capitulation. 'Sheriff, I would like your opinion, but I do not think justice would be served by an early trial. I think that he should be locked up whilst further investigation is made. There must be something in his private papers that will throw further light on his actions. You should make clear to him that he is no longer a prior, and is to be addressed merely as Brother Gregory from henceforth.'

The sheriff indicated his absolute agreement on both counts, adding 'some other information is bound to turn up sooner or later, My Lord Bishop. In the meantime we shall make Brother Gregory as comfortable as any other felon taking the hospitality of a Newcastle keep gaol cell. For his own protection he will be in solitary confinement, other prisoners often display an aptitude for lewd sport with such celibate inmates.'

'The church demands no further comforts than would be provided for any normal felon,' the bishop replied, sharply.

The sheriff nodded, bade his farewell and departed thinking. *I shall still put him in solitary; I will not be responsible for a dead monk, whatever the unspoken wishes of the bishop were intended to convey.*

***

The day after Katherine returned from Alnwick, following her successful meeting with the Abbot, Aidric broke the news that he wished to return to London, to ensure that Sir Walter was being looked after, and to see if his servant was attending him correctly, carrying out some of the more distasteful tasks. Jeanne, present during this discourse, made no objections, as he had mollified her by promising to return in one month's time, whereupon he hoped his stay at home might then be for a longer period. He did not need to hope, and Katherine's continued instructions brought a welcome smile to Jeanne's face.

Katherine gave Aidric a substantial amount of money, and a letter of introduction, whilst asking him to open up an account with a well known Italian banking family in the capital, and arrange for them to have a man pay periodic visits to Walt to check on his financial needs.

'One day,' she said, 'we may have such establishments in our northern towns, to avoid the need for family vaults and hiding places for cash, or to be dependent on such as the priory, and dubious priors to keep our savings secure. When you have the account settled I want you to get recommendations from the banker, or some other trustworthy person, for a lawyer. Appoint one on my behalf, and have him visit Sir Walter to receive his instructions and offer any advice as to the best course of action to secure his release. The lawyer can then look after your master's interests, leaving you free to return here for longer periods.'

'Thank you my Lady but I would still like to pay periodic visits to Sir Walter,' Aidric replied.

'Yes Aidric I understand. Once in the spring, and once in the autumn is sufficient once he has both a servant, and a lawyer.'

'Yes My Lady,' Aidric capitulated, there was little point in arguing, and she wanted him here, not wasting his time in London once a lawyer was appointed.

Aidric did not put the money in his saddle bags, but concealed it about his person where he deemed it to be safer. The numerous letters from Katherine, William, the children, Walt's uncles and aunts and Hugh Delaval went in his saddle bags.

Saying nothing to the family or to Jeanne about his immediate plans, he set off, as far as they were concerned, for his direct ride to London. In fact on that day he stayed the night at Tynemouth, this time at the more acceptable inn, where he had stayed with the family.

As soon as he had his horse settled with the ostler, he took a tankard of ale in the tavern, where this time he was well known to the innkeeper, who he engaged in conversation. After a few pleasantries, he steered the talk to matters of the priory, and learned of the strange visit of the man from Cumberland, asking questions here, and at the priory.

A visit to the priory and a talk to Brother Cornelius produced some surprising news, which somehow fitted in with his suspicions regarding the prior's actions, and Sir Walter's' missing papers.

Brother Cornelius told him that he did not know how long the prior would be away on the orders of the bishop, but it may be for some time, as he had a letter from the bishop appointing him Deputy Prior for the foreseeable future.

'What is it about a constable from Cumberland being here asking questions?' Aidric queried. 'Where in Cumberland, and what was it about?'

'Penrith I think,' the monk replied, 'and it was something about the disappearance of horses, and Brother Saul.'

'Anything about a man named Park?'

'I don't know, but now you mention that name, I do recall Park visiting the priory and being seen in the company of Brother Saul on more than one occasion.'

'One more thing,' Aidric asked. 'Have you occupied the prior's official office? If you are working there, have you come across any documents pertaining to the surrender of Sir Walter to the Sheriff?'

'I have taken over the office, but have seen no such document. The prior's private quarters are not open to me unless I become elected, so I would not know what he keeps there. If I should find something of interest, what should I do with it?'

'If it is Sir Walter's property, as you will understand if you do see it, you should hand it only to Lady Katherine, and no one else Brother Cornelius.'

Aidric thanked the good brother, congratulated him on his role as acting prior, and assured him that when it became necessary, he was sure to win the popular vote of the monks to be their permanent leader. He placed his hand on the monk's shoulder by way of encouragement and took his leave, heading for the inn, a meal and good night's sleep. Tomorrow he would depart for London, but via Newcastle and Penrith. In Newcastle he would call on the sheriff, and leave a letter there for him, regarding the disappearance of the documents at the Newcastle gaol. Then at Penrith he would call on the constable, where he was sure that, together, they would arrive at the full picture of the deeds, and misdeeds, of the parties concerned.

=====

CHAPTER 12

Good news for one and bad news for another

Aidric finally arrived at his lodgings in London on Friday the twenty-eighth of April 1322, following his interrupted journey, a little over two weeks since his short stay at Syhale.

Sitting now in the tavern below a loft divided into stalls by daub and wattle partitions, one of which was now his bedchamber for his stay in the capital, he held a tankard of warmed ale in his hand, feeling grateful that he had got through Aldersgate just as the curfew bell rang for dusk. A couple of minutes later and he would have been locked out and been obliged to sleep in the open at the mercy of delinquents who made their living by preying on such unfortunate travellers, or retrace his journey to find a hostelry. Now, with his immediate thirst quenched, he called over the comely serving wench, to order his evening repast. He was relaxed on the small bench shielded by a wattle screen against draft, as he reviewed his discoveries in the Tynemouth taverns, information from Brother Cornelius, and his surprise on learning that Prior Gregory was in prison for fraud at Newcastle. With these items of interest, and the revelations of the constable at Penrith, he was now sure that he knew exactly what had happened to Sir Walter's papers, and could not wait for morning, when he could impart the news to his master.

The following morning Aidric arrived at the Tower to visit Walt and was surprised when he was escorted to the cell, to find the door standing open and Sir Walter seemingly surrounded by many comforts. His manservant was busy making the place tidy, there was a small fire burning in the grate, and a pot of water boiling to make beverage.

'Good morning,' he said to Aidric, cheerfully, as he entered. 'What would you like to drink Squire, chamomile, rosehip, or will it be ale?'

Astounded, Aidric replied happily. 'This looks like an occasion for ale, Sir. Have you good news for me?'

'Only that I am being kindly treated by my gaolers, and I now have most of the comforts I require.'

283

The manservant finished what he was doing, and Walt dismissed him, saying he would see him again in the morning.

'Does he come every day?' Aidric asked.

'Yes for a couple of hours except Sundays, then I have to empty my own shit bucket, but I have not given up. I am working with the guards for a Sunday arrangement, but it will have to be with someone who works in the Tower. They will let in no outsider.'

Walt waived Aidric to a seat, and changed the subject to that which most interested him.

'Have you brought news of home? Have you brought letters? Are they all well? Did you find out anything about my missing papers?'

'Yes, yes, yes and yes are the answers to your questions Sir.' He delved inside his saddlebag and fished out a pile of letters.

Walt put them to one side whilst Aidric told him all the news of his family and how the estate was getting along without him, and finally he told him what he had discovered from his enquiries about the missing documents. Walt agreed with him that they must be secreted somewhere in the priory, but without a confession from the prior there was little chance of recovery. He was especially pleased by the news that Prior Gregory had been replaced, and was in prison. 'Not before time,' he remarked. 'Does Brother Cornelius know what to do if the papers come to light?'

'Yes, Sir, I have made it quite clear that he should hand them to Lady Katherine and no one else.'

'What other news have you for me?' Walt asked.

Aidric told him about the bank account he was to open with somebody called either Peruzzi or Bardi, and that he was to find a lawyer to engage, in case they found the documents, and to advise on their best course of action.

'I intend to set about these tasks tomorrow,' he said. 'I am told that both the bankers are Italian and hold accounts for the king. I just have to find one of them and make the arrangement that Lady Katherine wishes. I also have to find the lawyer, but I am sure one of the bankers can help in that matter.'

Walt had also learned a few things during the course of his imprisonment. 'There is no point in going to Banker Peruzzi or Bardi,' he said. 'I have made enquiries here, and they only bank for the king and the government. They say he does a small amount of private banking, but is unlikely to show any interest in the amounts we are wishing to deposit. Also those who practice law, and are not of a religious order, do so only on behalf of the king. If we are to have legal advice, we shall have to find a monk or priest who has studied the law. They can offer advice and help, without fear of being brought to a secular court. I suggest you seek advice from the abbot at Westminster. He may help to solve both problems.'

Aidric felt disheartened, He had arrived in London thinking all would be easy to organise, only to find out that the capital was not so far advanced as they thought in Northumberland. Rumours of banking and court lawyers were just that, for the court only. He bade Walt farewell and left for his lodgings, determined to speak to the highest authority that he could at the Abbey in the morning, to seek advice.

As planned, Aidric found his way to Westminster Abbey after he had broken his fast the following morning. Subsequent to a few questions to a priest he encountered, it became apparent that it would be a long process to gain audience with the Abbot, and he would be better speaking to one of the learned monks, of whom there were several at the abbey, who had studied medicine or law. The priest bade him wait in the courtyard, whilst he made enquiries.

After patiently waiting around, for what seemed to him about two hours, Aidric was eventually collected by the same priest, and escorted to a large library, where he was presented to a monk seated behind a desk covered with bound volumes of books.

The priest introduced the monk as Brother Peter, who was studied in the law of the land. The monk arose from his seat to welcome Aidric, and held out his hand in greeting.

Aidric took the proffered hand, and shook it firmly rather than grasping the forearm, more common with military types. 'Thank you for seeing me Brother Peter, I am Aidric Johansson, Squire to Sir Walter Radulf, who is currently residing in the king's tower prison, aside the river. He is expecting to face charges of rebellion, and other serious transgressions. He has been imprisoned since December last year. To this date, no formal charges have been brought, and he has not had an appearance in any court.'

Brother Peter listened patiently, while Aidric related the whole story of Sir Walter's fall from grace, and stated his need for someone who would be able to visit, and give legal advice, also someone who could manage his funds and keep them safe.

Brother Peter replied that he was in a position to do both, but would need permission to act from the abbot, and if Aidric would like to return later that afternoon, he could possibly finalise an arrangement. Aidric was astounded, it was going to take him ages to see the abbot, but the monk could achieve his answer, by this very afternoon.

A few hours later, back at the abbey, he was again shown to Brother Peter's presence, once again at the desk in the library. He wondered if this was the monk's normal place of work.

Aidric curiously asked. 'Did you study law in this library Brother Peter?'

This produced a roar of laughter from the good brother, and a round of shushes and hushes from others in the library. Brother Peter, embarrassed at his own lack of control, apologised, and then said quietly to Aidric. 'I studied law on behalf of the abbey, as did two other brothers at the same time. We graduated from Oxford University. Other brothers here have been to Oxford and studied medicine.'

'I am sorry Brother Peter, please excuse my ignorance. Where I come from, the only learning we have is in the abbeys or priories.'

'Well let us press on,' said the monk. 'Do you think I could speak with Sir Walter tomorrow morning?'

'I am sure you can Brother, but they may not let in two of us at the same time.'

'Leave that to me,' the monk replied. 'Shall we meet outside Middle Tower around two hours after daybreak?' He continued without waiting for Aidric's response. 'We shall return here afterward, subject to your master's agreement, and you can deposit his money with me, and I shall give you a receipt for you to convey to him. Future financial arrangement will be between me and your master. You will only need involvement to convey funds to London, as and when required. Such arrangement for this will be between you and him.'

Aidric took his leave of the monk and headed back to his lodging. He was tired, and looking forward to a good night sleep, which he achieved without effort, once he had partaken of the excellent game and ale pie that the inn offered for supper.

The next morning both Aidric and Brother Peter were allowed into the tower, but had to report to the gaoler, Sir Osbert Lancaster to gain permission to visit together. Sir Osbert granted permission, but only for the introductory visit. In the future it must be one at a time he insisted. Aidric did not see this as a problem as he did not to intend be here most of the time.

They were escorted to Walt's cell by one of the guards. Aidric was quick to note that he was still not actually locked in his cell, as the guard knocked and pushed open the door without using his keys. When asked about this after the guard had left, Walt said they generally now only locked him in at night.

Introductions followed, and Walt appeared to take an instant liking to the forthright manner of the monk. They had soon reached a financial agreement, and Aidric was instructed to hand over the money on the morrow, and bring the receipt to Sir Walter. Formalities out of the way, Brother Peter turned straight to Walt and said. 'I must inform you Sir Walter; that even if you had the document signed on behalf of the king, now is not a good time to petition for a hearing. I learned from the abbot this morning that the king's army defeated that of Earl Thomas of Lancaster, at Boroughbridge around the middle of last month, the earl was taken to Pontefract castle in late March, beheaded and put on view as a warning to all rebels.

The Destemper family are once again virtually in charge, and not only are the king's rebels being sought out for destruction, but also anyone who has crossed the Destempers. The next year at least could be a dangerous time for many. For a rebel who appears to have been overlooked, I would say that sitting quietly in this prison for a while until the political situation improves, would be the wisest move.'

Walt looked disappointed. 'So the steadying control of the earls and barons is finished, and the king's excesses are now to go unchecked again?'

'I am afraid so Sir Walter; and I would advise you to have a care what you say, and who you say it to. There are people in here, who may now wish to strengthen their allegiance to the king, with his position again apparently secure.'

With that final statement, the monk took his leave, along with Aidric, who promised to return on the morrow with the receipt, after he had deposited the money at the abbey; a task he would be happy to complete. The responsibility for the safety of the money had weighed heavily on his mind. The gold given him by Lady Katherine was concealed in a leather purse, securely fastened to a leather belt around his waist, which also served to suspend his braes and hose.

***

The ensuing years had passed slowly for all concerned. Aidric making regular visits to London, not twice but four times a year, and reporting that Sir Walt was still comfortable, but needed a continuous supply of money to retain his privileges. Katherine was deeply concerned about the amount of money she had already sent, but would never refuse him, even though with her diminished returns from the land, she had needed to borrow from her father. To add to her difficulties, Jon Monek must have found out about Walt's incarceration, because neither he, nor the money for the 1323 fleece shipment could be found when William went to collect in July of that year. No further wool was sent to Blyth for shipment, and they had to succumb to paying wool taxes in Newcastle. Katherine refused to go near the Tynemouth fleece fair.

Neither Aidric nor Walt knew of these financial difficulties, and William was sworn to silence. The last thing that must happen is that such news should get around bringing the possibility of restrictions being put on her credit with local traders. At the moment the only other person aware of her difficulty was her father, and he was discreet.

In the autumn of 1325 young Walter had finished his training at Alnwick Abbey. He was now home to take up his position as the fifteen year old master of the estate. Although he believed he was the temporary owner on the deeds, he had no illusions as to why this was done, and out of respect for his parents he liaised closely with his mother before making any financial decisions, and worked closely with his uncle William to learn the skills needed to command both his troopers, through Sergeants Guddal and Best, and estate workers through the bailiff and the reeve. Sergeant Richard Wilson who they had picked up at Mitford had been transferred, as previously suggested by Walt, to another troop on a nearby estate. There was no need for three seniors at Syhale, and Wilson never really fitted in with the Syhale men.

Only Katherine and William knew that the estate was officially owned by her father, since Prior Gregory's meddling soon after Walt's imprisonment. Young Walter was still unaware of the true situation, or of their dire financial difficulties, with so much money going to London.

Trouble with the Scots had not diminished. Bruce was pretty much in control of the area, and border raids sometimes now extended as far as Syhale. They were mainly raiding to drive off livestock and rarely in large bands, so the troop of soldiers at Syhale generally drove them off without too much loss of livestock. The thing that most worried Katherine was that the arrangement with Bruce, whereby their estates and those of a few friends and family were spared was no longer holding, probably as a result of Walt having handed over Mitford without a fight.

Katherine made Aidric promise that he would not tell Walt of this development, as he had worry enough while locked up in such a place. Aidric was not so sure about Walt being worried about his confinement too much, he seemed to be leading a fairly relaxed life, even though he was a prisoner. Knowing of his master's need for ladies' favours, Aidric thought *I will be surprised if Walt has not managed to organise a few female visitors by now, to help with the long afternoons.*

After young Walter had been home for almost year, William and Freda, satisfied that they were no longer needed at Syhale, expressed their wish to return to York, and resume their lives there. This was met with understanding by Katherine, and joy by young Walter, now sixteen, and eager to take the reins, without his uncle William being on hand to advise. He was sure he was ready to run the estate now, and if he needed male help there was Aidric to fall back on. After all he was his father's squire, and duty bound to support him in his father's absence. The only thing young Walter did not control was the purse strings. His mother kept strict control of the finances.

William and Freda departed for York on the first of September 1326, following tearful goodbyes from all the family and servants. The two of them had always been very popular. Just prior to leaving, they had taken the trouble to ride down to the mill, to say farewell to an appreciative Sergeant Heddon and Daisy.

It was on Sunday morning and barely a week had elapsed since William and Freda's departure, when Squire Elfric galloped into the yard shouting urgently for Lady Katherine. Young Walter was there as he arrived, and sensing the urgency of the squire's shouts, he ran inside to summon his mother. Elfric dismounted and met her on the doorstep; he was obviously very agitated and upset. 'It's your father My Lady, he has collapsed.'

'Have you summoned help from the healer?' she asked.

'No my lady, I am afraid there is no point, he died instantly. Your mother said he just clutched his chest and fell. She called your brother Richard, but there was nothing to be done. He was dead in minutes.'

Katherine although in some state of shock, called for her horse to be saddled. Young Walter shouted for his mount to be saddled as well. 'You are not going to ride over there alone,' he insisted.

'I shall not be alone' she snapped, 'Elfric will be with me.'

'Nevertheless, I shall come with you,' he said ignoring her sharp reply, in view of the shocking news she had just received.

There was a quiet funeral a few days later at Seaton Delaval church, with only close friends and family. Katherine accompanied her mother in her small covered carriage. Her father was a good old age she thought, at sixty six. Due to her mother's illnesses, she had always expected to lose her first, but then, her mother was still only fifty seven. She wondered about Richard. He was quite competent at running the estate, but he had as yet not shown much interest in finding a wife. She did not worry about his intentions, being sure that he did not have any of the inclinations attributed to the king, but she wished at thirty five years old, he would wake up and find himself a wife. He now had an aged mother to look after, and a wife would certainly be of help. She would have to try a little matchmaking, she thought. If the worst came to the worst, her mother could always come to the manor, but she would need Walt's permission first.

***

In London, Walt was reflecting on his situation. It was already September of 1326, he had now been in the tower over four and a half years, with no progress on trial or release. *At least*, he thought, *my life is not too onerous, just lonely without my loved ones and my freedom.* He looked forward to his visits from Brother Peter who would bring him up to date on the political situation.

The monk had previously told him that last year Queen Isabella, disgusted with her husband's behaviour, had gone to France and made a treaty of peace there. For some reason that the monk did not explain, the king had allowed his son Edward to join her and they had subsequently refused to return.

During the intervening years Walt had been acquainted with Dai Tudor on most days during their exercise period in the central courtyard. Dai showed great interest in Northumberland and the harsh life in the northern borders. He was most enthusiastic to learn that Walt had Welsh archers among his men and understood their reluctance to return to their homeland. Both men forged a firm friendship, with a common cause, freedom.

Brother Peter, on his next visit, had some new and exciting news to impart. 'Queen Isabella has formed an alliance with Roger de Mortimer, first Earl of March. They have raised an army to overthrow the king.' The monk paused to allow that news to sink in and waited for Sir Walter's comment.

'Well is that all, or is she going to do something with her army?' he asked.

Brother Peter watching Walt's expression with glee, continued. 'She landed in Essex two days ago, and is preparing to march on London.'

Walt's excitement was obvious. 'What of the king?'

'The king is scrabbling around trying to raise an army, but few have the stomach for another fight. I warrant he will not succeed,' the monk opined.

On the second of October, Aidric arrived bringing letters and more money for his master's comforts and legal advice, although he wasn't quite sure what that advice consisted of, during all the years of inaction.

He found out from the guard Matt, that Sir Walter had indeed had the occasional female visitor and was about to congratulate himself on his foresight when Matt told him hurriedly that he believed it was nothing improper. His visitor had been the gaoler's wife Lady Hilda Lancaster, but usually in the afternoon, and in the company of her husband. It seemed the gaoler had become quite friendly with Sir Walter and he and his wife were invited to spend time at Syhale manor when better times came. The crafty bugger does not miss a trick to improve his life here thought Aidric, proud now of his master's loyalty to Katherine, but feeling guilty for having thought otherwise. He wondered what other favours Walt extracted from his captors by his pragmatic attitude.

He handed Walt the letters knowing what one of them contained. He decided to tell him rather than wait until he read the letter.

'Sir,' he began hesitantly, 'one of the letters bears the sad news of the death of your father in law. We were all greatly distressed at his passing, and I am sure that Lady Katherine has included the full details in a letter so I will say no more until you have read them.'

'Thank you Aidric,' Walt said solemnly, 'I will read them later.'

Whilst he was there with Walt in his cell, Sir Osbert entered excitedly.

'I thought you would be interested to know Sir Walter, that the king and his guard have left London.'

'To engage the queen's army in battle?' asked Walt.

'No, it is reported that they have fled to the west after being unable to raise an army of sufficient strength to confront the queen.'

'Thank you, Sir Osbert; I shall discuss this situation with my lawyer when he next visits. Oh! And please thank your good lady wife for the delicious cakes brought to me yesterday evening. I look forward to our next meeting when it is convenient for you both. As you know Sir Osbert all my evenings are free and in your honour I shall make no other appointment without keeping you informed.'

Gaoler Sir Osbert left the cell laughing and promising to convey Walt's invitation and thanks to his wife.

Aidric stayed for two more days in London before setting off again to return to Syhale with some cheering news of the king's plight, which meant that it may soon be possible for Walt to present a petition, providing the king and his cronies the Despensers did not again seize the initiative. On his way home he thought about his master, and recalled the mention of an evening visit by Lady Hilda to deliver cakes. He tried to think it through. *Matt, the guard, had said nothing about evenings, but Sir Osbert seemed aware, so was something going on after all. Lady Hilda was certainly a good looking woman. Why would Sir Osbert allow her to be alone with his randy master?* He determined to ask some discreet questions on his next visit. Just out of curiosity, he would never betray his master's confidences.

***

Arriving at Syhale manor, Aidric was surprised to find an air of joy and hope in the household. He immediately assumed that the situation regarding the king's flight had reached Syhale. This was confirmed by Katherine, but that was not the main reason for their joy.

Katherine took him by the arm and literally dragged him into the house saying, 'come quick Aidric, I have something important to show you.'

She led him into the family room, bade Annie to provide him with the beverage of his choice and whatever he wished to eat and ran upstairs, soon to return waving a large canvas wallet. Aidric looked at her curiously, Katherine was grinning from ear to ear as she ceremoniously plonked the wallet on the table in front of him.

'Walt's lost documents signed by the three knights, the sheriff and the chamberlain,' she pronounced proudly as if she had personally sought and retrieved them.

A speechless Aidric took them and opened the envelope. He knew what should be in there and was amazed to see that both the royal promissory document and the testimony of the soldiers regarding the possession of Mitford castle were there. Recovering from his surprise and now realising why she was so buoyant, he excitedly responded.

'What fortune Lady Katherine, how did you come by them, are they the ones held by Baron Greystoke?'

'Sadly not Aidric. My son Walter has learned from Alnwick that both Robert de Umfraville and Baron Greystoke are missing, probably killed in France. Umfraville since March last year and Greystoke as long ago as 1323, and I have no idea what he did with his copy, although Walt said it was to be given to a sympathiser for safe keeping, nobody has come forward. This was the stolen copy and it was brought to me by the new prior at Tynemouth, Brother Cornelius. He found it last week by chance when he was inspecting what he thought was some damage to the end of a desk in the prior's private quarters, and discovered a secret drawer. He remembered your explicit wishes if he was to find any documents pertaining to Sir Walter and brought them to me at the earliest opportunity.'

'That is excellent news. Does it also now signal the end of hostilities between Syhale and the priory?' Aidric asked.

'Yes I believe so. Brother Cornelius certainly expressed the wish that we remain on a friendly footing and wished us good fortune for Walt's release. We have all heard about the Queen's landing but no more news as yet.'

'The king has been unable to raise an effective army to confront her, and has fled towards Wales. That is the latest news from London a week ago.'

'Can we hope then that Walt may soon be free?' Katherine asked.

'I think his lawyer will be watching the situation carefully to judge the correct time to petition. Too early could court disaster. If I may beg your leave now, My Lady, I would like to go home for the night to see my wife. Tomorrow I will return to London with the master's papers but via Newcastle, where I will seek a copy of the handover document from the High Sheriff or at least some deposition from him as to its existence to aid Sir Walters's petition.'

Katherine felt guilty, she was keeping Aidric talking when he could be with Jeanne, and yet here he was volunteering to return to London after only a night's rest with his wife.

'Yes of course Aidric, go now,' she replied hurriedly, taking his arm and virtually shooing him out of the house and onto his horse which was tied up outside the door.

***

In London, Brother Peter was also up to date with the latest news of the king. He was paying a visit to an excited Walt, who was eager to get his petition for freedom going.

Brother Peter explained that Queen Isabella and Mortimer were advancing towards London and gathering further recruits on the way. 'The king,' he said, 'is scrabbling around, trying in vain to raise an army to repel her.' Seeing Walt's eyes light up with hope, he rapidly advised caution, much to the annoyance of Walt who angrily asked the monk. 'What am I paying you for when all you do is tell me to wait, wait and wait again. This advice I get from my guards for free. I have been in this shithole for nearly five fucking years now and the bloody queen has been farting around outside Dover since September, is it not time she was at London's gates? And how much longer must I wait before you earn your bloody money?'

Brother Peter looked at him sorrowfully saying 'I know it is frustrating, Sir Walter, but please let me look after your best interests in this matter. Please remember that the king has been in sorrowful positions before and returned again to persecute his enemies, I want you free and alive, not free as a spirit in the Lord's domain. Incidentally, if you study your invoices, I charged you for our first consultation only, my visits to you have been pastoral and not as a lawyer. I will charge you again when we are ready to present your petition. Hopefully the documents you referred to will have been found by then, but I believe that with a new administration, I will still get you out. Also, the queen is not, as you put it, farting about near Dover. They had to avoid Edward's fleet, sent to intercept them and finally landed somewhere in Suffolk. I believe that they are now near Cambridge and should be in London any day soon.'

Walt apologised for his outburst. He now felt ashamed that he had spoken so thoughtlessly to the monk who had, as he said, visited him weekly and helped to break up his boring existence. With the monk's visits, and a visit from his gaoler, or his wife every couple of weeks bringing him gossip from the capital, life was just about bearable.

Brother Peter, understanding his state of mind, assured Walt that no offence was taken and promised to visit him again next week. 'Free of charge,' he added cheekily.

'Thank you Brother, I deserved that,' laughed Walt, as the monk left his cell.

After the monk had departed, Walt could virtually smell freedom, and the thoughts, sights and smells of his home seemed to be with him. He would awaken in the night and put out his arm to encircle Katherine, only to realise that he had been dreaming. No longer was he dreaming of dire punishments and waking in fear. He was dreaming of his wife and sons and the rolling hills of Northumberland. The friendly vision of the delectable Hilda Osbert had begun to quickly fade from his mind.

On the occasions of Hilda's evening visits, Sir Osbert had dismissed the guard, sending him into the city on an errand that he knew would take well in excess of an hour. Since Bannockburn, Osbert had not been a whole man, following injury on the battlefield. He knew his lovely wife had needs, and he had respected Walt's father who he had seen ride to his death in that battle. Always afraid that Hilda would leave him for a younger fitter man, he was prone to make what he deemed safe arrangements, for her occasional satisfaction. This time it had seemed a little more frequent than occasional, and Hilda a little too enthusiastic, but he did not worry. He was convinced that Walt would soon be on his way home to his wife, and that would be the end of it. Or it would be, until Hilda got the urge for love again.

***

Bishop Beaumont was intrigued when told that the High Sheriff was requesting an audience, and that he was accompanied by Squire Johansson of Syhale manor.

By the time he had finished the audience he was extremely angry, but not at the two men in front of him.

They had shown him the document signed by the chamberlain and the three knights who negotiated the handover of Mitford castle. He had also seen the deposition by the soldiers in their defence regarding the taking of the castle. The sheriff had brought with him the handover document and a copy made by his scribe, which the bishop reluctantly signed as being a true copy. He was obviously not keen to be involved with Sir Walter's petition, even though he now knew more about the truth of the events.

After some discussion where they pooled knowledge on the subject of where the documents had been found, and the information Aidric had learned in Newcastle, Tynemouth and from the constable in Penrith, they pieced together the whole sorry tale of the theft of the documents, and Brothers Saul and Gregory's involvement with the layabout Henry Park alias Arthur Mason.

'Brothers Gregory and Saul have stolen from the church, plotted to pervert the course of the king's justice and generally brought the church and my diocese into disrepute.' Bishop Lewis Beaumont pronounced angrily. 'Circumstances have already punished Brother Saul and that layabout Park so they are now in God's hands. It is up to me to ensure that Brother Gregory arrives at God's gate as well. I cannot forgive Radulf for his part in my abduction, but he is not guilty of murder or kidnap, and showed a kindly hand to the pope's nuncios. He is still a prisoner of the king, for who knows how long, so I leave his future to his majesty.'

Turning to the sheriff he asked. 'You have sufficient evidence I trust to bring Brother Gregory before my Bishop's Court, on charges of perversion of the king's justice and theft?' He added as an afterthought, 'I forgot fraudulently copying his bishop's signature for personal gain and revenge.'

The sheriff assured him there was plentiful evidence and he would lay the charges as soon as he returned to his office.

As soon as they left the bishop's palace, Aidric bade his farewell to the sheriff, and promised the return of the borrowed document after his master had been released.

'Would you not like to see the man charged?' the sheriff asked.

Aidric agreed that it would be pleasing news for his master, and agreed to a short delay in his leaving.

The sheriff saw no problem with keeping Brother Gregory in gaol after he laid the charges, until he could lay his hands on all the evidence. After all he still had to arrange for the Penrith Constable to attend the trial, and it would be months before the bishop was ready to hold court. He was sure the bishop would keep a low profile and not hold any controversial trials until the current political situation was resolved.

Brother Gregory had not been given the courtesies shown to Walt when he was imprisoned in the castle keep. He lay in a filthy cell and was shackled and chained to the wall. He had sufficient chain to walk around about half of his tiny cell. Relief of his bladder and bowels had to be done at the extremity of his chain in a small filthy wooden bucket. He tried his best to maintain some dignity and keep as clean as he could. He was led outside in a yard for a short exercise period in the morning, when he had to empty his bucket and could have a brief wash in a trough of cold water. There was no soap. His only relief was that there was a good amount of daylight coming through the barred window facing the south side of the keep. *Maybe,* he thought, *I could persuade one of the guards to bring me a bible.* He felt he needed some spiritual guidance.

It was while he was nurturing these thoughts that he heard the keys rattling in the door and the guard shouting for him to get to his feet, as he had visitors.

Brother Gregory had not had any visitors since he was locked up, and waited in anticipation for them to enter. Thoughts were racing through his mind. He was going to be released; there was no evidence against him for conspiracy. He had been foolish and forged the bishop's signature for the freedom of a poor man who wished to make good. That was all. His thoughts jolted to a sudden halt when he saw the High Sheriff, and who he was accompanied by. 'You,' he said, staring malevolently at Aidric, 'have not you and your traitorous master done enough that you must now come to mock me in prison.'

'Keep quiet prisoner,' said the sheriff with dignified authority. 'I have come to inform you that the Bishop has heard your case and seen the document you stole and hid in your desk. You are charged with perversion of the king's justice, theft, forgery and conspiracy to defraud. You will appear in the Bishop's Court in due course. The sentence for such crimes is death. The manner of your death will be resolved by your plea. A plea of guilty will see you hung and a plea of not guilty will likely result in a more prolonged and entertaining death, for the citizens of Newcastle.

The sheriff then handed a copy of the Holy Bible to Brother Gregory saying, 'The bishop suggested you have this in order to help you make your peace with God before you arrive at his gate.'

As the sheriff was handing the book to the monk, Aidric saw him turn white, as all the blood drained from his face. It became obvious that he was overcome with fear as his mouth dropped open and the front of his robe became wet with a puddle appearing on the floor below him. An embarrassed and disgusted Aidric turned on his heel and departed as the monk began to whimper,

'Oh My God, I have already been found guilty.'

***

It was just over a week later on Saturday the thirtieth of October that Walt received a surprise visit from Aidric. His young manservant had finished his morning tasks, and had remained, as he had been doing for the last couple of years when no visitors were expected. Walt had made an agreement with the lad's father in return for certain privileges. To the best of his limited ability, he was teaching him to read and write Latin. He found that the lessons had the twofold effect of not only tutoring the boy but refreshing and improving his own command of the language. Young Gerard was learning well and it gave Walt a sense of satisfaction as he could equate the task with his own son's learning at Alnwick. He had formed quite an attachment to the lad in the absence of any other youthful company as he was familiar with at home, and it was during one of these lessons that Aidric arrived unannounced and walked into his cell. He knew the boy as a servant and had never before paid him much attention as he had normally departed as soon as he arrived.

Aidric greeted his master and waited for an explanation.

Walt closed the books and told the boy it was enough for today and he would see him again on the morrow.

After the lad had left, and noticing the quizzical look on his squire's face, he said. 'I am teaching the lad to read and write Latin, Aidric. Is that a bad thing?'

'No Sir,' said Aidric jovially, 'now I know how you got around the grumpy guard Geoff.'

'And how is that then Squire?' Walt asked with a smile.

'Do you not agree that the boy bears a striking resemblance to the said guard, Sir Walter?'

'You have me Aidric, you are correct, it is his son Gerard. I still have the other servant for the more odious tasks. Gerard is more for company than service. Now enough chatter' what are you doing here so soon? Do you know that the king fled to Wales? Have you brought important news?'

Aidric ignored all but the last question as he triumphantly produced the wallet from his saddlebag and laid it before Walt, who did not need to be told what it was. His face lit up and he grabbed hold of Aidric and hugged him in a most uncharacteristic manner. Seeing his squire's embarrassment, he immediately released him, and turned his attention to the envelope, opening it to find not only his original documents but a copy of the sheriff's handover document for Mitford castle, signed and dated a week ago by the sheriff and certified as a true copy, reluctantly Aidric told him, by Bishop Beaumont.

Aidric went on to tell him of the fate of Prior Gregory, and his fear when confronted with the almost certain fact that he was going to be executed for his crimes. The fact that he was to face the very court of the man whose confidence and trust he had betrayed, to the great embarrassment of the church, and the presentation of the Bible with the bishop's advice was sufficient to convince Brother Gregory that he was to be found guilty and executed.

'The wheel is turning now,' Walt replied, 'only a couple more turns my friend and we shall be together riding the hills and dales of Northumberland again, and I shall be with my beloved wife and sons.'

'One more thing, Sir, before you read your letters I must tell you that, sadly, your uncle and aunt from Felling have both died of a fever, Sir Adam in late September and Lady Dorothy a few days later. Master Matthew also had the fever, but being young and strong he recovered.'

Walt said a short prayer for his uncle and aunt before asking. 'How is Matthew coping alone? Is there a wife in sight yet?'

'He is managing well Sir, and no, there is no prospect of marriage yet.'

After handing his master the usual purse of gold florins from Lady Katherine, a tired Aidric made his excuses, and left Walt in jovial mood thinking about his freedom. He would stay the night at the inn nearby and make his way back home to Syhale and his wife tomorrow. He would not be returning to London until the spring. He had done all he could and now it was up to Sir Walter and his lawyer to judge what action to take next. Arriving at his lodgings Aidric remembered that he had completely forgotten to seek information on Sir Walt's possible liaisons with his gaoler's wife. *Oh well,* he thought. *It is probably best left unsolved.*

***

Aidric arrived home nine days later after some delays due to inclement weather. This time he did not go first to the manor, but straight to his holding and Jeanne. Nothing was going to distract him this time from the immediate delights of her warm and passionate welcome. It was early evening as he arrived, and he found the trooper who was helping to supervise the farmhands about to leave for the day and return to his barracks at Syhale. The man was about to shout the news to the house, but Aidric held his finger to his lips for silence, and indicated the soldier should head off home quietly. As he passed by, Aidric said in a low voice. 'I would be appreciative if you would not mention my return. I shall report to Lady Katherine in the morning when I am cleaned and refreshed.'

The trooper nodded his agreement, thinking, *I bet you will you randy bugger.*

Aidric quietly dismounted and tied up his horse. Going quietly into the kitchen he saw Jeanne, with her back to him, and bent over a small pot gently stirring it with an iron kitchen ladle. The sight of Jeanne's vulnerable rear end was too much for Aidric, and in two quick strides he was across the room, and her skirts were thrown up around her shoulders.

Jeanne's reaction was instant. The iron ladle came out of the pot and over her shoulder with the speed of a striking viper. The last thing Aidric remembered for a while was the tremendous blow to his head and darkness.

When he recovered consciousness, he was lying on a horsehair-filled palliasse that Jeanne had brought from their bed. His eyes gradually focussed and he could feel somebody bathing his head gently. He moaned, as he realised it was Jeanne.

'You lovely stupid man,' she said. 'I thought I was under attack. This was not going to happen to me again as long as I was alive, so I did what I had to do. Why did you not announce yourself, I would have lifted the skirt for you.'

'Not so much fun' he said.

'So long as it was worth the pain,' Jeanne said.

Deciding he had recovered enough she set out to fulfil his desires.

'I will never tire of you my love,' he said later, as the couple lay exhausted on a palliasse before the fire.

'Nor I of you Aidric; come now let us eat. You take the potage, there is not enough for two, and I will get some bread and cheese.

'We shall share, and have a little of each,' he said.

While they were eating he brought Jeanne up to date on the latest developments.

'I know something you don't,' she said when he had finished.

She flounced off from the table and busied herself with the dirty plates and pots. A frustrated Aidric chased her across the room and pulled her away, kissing her and ordering that she stop teasing and tell him what she knew.

'Hugh Despenser the elder was hanged at Bristol on the twenty-seventh of October.'

'What about the King, and his favourite the younger Hugh Despenser; the one who signed Sir Walter's document.'

'No news yet,' Jeanne told him as she was washing their dirty supper plates and pots. 'Perhaps they have not caught them yet.'

'Come on Jeanne,' Aidric coaxed, 'this is no time to clean pots, let us be off to bed.'

Jeanne complied willingly and there was no further discussion of the master, or politics, in the Johansson house that night, as with the fire damped down, the pair went into their small sleeping chamber taking the palliasse with them.

The next day, after reporting all new developments to Katherine, who was particularly pleased to hear of the fate to befall the old Prior of Tynemouth; Aidric did the rounds of the estate peasants collecting rents with young Walter. He was surprised how soon the lad had got a grip on things and the respect he had already gained from the workers. *If only we had all the land back,* he thought, not recognising the fact that it was never his land and he was just a squire. What was his master's land he looked upon as his own in terms of responsibility; and that was enough to make it the same by his reckoning.

That week they had a raid by reivers and a quantity of sheep were driven off. Aidric gave chase with ten soldiers led by Sergeant Guddal, leaving Sergeant Best at the manor with the remainder. After a day's chase the reivers realised that they were not going to escape with the flock and deliberately scattered them to delay their pursuers while they made their escape. Aidric stayed with two men to round up the sheep, leaving the sergeant and eight soldiers to pursue what they believed were around five robbers. Having rounded up the sheep they set off for home at a leisurely pace, and were just passing the mill when they were caught up by the sergeant and the remainder of his section.

'Well, what happened?' Aidric enquired.

Galeron answered. 'We believe there were five or six of them, we caught three, and the remainder got away.'

'So where are the three you caught?'

'I had them hung them from trees by the road as a warning to others. They claimed to be Scots but they were no more Scot than you or I. It is my belief they thought we might spare them if they were taken to be Scots.'

'Well done Sergeant Guddal,' Aidric replied, 'a thief is a thief, no matter where he is from, and the king has even less influence in our northern land than ever before. We must dispense our own justice. It seems that things will not improve until we have a strong monarch who is willing to involve himself in affairs north of York.'

When they returned to Syhale, young Walter, who had been away at Seaton for the day was sorely disappointed that he had missed all the fun, and an opportunity to demonstrate his swordsmanship and ability to attack from horseback.

Later in the afternoon Aidric made his way home and wondered why life had been so kind to him. He was a free man and had a smallholding and a wonderful wife who he knew adored him, as he did her. Nothing could spoil their happiness now. All they needed was the return of the master to make their life complete.

=====

CHAPTER 13

Freedom

By November, Walt's patience was running low. He was keen to get on with his petition but Brother Peter was still advising caution, however he had prepared the petition and presented it to Walt for approval.

He had made a short reference to the document signed by the knights whereupon it was agreed that Sir Walter be granted life and limb. He had then gone on to plead pardon for all felonies, robberies and homicides.

Walt objected to homicides stating that he had committed none. Brother Peter, to whom Walt had told everything over the years, reminded him of the execution of the robbers.

'Best we cover it,' he said. 'If they don't find out about it no matter, if they do then you will have been pardoned. We will hold these other documents of yours to be presented as a last resort. The sheriff's document refers to the knight's document, and we hold back the one signed by a Despenser who may be distinctly out of favour.'

Walt sighed and agreed as he knew he must.

The following week Brother Peter brought the news that the king had been captured and was imprisoned in Monmouth Castle. Things seemed to be moving fast now, but not fast enough for Walt. It was over a week later before he received the news that the younger Hugh Despenser had been captured and conveyed to Hereford to await the pleasure of the Queen and Mortimer, who, it was said, insisted on being present to orchestrate the manner of his death. Brother Peter said the Queen thought of it as God's retribution for the unnatural liaison with her husband. The following week he told Walt of the horrific death that had befallen the unfortunate Hugh Despenser the younger.

It had taken place in Hereford and on the twenty-fourth of November, in front of assembled townspeople, with Queen Isabella taking a grandstand seat with her lover Roger Mortimer as the unfortunate Despenser was hung drawn and quartered.

Walt pressed the monk for details but he refused saying that he did not hold with torture and sadistic acts of revenge which was no part of God's work. Walt was disappointed but the monk was not to be swayed.

Realising that there was no more to be gained by pursuing this line, he again pressed the monk to proceed with his petition, but Brother Peter held fast, saying that everything was prepared and he would be the judge of the correct time for submission. He confirmed that the latest development was a good omen for Walt's future but urged him to be economical with his conversation as a wrong word could jeopardise all his hopes.

There were no more immediate political developments affecting Walt's position and he soon found himself involved with preparations for Christ's Mass following a welcome note from the constable. The very fact that he had to make such preparations gave him good cheer. He looked again at the note he had been handed by his gaoler Sir Osbert. It was an invitation to attend the Christ's Mass at the Chapel of St. John and afterward to festivities at the Constable Tower as guests of the constable, Sir Henry Plantagenet and Lady Maud.

The gaoler had given him permission to have the freedom of the castle, within the inner walls. This allowed him to see the tailor who obtained some suitable clothing and carried out the necessary alterations in order that he may present himself in a knightly manner at the occasion.

Walt was pleased to find that these privileges had also been afforded to Dai Tudor although he was not invited to the constable's festivities, probably because he was not a wealthy man and a former constable of a small town, therefore nowhere near the ranking of the Tower Constable and not a knight. However, Walt was interested to see what transpired and if Sir Henry actually spoke to him. There definitely seemed to be a more relaxed atmosphere among the staff at the tower since the news of the king's arrest. People no longer conducted their business as if walking on eggshells.

On the 25 December 1326 Walt rose at dawn to attend Matins in the chapel. It was very cold and windy as he made his way toward the White Tower, pulling his cloak tightly around his body. Making his way to the far side, he entered the Chapel of St. John, pausing just inside the door to let his eyes become accustomed to the dim light within. He did not know where he should sit, but noticed that toward the altar there were rows of pews that seemed to be more elaborate and with wider spacing than those further back. He decided that these were probably all earmarked for the hierarchy of the tower, and wished he had not been so early, arriving when there were only a couple of worshippers present and nobody at the front. To his great relief a seminarian noticed his dilemma, came forward and showed him to a suitable pew. He was then able to take advantage of his early arrival, as he watched the remainder of the congregation arrive. He saw his gaoler Sir Osbert Lancaster arriving with his wife Lady Hilda, who looked over to him and gave a cheeky little wave. Walt felt a small surge of affection for the obliging lady, and flattered that she had sought him out for recognition. He was now ever more confident that he would be out of the tower prison before long.

The last to arrive were the constable, Sir Henry Plantagenet and Lady Maud. This constable, he knew to be a very important man in the capital. He was responsible for the security of the tower, its military garrison and all the prisons and their occupants. His position was plain to see, if the fine clothes worn by he and his lovely wife were to be counted. Lady Maud was enveloped in the most colourful and expensive looking silks from the orient. Walt could not bear to think of their cost. The constable was wearing an elaborate uniform with intricate brocade work of red and gold. He was a tall man, looking fit and muscular with a pleasing countenance. Following the service Walt returned to his cell where he broke his fast on a hot bowl of porridge and a mug of hot rosehip beverage.

Walt's next surprise was when young Gerard turned up to do his duties. He had seen him at Mass with his parents, but did not expect him to work today and made his thoughts clear to the lad.

'Just do the commode for you Sir Walter,' Gerard said. 'Then if it is alright with you I would like to read a short passage from the Bible to you.'

'Good grief Lad! You think I have not had enough religion so early in the morning? What is it you would like to read to me on Christ's Mass day Gerard?'

'The Holy Bible, Sir, the section of the testament referring to Christ's birth, and I would be grateful if you would hear me, and give help if I have difficulty.'

'I imagine young man that you will experience some difficulty as I think we need a deal more schooling for such a task.'

Gerard looked a little crestfallen. 'Please, Sir Walter, I wish to read a passage to my parents as a special treat for them this afternoon.'

'Very well Gerard,' Walt said taking the bible to his table. He opened it at Matthew Chapter 1, and suggested they do from verse 18 to 25 as this was probably the simplest description and does not go into great detail.

Gerard was happy with this, and set about reading the section to Walt, using the skills he had learnt to sound any Latin words with which he was unfamiliar. Walt was surprised at his effort, considering the lad had not a complete understanding of what he was reading. With his limited knowledge of Latin, Walt was able to teach the boy the general gist of the verses, in the hope that his wish to impress his parents may be achieved.

'Have you been doing a lot of practice at home then?' Walt questioned, when they had completed the exercise.

'Yes, Sir, I am determined to gain some education. I would never say this to my father but I do not want to be a prison guard or a soldier, I would like to be a merchant of some sort, and for that I must have reading, writing and numbers. I have been doing numbers with a friend who was schooled by monks.'

Walt was impressed by the lad's efforts to better himself and his sensitivity of not deriding his father's work.

'Well Gerard,' he said. 'I suggest for further adventures into Latin, you find a priest or a monk as tutor, but now we had better get as many hours in as possible over the next month, as I do not know how much longer I shall be staying here as a guest of the state.'

'Thank you, Sir; I shall be sorry when you leave.'

'You have my permission Gerard, to be just as sorry as I shall be happy.'

That seemed to amuse Gerard, as he requested that he go through the passage once more before he left.

Alone again and feeling a necessary urge to please God and hope he noticed, Walt headed again for the chapel to attend Sext at noon. There would be plenty of time afterward to make himself ready for the afternoon festivities in Constable Tower.

He was collected by Sir Osbert Lancaster and found Lady Hilda waiting in the courtyard when they emerged from London tower. Walt was surprised to see her talking to Dai Tudor, also dressed for a function. Sir Osbert explained that he had reminded Sir Henry of Dai's status as Constable, prior to imprisonment, and he had decided to include him in his guest list. There would not be many people present he was told. From the tower staff, only the senior officers and from the prisoners there were only Walt and Dai Tudor.

'Just a small gathering,' he said.

There appeared to be around thirty people around the banqueting table, with Sir Henry and Lady Maud centrally placed. Their most senior officers and their wives were arranged on either side and opposite to them. The remainder were spaced out to the ends of the table on each side. Walt found himself sat next to Lady Hilda, with Dai Tudor opposite and a tower guard he did not know to his right. He took his first opportunity to introduce himself to the man on his right.

'Good afternoon, Sir, may I introduce myself, I am Sir Walter Radulf of Syhale, prisoner of his majesty.'

'Not for much longer I warrant,' said his neighbour laughing, and turning to offer his hand to Walt. 'Sir Matthew Witham, quartermaster,' he said taking Walt's hand firmly, 'and to my right my lady wife Barbara.' Barbara took her cue and stretched across her husband to lightly take Walt's hand.

Food began to arrive on the table, along with jugs of wine decanted from oak wine barrels. Conversation dwindled as everyone began to tuck in to the various courses of delights and quaff copious quantities of wine. Walt gave the impression of joining in with the wine quaffing, but in reality he was taking the drink more slowly. This to him was a strange situation, apart from being Christ's Mass; listening to the conversations around him, he would be forgiven for thinking that it was also a celebration of the king's departure from the political scene. He just hoped it was not premature, which was why he wished to keep his head clear and watch his tongue. He felt a gentle stroking on his thigh, looking to his right he saw Hilda smiling at him. Startled and hoping nobody saw their momentary gaze at each other, he gently shook his head and picked up her hand, placing it upon her own knee.

Small talk was the order of the day during the meal, nobody wanted to get into deep conversation whilst stuffing themselves with the various courses being delivered just about as quickly as they could be eaten. Once the meal was over and the trenchers and leftovers cleared away, they were left only with the ample supply of wine and large bowls of apples on the table. This seemed to be the signal for people to arise from the table and excuse themselves, to obey calls of nature, and generally begin to gravitate into groups and engage in more serious conversation. This was the part that Walt was dreading, and had kept a clear head for. He told himself that he must be prepared for anything, even maybe insults, and he must not lose his temper.

Walt looked towards the constable's position where the seat next to him had been vacated by his wife. He immediately regretted this action as he caught the eye of Sir Henry who beckoned him over to the vacated seat. As he arrived next to Sir Henry, the constable held out his hand and took Walt's forearm with a firm military style grip.

'Sir Henry Plantagenet and you, Sir, I gather are the notorious rebel, Sir Walter Radulf.'

Walt was speechless; he did not know how to respond, to admit being a rebel or to say something in his defence.

Sir Henry, anticipating his dilemma, roared with laughter, slapped him jovially on the back saying. 'Come now, Sir Walter, you are among friends or you would not be at this gathering. I wager you will be submitting your petition for freedom within four weeks.'

He bade Walt sit in the seat vacated by his wife and engaged him in conversation by asking about the Mitford episode. Walt guardedly told him all the truth he thought he should hear, no matter which monarch he may support. In essence he stuck to the story as explained in the handover document and the soldier's deposition. Sir Henry was sympathetic and said he could well envisage the difficulty of being between two such hard places where a wrong decision could mean his head.

'You did the right thing getting rid of the Scots and then not allowing them back in. Now tell me something of Robert Bruce, what did you think of him? I understand your father died at Bannockburn, you must have hated the man.'

Walt again gave him a sanitised version of his meeting with Bruce, having skipped quickly over the reason he fled to Scotland in the first place, with another heavily edited account, but leaving enough truth to be believable. Walt was happy for Sir Henry to believe that version of events without him having to lie. It was with relief that Walt spied Lady Maud returning to her seat and stood to vacate it. Sir Henry was having none of it. He pulled Walt back down and told his wife to sit in the next seat alongside Walt, which was vacant. Sir Henry introduced the two of them and Walt was then relieved to see that Sir Henry had his attention turned to another man, now leaning over his shoulder and whispering to him in earnest. Lady Maud was not going to let him off scot free, though to Walt's relief, she was not interested in his political escapades but in his home and his family. These were subjects upon which Walt could pontificate until the cows came home. She listened intently and occasionally threw in a question. Although she was a good listener, Walt could not help feeling that she showed a glimmer of relief when Sir Henry caught her attention and suggested that they should circulate among their guests.

This was also a relief for Walt, who immediately sought out Dai Tudor for some uncomplicated conversation, and a little more of the wine he had been studiously avoiding. Dai had been questioning Sir Osbert and found out that he and Walt were the only political prisoners left in the Tower. The others had already been released or long gone for execution. There were still quite a few criminal prisoners detained for serious crimes such as piracy and murder of a lord and such like. All were awaiting trials which had been long delayed because of the political situation.

***

The fate of the Despensers and the king's imprisonment had also reached Syhale manor. Katherine was heartened by such news, believing that the door would soon be opened for Walt to leave his prison and return home to his family. She did not want to appear over optimistic, but determined that they would make this coming Christ's Mass celebration a period of special prayer and aspiration for their reunion with their husband and father. *They would wait until Walt's return to throw a grand feast for all, and be damned with the expense,* she thought.

My boys, she thought proudly. Young Walter was a man already and not yet seventeen. He was now running the estate with confidence and had already won the respect of the workers for his uncompromising discipline but fair treatment. He was not afraid to mete out serious punishment for laziness and other misdemeanours or the summary hanging of reivers caught rustling estate stock. On the other hand he would give praise and reward where it was due.

Alex was at Alnwick Castle undergoing his training for future knighthood and Hugh would be there in another six months when he finished his schooling at the abbey. James and John were both normally at the abbey under tuition of the monks, except that now it was Christ's Mass and they were all home with their doting mother.

They were a lively lot and in particular young Walter and Hugh needed a strict rein on their off duty behaviour. She did not want any pregnant serving girls, as both the boys, and the young girls on the manor and in the village seemed to have a very natural fascination for each other. *A bit too natural,* thought Katherine, remembering their father's antics with Freda. She thought perhaps she should ensure the old barn was securely locked, but immediately dismissed the idea as paranoia. *Anyway,* she thought, *we shall have the best time we can without Walt and celebrate the hope of his homecoming.*

She had a better idea for the old barn; she called the reeve and instructed him to have it cleaned out, and to build a central stone fireplace and spit for a hog roast on the twenty-fifth of December. The estate would donate a hog and some ale for the workers to celebrate the inevitable homecoming of Sir Walter. Whatever they did in the manor, it would be unwise to let the workers and soldiers think that there was no certainty of their master returning.

Young Walter did not disagree with this decision but was annoyed that his mother had instructed the reeve without discussing it with him first. He was also concerned that this potential homecoming celebration was a little premature and costly. It had not escaped his attention that their Steward Turstan Gathergood was no longer in their employ and nobody; least of all his mother would discuss the reason. Surely, whatever happened to the king there were legal arrangements to be made, and the agreement of the new powers, whoever they may be, before his father could be released.

Young Walter's misgivings aside, the soldiers and the workers had a grand celebration on Christ's Mass; all convinced that next year was to be the end of separation for the family. After a quiet, reflective, but substantial meal on the twenty fifth, the family settled down to wait for news. The three youngest boys had to return to Alnwick on the Monday the fifth of January to continue their respective training courses.

For the rest of them, January brought the normal run of the mill tasks, and after the festivities and hopes, things all seemed a little dull. With no news of Walter's release their expectations were now being considered with reason, instead of wine and ale.

Assuming that Walt would soon be released, Katherine had one outstanding problem to resolve, her brother Richard. *What to do about Richard, the debt and the deeds?* she thought.

It was imperative that she unburdened herself to Walt before Richard could put in his two penneth. Her son Walter had gone to Aidric's farm with Jeanne to help her resolve a problem with one of the serfs, so she would be able to slip away without him insisting on accompanying her. Knowing her son's aptitude for bringing out the worst in her brother she decided to take the opportunity for a private talk. With Galeron as escort she arrived at the Delaval tower just before midday, when she was sure that Richard would be there for his meal. Leaving Galeron with Watson, the groom, Katherine ascended the staircase, announced herself to the maid and went straight to the family area, where her mother was sat crocheting, attended by her servant Cecily. She kissed her mother, and explained that she thought it would not be long now before Walt was released and home again.

'Humph,' said Isobel, 'until the next time he gets himself into trouble and leaves you and the children to fend for yourselves.'

'Mother!' replied a shocked Katherine. 'I have never heard you speak of Walt in such a manner before. What has got into you?'

Isobel did not reply and the pair sat silently until they heard voices denoting the return of Richard and his squire. Richard entered the room, closely followed by servants bringing the midday repast and a jug of ale. After a cursory greeting from her brother they sat down to eat. Richard did not seem to notice the strained atmosphere between Katherine and their mother, and chatted happily about his plans for Delaval land this year.

Katherine wondered if these included Syhale demesne. As soon as there was no longer reason to delay, she bade farewell, kissed her mother, and asked Richard if he would accompany her to her horse.

Once outside, she took him by the arm and steered him towards the tower's kitchen garden.

'Why are you taking me into the garden Sister?' Richard queried.

'Walt will be home in a matter of months, and I do not want you to talk to him about our deeds and our finances until I have had chance to explain first.'

'Worried your Saxon warrior will knock the shit out of you for losing his last plot of land?' Richard scoffed. 'You can tell him, he will not get the deeds back until the debts are cleared.'

'There is no need to be so bloody pleased about my predicament Richard' she said, shocked at her own turn of phrase. 'Why do you hold so much resentment of Walt and his family after all this time? Surely it cannot be still about Freda rejecting your advances at the Michaelmas fair in September '05.' Immediately she had said it, Katherine knew it was a mistake when she saw him redden.

'God damn you Sister and all your new clan. I shall keep my peace on the matter but there will be no deeds until I am fully repaid, and any more remarks like that may see no deeds at all.'

Katherine was appalled, her brother's state of mind was worse than ever. 'What have you been saying to Mother?' she asked.

'None of your bloody business, now piss off home before I change my mind.'

Katherine did not acknowledge his last statement, she turned about and walked to the stable, where she collected her horse and escort, mounted and left at a dignified walking pace.

Inwardly she was furious. *I would as well have gone to Prior Gregory for loans as my brother. He has now succeeded in poisoning our mother's mind against my family,'* she thought.

***

It was nearly the end of January 1327 before Walt received another visit from his lawyer. He was beginning to worry that he had been deserted when there was a call of 'Visitor for Sir Walter,' from Matt, the guard, to avoid him being surprised by the sudden appearance of his visitor through the unlocked cell door.

Walt was more than a little relieved to see Brother Peter walk in through the door.

'I thought you had abandoned me' he said, with the relief visible on his face as he slowly broke into a wide grin.

The good brother laughed as he replied. 'I wanted to wait until I had news worth conveying, and now I have. You may now present your petition. The king has abdicated the throne in favour of his son Edward.'

'But Edward is a mere boy, what is he, not much more than fourteen I would wager, when did this happen?' asked Walt.

'I am told it was on twentieth of this month, but the news took a little time to be verified. As for him being a boy, I am sure that the country will be run by Queen Isabella on his behalf.'

An excited Walt lost no time in signing the prepared petition the monk had brought with him. This was to be submitted without delay, addressed to the king, although it would most likely be reviewed by Queen Isabella, said to be acting as regent.

In early February, soon after the coronation of the new king, Walt had a visit from Aidric, bringing news of life at the manor and another bunch of letters and money. He told Walt about their celebrations in the hope that he would soon be home.

Walt laughed heartily throwing the letters in the air, 'I am sure there will soon be no need for letters,' he said. 'Soon, I believe I will impart my news directly to my loved ones.'

He went on to tell Aidric that the petition had been signed and presented by Brother Peter, and all they had to do was wait a while longer and hope that it was well received.

Aidric's response was enthusiastic and immediate. 'I shall stay in London and wait as long as it takes.' Thinking he detected a look of disapproval on his master's face, he quickly qualified his statement. 'No longer than two months, with your leave, Sir.'

'You want me to pay you for sitting around on your arse for two months?' Walt asked with a serious scowl on his face.

Aidric began to stammer an apology, as Walt burst into laughter and slapped him heartily on the back, whilst still laughing at his little joke.

'Of course you can stay dear friend,' he said, 'but you had better visit me every day.'

Five weeks later came a day Walt would never forget. It was the fourteenth of March 1327. He was playing a game of chequers with Aidric when Geoff the guard called. 'Visitor for Sir Walter.'

'Must be the lawyer, they would not let any other in to see me while you are still here.' Walt said.

Aidric, sitting with his back to the door, was surprised when Walt suddenly stood up with a deference that he would not normally show to Brother Peter. He turned to see that it was the head gaoler Sir Osbert Lancaster, and quickly rose to his feet in respect to the master of London Tower. Sir Osbert waved them to be seated and wished them good morning; following which he ordered the two of them to report to Constable Tower in one hour's time with regard to Sir Walter's appeal.

'I have already despatched a messenger to the abbey to fetch your lawyer,' he added as he turned on his heel, and left as sharply as he had arrived with no further explanation.

The two men looked at each other with smiles of anticipation. Aidric was the first to speak. 'I think this will prove to be your lucky day, Sir.'

'I hope so Aidric, I hope so,' Walt replied. He stood for a moment at a loss what to do next, before sweeping the chequers into their box and announcing that he intended to change his clothing to something more appropriate for the anticipated occasion.

Aidric said nothing, but just hoped that they were not going to be disappointed.

One hour later he was collected by Sir Osbert and was pleasantly surprised but curious to find Lady Hilda waiting in the courtyard to accompany them to the Constable Tower.

Arriving at the Tower they were immediately shown to the grand hall where there was frantic activity as servants were quickly placing flagons of wine and ale together with numerous and varied morsels of food in platters on a long table supported by trestles.

Walt noticed that the constable and his wife Lady Maud were standing at the end of the room near the fireplace talking to Brother Peter. All appeared to be in a jovial mood and this gave him good heart. The constable noticed their entrance and immediately called Sir Osbert to join them with his party.

Following the normal courtesies of greeting, the constable announced without further preamble. 'Sir Walter, I have here in my hand the royal response to your petition for a pardon.' He paused for what seemed like an age, while all about him held their breath, before continuing: 'Your plea has been scrutinised by Her Majesty Queen Isabella acting as regent for the young king. Having carefully considered your plea and the supporting documents signed by the knights, Sir Ralph Greystoke, Sir Robert de Umfraville and Sir John de Eure, together with the deposition signed by your troop of soldiers at Mitford, the Queen has accordingly, and on behalf of his majesty the king, decided that you have been poorly treated, and therefore offers you a full pardon on all counts, and also the full restoration of your lands. The pardon was dated yesterday the thirteenth of March.'

Sir Henry then held out his hand to congratulate Walt, and wish him well for the future. He did point out that the restoration of his lands may be a protracted affair as those currently in possession on the king's authority might be reluctant to relinquish them while the deposed king was still alive, and they saw a chance to hold on.

Walt was ecstatic and had little interest in the problems, he was free, and that was the main thing. Any difficulties he felt capable of dealing with, now he had a royal pardon.

When everyone had finished congratulating each other and he had a moment to think, Walt suddenly turned to Brother Peter.

'I thought you were not going to use the documents from the knights and the soldiers?' Before the monk could reply he continued. 'How can you have, they are still wrapped up in my cell?'

'I did not submit those documents the monk replied; the constable has told me it was he.'

Walt looked to Sir Henry for an explanation.

Sir Henry laughed. 'There is nothing mysterious about it. When Sir Ralph left Mitford with the documents he told you that he would deposit them with someone sympathetic to your cause.' Walt nodded his agreement.

'Well,' continued the Constable. From there it is a tale of two Henry's. The sympathetic person was Sir Henry Percy, whose grandmother was a Plantagenet and he is therefore related to me and known to me, the other Sir Henry. When he heard that you were to be sent to the tower he sent them to me by urgent messenger, with the request that they were only to be used in an emergency, should you be in imminent danger or as part of a plea, but only if considered they would be advantageous at that time. I believe that on return to Northumberland you owe your friend a token of your gratitude.'

'I owe thanks to you too, Sir.' Walt said taking the constables forearm and shaking it vigorously.

The constable returning his firm grasp, said. 'Now, enough of this; let us make a little merry but not too much if you will be on your way today. Our groom has prepared a riding horse and a pack horse for you for when you leave, you may consider them a present from his majesty by way of small compensation for your incarceration without trial.

Walt thanked him, thinking he was lucky there had been no trial as he would more than likely have been here for life.

With that they began to partake of the food and beverage and the general conversation.

Walt waited patiently for an opportunity to speak to the constable alone, and asked about his friend Dai Tudor, and his chances of release. Sir Henry was sympathetic but said that the man had not only had his property seized but his money as well, leaving his wife destitute, whereby she had taken her own life shortly after his imprisonment.

Walt was horrified by this news; Dai had never mentioned such a tragedy.

'Can he be allowed to attend this meeting that I may speak with him before I leave?' He asked the constable.

Sir Henry agreed and immediately called a servant, ordering the man to fetch the prisoner Dai Tudor from London Tower.

While they were waiting for the Welshman's arrival, Walt asked Brother Peter if he would act on Dai's behalf and prepare his plea. 'I will bear the cost of your services in this matter' he assured the good brother. The monk agreed, and there followed a short consultation with Sir Henry who consented to facilitate the action and write a recommendation for pardon.

Ten minutes later the servant arrived with the bemused Welshman, who on learning what the occasion was, pronounced himself overjoyed for Walt's good fortune and hoped he may follow him soon. He made no mention of his own position or plea for help.

Walt realised that it was more than likely a matter of principle for Dai that he would not beg help from an Englishman. He waited patiently until the Welshman had settled down and appeared relaxed.

Once Dai had himself a leg of chicken in one hand and a mug of ale in the other, Walt drew him to one side and explained what he had done. He did not get the rebuff he expected, but merely a weak protest.

'But how am I to repay you, I am destitute and without a position.'

'I shall resolve that before I leave. Accompany me to my cell when I go to pack for my journey.' Walt replied.

Leaving the Welshman talking to Lady Lancaster and Aidric, Walt sought out Osbert. The result of his conversation with Osbert was that for a small consideration to the guards, the privileges Walt enjoyed would be transferred to Dai Tudor when Walt left, and the Welshman would occupy the cell that Walt had fitted out for himself.

Walt arranged with Brother Peter that he should prepare his bill today at the Abbey as soon as he left the tower. Leaning closer to the monk to avoid eavesdropping he whispered 'Following settlement I will open a new account for the Welshman to be billed to me at Syhale. You should send future bills by trustworthy messenger and I shall return the money by the same man.'

Promising to have his account prepared, the monk bade a hasty farewell and hurried off to the abbey to complete the task. With these arrangements complete, and after a grateful farewell to Sir Henry, Walt headed for his cell with Aidric and Dai Tudor. He was surprised to find a new and fashionable tunic hanging from the hook on the wall behind the door, along with a sword, belt and scabbard. Below on the floor was a pair of riding boots.

'From Sir Osbert, and his lady,' remarked a smirking Geoff, who had followed them in to see if there were any rewards in the offing before Walt departed.

Walt explained to Geoff that Dai Tudor was now to occupy this room and that he had made adequate arrangement with Sir Osbert for reward for all three guards to offer him the same courtesies he had received.

With the guard out of the way he changed into his new clothes, gave a couple of florins to Dai and told him to make his way to Syhale if he had no place to go following his release. 'You can always find a place with the Syhale troopers,' Walt said in jest.

Dai countered. 'Methinks I am a little too old for cavorting around with a troop of mounted cavalry Sir Walter.'

'Seriously Dai, there are always places in one of the villages or towns for a trained constable.' Walt told him.

After bidding farewell to Dai, Walt descended to the courtyard, with Aidric carrying a small bag of personal belongings and Walt's old clothes, in case of need. They headed for the stables where their horses would be prepared, and no doubt a final farewell to his genial gaoler and lady wife.

Arriving at the stables they were surprised to see not only Aidric's horse prepared for the journey, but a magnificent black destrier saddled and ready with saddlebags and rolled groundsheet behind the saddle.

A surprised Walt, seeing the destrier and Sir Osbert standing nearby, asked 'are you escorting us to the city gates Sir Osbert?'

The bemused gaoler slowly understood, and gave a hearty laugh. 'This is your destrier, Sir Walter, we could obtain naught else which is fit for a knight. God speed your journey home.'

A third horse was also harnessed with packsaddle and two packs, which appeared to have at least some contents, a quick check showed that they had been provided with a limited amount of food and a tinder box should they need to spend a night in the open. Aidric added the bag of personal possessions he had carried from the cell, and they were ready to leave.

After a firm handshake from Sir Osbert, and emotional Norman French kisses on the cheeks from Hilda, during which she whispered, 'I shall miss you my love,' they mounted their horses and rode from the tower, with Aidric having witnessed the whispered words but not heard. *I was bloody right, I knew it. They were lovers.* He thought as he remembered Lady Hilda wiping a tear from her eye, as they turned their mounts to depart.

Walt did not look back as they left the Tower. Their first stop was at the inn to collect Aidric's travel equipment and pay the innkeeper any outstanding debt. There was one further stop at the abbey to settle accounts with Brother Peter, and then they headed north towards the Aldersgate to be free of the city before dusk and the curfew. Knowing they would not get far before dark, and that it was not a good idea to sleep rough anywhere close to the city due to the number of footpads and robbers on the prowl for unfortunates who had been locked out at curfew, Aidric suggested that they take a bed at an inn in the village of Isledon, around three miles from the city gate, on their road to the north.

After leaving the city through the Aldersgate, Walt took only one backward glance and declared. 'I am not sorry to see the back of the smoky smelly hellhole.'

Now, he just looked forward to returning to his land apart, Northumberland, and his wonderful wife and sons. He urged his destrier forward with an urgency that left Aidric struggling to keep up whilst riding his own mount and leading the slower packhorse.

Walt only looked back when Aidric called to request a reduction in pace as he could not coax more speed out of the dubious pack-horse. They were currently passing through the shack and makeshift shelters of the outskirts of the city. A place where no gentleman would want to linger and was best left behind without delay. Walt reined in and waited for his squire to catch up. 'What was that place you said was the first village outside the city where decent lodgings can be obtained Aidric?'

'That would be Isledon Sir, an inn known as The Angel. It gets very crowded and chambers are not always available, but they have plenty of dormitory space in the loft.'

'It will have to do Aidric. Despite my urgency to be in Syhale I find myself more than a little sleepy after the generous quantities of the constable's excellent wine I have quaffed.'

They walked the horses at a slow but steady gait, occasionally needing to draw their swords to forcibly fend off persistent beggars and avoid them getting too close, where they might try to harm them with concealed daggers.

The shacks thinned out and as they passed by tilled fields, Walt again began to long for home and Katherine's arms about him. *My Sons,* he thought, Young Walter would be almost a man at seventeen and the youngest John now nine years old. *I am sure they are all fine young gentlemen,* he thought. From what he had gleaned from the constant supply of funds for his comfort sent by Katherine, their demesne must be doing very well and this would give him the opportunity to please his wife, by giving up all the activities she disliked and living a law abiding life, loyal to the new king, who had been so gracious to him. A feeling of impatience interrupted his deliberations. 'How far now to this inn?' he called to Aidric.

'Less than a mile now Sir, soon be able to get our heads down.'

'Not before a couple of ales, my mouth feels as if I have been chewing sawdust.'

'Yes Sir,' sighed Aidric quietly, himself looking forward to a good night's sleep before their long journey on the morrow.

=====

29546725R00187

Made in the USA
Charleston, SC
16 May 2014